Avai...
from Mills & Boon®
Special Moments™

THE SECRET SHE KEPT

Jake looked Savannah over from head to toe, a slow perusal, missing nothing.

He noticed the fullness of her bottom lip, slightly moist. Her sweatshirt hugged her body, making it easy to imagine the curves without the clothing in the way. Her fingers were in the front pockets of her jeans, elbows resting lightly against the door. Her back was arched and he could pretend that was to move her body closer to his. His pulse throbbed with the thought and he took a step towards her, so that a mere foot separated them.

He was drawn to her like a bee to sweet nectar.

"Well?" she said and he fought to remember what she'd asked him before…

She could easily have pushed him away but she glanced again at his mouth and in that moment Jake saw the truth in her eyes. She wanted him to kiss her. Savannah still wanted him, whether she would allow herself to or not.

A KISS TO REMEMBER

"I'll be in touch," Nora said as she walked away.

She started for the gate, then doubled back, realising she ought to give him a business card.

"Thank you." He accepted the card and their fingers brushed. The contact was minute, but it was enough to send an electric zap down the length of her arm. She yanked her hand back and the corner of his mouth lifted in subtle acknowledgement. She eyed him suspiciously. Had he felt it, too?

But he offered nothing, saying "I look forward to hearing your ideas," before ascending the front steps and disappearing into the house.

Nora stared down at her fingers, all too aware of her physical reaction to Ben's brief touch. Grimacing, she wiped her hand on the back of her jeans and stalked to her truck. She'd never been the type to act all fluttery and girly over a guy. Wasn't her style.

Nora glowered at the house, more specifically at Ben inside, and jerked her truck into gear. Not gonna happen.

All the characters in this book have no existence outside the imagination of the author, and have no relation whatsoever to anyone bearing the same name or names. They are not even distantly inspired by any individual known or unknown to the author, and all the incidents are pure invention.

First published in Great Britain 2010
Harlequin Mills & Boon Limited,
Eton House, 18-24 Paradise Road, Richmond, Surrey TW9 1SR

The Secret She Kept © Amy Knupp 2009
A Kiss To Remember © Kimberly Sheetz 2008

ISBN: 978 0 263 87940 7

23-0110

Harlequin Mills & Boon policy is to use papers that are natural, renewable and recyclable products and made from wood grown in sustainable forests. The logging and manufacturing processes conform to the legal environmental regulations of the country of origin.

Printed and bound in Spain
by Litografía Rosés S.A., Barcelona

THE SECRET
SHE KEPT
BY
AMY KNUPP

A KISS TO REMEMBER
BY
KIMBERLY VAN METER

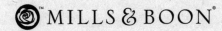

MILLS & BOON

THE SECRET SHE KEPT

BY
AMY KNUPP

Amy Knupp lives in Kansas with her husband, two sons and four cats. She graduated from the University of Kansas with degrees in French and journalism and feels lucky to use very little of either in her writing career. For more about Amy's books and writing life, visit her website at www.amyknupp.com.

Heartfelt thanks go out to:

Sharon Long and Jan Kenny.
Sharon, for redirecting me midstream when I need it (usually) and Jan, for providing feedback at the eleventh hour (as well as the eighth, ninth and tenth). Thank you both for listening, brainstorming, arguing, laughing and cheering me on.

Roxana Laing, for helping me with art details, as well as offering ideas for my story.

The Writeminded girls, Jaci Burton, Stephanie Tyler, Larissa Ione and Maya Banks. You inspire me every single day with your humour, your work ethic and your fantastic books.

Kay Stockham and Suzanne Cox, the very best FNGs ever. You guys keep me (almost) sane.

Mum and Dad.
Your support means the world to me.

Justin.
Yep, again. I couldn't do what I do if you didn't do what you do. Thank you.

CHAPTER ONE

SAVANNAH SALINGER DIDN'T like surprises.

Especially when the surprise was Jake Barnes, living, breathing, looking far too good—and standing four feet in front of her. In *her* office. Where she was supposed to be in control.

"Jake," she said, damning the waver in her voice. She stood and walked out from behind her desk toward him. Her heart jackhammered with a suffocating fear she couldn't take time to either rationalize or dismiss. All she knew was she couldn't let him see how his reappearance affected her. Could *not* let him notice her hands were shaking and sweating.

"Savannah." His frown disappeared as he eyed her with blatant approval. "What a surprise." He eased his mouth into the grin she remembered well—sixty percent cocky, forty percent pure sexy. Fortunately, Savannah was one hundred percent immune to male charm—his and everyone else's—these days.

"What in the world are you doing here?" she asked.

"I have a meeting with Zach Rundle," Jake said. "Two o'clock."

"He has…" She stepped over to Zach's desk, which lay

along the back wall, and glanced at the oversize October calendar where he jotted down his appointments. "A two o'clock with the owner of the Levine land."

She peered up at Jake, eager to determine his reaction to being wrong about his meeting. Anxious to get him out of there.

"That'd be me."

She tilted her head in confusion. "I thought the owner was…Odessa Levine."

"I'm here on her behalf. She's my grandmother."

Savannah opened her mouth, then closed it again. "So we're working with you."

"For now."

"You're the one who's going to sell us the land?" She watched his face for a clue to his plans.

"We'll see how it goes," Jake said, shrugging one shoulder and gazing around the room.

Crossing her arms and leaning against the front of her desk, Savannah perused him, refusing to be intimidated by his nonchalance. Or his good looks.

His dark hair was just long enough to be messy on top, in a fresh-out-of-somebody's-bed way that could pique a woman's imagination. Eyes the color of melted chocolate followed her, missing nothing. He was all angles and tautness and confidence.

"Does Zach realize he's meeting with you instead of your grandmother?"

"I do." At that moment Zach, Savannah's boss and brother-in-law, entered the undersized, overfurnished construction office from the back shop area. He wiped off his hands on his jeans, brushed his brown hair off his face and extended a hand to Jake. "Zach Rundle. You must be Jacob Barnes."

"Call me Jake. Pleasure."

"You never mentioned his name," Savannah said stupidly to Zach.

"You two know each other?" he asked.

"We grew up together." Her chin rose a notch as she met Jake's eyes.

"It's been awhile," Jake said in that deep, husky voice of his, returning her stare, their past hanging heavily between them.

"What are you doing back in town?" she inquired, striving for friendliness.

"Family stuff. Researching land options for my grandma, for one thing."

Zach switched into business mode at the reminder, and the two men headed into the adjacent conference room and shut the door. Savannah slumped into her chair, relieved that Zach hadn't invited her to join them, as he often did.

She closed her eyes, wondering what to do about Jake, and about the way her heart was pounding. Keeping him out of her personal life was of the utmost importance. Yet buying that land from Jake's grandmother was vital to Zach and the company, which of course meant it was vital to her. She had to play nice and focus on their business goal until Jake got the heck out of town. And hope like crazy he'd leave none the wiser.

JAKE STRETCHED HIS LEGS out under the conference table as Rundle went to grab a folder he'd left on his desk.

Fancy running into Savannah Salinger here, on his

second day back in Lone Oak. Sure, it was a one-horse town, but he'd barely left his grandmother's house where he was staying since getting in. Hadn't really encountered anyone besides his grandmother and sister. Nevertheless, the odds of meeting up with the one woman who'd always gotten his attention were slim to none. Especially at a construction company.

He let his mind wander to the last day he'd seen her—his final day in Lone Oak. Nearly twelve years ago. He could still recall her eyes lowering with regret. Embarrassment. Loathing, for both herself and him.

Jake straightened in his chair, every muscle in his body tense as he fought to push the memories aside. He needed to be on an even keel for this meeting, not affected by this hardheaded woman from his past.

Rundle walked back into the room, said hardheaded woman following him.

"Savannah's my detail girl," Rundle said. "She keeps track of everything, so I invited her to join us."

Jake nodded, reminding himself this was just like any other meeting he'd had back in Montana. Merely business.

He tried not to focus on how her sweater stretched across her chest as she settled in the chair next to Rundle. When Jake raised his glance to her face, tension buzzed between them.

"Why don't we get down to business, unless you two have some more catching up to do," Rundle proposed.

"We're caught up and then some," Savannah said.

Jake leaned back in his chair and motioned for the other man to go ahead.

"We're very interested in your grandmother's land."

"You and a long list of others," Jake said. "Seems it's in a particularly hot spot."

"It is. It's along the route the new road will take."

"The one that will shorten the commute time to the university."

"Supposed to turn Lone Oak into a bedroom community. God knows this town could use a boost, before it falls off the map."

Jake leaned forward and rested his elbows on the table. "My grandma has lived on that land for ages. Its value is more than monetary to her. She wants to have a say in what it becomes."

"May I inquire why she sent you to meet with us?" Savannah said.

"She's eighty-one years old. Her mind is sharp, but she has trouble getting around."

"So you came back to town to handle this for her?" Rundle queried.

"I came back for other reasons, but she asked me to check into options while I'm here. I build high-end custom log homes in Montana, so I know a bit about property development."

"I'd say you probably do." Rundle sat up straighter.

"I'd like to get an idea of what you intend to do with my grandma's land."

"We plan to build a whole community. Single-family dwellings, apartments, a couple commercial buildings, a community center with a pool, convenience store and gym. Trees and green space."

"Sounds pretty progressive for Lone Oak, Kansas," Jake said. But he was intrigued. He'd expected the status quo.

"Maybe. Or maybe changes would return the town to what it used to be. Make it once again a friendly community where folks could get to know their neighbors, walk to the store for a loaf of bread."

"That sounds promising," Jake murmured. "My grandmother wants something developed that will be important to people."

"What's more important than homes?" Savannah asked, her tone defensive. "A neighborhood where people can put down roots, settle in, stay for years. That's the goal."

Zach glanced sideways at her, as if he wasn't used to her speaking up at meetings.

"You'll be hard-pressed to find a better plan for your grandma's land," she continued. "Unless you consider a sprawling industrial park a decent idea—"

"What Savannah's trying to say," Rundle interjected, "is that we invite you to hear everyone out. Meet with the others who've expressed an interest in the land. We feel confident our vision is the best thing for Lone Oak."

"I've got another meeting this afternoon, as a matter of fact," Jake admitted. "But I can tell you're both very passionate about this scheme."

Savannah always had been passionate, to a fault. They'd argued over many subjects through the years. It was nice to find growing up hadn't mellowed her.

Jake posed several questions. Rundle had answers for everything, albeit vague ones. But Jake couldn't fault him for that. The guy had no reason to trust him yet. Only an idiot would hand over detailed plans at this stage.

Jake studied Rundle, from his plaid flannel shirt over a

white T-shirt to his calm, steady gaze. Rundle was a couple of years older than him—Jake remembered his name, recalled how his brother had been responsible for the accident that killed Savannah's mom. Interesting that Savannah was working for him and seemed to have gotten over the past. He discovered nothing that suggested arrogance or dishonesty in Rundle now, and he appreciated that. His first impression was that he could work with this guy, and first impressions were usually reliable for Jake.

The worst part of Heartland Construction so far was that Savannah came with it. But he wasn't going to let the past or a woman get in the way of what was best for his grandmother whatever that turned out to be.

Having all the information he required for now, Jake stood and exchanged business cards with Rundle.

"Thanks for your time," the man said. "Give me a call if you'd like more information for Mrs. Levine."

"Will do."

The three of them strolled out of the conference room. Jake shook hands with Rundle again and left, thinking about the development they'd discussed. The project was actually something he could get behind. But ultimately, the decision was his grandmother's. He would advise her as much as she wanted, but the land was hers.

"WHAT'D YOU MAKE OF THAT?" Savannah asked once Jake had left.

Zach put his files down and shrugged. "He was impossible to read. Could go either way. Sounds like he knows his stuff, though."

"What if he chooses someone else?" She hated so

much that Jake Barnes was in a position to affect their entire business.

"Then we find another project." He pulled his attention from the papers he'd been shuffling. "You're too worked up about this, Savannah. There's not a lot we can do except present our case the best we can. We just did that."

In other words, they were powerless. Savannah dragged her hands through her long hair with a huff of frustration. "I have to go get the kids," she said as she extracted her purse from her bottom desk drawer. "I'll see you in a while."

As Jake got on his Harley, helmet in his hands, someone exited the front door at Heartland. Savannah. He was parked along the street about two doors down from her, and couldn't help observing as she moved quickly, single-mindedly, ignoring everything around her.

She headed toward the beat-up blue minivan parked in front of him, her wavy, reddish-brown hair flying behind her, and was about to climb in the driver's side when she spotted him. Savannah stopped in her tracks, those brown eyes of hers focused on him.

She tossed her purse into the van, then stared at her feet for a moment, as if gaining control of her temper or else gathering her nerve. She'd never been the type who needed to bolster her courage. Never worried much if she lost her temper, either, now that he thought about it. He watched her curiously from behind his dark glasses.

He noticed her shoulders rise before she turned toward him and approached. That was strange. Atypical for this normally confident, look-out-world-I've-got-something-to-say woman.

She had plenty to be confident about, too. Dressed in slender black pants that showed off her long legs, and a sweater that fell midway down her thighs and was clasped by a single tie across her chest, she somehow managed to appear sexy and professional at once.

It would've been better for him if she'd aged ungracefully. He didn't want to be attracted to her. Instead, she was just as appealing as she had been as a teenager. More so, actually, because now her curves had filled out completely and she had a look that said she'd lived life and had an inner strength to deal with whatever it threw at her. And yet, as she moved toward him, he detected a hint of…uncertainty.

"Hi," she said softly as she drew to a stop right next to him.

"Hey. What's up?"

She chewed the inside of her cheek briefly. "Zach's plan is the best you'll find."

"I have to make sure of that."

"How can you argue about a place where people want to raise their kids?"

"I can argue anything with you."

She scowled at him, then glanced over her shoulder. She took a deep breath and put her hand on his bike. He eyed her, waiting for her to remove it.

"I never pictured you on a motorcycle."

"You pictured me, though, huh?" He shot her a lopsided grin.

That was all it took to get her to drop her hand. "I didn't say that…." She crossed her arms. "Still just as cocky as ever, I see."

"That's the way you always liked me."

"I never liked you."

"That's not exactly how I remember it."

She swallowed and pierced him with those eyes. "Back to the land… Are you going to sell it to us, or are you just going to play games?"

"You really think I'll tell you my plans?"

Fire flashed in her eyes. Here was a much more familiar Savannah than the one he'd seen so far. A thought occurred to him. "Is there something between Rundle and you?"

Savannah laughed for the first time, and he was yanked back to the days they'd run in the same crowd. That laugh had always made him want to hear it over and over.

"Me and Zach?" she said. "Seriously?"

"You can't expect me to believe you don't have a man in your life." Jake didn't allow himself to consider why he wanted to know.

"I don't. And if I did, I can tell you with total certainty it wouldn't be Zach. He's my brother-in-law."

Jake felt the tightness ease out of his neck. "Seems your interests are pretty wrapped up in this company. Your livelihood, your brother-in-law's, your sister's…"

"That's why I'm standing here in the street, talking to you."

"Wouldn't be caught dead with me otherwise, would you?" Anger from the past seeped into his voice.

One of Savannah's knuckles cracked and Jake remembered that had always been the telltale sign she was pissed, liable to tear someone's head off. Getting a reaction from her satisfied some twisted part of him deep inside.

"Hard to be caught dead *or* alive with someone who disappears for almost twelve years."

"If I recall correctly, I disappeared after you told me to get lost."

She hesitated then. "Are you saying you left because of me?"

Jake couldn't help chuckling as he shook his head. "Don't flatter yourself, sweetheart."

He would never admit the impact her blowing him off had had on him. But it had only been one part of what had convinced him to leave.

Savannah frowned, and he could swear her thoughts turned the air blue. But instead of letting loose as she once would have, she spun on her heel and stalked to the driver's side of the van.

Jake watched her retreat, wanting like crazy to hate her. The fact was, though, that after all these years she still got his blood pumping and his brain fantasizing.

CHAPTER TWO

"YOU HAVEN'T BEEN BY the hospital yet, have you?" Jake's sister stood in the middle of their grandmother's spare bedroom with her hands on her slender hips, her shirt riding up just enough to reveal some kind of flashy jewelry in her navel. Jake noticed the tattooed claw of a dragon wrapped around an Asian-looking flower at her hip and would've laughed if he hadn't known she would tear into him for that, too.

"You've got me here for a week," Jake said. As he glanced from Emily to their maternal grandmother, who was perched on the antique armchair in the corner, he felt something inside himself softening. "Ten days, max."

"You've already been here for two full days." Emily continued to stare at him, her green eyes somehow conveying both steel and affection. "Shouldn't need half that long to do what you came to do."

Jake bent down and took an armload of books from one of the shelves, then carried the pile to the side table next to his grandma. Thinning out her bookshelves—stacked three books deep from the bottom—was yet another task Odessa had decided Jake should tackle while in town. "I came back for *you*, Em. Not for him."

"I told you I appreciate that, but a visit's overdue. If you don't do this now, it'll be too late."

The tears in her eyes were like a physical blow. It wasn't often his hard-shelled little sister cried. Her pleas over the phone had been the only thing that convinced him to return to Lone Oak, for the first time since he'd left.

Jake faced his grandma and picked up the top book from the pile. "John Jakes. *Heaven and Hell.* This sounds like something I might be able to relate to."

"It's part of a series," Odessa Levine said, running her hand over her straight, grayish-white hair. "One you'd probably enjoy if you'd sit still long enough to read it."

"I'll save it for my retirement."

"I'll give it to the library," she said, struggling to prevent the corners of her mouth from tipping upward any more at her grandson's hopeless lack of interest in reading.

"He's dying, Jake." Emily broke in. "You have to set aside your testosterone-induced grudge."

"I said I'd see him. Just not today."

Probably not tomorrow, either.

Trying to make peace with his dad after all these years held about as much appeal as reading the entire works of Shakespeare—which he was sure his grandmother had here in her collection somewhere.

His old man had never been reasonable or the least bit concerned about family ties. If he had, maybe he would've apologized before now. But Jake hadn't waited around for any miracles.

"Maybe it'll go better than you expect with your father." Odessa spoke as she sorted her books into two piles, keepers and ones for the library. This had to be done periodically, she'd explained in earnest, to make room for new books. That, or build an addition onto the house.

"Better than I expect would mean we don't kill each other. I'd never dare to hope for an apology."

"He's different now," Emily stated. "These past few weeks he's been...forced to consider something besides work."

"For the first time in his life."

"That's true. I'm not going to make him into something he's not," his sister said. "He's still the workaholic dad who was never there for us. But facing death has made him reflect."

"He's scared," their grandma said. "Fear does something to people. So does waiting to die."

"If he's so different, why aren't you there now?" Jake asked Emily.

"I visited him this morning. I try to go by every day either before or after work."

"So what else do we have to get done while I'm in town?" Jake asked, knowing any more talk of their father's supposed change would just end up in a disagreement. He collected another stack of books and carried them to the table for sorting.

"We need to go through his house and everything in it," Emily said. "He won't be coming home."

"You going to sell the house? Or move in?"

She shook her head. "I have my own place and I'm happy there. I figured we'd sell it."

"That'll be up to you. I don't plan to be in his will. Don't want a damn thing from him."

Instead of disputing Jake's assertion or scolding him, Emily nodded once, her jaw tight. No matter how unconventional in appearance she was, she'd always liked to dream about being part of a conventionally happy family.

Jake had given that up years ago.

Emily pulled her cell phone from the pocket of her black cargo pants and checked the time. "I have to get to the shop for an appointment."

She stuck the tiny phone back in the pocket, bent to plant a quick kiss on their grandmother's forehead, then turned toward Jake, arms open.

"I'm glad you're here," she said as she hugged him. "Even if you're not."

He held on to her, still processing how much she'd changed in the past four years. "It's great to see you, Em. I'm sorry it's been so long."

Which was the truth. He understood now how stupid he'd been to stay away just because of his dad. He'd flown Emily out to visit him a few times, and their grandmother as well, but it was never often enough.

"I'm taking you to Dad tomorrow." She was halfway down the hall when she spoke

"I'll go by myself." When he was darn well ready. "Demanding woman." Only his grandmother could hear the last bit.

"I'm on her side, mister," Odessa said. "If your dad dies and you haven't even tried to make amends, you'll likely regret it one day."

Jake seriously doubted that. But he knew better than to continue this argument. He'd never win.

"Would you like to hear more about the meetings I had today, or do you just want to talk books?" he asked.

"Let's go to the kitchen to discuss the land while I make

dinner. We can finish the books tomorrow so you can haul them to the library."

Jake pulled her walker around in front of her and moved to her side to help her stand.

"Thank you," she said, then made her way out of the room.

When they arrived at the kitchen, Jake got glasses down for iced tea and his grandma removed the lid from the Crock-Pot on the counter. The aroma of home-cooked ribs made Jake weak in the knees.

"Needs another thirty minutes. Sit down. I'll fix the tea," she told him.

He looked at her skeptically.

"Sit," she repeated sternly. "Quit treating me like I'm helpless. I know I've gotten slower, but if I just give up and stop doing everything, you might as well check me into the old folks' home."

Jake grinned and pulled out two of the chairs at the rectangular farmhouse-style table, then settled into one of them.

"So tell me about these meetings. Anyone worth talking any further to?"

"Both of them, frankly."

After adding barbecue sauce to the meat, she made her way to the table, steering her walker with one hand and holding a glass of tea in the other. As she put the glass down, her hand shook.

"Grandma, would you sit down and let me get the other glass?"

She stopped and stared at him, silently, daring him to say another word.

Jake held his hands up in surrender. "No mystery where the stubborn in this family came from."

When she finally returned with the second glass and lowered herself to the chair opposite his at the table, she began peppering him with questions about the development companies he'd met with.

"Sinclair Harris would like to build big beautiful custom homes on large lots," he told her. "With rolling green lawns and long curving driveways. He's got big ideas."

"Does he realize no one in Lone Oak could afford his mansions?"

"He's of a mind that professors from the university would move into them, in addition to some folks here who he claims could manage financing."

"What's so great about that plan?" his grandmother asked. "What am I missing?"

"You said you wanted the area to look nice. This would definitely be impressive."

"Until the houses decayed from no one living in them."

Jake nodded, acknowledging she was more familiar with the community now than he was.

"What about the other company?"

"Zach Rundle proposed building an old-fashioned neighborhood." He explained in more detail what the man had told him. When he finished, his grandmother gazed at him thoughtfully.

"What do you think?" he asked.

"*That* sounds impressive. But I believe I'm in way over my head." She took a sip of tea. "I shouldn't have kept the land so long. Now I'm not sure I can handle this."

"Of course you can, Grandma. I'm here to help you."

"For a little while. What do I do when you're gone?"

"You call me when you need me. But if I remember right,

you're capable of handling just about anything on your own."

"Tell me about the people you met with. Are they decent folks?"

Jake didn't hesitate. "Based on one meeting, I'd say so."

"If this were your land, what would you do?"

He tapped his fingers on the table as he eyed his grand-mother. He knew what his instincts were telling him, but sometimes it was necessary to let reason catch up. Jake thought about the men he'd met with today, about their projects. The call was an easy one. "I'd go with Heartland."

She took another sip of tea, then watched the ice bob as she swirled the glass. "Very well. I believe I'd like to meet these people from Heartland. What's next?"

TUTTLE'S DINER WAS still the only burger joint in town after all these years. That point was driven home for Jake as he sat with his grandmother and her book club at a long table on one side and, when the Monday evening dinner crowd thinned out, spotted Savannah in a booth on the other side.

The place hadn't changed at all since he'd been here. Still the same decor, or lack thereof, still the same aromas from the kitchen. Even the specials handwritten on the board next to the cash register were the same, if memory served him correctly. The sameness was comforting in a way Jake had never expected anything in Lone Oak would be.

"Maybe Jacob could provide us some male perspec-tive," one of the women—either Grace or Mary, he thought—said with an eager grin.

"I haven't read the book," he replied for the seventh or

eighth time. Nor had he been paying attention to their discussion. "But the general male perspective is that the woman is usually right, unless it involves tools or cars."

The group of women, ranging in age from their mid-fifties to his grandmother's eighty-one, chuckled and made sounds of approval.

"If you'll excuse me, ladies, I see an old acquaintance." Jake probably scrambled up too quickly, but he'd been sitting with his grandmother's friends for well over an hour, and while they were all welcoming and tried to include him, he'd had enough discussion of Jane Austen for one day.

He stopped at the counter and requested a refill for his coffee, and as the waitress topped off his cup, he glanced around at the other customers. He spotted a couple of people who seemed vaguely familiar, but no one he could put a name to. He looked over at Savannah again. She didn't appear to have noticed him yet.

Not until he reached her table did it hit him that she was sitting across from two kids.

"TWICE TODAY. Must be my lucky day."

Savannah jumped in her seat at the sound of Jake's voice. She peered up at his hulking form at the head of their table, then at her children, and she had to fight down the urge to escape. Maintaining a calm facade as she forced a smile was all she could do.

"Jake. What are you doing here?"

"Brought my grandmother up for her book club meeting." He gestured to the table of women on the other side of the diner.

"Is that Mrs. Pope over there?" Savannah asked. "She was a teacher at the grade school until she retired last year."

"Grade school, huh?" Jake eyed the kids curiously, then gestured to the booth she was sitting in. "May I? I'm Jane Austen-ed out."

Savannah glanced nervously at Allie, who'd eaten half her meal before pulling out her sketch pad and losing herself in her drawing. Because she couldn't think of an excuse to turn him away, Savannah moved over so he could sit down.

Jake smiled at Logan and Allie, then faced her. "You said there wasn't a man in your life. I guess I didn't know you had a family."

"What with you leaving town for so long, I'm sure there's a lot you don't know." As soon as she said it, she silently scolded herself for getting defensive.

Jake watched her for a second too long, then addressed the children. "My name's Jake." He extended a hand to Logan, who got up on his knees in the booth and shook it for all he was worth. "What's your name?" Jake asked.

"Logan Michael Moser. This is my sister, Allison Elizabeth Moser. Mom's name used to be Savannah Elaine Moser, but her last name changed to Salinger because she got divorced."

Savannah cringed. Why couldn't she have *two* children giving her the silent treatment instead of just one?

Jake glanced at her, a smirk on his face. "Saves me a couple of questions, anyway," he said. "Would that by any chance be Michael Moser?"

"You know it is." She raised her chin, daring him to say anything about her choice in husbands.

Jake focused on Allie, as if finally noticing she hadn't even acknowledged his presence. "Allison Elizabeth. That's a pretty name," he said to her.

Allie continued to ignore him, working away with her pencil on the sketch pad on her lap.

"Allie," Savannah said firmly.

Her daughter glared at her, then uttered a curt "Hi" to Jake.

"She gets involved in her drawings," Savannah said, unsure why she felt it necessary to explain away her daughter's behavior. The truth was this was status quo, and had been for the ten months since the divorce was finalized. In fact, Allie's anger had begun when Savannah and Michael first split up. She apparently blamed Savannah more than Michael, because she treated him with a fraction of the hostility she showed Savannah.

"You like to draw?" Jake asked Allie. "I drew a lot when I was your age."

That piqued Allie's interest. "Did you draw horses?"

At that instant, it all came rushing back to Savannah—how Jake had been into art during grade school, working extra hard on his projects in art class, proudly but quietly accepting the teacher's continuous praise. It was the one area in which Savannah hadn't had a hope of competing with him. Maybe that was why she'd blocked it from her memory until now.

She tuned back in to their conversation, her stomach gurgling with nausea. Jake was listing shows and contests where Allie could enter her drawings.

"I didn't realize you were still active in the art community," Savannah said.

"I'm not. I haven't been for years, but I'm certain those events are still around. Now it's probably easier than ever to hook up with them. Just look online."

"Can we check on the Internet, Mom?" For the first time in weeks Allie was animated. While that brought a small measure of joy to Savannah, she was also ticked off that Jake was the cause of it.

"Of course we can." She strove for offhandedness, as if having a normal conversation with her daughter was…well, normal.

"Can Jake help me?"

Not on your life. "We can handle it ourselves."

"Mom—"

Savannah held up a hand and gave her daughter The Look, the one that stopped whining in its tracks. And now garnered a hateful glare from her once sweet little girl. Savannah sighed inwardly. "Tell you what," she said without thinking. "When we get home, we'll check into signing you up for that art class you've been hounding me about."

"Really?" she asked, eyes bright.

"Really." Savannah forced a grin. No way would she let Jake be the only one to make her child happy.

Allie squealed and bounced in the booth. "Thanks, Mom! Can we go now? I want to get home and fill out the application right away."

"Logan's still eating, honey. We'll leave soon."

Savannah knew already this was the absolute dumbest thing she'd done for some time. She couldn't afford art classes. Was doing well to afford dinner out one night a week. She'd always been prone to doing stupid things when Jake was around. Why did she lose all semblance of sense in his presence? Besides, what did it matter if Allie thought he was nicer? Of course she would. He didn't have to discipline her or tell her no.

"When are you leaving Lone Oak?" she asked him abruptly.

"Another week or so."

"Don't you have to get back to your job?"

"Believe me, I would've been happier not leaving my job at all. But it's good to see my grandma and sister."

"What about the rest of your family? Your dad? Is he still living?"

"For another couple weeks, or so the doctor says."

Savannah looked at Jake sharply to make certain she'd understood right. "He's dying?"

Jake checked to see if the kids were paying attention, but Allie was drawing again and Logan was pushing a French fry around on his plate and making race car noises.

"Cancer. That's the real reason I'm back." His jaw locked tight and he frowned, but she got the sense it wasn't out of sadness.

"I'm sorry," she said, and meant it. She remembered he and his father hadn't been very close, but she didn't wish losing a parent on anyone. She'd been through that when she was fourteen, and understood what hell it could be.

Jake didn't respond and she didn't know what else to say, although his unspoken emotions were pulling at her, making her want to find out more.

"So you build log cabins in Montana."

"Homes. Big custom jobs. I just got the biggest break

of my life, and here I am back in Podunkville to make up with the old man, who couldn't care less about seeing me."

"What kind of break?"

"You familiar with Tony Clayton?"

"Familiar?" He was only one of the biggest names in Hollywood right now. "Just a bit."

"I'm building a house for him."

"Wow. That's great. A big break, like you said."

"If I make him happy, he's got friends. A bunch of overpaid friends who love to buy second and third homes out in the middle of nowhere."

"So you're hoping this will get you all that business."

"That's what I've dreamed of ever since I started. I've worked toward it for years, and now I'm so close I can taste it."

"Your dad's timing isn't the greatest, huh?"

"Nope." Jake frowned again and admitted, "I haven't spoken to him since the day I left town."

The huskiness in his voice made her wonder at all the things he must be going through. She damned herself for caring, but couldn't seem to help it.

Logan shoved his last fry into his mouth and that was all Savannah needed to excuse them. "We have to go."

Jake glanced over at his grandmother. "And I better return to the hen party. Nice to meet you, Logan and Allie." He held his right hand up for a high-five from Logan, and shared a brief smile with Allie before standing.

Savannah watched him walk away, reminding herself distance was exactly what she required. Especially since she apparently couldn't help herself from caring, no matter how dangerous that was.

CHAPTER THREE

SAVANNAH SWORE as she walked down Main Street toward her office. The double mocha latte she'd just bought overflowed the lid of the cup and burned her wrist. She slurped up the spill before it could run down her arm, but didn't take time to reposition her load. She'd taken the kids to the office after school, as she usually did, then left to buy them a snack. Zach was there somewhere—his truck was out front—but he hadn't been in the main office when she and the children had arrived from school ten minutes ago. Judging by the closed conference room door, she'd guessed he was with a potential client.

Logan and Allie were generally well-behaved kids, but too many things could happen in the blink of an eye, especially with a rambunctious eight-year-old boy unsupervised. She never wanted Zach to regret letting her bring the kids to the office after school each day.

The aroma of chocolate chip cookies fresh out of the bakery's oven wafted from the paper bag in her other hand, making her wish she'd grabbed a cookie for herself, too.

Normally, she packed after-school snacks to save money, but this morning she'd had one crisis after another. Allie had experienced one of her preadolescent hormone imbalances, triggered by finding that the one and only shirt she wanted to wear was still in the dirty laundry. Logan's volcano model for school had somehow suffered nearly irreparable damage overnight, which he blamed on Allie, which started the second shouting match before 8:00 a.m. And that was just the beginning of the morning love in the Salinger-Moser family.

Savannah opened the door to Heartland with three fingers of her left hand. Logan was crouched beneath the spare chair along the wall by the copy machine, aiming his gun, made of LEGO blocks, at his sister. The conference room door was now open.

When she glanced at Allie, Savannah stopped dead. Her daughter, sweet, innocent and unsuspecting—okay, sweet was an exaggeration lately—was sprawled on her stomach on the floor between Zach's and Savannah's desks. Talking to *Jake*, who'd pulled out Savannah's chair and was lounging in it, a smile on his face.

Savannah bit back the exclamation of alarm on the tip of her tongue. She wasn't usually one to panic, and showing fear now would only cause suspicion.

Opening the paper bag, she walked toward her son and held out a soft, luscious-looking cookie.

"Come on out, Logan. You can't eat this under the chair."

"Aw, Mom. You blew my cover."

Savannah cracked a smile in spite of her preoccupation and held out the snack, waiting for him to disentangle himself and emerge.

"Thanks," he said as he grabbed it, breaking it into pieces in his haste.

Savannah braced herself and turned toward Allie and

Jake. "What are you doing here?" she inquired, hoping to sound casual and unconcerned.

"I brought my grandmother in to meet with your boss."

"Where *is* Zach?"

"In the back with her. She wanted to see the custom cabinets the guys are finishing up for someone's house. Next thing you know she'll have some in her kitchen. Logan had me at gunpoint and here I am."

Here he was. She nodded in spite of being entirely unhappy about the situation, and set her coffee, now only half-full, on her desk. Could she dare hope that this second meeting meant Odessa was going to sell to Zach? Savannah couldn't bring herself to ask; she'd find out from Zach later. Instead, she gave Jake a scowl that anyone with a clue would know meant *get out of my chair.*

"Allie here tells me she just had a birthday. Eleven years old. Getting close to being a teenager."

Allie smiled at him, that bright, easy, pre-divorce smile. Savannah barely noticed, though, freaking out anew that her daughter was getting so comfortable with Jake. She wasn't typically a chatterbox.

"Could I have my desk back, please?" Savannah wiped every trace of fear off her face and moved in on him, her tone almost amiable.

Jake remained where he was, his long, muscular legs stretched in front of him. He looked Savannah up and down slowly, and apparently finally grasped that she wasn't in the mood to joke around, because he stood and moved out of the way.

She put her purse in her bottom desk drawer and handed the cookie bag to Allie, who set it aside, then intently

resumed her latest horse drawing. Jake was heading toward
Logan, and Savannah couldn't wait for him to leave, before
he lured both her children into liking him.

"Can we talk outside for a second?" she asked him.

He studied her for another moment before nodding. "If
my grandma comes in, please tell her I'll be right back,"
he said to the kids.

Jake followed Savannah out the door. She tried not to
feel the heat of him directly behind her, but she couldn't
help being hyperaware of his closeness. She'd always had
that problem—knowing exactly where he was in the room,
what he was doing, who he was talking to, even if she was
in the middle of a conversation herself. Always, ever since
they were kids.

Once outside, she took several steps down the sidewalk,
away from the Heartland office, so the kids wouldn't see
them out the window.

The wind had risen that afternoon and the first hint of
fall filled the air. She turned to face Jake and the breeze
blew her hair into tangles behind her. She made a mental
note to drag the kids' jackets out of storage, and hoped
they'd still fit.

Jake leaned a shoulder casually against the stone facade
of the ancient building. He was close enough that she
caught his scent—outdoorsy with a hint of aftershave. It
did things to her, jump-started some kind of physical
reaction. Their silence grew as she studied the individual
fibers of his navy-blue T-shirt. Inching back a step would
be wise, but Savannah didn't like the message backing off
would send.

JAKE HADN'T BEEN THIS close to Savannah for almost twelve years, yet the reddish brown waves of her hair were still so familiar, the toffee color of her eyes the shade in the recurring dreams he tried to forget about.

"What's up?" he said, annoyed that he could still fall under her spell after how they'd ended things so long ago.

Savannah's eyes shot from his shirt to his face. "My kids have been through hell with this divorce."

"Losing a parent's tough. We both know that first-hand—"

"Right." She cut him off abruptly. How could he forget how she avoided talking about personal subjects? That it was something they had in common didn't matter. "They're still reeling from it. Especially Allie."

"I'm sorry to hear that."

"Stop being so nice to them. Please." Her chest rose as she took a deep breath. "What I mean is, don't go out of your way to get them to like you."

"Who says I have to go out of my way?"

The joke was met with a glare.

He frowned at her. "Let me see if I understand this. Your kids are hurting, so you want me to be mean to them."

"Don't you dare be mean to them. Just…leave them alone."

"I'm not attempting to be their best friend, Savannah. I was just talking to them, treating them like people."

She closed her eyes for a moment. "I know. What I'm trying to say… Allie's responded to you more in the two times she's met you than she has to me in nearly a year. She's hungry for a grown-up she can love and trust, and you seem to fit the bill because you like to draw horses."

"And you're afraid she'll get attached, then I'll leave."

"You're only here for a visit. She *will* be let down. I don't want her to lose anyone else."

"Don't worry. I won't encourage her—"

The door to the office opened and shut, and he pivoted to find Allie walking toward them. Jake automatically smiled at her as she sidled up next to him and handed him a piece of paper—the horse drawing she'd been working on. At the top, she'd written in fancy block letters, "For Jake."

"His name is Frosty," Allie said.

"He's a beauty. You've got some serious talent, Allie." As he gazed down at her, she shyly dropped her gaze to her feet.

Jake noticed the beaded butterfly clasp holding her shiny blond hair in a ponytail, and then his eyes were drawn lower, to her neck, about two inches behind her ear.

He did a double take. Veered away and looked back a third time to be sure.

Holy mother of…

She had a birthmark there. Faint brown, just larger than a quarter, in the shape of an upside-down crescent moon.

Jake knew his eyes were bulging, but he tried to hide his astonishment by avoiding eye contact with the little girl next to him. Coherency escaped him.

He closed his eyes briefly. When he opened them, they automatically sought out the birthmark again, and he broke out into a sweat.

It was the exact same shape, in the exact same place, as his sister's.

CHAPTER FOUR

SAVANNAH'S GAZE WENT from Jake to Allie and back as he leaned against the stone column and covered his eyes with his hands. He was acting weird, as though he was fighting off a sudden migraine or something. Savannah couldn't figure out what she'd missed.

"Jake?"

He didn't appear to hear her.

Allie glanced up at him then, as if finally noticing his strange behavior. "You don't like my picture?"

Savannah glared at him anew, daring him to ignore her daughter's hurt feelings, but he didn't react.

"It's great, Allie," he said after a moment's hesitation. "The best." He held the drawing out in front of him and stared at it, as if just now appreciating all the detail. "I'll hang it on the refrigerator at my grandmother's house."

"Can I visit you sometime so I can see it hanging?"

"I don't think—" Savannah began.

"Hey, Allie, I have to talk to your mom about something really important. Could you go check on your brother?"

Savannah observed him more closely, her heart picking up speed. Something was definitely wrong. She turned to her daughter. "Go. Make certain Logan's not bothering Zach. I'll be there in a couple of minutes."

Allie's eyes sought out Jake's, but he didn't meet her gaze. She pivoted and headed toward the office, shoulders sagging. How had she become so eager for Jake's attention so quickly? She'd have to unlearn that, and fast.

Jake slid down until he was squatting, braced against the column behind him. Savannah was so unaccustomed to him showing any sign of weakness that she wasn't sure how to react.

"Are you…okay?" she asked finally, in a low voice so Allie wouldn't hear.

Her daughter opened the office door, then looked back at them once again before slipping inside, out of earshot.

Jake sprang up angrily and pushed himself away from the column. "When were you going to tell me?" The tightly controlled rage in his voice was unmistakable.

"Tell you what?" But something inside Savannah knew, even before her brain processed the message. She crossed her arms protectively over her chest and sought out the support of the stone wall of the building.

"When were you going to mention that Allie's mine, Savannah?"

Dizziness made her vision blur. She closed her eyes and feared she might throw up as she fought the bile bubbling from deep inside.

"When?" His demand made her jump, and his anger sparked her own.

She uncrossed her arms and straightened, then stepped forward. She shook all over, and clenched her hands to fight the trembling. "I wasn't going to tell you. You were gone."

"It's true then. She's my…daughter." He ran a hand

through his hair, staring into space, unseeing. The tic in his jaw belied the eerie calm that fell over them.

"How did you figure it out?" Savannah asked quietly. "She doesn't resemble you at all—"

"She doesn't resemble me so you planned to take the secret to the grave with you, didn't you? The birthmark on her neck. It's the same as my sister's. Same shape, same place. My dad's mother had it, too. Apparently, it shows up in our family among the females."

Savannah would never have guessed. She'd kissed the mark countless times, but had never reckoned it might make such a difference in their lives. Ever since Jake had returned to town, she'd soothed herself with the reassurance there was no way he could find out the truth….

Savannah slumped against the wall again, in desperate need of its solidity. Her head fell back and hit the stones, but she barely felt it. Her mind became numb. She couldn't form a thought, knew only that her world was falling apart. The security she'd clung to since the divorce was evaporating like a cool mist on a scorching day.

Her chest constricted as she considered Allie. Her baby. Her daughter, who already hated her, yet would need her more than ever if she learned the truth.

Jake had paced down the sidewalk. Savannah took several steps after him.

"You can't tell her. It'll crush her. She's been through so much—"

"Whose fault is that?" He rounded on her, fury in his eyes. "What the hell were you thinking, Savannah?"

She glanced about to make sure no one could hear. "This isn't the place to discuss the subject."

"Forgive me if I'm not too concerned about that."

"Consider Allie, Jake. For one second, think about that little girl and what it will do to her life if she's the talk of the town because of something somebody overheard on the street."

He closed the distance between them, anger radiating from him in waves. He backed her against the wall until their thighs touched.

"You know what I'd like to do right now, Savannah? I'd like to wring your neck!" But he shoved his hands into his pockets. "How could you keep this from me? For all these years?"

In some corner of her mind—a corner she usually kept dark—she'd known this could happen. But she'd never imagined how awful the reality would be.

"I refuse to discuss this with you in the middle of downtown on a public sidewalk," she said. "If you want to talk, we talk later. Tonight. After the kids are in bed. I have to go to them now."

She inched from between him and the wall, but he grabbed her wrist, conveying that he wasn't about to let the matter drop.

"Let me go," she said through gritted teeth.

"Where can I find you tonight? Because we *will* be discussing this in a lot more detail."

"Fifth and Vine. A red duplex. I live in the one on the left. Don't come before nine, because the kids will be awake."

He nodded once but still didn't release her. She pulled on her arm, but he held tight as he stared at her. "I can't believe you didn't tell me."

"Kind of hard to tell you when you *ran away*." She yanked her hand downward and freed herself, then walked toward the office. At the door, she paused and schooled her features to reveal nothing of the tempest inside her.

"Tell my grandmother I went to move her car closer."

Savannah made a point of not glancing at him as she entered.

"Mom! Make Allie stop staring at me like that."

"I'm not staring at him," she said. "Brat."

"Allie. Don't call your brother names. Logan, get your homework out, go to the conference room and start on it."

The little boy groaned, but Savannah barely noticed.

Zach entered from the back room then, helping Mrs. Levine through the doorway with her walker. Thankfully, they'd missed the bickering.

Zach introduced the women and Savannah forced herself to be polite. "It's nice to meet you."

"You, too, dear. Any idea where that grandson of mine is?"

"He went to get the car." Savannah assumed Zach's place to help her to the door.

Mrs. Levine smiled warmly at her. "This young man's got a talented crew. Those custom cabinets are lovely."

"I keep begging them to do some furniture for me, but they claim paying customers come first," Savannah said, vaguely wondering how she was managing to speak coherently, making small talk with Jake's grandma as they headed to the door.

Jake opened it from the outside just as they reached it, and gently took his grandmother's arm. Savannah tried to avoid eye contact and any kind of conversation, but she met his eyes automatically when he touched her arm.

"I'll see you later." His quiet words sounded like a threat.

She let the door swing shut once Jake and Mrs. Levine had cleared it, and went to her desk. There, she sat and shuffled papers to appear busy, even though she couldn't possibly focus on work.

Zach didn't seem to notice anything was wrong. "They're decent," he said. "Had some interesting ideas."

Suddenly, now that she had a crisis to deal with, the land deal wasn't so pressing to Savannah. "What kind of ideas?"

"They proposed forming a partnership just for this project. Mrs. Levine is very interested in what we'd do with the land. She wants to keep her immediate property and the home she lives in, which is close to one edge of the forty acres."

He continued explaining something about varied floor plans and cohesive styles of homes, but Savannah found it difficult to pay attention.

"So where did you end it?" she asked when he stopped talking and waited for her to say something.

"I'm running their partnership idea by my lawyer, first off."

"You're thinking about proceeding?"

Zach strolled around his desk. "I don't think I can pass it up. If this is the only way the project will happen, I can work with a partner. Besides, it'll be cheaper for us in the short term."

"Cheaper's good."

"Tell me what you know about Barnes."

"I thought it was Mrs. Levine's land."

"He'll be in on it, too."

"He doesn't even live here. Why involve him?"

Zach gave her a puzzled look. "Because Odessa Levine wants him involved. She holds all the cards right now. Is there a reason I shouldn't work with him?"

Now Zach seemed suspicious of her, which wasn't at all what Savannah wanted. She struggled to provide him with an honest response.

"Jake is…diligent. Competitive. Loyal until you cross him, then he carries a grudge…."

"Have you crossed him?"

She wouldn't call it that, exactly. "We've known each other since kindergarten. Competed in everything."

"Is that all?"

"What do you mean, is that all?"

Zach studied her, and that made her antsy. She checked her watch, only to find she still had almost an hour to go before she could bow out for the day.

"Maybe what I should ask is whether you can work with him if we make this deal."

"Of course. We need this to happen."

"Last chance. If there's anything I ought to know about Barnes, now's the time to bring it up."

She shook her head. "Go for the deal." Her voice lacked enthusiasm, but it was the best she could do.

Zach stared at her, so she picked up a pen and drew lines under the words on the top paper, as if she was reading intently. Finally, she heard him sit down, reach for the phone and dial.

Savannah propped her elbows on the desk and shielded her eyes with her hands, still acting as though she was hard at work—when in fact tears threatened. She couldn't let them fall.

What was she going to do? What if Jake told Allie the truth? Her throat swelled and seemed to cut off her oxygen. The tears overflowed at last, dropping onto the paper and turning it into a black-and-white smear.

She sucked in air as quietly as possible, fighting to breathe evenly. Perhaps in a few years, when Allie was old enough to understand, she could handle the news. Right now, after the divorce, Savannah had to rebuild Allie's world. She couldn't bear the thought of Allie having another reason to hate her.

She eyed Allie sideways, from under the cover of her hands. The young girl was sprawled on the floor, drawing again, totally unaware. Good. Savannah wanted to keep her in ignorant bliss for as long as possible. Wanted to mend the rift between them and get their relationship back on track before hitting her with another life-altering shock.

Allie was independent, determined to do things her own way. Her butterfly ponytail holder was so little-girl, her concentration on her artwork so grown-up. She was at that awkward stage, no longer a young child but not yet a teenager. Soon she'd be in middle school and face the craziness that was adolescence.

Savannah ached to hold her and tell her everything would be okay, but she knew too well what reaction that would get.

Tears overflowed anew and Savannah plucked a tissue from the box on her desk to sop them up before anyone noticed. Jake had to understand what was best. He might be mad as a bull at her, but he had to step back and acknowledge how much it would hurt Allie to tell her.

Her jaw stiff, Savannah dabbed her eyes with the tissue once more and took a fortifying breath. Her control was back and she wouldn't permit it to slip away again.

CHAPTER FIVE

JAKE ROUNDED THE CORNERS on the gravel roads too fast and nearly planted himself and his bike in a ditch several times, but he didn't slow down.

He'd been riding for hours. If he'd gone in a straight line, he'd be halfway to Montana by now. The freedom the road offered, however, was an illusion, one he fell for less and less the longer he rode.

All of a sudden he was a father. Something told him that even if he'd had years to digest the news, he wouldn't be used to it. *A father.*

His daughter was eleven. Hardly a child anymore. And all he knew about her was that she liked to draw horses and could be moody and withdrawn around her mother. Something inherited from each of her parents, he thought resentfully. He wondered what else she'd gotten from his DNA besides the talent for art and the birthmark.

The sun had set hours ago, darkening the hilly fields so that he could barely make them out in the dim moonlight. He was just outside Lone Oak now, only minutes away from nine o'clock and the chance to confront Savannah and get some answers out of her.

Just the thought of her made his blood boil. Who did

she think she was, to control everyone else's life? Sure, he'd fled Lone Oak, and he'd admit he'd made damn certain no one could track him down. But a lot of years had elapsed between the night he'd taken off and tonight. Plenty of time for her to find him and fess up.

He made his way to Fifth and Vine quickly, his pulse speeding up as he arrived at her house.

The red duplex could use a coat of paint or two. The place was on a hill, and Savannah's side sat atop two single-car garages. Jake pulled his bike up close to one of them and ascended the crumbling concrete steps.

A screen door was all that kept him out. Peering in, he could see a short hall, with heavy wooden doors on either side. He entered and knocked on the door to the left.

It opened almost instantly, but instead of stepping back to let him in, Savannah barreled into the hallway. She led him outside, down the concrete stairs, and seated herself on the second step from the bottom.

"Nice to see you, too," he said to her back.

"Keep your voice down, please. I don't want to wake them up."

He ran a hand through his hair and glanced around the quiet neighborhood before relenting and sitting down next to her.

"Still mad?" she asked.

"What the hell do you think?" he shot back.

A knuckle cracked in the otherwise hushed night. "Try to stop making it all about you for a minute, and listen to me. You cannot tell Allie about this."

"She has every right to know, Savannah."

Her left hand flew to his knee and gripped it. "You can't. She can't handle it."

He shook his head, weary in every cell of his body. "You haven't changed a bit. You're still all about control, aren't you?" He chuckled, a cold, humorless sound emanating from deep in his throat. "I'd think that after being married and having to play nice with others you'd tone it down a little, but you're still every bit as dedicated to being in charge."

"This isn't about me."

"Oh, yes, it is. You're the one who's been manipulating other people's lives in order to hide the big embarrassment of sleeping with me."

Savannah's jaw dropped and she stared at him. "If that's your opinion, then it just goes to show you don't have the first clue about being a parent."

"I haven't had the chance to be a parent. That was taken away from me."

"You took it away from yourself by leaving town."

JAKE BOLTED UP and paced down the driveway. Savannah waited, her tension skyrocketing.

A couple of minutes later, he came back, his arms crossed over his chest. "What I want to understand," he said in an obviously restrained voice, "is why you've kept this a secret from me. Why you thought I didn't deserve to know I have a child."

Savannah really had no desire to get into the subject, had no desire to relive the past or remember that awful period when she'd been so alone and expecting a baby. Had no desire to justify the decisions she'd made, even though she still, today, firmly believed they'd been the right ones.

But she had to. There was no way out of it. Jake would never stop pestering her until she explained, and she yearned for nothing more than for him to leave her and her children in peace.

"You want to know all about it?" she asked.

He raised his brows expectantly.

"Fine." She gazed at her lap for an eternity, struggling to figure out where to start. What to say. Finally she rubbed her hands over her thighs and jumped in at the beginning.

"I was back at college for spring semester, a month or so after we were together. I did a pregnancy test. Four of them, actually, hoping that if I kept trying, one would give me the answer I wanted. But no, they were 100 percent accurate. I freaked."

Jake sat on the step next to her, but maintained his distance. Distance was what she wanted, Savannah reminded herself.

"I came home the following weekend," she told him. "I'd heard you'd gone before I returned to school, but I thought maybe you'd be back. I went to your house and your sister told me you'd left town permanently. She had no idea where you were."

Savannah wasn't about to go into detail about how his absence had sent her into another downward spiral. She'd needed him then, needed someone to face such an insurmountable problem with her. Someone who was as affected by it as she was.

"You'd run away," she said.

"I didn't run away. If you want to get technical, I was sent away."

"What do you mean?"

He was quiet for several moments. "My dad kicked me

out of the house. He was bent out of shape because I was gone all night that time—with you, but he didn't know that. My sister had gotten picked up by the cops. My dad was in Kansas City for a conference and had to leave early to deal with her problems. He was livid I wasn't around to do so."

"You were always handling your sister's problems. Problems your dad should've dealt with."

"That's why I blew up. That particular battle had been brewing for years—ever since my mom died—and we finally let it all out." He swallowed, staring off into the distance. "It was ugly."

"So instead of just getting out of his house, you got out of town."

"Right."

Neither of them said anything for a long while and Savannah found herself waffling between sympathy for Jake and anger that he hadn't been there for her.

At last, he broke the silence. "You can't hold it against me that I wasn't around. I had no idea what you were going through. Maybe if you hadn't told me what a big mistake sleeping together was, if we'd still been together, I wouldn't have left so easily."

"Don't put the blame on me, Jake."

She had wondered frequently, though, how her life would have been different if she hadn't run scared from him. That was what had happened, even though she'd denied it to herself back then. The morning after they'd made love, she'd flipped out. The feelings Jake had evoked in her were way too intense and out of control and she couldn't handle them.

Then *or* now.

"Michael was home from college that weekend, too."

"Moser."

"Yeah."

"Whom you married." He said it as an accusation.

Savannah stood, unable to keep sitting by Jake, zigzagging between past emotions and the spectrum he was putting her through now. Just being around Jake was like trying to sprint through quicksand.

"Michael and I were friends. We'd already dated several times."

"I remember."

"We went out that weekend. I called him because…well, I guess I wanted to talk about it. I hadn't told anyone and I knew I could trust him."

She'd also known he was "safe." He didn't make her do or feel crazy things the way Jake did.

"We had dinner at Tut's and I was rotten company. Afterward, we went on a long drive and I told him everything. He was really understanding. Offered to help."

"So he popped the question."

Savannah glared at Jake. "No, he didn't pop the question. He offered to help me find you."

Jake apparently had nothing to say to that.

"We tracked you to the bus depot in Denver. He and I even drove there the next weekend, hoping to uncover a clue to where you were."

He shook his head. "I didn't want to be found."

"Obviously. Michael and I hunted for you for weeks. We drove all over to small towns, asking people if they'd spotted you. Called hospitals and police stations.

"My dad never suspected what was going on. I missed

a lot of classes, and when spring break rolled around, my pregnancy was starting to show. I hid it for a while, but I knew I had to tell my father. That's when Michael proposed and I quit school."

JAKE CLAMPED HIS JAW SHUT to keep his comment to himself. Michael Moser had been good enough for her, but *he* hadn't. That she'd turned him away after one night burned him to this day. One nearly perfect night that he could still recollect clearly… Her pale silky skin, ghostly white in the moonlight shining in through the window. The long slender body that had sent him into orbit. The waves of reddish brown hair that had covered her delicate shoulders. He hadn't forgotten a single detail.

That night had resulted in a little girl, he reminded himself.

"What's she like?" he asked, emotion softening his voice.

"Who?"

"Allie. Tell me about her."

Savannah studied him in the near darkness and moved closer, then sat down next to him again, lost in thought.

"She's smart. Not just book smart—she grasps things about life. You already saw she's a talented artist. I never realized she got that from you. I'd forgotten."

"What'd she get from you?"

Savannah smiled, but the smile faded into a grimace. "She's as stubborn and independent as anything."

"She got your eyes," Jake said, surprised at the tenderness he felt toward the child he'd only met the other day.

"She got my big feet and my tangle-prone hair. She's a shy child, normally. Total introvert."

"Where did *that* come from?"

"Some recessive gene buried deep inside one of us, I guess."

"I want to get to know her," Jake said without thinking. Once the comment was out, he didn't retract it. He couldn't deny its source was more than mere curiosity about the person who shared half his genetic makeup.

"That's not possible." Savannah's voice lacked all hint of the gentleness it had held when she'd described Allie. Now it was hard. Unrelenting.

But that was too bad, because Jake wasn't about to be denied. He'd missed eleven years with Allie and he refused to miss more.

"It'll have to be possible. She's my daughter, Savannah. You can't prevent me from getting to know her."

She popped up off the step again.

"Tell me how you're going to work that. 'Hey, Allie, this strange man who just showed up in town out of nowhere wants to hang out with you, and I'm okay with it, even though he's a virtual stranger.' She'll think I've lost it."

"So let her think that."

"You don't understand. She is not at her best now. She's hurting and she hates me. I can't do anything to push her further away."

"I thought you said this wasn't about you."

She spun around and faced him. "It's about *her,* Jake," she hissed. "All about Allie. I can't let her find out that the man she's called Dad all these years…isn't. Not right now. Can't you understand how that might shatter her already very fragile world?"

Jake struggled to see things from the point of view of the daughter he barely knew. Wouldn't she want to have the truth? He couldn't quite imagine what discovering something so shocking and fundamental about who you were would be like. Would it hurt her or help her to learn he was her father? The last thing he wanted was to hurt Allie in any way.

"I'll agree to hold off on telling her. For a little while. It'll probably be easier on her if we get to know each other first."

Why he expected that to appease Savannah or make her reasonable, he wasn't sure.

She shook her head vehemently. "We haven't decided you're going to get to know her."

"I'm her father."

"You could pick up and go at any moment. In fact, aren't you leaving soon?"

"I'll be here for a few more days, and then I'll be back several times if things work out with my grandmother's land. But leaving town doesn't mean walking out of Allie's life. There are such things as phone calls and e-mail. She could even fly out and visit."

Fear washed over Savannah's face. "She's not old enough to do that."

He stood and walked up to her. "I'm going to get to know my daughter. We can work together on this, or you can piss me off and push me. Trust me when I say that won't be to your advantage."

"Are you threatening me?" Her teeth were clenched and her eyes held a vicious protectiveness he'd never witnessed.

"Just explaining where I'm coming from."

"Are you telling me you'll take legal action?"

"I didn't say that, did I?"

"Sure sounded like you did."

"I don't want this to be ugly, Savannah. We have a child together, and both of us have some rights in the matter. All three of us. Allie has the right to know who her father is, and I have the right to know her."

"Simple, isn't it?"

"Dammit, Savannah! There's nothing simple about it. I just found out several hours ago that I have an eleven-year-old daughter I never knew about. You tell me what's simple about that."

"Lower your voice," she said coldly. "You may have rights as her father, but the minute you do her harm is the minute you give those up. Having her overhear you would qualify as doing her harm."

Jake pressed his thumb against his lip. The one thing Savannah was correct about was that if Allie overheard them arguing about his being her dad, it would hurt her.

"You're not the only one who's reeling here," Savannah said. "For almost twelve years, I've been in this without you. Now, suddenly, here you are, barging in and insert-ing yourself into our lives. Wanting to take my daughter to Montana. It doesn't work that way, Jake."

"Does anyone else know about me?"

"No one. No one even knows I was with you."

Didn't that just figure. She was too embarrassed by her terrible lapse in judgment to tell anyone.

"What's your family going to say?" he asked.

"My family isn't going to find out."

He shook his head in disbelief. "You don't get it, do you? The secret is out. You can't go back, Savannah. I'm her father and I'm not going away. The truth is no longer something you can shove under the rug and pretend everything's okay."

"You think that's what I've been doing?" There went the knuckle crack. "You have no concept what it's like to make the decisions I've had to make by myself because you took off. Keep the baby or not. Marry Michael or not. Let my family in on who the real father of my child is or not. Tell Allie or not. Track you down or not. Not a day's gone by that I've pretended everything's okay."

He held up a hand. "Okay, I get it. I'm sorry." He reached out to touch her arm. "Let's take some time so we can both get used to things."

She pulled away from him.

"We'll talk about it again in a couple of days," he stated.

"You don't understand that I don't want to talk about it ever, do you?" she said.

"Oh, I get it just fine. *You* don't understand that now that I know I have a daughter, I can't walk away."

He stared at her for several seconds and then did just that…walked away. But he'd be back.

CHAPTER SIX

JAKE DETESTED HOSPITALS. The smell, the sounds, the harsh lights everywhere. He supposed that was a natural reaction when you'd been through what he and Emily had with their mother.

He stopped at the information desk and asked for Dean Barnes's room number. The volunteer typed in the name, her nails clicking on the keys. "Room 204," she said, and smiled up at him. Jake wasn't able to fake a smile back.

As he made his way to the elevators, he saw the hallway that led to the emergency room. Against his will, he paused, regarded the corridor to the waiting area, and broke out into a cold sweat.

The whole scene came back to him vividly—he and Emily in the uncomfortable, crowded lobby, praying, holding hands... He'd been twelve and Emily six. He remembered fearing the worst and having those fears confirmed when the doctor emerged too soon. Too soon to have rolled their mother to surgery, or to have spent much effort saving her.

Because it'd been too late.

She'd ended her life with a bottle of pills, and no one at the hospital had been able to do anything for her.

Their father had arrived not long afterward. He'd been teaching a class at the university, fifty-five miles away. Jake had tried numerous times to reach him at his office before he'd finally gotten through, and he'd thought then, surely, his dad would step in and make everything a bit more bearable. A little less nightmarish.

But no, he hadn't. He never did. Instead of helping his children through their grief, he'd buried himself even more in his job. Ironic, since Jake maintained that a big part of his mother's problems had stemmed from her husband's workaholism.

Jake shuddered and hurried past the hallway to the elevator.

Once he stood outside of room 204, he leaned against the wall, thinking that maybe sitting in the E.R. waiting room and remembering the hellish past would be preferable to walking through that door and speaking to his father.

He pushed off from the wall and entered, not giving himself a chance to rethink the visit. This was why he'd returned to Lone Oak. He was doing it for Emily and Emily alone.

The sight of the figure in the single bed stopped him in his tracks. Jake turned and checked the number on the door, which he'd left ajar, to verify this was the right room. The man in the bed did not look like his father.

He was sleeping, and the body outlined by the sheets was half the size his dad's had always been—not fat, just wide…sturdy. Tubes snaked from bedside machines and IV drips, and monitors periodically beeped.

When Jake had left town, his dad had had thick, dark

brown hair. Now it was fully gray. His face was thin, bony, almost unrecognizable. His father opened his eyes, and Jake caught a glimpse of the man he remembered. But those hazel eyes were weary. Filled with defeat.

Jake could tell when recognition struck. His father didn't smile, exactly, but something in his face lightened. "Am I imagining things?" he asked in a weak, gravelly voice. "Is it really you, son?"

Jake took one step forward, feeling uncomfortable. "It's me."

Dean Barnes worked one arm from under the blankets and held it out. Jake looked at the bony, pale hand for several seconds, torn. Torn because this man who barely resembled his father was heartbreaking, but had caused so much resentment and anger in the past.

Jake touched his father's hand, then pulled over a chair to sit on, carefully keeping his distance.

"It's nice to see you," Dean said. "Been too long."

Jake worked to keep his comments to himself. While he couldn't get rid of the years-old anger, he did have the sense to go easy on this man. This dying man. Even as Jake stared at his father's emaciated body, he couldn't quite wrap his head around the fact that Dean was losing his battle with the big *C*.

"Emily asked me to return."

"I'm glad."

A nurse arrived then and Jake stood to get out of the way, relieved at the interruption.

"This won't take long," she told him as she rolled in some equipment.

"I'll wait in the hall." He slipped out before anyone

could protest. Exhaling deeply, he leaned against the wall, searching for a happy memory of his father. After his mother died, there had been very few good moments, but before that… There had to be something.

By the time the nurse emerged a few minutes later, he'd dredged up one happy memory. He'd been five or six, and his dad had bought him his first real wooden bat and baseball. They'd played out in the yard for hours. It was one of the only occasions Jake remembered his dad playing with him.

"All done," the nurse said, her voice friendly yet concerned, conveying sympathy for their situation. Sympathy, Jake realized, that was wasted on him.

He was sad, but not because his dad was wasting away. Maybe that would come. Perhaps when his father passed on. Right now his throat tightened at the realization of all they'd missed throughout his life. The family that wasn't…

His thoughts turned to Allie, his little girl, who made him want to smile even now as he thought about the horse drawing she'd given him.

Sadly, he and his dad had shared almost no connection in the nineteen years they had lived under the same roof. Jake had missed the first eleven years of Allie's life, but he had hope for the future. He wanted to make their relationship special, wanted her to have good memories of things they'd done together, moments they'd shared. He wanted to have everything with Allie that he'd missed with his dad.

With Dean it was too late.

Jake straightened and went back into the room, but his father had fallen asleep. Jake watched him for several minutes, again searching for childhood memories of them together, but the truth was his dad had been at work most of Jake's waking hours. He remembered hearing him slip in the back door after Jake had gone to bed. There were occasions when Jake had woken up as his dad told him good-night and pulled up the blankets, but those were fuzzy. Jake wondered now if they'd been real or just what he'd hoped for.

He could feel his pulse pounding in his temples. He had to get out of here. He would have to come back; he couldn't leave things like this. But he couldn't take more tonight, and maybe his dad couldn't either. Dean had acted friendly, but Jake was certain they'd both felt awkward.

He walked out of the room before his father could wake up.

THURSDAY AFTERNOON, Savannah rubbed her aching neck and struggled once again to concentrate on the work in front of her. She hadn't slept much last night, or the nights before—ever since Jake had found out the truth about Allie and decided he wanted to be part of her life.

The kids, for once, were avidly doing their homework, Allie in the conference room and Logan next to Savannah on the floor. She'd promised them that if they could finish their assignments before she was done with work, she would let them each rent a video. She was a firm believer in parenting by bribery at times, and this was one of them. Her headache had persisted for days now, and she acknowledged she'd been rotten company and a grumpy mother. Both kids probably deserved more than a video rental for putting up with her mood, but that was what she could afford today. Maybe Michael could spoil them this weekend.

She frowned. She still wasn't used to losing her kids every other weekend. They were fortunate their dad cared enough to fight for some regular hours with them, she guessed. Sharing was hard to adjust to for everyone, though. All those instances over the years when she'd secretly wished to be alone in the middle of a sibling battle, and now she finally could be. She just had to learn what to do to keep from missing the kids.

The door from the shop area opened and she glanced up, expecting to find Zach, but not Jake right behind him.

"Hey," Zach said, and immediately busied himself with the phone messages that hadn't been urgent enough to forward to his cell phone.

"Afternoon," Jake said, not smiling. He was still upset, obviously. Well, join the club.

Savannah stared at him, unable to think of a thing to say. She couldn't quite act as though everything was fine, not when she was terrified of what his being around would do to her and her kids' lives.

"Is there any coffee?" he asked, and Zach pointed to the conference room, where they kept the coffeepot and cups.

Jake sauntered in that direction and Savannah hastily popped out of her chair to follow him.

She needed to chill. She knew that, but she couldn't seem to do it.

"Coffee?" he inquired smugly.

"No, thank you. Just checking on my daughter." She shot him a glare of warning—possible because Allie didn't even glance her way. "Why are you here, Jake?"

He poured brew into a disposable cup, his back to her. Then he turned, and she couldn't help noticing how appealing he was even after being, she'd guess, on the future job site with Zach—hair tousled, dusty T-shirt stretched across his sculpted chest.

"I'm here for my grandma. Until I leave town, she's put me in charge of her interests."

"I thought you were in the middle of a crucial project back in Montana."

"I am. Now I'm in the middle of two crucial projects, one in Montana and one in Kansas."

"I just find it coincidental that—" Savannah glanced pointedly at the back of Allie's head "—with everything going on, you decide to invade *here*. Now."

"Interesting choice of words." As he spoke, he ambled toward her. "You make it sound like it's all about you." He stopped right in front of her. Far too near. Infringing on her personal space and then some. "It's not."

Savannah glanced toward Allie again, noticing she was drawing instead of studying. Her daughter appeared to be ignoring them, but Savannah had learned that little ears were usually tuned in when you didn't want them to be.

"Allie, why don't you pack up your stuff. We'll be leaving in a few minutes. Did you get your homework done?"

"Yesss," Allie answered impatiently. But she did as Savannah requested, without ignoring her or fighting. She put her pencil into a pink canvas pouch full of art supplies, and zipped it.

"We're renting videos tonight," Allie told Jake.

"Videos? Cool. What are you going to rent?"

"*High School Musical.* It's my very favorite movie."

Who was this child who was volunteering all kinds of information without being prompted?

"That sounds fun," Jake said, brushing a lock of hair behind her ear as she walked past him.

"You could watch with us."

"No, he couldn't." Savannah practically snapped the words. "Go tell Logan to pack his stuff."

Jake started to trail Allie from the room, but Savannah reached out to stop him. He looked down at where she held his arm and she dropped it fast.

"You touched her," she said in a low voice. "You're being affectionate with her. You're trying to get her to like you." Her words were crazy, she acknowledged, but she felt desperate, as if he was stealing her child away.

He stepped closer, so they were inches apart, and spoke softly, gently. "Savannah. You're being ridiculous. Relax."

Being so close, she could sense his heat, the energy that pumped through him, and she wanted to lean closer. Wanted to hang her head and bury it in his chest, because yes, she was overreacting and she knew it. But…

"I can't relax," she said through gritted teeth. "She's my daughter."

Their eyes met, and the fact that Allie was *his* daughter, too, hung between them. Savannah stepped away, annoyed with herself for the momentary urge she'd had to move nearer to him. She pulled him farther into the conference room, out of sight of the others.

"You're using this project to get closer to her, aren't you? That's why you did it."

He eyed her in disbelief. "I didn't even know about her when my grandma decided to meet with Zach. It's been her decision all along. Completely unrelated to what I learned the other night, after our meeting. Do you really think I'd jeopardize my deal in Montana just to mess with you?"

"You said yourself you wanted to be in Allie's life."

"And I'm going to be in her life. I don't have to play games to accomplish that. Not my style, honey."

With that, he left the room, said goodbye to everyone and went out the front door.

Savannah sat on the edge of the table. She was an idiot. She didn't really believe he was using the construction deal to get closer to Allie. She knew how insane that was now that he was gone. But seeing him saunter into the room with her daughter had sent Savannah into a panic. Made her slip into her annoying out-of-control-because-of-Jake mode.

She put her feet on a chair and lay across the table. The fact was more than just Jake's knowing about Allie bothered her. Added to it was a bone-deep fear that her relationship with her daughter would get even worse.

The sound of Logan giggling at something snapped Savannah out of her self-pity fest and made her realize how easily one of the kids could find her here being pathetic and ashamed. She wearily sat up and slid to her feet, wiped the tears away, then busied herself tidying the coffee area. Which really wasn't messy. She just needed a few moments to regain her composure before facing everyone.

So much for not losing control again.

CHAPTER SEVEN

"MICHAEL ISN'T ALLIE'S biological father." Savannah squirmed and closed her eyes for a moment, then got the nerve to face her two sisters, who were seated on the couch next to her. They'd been bugging her the entire car ride to the bridal shop to tell them what was wrong, why she was so uptight. Now they knew.

Katie, the youngest Salinger sister and the bride-to-be, was smiling, clearly not believing what Savannah had said. She pulled her light brown hair up to the back of her head and secured it with a hairband. Lindsey, the oldest, grabbed Savannah's arm, brown eyes wide, her other hand resting protectively over her pregnant belly. Katie noticed, and then she, too, became serious.

"You're not joking, are you?"

"I wouldn't joke about this," Savannah said as she bolted off the couch and paced.

The fitting room was as big as a living room, in order to accomodate three different pedestals surrounded by mirrors, long wedding-dress trains, and the number of people who invariably accompanied a bride to such ordeals. Today there were just the three Salingers. The other bridesmaid, Eve, couldn't make it, and would have to drop by for her final fitting later that week. Claudia, their stepmother, was also absent, on a weekend trip to Vegas with their dad. This was the last fitting before Katie and Noah's wedding, and the sales associate had gone in search of their gowns.

"Whoa," Katie said. "Scandal in the family. Who, pray tell, *is* the father?"

"Katie," Lindsey scolded. But she, too, waited for an answer.

"Probably someone you don't know. His name is Jake Barnes."

"No way! I totally remember him," Lindsey said. "You used to talk about him nonstop."

The saleslady arrived just then, lugging Katie's dress. "Here is the bride's," she said. "Let's start with you and then I'll go get the other girls'."

Katie slipped her jeans and sweater off her perfect size-six body and walked over to where the woman was removing the plastic covering from the gown. "Thanks—" she read the woman's name tag "—Beth. I don't remember Jake." The last was said to Savannah and Lindsey.

"You could stand to eat a sandwich or two," Savannah said at the sight of her sister's thin frame.

"Stop," Katie said. "I'm starving. Now, who's Jake?"

The bridal shop they were in was located in Topeka. The fact that they didn't know anyone in the city was the only reason Savannah dared to continue the conversation.

"He was in my class from kindergarten on. We competed in everything. Something about him has always egged me on. At first the rivalry was natural. Then he started taunting me and encouraging it. I used to hate him," Savannah said.

"I'm not sure *hate's* the right word," Lindsey mused. "I recall how much you talked about him. Usually complaining, yes, but an unnatural amount of it. I used to think you had a crush on him." She took the dress from Beth and began digging through the layers of material to try to slip it over Katie's head.

Savannah made a sound of disgust, a cross between a grunt and a laugh. "He's always made me crazy. He gets my pulse up every time I'm in contact with him, and I don't mean that in a good way. Not always, anyhow."

"He gets under your skin," Lindsey said.

"Yes. Exactly."

"Then how in the world did you end up sleeping together?" Katie asked this from inside the dress, so she didn't immediately catch the glare Savannah shot her.

When Katie's head finally emerged from the white satin, Savannah made a discreet gesture toward the salesclerk, and Katie mouthed, *Sorry.*

Savannah helped Lindsey arrange the skirt of the wedding dress as the woman left the room.

"It's not like we're ever going to see her again after we pick up the dresses, Van. She doesn't care what we're talking about. So, how did this happen?"

"The usual way."

"She means how did you and Jake get together," Lindsey said as she started fastening the million little hooks down the back of Katie's dress.

Savannah stood aside to admire her sister. "You're stunning."

Katie attempted to turn and primp, but the dress didn't seem easy to move in. "Thanks. Now answer the question."

Savannah sat on a stool in the middle of the room and crossed her arms. "We were at a party one night during winter break my freshman year in college. My friends— the ones I'd ridden there with—had an accident when they went out to pick up snacks. I'd stayed at the party but was pretty freaked out when we heard the news. Jake became Super Caring Guy and took me to visit them at the hospital in Layton so I could stop worrying.

"After I'd gotten reports on all of them—they wouldn't let me in to visit Lisa, who was hurt the worst—neither of us was in the mood to return to the party. We didn't want to go home, either."

Savannah stood again, unable to sit still. "This is the embarrassing part. We went to an old barn near his house. The owners only used one part of it, for a couple horses. It was warm and private."

"The proverbial roll in the hay," Katie said from up on her pedestal.

"Hey, watch it. All I have to do is push you and you'll be tangled in satin for a week." Savannah managed a half grin in spite of how uncomfortable she felt baring all.

The fact was she'd needed to confide in her sisters. Needed to talk to someone about the insanity she'd been going through this past week.

"For once, Jake wasn't trying to get to me and I wasn't trying to one-up him. We just…talked. Something clicked. We connected over losing our mothers, and so much more. We spent the whole night there and it was… well, it was the best sex of my life."

Beth reentered the room, carrying two coral dresses. "Usually, it's the bride we overhear saying that," she commented with a grin, and if Savannah had been the blushing type, she would've been beet-red.

She took her gown and laid it over the end of the couch while she undressed. Lindsey was nearby, doing the same.

"Wow!" Katie called, from the perch where she was stuck. "Your bump has become a bulge!" She pointed at Lindsey's belly.

"I want to touch," Savannah declared, shooting back in time to when she'd been pregnant. "May I?"

Lindsey rolled her eyes and nodded. "A girl can't keep anything private anymore, can she?"

"Hey, I just told you the biggest secret of my life. The least you can do is let me feel the baby kick."

"He's apparently napping this morning."

"The seamstress will be in in a few minutes," Beth told them. "I'll help you two get your dresses on. I hope that baby hasn't grown too much." She looked doubtfully at Lindsey's middle.

Once they were all in their gowns and waiting for the seamstress, Beth left the room to help another bridal group.

Lindsey studied herself in one of the mirrors. "I'm never going to forgive you for getting married while I'm pregnant."

"You're gorgeous even with the bulge," Katie said, and faced Savannah. "So you went back to school, found out you were pregnant? Then what?"

"I attempted to find Jake. He'd left Lone Oak right after our night together. I didn't know what else to do. I couldn't handle it by myself. Mom was gone…."

Both her sisters nodded.

"God, I missed her then."

"I can imagine," Katie mumbled, her face drawn. "Did you find Jake?"

Savannah shook her head. "I tried for weeks. Michael and I had gone on a few dates before the Jake night, and he helped me search. I don't know how I would've gotten through everything without him."

"Why didn't you tell *me?*" Lindsey asked. Savannah could hear the subtle hurt in her voice.

"You were at school, sixty miles away."

"You could've called. I would've been there for you."

Savannah studied her. "Are you now?"

Her sister averted her eyes, smoothed coral satin over her belly, chewed her lip. "I don't understand why you didn't tell me. I came home from school often enough. Getting pregnant by the wrong guy—that's huge, Savannah."

"You think I don't know that? It wasn't something I was proud of, believe me. Once I told Michael, I couldn't figure how anyone else could help me. Only Jake."

Lindsey hesitated, as if imagining what Savannah had gone through back then. "So Michael knew from the beginning you were pregnant with Jake's kid?" she queried. "There was no chance Allie was Michael's?"

"Michael and I never slept together. Not until after Allie was born, actually. When it was obvious we weren't going to find Jake, and I started to show, he told me he was in love with me and offered to marry me and raise Allie as his own."

"Wow," Katie said. "I had no idea."

"No one did," Savannah said. "No one could."

"So does Jake know he's Allie's father?"

"He does now. I confirmed it after he met Allie at my office."

"Oh, my God! That's the guy in the new development, isn't it? Jake. And Odessa Levine." Lindsey said. "I hadn't put the name together with *your* Jake."

"He's not my Jake."

Lindsey closed her eyes for a moment. "Zach doesn't know. You haven't told him, right?"

"I haven't told him, but he knows something's weird between Jake and me. I don't exactly act normal when Jake's around," Savannah said.

"That's wild." Katie shook her head.

The seamstress knocked and entered. "Sorry to keep you ladies waiting."

"Oh, that's okay. We've managed to entertain ourselves," Katie said with a friendly grin. "Lindsey's going to require another yard of satin, though."

Half an hour later, they were back in their regular clothes and walking out to Savannah's minivan. Their discussion had turned to wedding topics ever since the seamstress interrupted them, but Savannah was still preoccupied.

"There's one more thing," she said when they'd all shut their doors, Lindsey in the passenger seat and Katie behind them in the middle row. "Jake wants to get to know Allie. And he wants to tell her the truth."

Lindsey shook her head, as though Jake's idea wouldn't work at all. "Did you tell him she's still adjusting to your divorce?"

Savannah nodded. "What am I going to do?"

"I'm not sure. I think you have to prevent him from

telling her for a while," Lindsey said. "She's not in the right frame of mind to hear that kind of news."

"How long will he be in town?" Katie inquired.

"Another few days. And then he'll be back on and off, he said. Enough to turn our lives upside down."

"You have to give him full access to Allie, as long as he promises not to tell her until you agree." Katie was leaning forward between the two front seats.

"Are you crazy?" Savannah said. "Allie's already met him and considers him the coolest thing since Hannah Montana."

"That's okay," Katie replied. "Let him do things with her if he wants. You can't afford to let this get ugly."

"Did he mention legal action?" Lindsey asked.

"Not really. He did make it clear he'll go as far as he has to."

"I feel being flexible with him is the only way. Don't fight him. Give him what he wants as long as he won't tell Allie he's her father. How much will he really take you up on it when he's hardly going to be in town?"

"She has a valid point," Lindsey said.

"Jake is stubborn. He'll take me up on it as much as he can."

"So what's so bad about it, as long as Allie doesn't learn who he really is? If she likes him…"

"I know that's gotta be scary to think about," Katie said. "But if you're nice and accommodating, he has no reason to push things."

"I don't want them to be alone together. That would make me insane with worry."

"Then be sure to let him know you'll always be with them."

Savannah stared straight ahead, tapping on the steering wheel. "I don't like being around him."

She felt Lindsey studying her, which had always made her fidget. "How do you feel about Jake?"

"I loathe him."

Lindsey had one eyebrow raised in complete doubt.

"Mostly. He pushes my buttons. Makes me do stupid things, say stupid things. I basically morph into this out-of-control idiot whenever I'm with him."

"You want him," Katie said.

"Shut up."

"There she goes with that protesting-too-much thing," Lindsey told Katie.

"Make fun of me all you like, but it doesn't matter if I want Jake or not. I'm *not* going to have a relationship with him."

"I don't get it. You have a kid with him. You want him. He probably wants you. What's the problem?" Katie asked.

Savannah twisted to face her little sister. "*You're* asking me? Miss I'm-Not-Going-to-Fall-for-Noah?" She turned back around. "The problem is that I have tried marriage. Tried and failed. As my dear ex pointed out ad nauseam, I like control too much to be in a partnership of any kind. He's absolutely correct. So while I might have once been dumb enough to believe I could make a marriage work, I won't be making the same mistake twice."

They were all silent for a few seconds.

"That's really sad, Savannah." Katie sat back and buckled her seat belt.

"You guys don't understand what it's done to us. To the kids *and* me. I won't do anything to put any of us in danger of going through that again."

Lindsey shook her head. "You have to do what you feel is best, but let me just say I believe you're making a mistake. Maybe you're meant to be with Jake."

Savannah scoffed and started the van. "You've never even met him."

"No, but he's working closely with Zach. Besides, it sounds like I might, if he's going to be in Allie's life."

"Sounds like," Savannah said. "I know you guys are right. I'll make an effort to be nice. And accommodating. Even though that goes against every fiber of my being."

CHAPTER EIGHT

JAKE MADE HIS WAY UP the stairs to Savannah's place late Sunday afternoon, knowing full well she didn't want to see him. Several days had passed since he'd learned Allie was his daughter, and he'd been fixated on all the years they'd missed. He shared the blame for that, but only to a certain point. He still thought Savannah had had plenty of opportunity to track him down and tell him he had a daughter. He couldn't deny that continued to tick him off, and probably would for a while.

He knocked on her hallway door, hearing a TV on inside and sensing movement. But no one answered. He knocked again and heard Savannah's voice just before she opened the door.

"You need a peephole," he told her. "What if I happened to be a serial—"

"If I'd had a peephole, I wouldn't have opened up," she said in a low voice so the kids didn't hear.

Logan was watching cartoons in the living room, but Allie was nowhere in sight.

Savannah hesitated, then smiled—a forced one, he would guess—and moved back to allow him to enter. "To what do we owe the pleasure?"

Her hair was piled sloppily on top of her head and she wore an old sweatshirt and sweatpants with a hole in one knee. Her eyes were weary and had shadows under them, as if she hadn't slept for a couple of nights. He stepped past her and looked around. "Hey, Logan."

The boy turned his attention from the TV and smiled when he saw him. "Hey, Jake! How come you're here?"

"Logan, that's not polite," Savannah said to her son. She turned back to Jake. "But I'm dying to know as well…."

Allie emerged from a different room then and her face lit up when she recognized Jake. He couldn't deny the power her smile had over him. His *daughter*. And she seemed to like him.

"Hi," she said somewhat shyly, but she moved closer.

"What are you drawing today?" he asked. "More horses?"

"I'll show you. Wait a minute." She went back to the bedroom.

Savannah appeared nervous, still hanging near the door. "Why'd you stop by, Jake?"

"I thought maybe we could all go somewhere for dinner." He glanced toward the kitchen but didn't smell any food cooking. "Did I catch you in time?"

Allie came out of the bedroom again just as he spoke. She cheered and pulled at her mother's sleeve. "Can we, Mom?"

Savannah eyed her daughter. "I already have meat thawed."

"Please?"

"You can save it for tomorrow. It'll keep," Jake said.

He studied Savannah's face and could tell she didn't

want to go. But if she said no, she'd be the bad guy, and she knew it. Jake was sure he'd hear about it later, but he didn't care. Getting an earful wouldn't be enough to keep him from spending time with his daughter.

"I'd have to take a shower," Savannah said. "I smell like kitchen cleaner."

"We'll wait."

Allie jumped up and down and said, "Yay!" Then she held out her drawing to Jake. It was of a saddle propped up against a barn wall.

"You drew this yourself?" he asked with a smile, knowing she had.

"I used a picture from a magazine."

"I really like it, Allie."

Savannah leaned in to view the drawing upside down, and Jake was shocked that Allie hadn't shown her yet. He remembered that when he'd been Allie's age, he'd always rushed to show his mom his latest work—until she'd died. Now that he thought about it, that was when he'd stopped drawing altogether.

"It's wonderful, honey," Savannah said, but Allie didn't respond.

Jake spotted the hurt that flickered over Savannah's face. She met his gaze then and he braced himself.

"Why don't you go put this on your bulletin board, Allie." As soon as their daughter skipped off, she moved closer and spoke quietly. "You don't have to manipulate me. I've made up my mind to let you get to know her—as long as I'm around, too."

"I'm glad to hear that. It'll make things a lot...friendlier."

"Right. Just remember that. Stop playing games and we'll all be fine."

Her eyes shone with fear and he understood she wasn't happy about any of this. That suited him, because he wasn't, either. But he'd take what little she was offering. The one thing he knew about Savannah was that giving over any control to him killed her. His point wasn't to control. He just wanted to get acquainted with Allie. Being with her mother wouldn't exactly be a hardship, unless they fought nonstop.

Savannah stared at him a long while, those brown eyes piercing his. "I'll just be a minute."

She retreated into what he assumed was the master bedroom. Her sweats hid nothing of her shape and he couldn't help admiring how nice her curves were. He shook his head, determined not to think of her in the same way he had for years and years. He'd had no chance with her in the past, proved by her almost immediate rejection of him after their one night together, and had even less of one now. The only thing he wanted here, he reminded himself, was to form a relationship with his daughter.

SAVANNAH TOOK the fastest shower of her life, praying that Allie was still hidden away in her room with her sketch pad. Savannah didn't think Jake would reveal anything critical but she still didn't want them together without her there.

She dried her hair, then threw on jeans and a black hoodie. Skipping makeup, she found her tennis shoes and slipped them on. She was *not* going to look good for Jake. The second she was alone with him she was going to wring his neck, as a matter of fact. He'd said he didn't play games, but that was exactly what he'd done by asking them to dinner when Allie could overhear. Didn't matter that Savannah had decided to go along with her sisters' advice. How he'd gone about getting to see Allie was the issue.

Savannah poked her head out of her bedroom to note where everyone was. Both kids lounged on the couch with Jake, watching Batman cartoons, from the sound of it.

"Jake?" She motioned for him to join her.

He followed her into the kitchen, which was walled off from the living room and dining area, so the kids couldn't see or hear them.

"Where are you planning on eating?"

He shrugged. "Tut's would work. There aren't a lot of choices here, right?"

"I don't want to go where people will recognize us. In Lone Oak, less than a dinner together could start rumors flying."

"And wouldn't it be terrible if everyone thought you and I were together?" he said sarcastically.

"No, it would be terrible if anyone ever suspected the real reason you're with us."

"You know what, Savannah?"

He advanced on her until they were inches apart and she was backed against the counter. Which didn't take much in this small space. She could smell him and was annoyed that his scent was so familiar, that it still stirred something deep within her after all these years. Even more annoyed that a part of her had the overpowering desire to have it envelop her.

She shook off the weak moment.

"I didn't do anything wrong here," he said. "I'm the one who was kept in the dark and lied to for eleven years."

"I never lied to you." She stood her ground even though their closeness was making her lose her concentration.

"You never told me the truth."

"I've told you why."

"Somehow it's not making me feel any better."

"So now it's all about you, huh?"

He stared at her for a moment and then his lips twitched with the hint of a grin. "I'd almost forgotten what a world-class arguer you are and how much fun arguing with you can be."

"This is fun?"

"Beats sitting around at book club with a bunch of old women." Then he did smile, and it made Savannah's heart catch. She hadn't seen that genuine Jake smile, the not-trying-to-charm-the-ladies one, since he'd been back. Which was a good thing, because the sparks it sent through her were powerful and dangerous.

"We've agreed to dinner, right?" he asked, his eyes penetrating and his body still crowding her, making her want things that she would never take.

"I suppose."

"Let's just go with that. Find out if we can get through it without arguing more. For the kids."

She hesitated briefly, then ducked away from him. "You're treating?"

"I'll treat."

"And we can go where no one will know us?"

She could tell that pained him, but he agreed. She

hollered at the kids to get their shoes and jackets on, and practically rushed from the kitchen to escape the close quarters.

"WHAT'S PERSPECTIVE?" Allie asked Jake after she'd finished her pizza and pulled out her pad of paper.

Savannah shoved her last bite of salad into her mouth. She was ready to be done and out of here. When the hostess had led them to this booth, Jake had insisted on sitting next to her. Instead of acting as though it was a big deal, Savannah had gone along with it, but ever since, they'd been inches away from each other, their thighs sometimes touching.

She wished she could say she wasn't affected by his nearness, the warmth of him along her side, but she'd be lying. She kept inching away surreptitiously, but there wasn't a lot of extra space in the booth.

They'd decided it would be best to get out of Lone Oak if they didn't want to be recognized, and Jake had suggested a pizza place in the nearby university town that his sister swore was the best. So here they were at Luigi's, in Manhattan, Kansas. Savannah had to agree with his sister's assessment. They even had goat cheese for Logan, who was allergic to regular cheese.

Her son frowned at Allie's question. "Can't we go play foosball again, Jake?"

"Logan, we're done with foosball for the night," Savannah said. "Let Jake sit and relax."

"Relaxing is boring."

"Sometimes boring is okay," Jake told him. "I don't think I can handle getting beaten again tonight."

That put a smile on her son's face. She opened her purse

and pulled out the small plastic bag of Lego blocks that she always toted around.

"Smart," Jake said.

"Coping mechanism. Little boys don't do sitting still very well."

Allie pushed her tablet toward Jake expectantly. He turned to a blank page and started sketching something, trying to explain what perspective was. He spoke in terms an eleven-year-old could understand, and Savannah remembered he'd taken care of his little sister after their mom had died. He'd always been pretty close-mouthed about it, but keeping things private in a town the size of Lone Oak was hard.

She had to give him credit for being attentive to *both* her children. He'd played foosball with Logan and paid just as much attention to him as to Allie. That endeared him to Savannah more than she cared to have him endeared.

Between that and the attraction that wouldn't quit, she would have to be doubly on guard whenever they were together.

As Jake finished his sketch, a woman approached their table, someone who'd just come in from the street. She wore black leather pants, a colorful tank top beneath a transparent black shirt, and had multiple earrings and studs in her ears and an emerald stud on the side of her nose.

"Emily," Jake said, standing and putting his arm around her. "You're supposed to be working."

"I'm on break. Called in an order for takeout."

Jake stood back and motioned to Savannah and the kids, introducing them. "This is my little sister."

Oh, yes, his sister. Savannah should have remembered her name. She would never admit to the flutter of jealousy she'd felt before realizing who the woman was. Savannah held out a hand to Emily and greeted her.

"I have to grab my food and get back. No one's there to answer the phone in case it happens to ring for the first time all afternoon." She rolled her eyes. "Stop by the shop when you're done if you want."

"We might do that. See you," Jake said, and sat back down.

"What kind of shop? A toy shop?" Logan asked.

Jake chuckled. "Nothing quite so interesting. Just tattoos."

"Cool!"

"You can have one when you're thirty," Savannah told her son.

"What kind of tattoos does she make?" Allie inquired, suddenly interested.

"Whatever you want," Jake said.

"Same rule of thirty applies to you."

"Do you have any tattoos, Jake?" Allie's eyes skimmed his arms and neck.

"I have one on my back," he told her. "Maybe sometime you can have a peek."

"What's it like?"

"It's a design. Kind of tribal." Jake borrowed her pencil and a napkin and sketched it.

Allie found a blank page in her pad and began drawing something. Logan asked Jake questions about having a sister, apparently thinking having sisters gave them lots in common. While Jake chatted with him and polished off a final piece of pizza, Savannah longed to be back home, safe from the thoughts this man made go through her head.

Several minutes later, Allie held up her notebook. "How do you like it?"

"What is it?" Logan asked.

"A tattoo, dummy."

"It doesn't look like anything," her brother said.

"Tattoos don't have to be objects," Jake told him. "Sometimes a design is so neat it doesn't have to be anything. That's really cool, Allie."

"Thank you," she said, her shyness disappearing.

"I believe you have talent at more than just drawing horses."

"She does," Savannah confirmed. "Horses just happen to be the thing right now."

"At my school art show, I'll have lots of stuff on display. You could come, Jake. It's on Thursday."

"What time does it start?" he asked promptly.

"Six-thirty."

"Sounds like fun. Maybe I'll show up."

Savannah didn't like the idea. Michael was supposed to be at the art fair, and just thinking about how awkward that would be made her squirm. "It'll mostly be just family."

"My teacher said we could invite anybody we want to," Allie announced.

"Jake probably has things to do, honey. It's during dinnertime."

"We'll see," he said in a tone that, to Savannah, held the trace of a threat.

She eyed him sideways, shooting a silent warning his way, but all Jake did was smile smugly and announce it was time to go.

"YOU DIDN'T HAVE TO STAY," Savannah said grudgingly as she walked Jake to the door of her place. He'd waited in the living room while she'd tucked Allie and Logan into bed.

"Oh, I know."

She stepped out into the hallway with him, then shut the door. "So why did you?"

"Thought I'd apologize."

"For?"

They descended the concrete stairs to the driveway in silence. His bike was pulled up along the edge.

"Exposing your children to the world of tattoos," he said with a crooked grin.

"I don't know if I'm more worried about Logan wanting to get them or Allie wanting to design them. I've never seen her so interested in something," Savannah leaned against the garage door with a wry smile.

"How many designs did she do on the way home? Four? Five? And they were decent."

"Don't tell her that." She pushed a strand of her hair behind her ear. "Have you visited your dad yet?"

Jake perused her from head to toe, missing nothing. He noticed the fullness of her bottom lip, slightly moist from her tongue. Her sweatshirt hugged her body, making it easy to imagine the curves without the clothing in the way. Her fingers were in the front pockets of her jeans, her elbows resting against the door. Her back was arched, and he could pretend that was to move her body closer to his. His pulse throbbed with the thought, and he stepped toward her, so only a foot separated them.

He was drawn to her like a bee to sweet nectar.

"Well?" she said, and he fought to remember what she'd just asked him.

"My dad. Yeah. I visited him."

"How'd that go?"

"Wouldn't really call it a rousing success. It was awkward as hell. He was friendly, acted glad to see me."

"But you…weren't."

Jake shrugged. "I've got a lot of years of being pissed at him to get over."

She nodded and glanced at his lips, which was all Jake needed to make him move closer yet.

"Kiss me and my knee will go up faster than you can apologize." She smirked when she said it, her hot breath caressing his face and making him yearn even more to kiss her.

He laughed. "Do you get a lot of dates like that?"

"I don't date."

She could have easily pushed him away, but she glanced again at his mouth, and in that moment, Jake discerned the truth in her eyes. She *wanted* him to kiss her. Savannah still wanted him, whether she would allow herself to admit it or not.

For a minute, he let himself get lost in the desire in her eyes, in the heat that pounded through his veins. Then he forced himself to take an excruciating step back and make her consider what she was missing, even though not tasting those lips or sliding his hands across her skin nearly killed him.

He stared at her for a minute longer, then pivoted and got on his bike. "I'll see you soon. Before I fly out next weekend."

She was flustered. Bothered. Exactly what he'd aimed for. He grinned to himself, put his helmet on and rode off.

SAVANNAH WATCHED Jake ride down the dark street, and didn't move for another five minutes after he was out of sight.

Damn him. He made her body want his, crave him, even though her brain knew much better than to even entertain the idea. She was still shaking from the closeness and that look he'd bestowed on her—one that said he'd like to eat her up inch by aching inch.

The wind was cold now but she stayed where she was, willing it to cool her body and erase the painful tightening deep inside. When her fingers were nearly numb, she finally gave up and went back in, although the empty longing had yet to go away.

CHAPTER NINE

MONDAY AT WORK, Savannah spent too much time reflecting on the night before with Jake. She had a stack of papers to read through, but though she didn't want to think about him, she couldn't seem to get him out of her mind.

She sat at her desk after Zach went home, feeling guilty that she hadn't gotten nearly enough done. She'd promised herself she'd check at least two more items off her to-do list before leaving, and she was at last finished. Just one more task to attend to for Allie. The kids were strangely calm and content—Logan with his Game Boy and Allie with her pencils and sketch pad.

Savannah's obsession with Jake was twofold. There was still the anxiety that lit up like a match to a puddle of gasoline whenever he was with Allie. It was mostly irrational, Savannah realized. She'd figured out he wouldn't reveal their secret without letting her know first. He *would* force the issue someday—and probably soon—but his style wasn't to go behind her back. He'd be up front about it. And Savannah would do everything in her power to convince him to hold off.

Then there was the other half of her obsession—the attraction. The memory of how she'd felt close to him on the driveway last night, and in the booth at the pizza shop. Being near him now brought back how being with him years ago had felt, somehow made the memory fresher and a lot more vivid.

Memories aside, her body still reacted to Jake's, and it ticked her off.

Savannah shook her head and focused on the task at hand. She grabbed a sheaf of card stock and went to the large paper cutter next to the copy machine. Allie had it in her head that she was going to create her own postcards with tattoo-like designs, and she'd asked Savannah to cut some card stock into fourths.

Savannah lined the thin stack of paper along the straight edge of the heavy-duty cutter, trying to ensure the cards would all be the same size. Just as she was about to pull the blade down, the front door opened.

"Hey," Jake said.

Savannah's hand slipped and she caught two of her fingers under the blade. "Ouch!" Pain surged through her, and she saw blood welling before she instinctively grabbed the injured fingers with her other hand. "Don't sneak up on me!" she cried, shaking with fury at her clumsiness.

"I just walked through the door. No sneaking. Came to drop off some papers for Zach." Looking concerned, Jake led her to Zach's empty chair, setting a file folder on his desk as he bent over her. "Let me see."

Vaguely, Savannah thought that if she let go of her injured fingers, they might fall off. She squeezed harder, and tears filled her eyes.

"Allie? Bring some paper towels," Jake hollered. "Quick."

Savannah leaned forward in the chair, feeling light-headed. Her eyes were shut, but she opened one and removed her hand enough to find…blood. Lots of blood.

"Jake." Her voice wobbled. "Can't stand it…"

"It's okay, Savannah. We'll handle it."

She shook her head, which made everything swim. "Not good with blood."

He eased her lower, so her chin was between her knees. "No passing out. It's okay. You're okay."

He gently gripped her injured hand, and Savannah felt more pain as he pressed a towel to it, but she didn't care. She was focused on not falling out of the chair or humiliating herself any more.

"It's all right, Allie." Jake's voice sounded muffled now, but on some level Savannah appreciated that he was making an effort to comfort her daughter. "Is Zach here?" he asked.

"He went home," Savannah said. "We can call him…."

"Shh. Let me check."

She started to sit up, but Jake gently pushed her back down.

"No. Let me." He held her hand tightly and she understood he was surveying the damage. "Oh boy," he muttered in a low voice.

"What?" She shifted again, but he restrained her.

"The bone in your index finger is visible. You'll need stitches."

The spinning increased and she put all her effort into sucking in deep gasps of air and letting them out slowly.

"Get your brother to pack up," Jake told Allie, and Savannah was aware of her going into the conference room and doing as she was told. "We're driving you to the E.R."

"What about Noah?"

"Who's Noah?"

"Doctor. Brother-in-law to be. Dr. Fletcher's office."

"Know the number?"

She didn't, and told him where to find a phone book.

While he was dialing, Savannah lifted her hand toward her face, which was still buried between her legs, and moved the paper towel aside. She wanted to see her injury....

No, she didn't.

"Out of luck," Jake said. "They've gone for the day. E.R. it is."

Allie and Logan were hovering close by now. Savannah could feel their concern. "I'm all right," she told them, trying to sound brave.

"She just needs stitches, guys," Jake said.

"Why is she acting like *that?*" Logan, a veteran of many stitches, inquired.

Savannah didn't hear an answer. Instead, Jake appeared at her side. "Ready to stand?"

She drew in a few more slow breaths and nodded. The key was to not look at her hand. She could do this as long as she didn't glimpse the red stuff.

"Where are you parked?"

"Out front, down the street."

After asking for her purse, which Logan fetched, Savannah directed Jake to lock up for her. All this she did without a glance toward her throbbing fingers.

JAKE THOUGHT NOTHING OF going after the van down the street and picking up Savannah and the kids where she'd stopped and sat on the sidewalk. Caring for Savannah's family came naturally. Which would scare the crap out of him if he stopped to analyze it.

Savannah let him do everything. Drive to Layton to the emergency room, answer the questions and fill out the forms at the check-in, dig through her purse for her insurance card, guide her into the little examining room.

The doctor gave her a painkiller and numbed her fingers, and Jake knew the exact minute the drugs kicked in.

"You can go now. I'm fine," she told him.

He ignored her.

"Mom, it's my first art class tonight," Allie said. "Am I going to miss it?"

"Darn it." Savannah motioned for her purse and pulled out her cell phone. She dialed and waited, but obviously got no answer. "Where *are* those people tonight?"

"Who?" Allie asked.

"Katie. Noah. They've disappeared."

"I'll take Allie to her class," Jake said. "Logan can come with me, and then he and I will drive back to get you. Unless you need us here."

"No. And no."

Jake noticed both kids looking at their mother strangely, curiously.

"Savannah, it's a ten-minute drive back to town."

"We have to pay for class whether I go or not," Allie stated, and he wondered if she was parroting something Savannah had said earlier.

Savannah dialed another number, ignoring all of them. Allie seemed close to tears and Jake reassured her that she'd get to her art class.

Savannah clicked her phone off and swore.

"What's wrong, Mom?" Logan asked.

"Lindsey can't come."

"Kids," Jake said, his frustration mounting, "hang out in the hall for a minute, please. I have to talk to your mother."

Savannah started to object, but he sent her a look that shut her up for once. Logan and Allie went out the door and shut it gently behind them.

"What's that all about?" Jake asked, his patience gone.

"I don't want you to have to chauffeur my kids around...."

"She's mine, too." He drew closer. "I thought we were over this."

"Over what?"

"You not trusting me."

"Of course I don't trust you. You want to rock her whole world by telling her the truth."

"It'll happen soon—make no mistake about it. But I hadn't planned on springing it on her tonight on the way to art class."

Savannah cracked one knuckle on her uninjured hand, but didn't say anything.

"Savannah, this is stupid. You've paid for the class. She wants to go and you can't take her. I'm offering."

She dialed again.

"Who now?" he asked.

"Michael," she said into the phone, and explained where she was and that Allie had a class tonight. She hung up within thirty seconds. "He's on his way."

Jake shook his head and chuckled humorlessly. Once

again, she'd chosen Michael over him. Her ex. She trusted the man she'd divorced more than she trusted him.

He sat back in the horribly uncomfortable chair and stretched his arms behind his head, watching her.

"What are you doing?" she asked.

"Staying with you."

ANY OTHER TIME, Savannah would have protested, but her energy was sapped and her fight just about gone. "It won't be pretty," she warned him—futilely, she knew.

"I'll hold your hand." Jake grinned when he said it, and Savannah embarrassingly thought that might not be so bad. She was such a baby when doctors and needles were concerned. "Where's Michael going to meet the kids?"

"Here. I don't want them waiting in the lobby by themselves."

Jake leaned forward and put his elbows on his knees, appearing ill at ease.

"Are you worried about seeing Michael?" she inquired.

He met her eyes, pausing a moment to absorb what she'd said, then laughed. "No. I'm not worried about Michael. Just don't like hospitals much."

"Who does?" Especially when they were planning to drag a needle in and out of your skin.

"My mom died here. My sister and I waited by ourselves out in the lobby. Talking about whether to let your kids wait out there brought it back."

"Jeez, Jake. I'm sorry." Images of what it must've been like for him and his sister ran through her mind and made her shudder.

She climbed down from the examining table to open

the door and let the kids back in the room. On her way, she stopped next to him and put her uninjured hand on his shoulder.

"Go get your kids," was all he said.

They waited in the way-too-small room until Michael arrived. That took forever, but the doctor still hadn't showed.

Savannah hovered at the door, because she in fact *was* nervous about having Michael and Jake together. If she knew her ex, he'd have an opinion about Jake being with the kids. Specifically Allie.

But she spotted him approaching, and sent the kids to him before he got to the room. They would probably tell him who was with her, but at least there wouldn't be any awkward Lone Oak High reunion moments to suffer through.

Then she turned around and realized she was trapped in that small space with Jake. She gave serious consideration to running after the kids and begging at least Logan to stay.

Her eyes met Jake's and she glanced away. A nervous energy hung in the air between them, and she didn't want to think about what that meant.

"Nice," Jake said.

Savannah climbed back up on the table. "What?"

"The way you orchestrated that so Michael and I didn't come into contact. Which one of us are you protecting?"

"Neither. I'm protecting my own sanity. I don't want you two digging at each other."

Finally, a short, fifty-something doctor strode in and greeted them. "How are you folks this evening?" he asked.

"I'll be better once I'm out of here," Savannah told him. "Not a big fan of needles."

"You won't feel anything but a slight tug."

That didn't ease her fears much.

She must've looked as green as she felt, because Jake stood and walked to her side. "Okay if I hold her other hand, Doc?"

"Of course."

He gently took Savannah's hand in his work-roughened one and ran his thumb over her fingers. She was too nervous about getting stitches to appreciate the tenderness of the gesture, though. She faced away from the doctor and his needle, toward Jake. "You'll never let me live this down, will you?"

"Not a chance, Chicken Little."

She clenched his hand in response to the "slight tug" on her injured fingers, then clamped her eyes shut and broke into a sweat.

By the time the procedure was over, Jake was even closer and her head was resting against his chest. In coping mode now, she breathed in the scent of him, over and over. Listened to his heart beat. Steadily. Quickly?

The thought disappeared when Jake tightened his grip on her good hand. "Savannah. All done."

She sprang upright faster than a teenager caught making out in a car. But Jake didn't release her. She tried to pay attention as the doctor provided care instructions, but caught very little of his advice. The urge to get out of this tiny room before the walls closed in on her was growing....

She shut her eyes again until Jake pulled her off the table to her feet. The doctor was gone.

"You okay?"

She didn't reply, just headed for the door. Once out in

the hallway, she leaned against the wall for a few seconds, willing the dizziness away. Then she finally straightened, starting to feel better.

"You're really a mess, aren't you?" Jake noted, falling into step next to her.

"I'm fine."

"Ma'am! You forgot your papers." A nurse jogged down the hall toward them. "Just sign them and you can go."

Savannah stopped at the nurses' counter, signed, and waited for her copy.

"So fine you forgot to get your discharge papers," Jake said.

"I told you I hate needles—and blood. But I'm much better now." She began walking again. "Isn't this where your father is?"

It was a guess, but his hesitation confirmed she was correct.

They went through the double doors to the lobby and she stopped. "Do you want to visit him before we leave?"

"No." The response was immediate.

"Don't you think you should, while we're here?"

"*Should* should be a dirty word."

"That wouldn't prevent you from using it."

Jake looked down at her, considering. "You want to get home and rest. I can do it another day."

"All right, Chicken Little." She started toward the exit.

"Wait," he said. "Let's go." He indicated the hall that led to the main elevators, and Savannah followed him.

"I'll stay in the hall," she murmured as Jake slowed outside a room on the second floor.

"You wanted me to visit him so bad you can come in

with me and suffer the awkwardness." He was trying for offhandedness, she could tell, but didn't quite pull it off. He suddenly wouldn't meet her eyes, kept glancing at the closed door of room 204.

She figured she owed him one and clasped his elbow. "Party on."

That got half a smile out of him. He opened the door and they went in.

JAKE WISHED HE HAD WARNED Savannah about his father's sickly appearance. Her eyes widened when she saw him, and she gripped Jake's arm.

The old man was sleeping. Because he was facing them, it was easy to tell how hollowed out his cheeks and eyes were.

Savannah regarded Jake and he struggled not to let his reaction show.

"Maybe we should go," he said quietly.

His dad's eyelids lifted and he focused on them groggily. "Jacob? Are you back?"

Jake stepped forward. "It's me."

Dean squinted at Savannah. "That's not Emily."

"It's Savannah. A…friend of mine."

His dad slowly nodded at her. "I'm sorry. They've got me pumped full of morphine. Brain's a little fuzzy. Mind helping me sit up?"

Jake grasped his shoulders and repositioned him, then pushed the button to raise the head of the bed. His dad's arms were alarmingly bony, lacking any muscle.

"Thank you," Dean said once the bed's motor stopped and he was resting at a forty-five-degree angle. "I'm glad you came."

Jake couldn't quite say the same, although maintaining a grudge when his dad was so clearly close to dying was hard. "It's Savannah's fault. She tried to chop off her fingers." He gestured toward her bandaged hand. "Had to bring her in for stitches."

Savannah smiled and waved her injured hand. "Good times," she said.

His dad stared at her for several seconds and then smiled. He gazed at her a little longer, then turned his attention to Jake.

"Jacob, I'd like to talk to you."

Jake tensed. He knew this wasn't going to be about the weather or any cute things he'd said when he was a toddler. He glanced at Savannah, thinking she was probably sorry she'd come. "What's going on?" he asked his dad.

"Well…I'm dying."

His father's humor had never been tongue-in-cheek, so surely he realized he'd stated the obvious. Jake had no idea what to say to that so he just stood there.

"Pull up a chair. You, too, if you want," he said to Savannah, "although this could bore you to tears."

Jake drew over a chair with wooden arms. He offered it to Savannah, who shook her head and mouthed that she was fine. Once Jake sat, though, she lowered herself to one arm of the chair.

They perched there, waiting for his dad to speak. The old man didn't rush. He moistened his lips, and Savannah inquired whether she could get him a drink. He nodded and she walked around to the tall table by the window, to the mustard-colored, plastic pitcher.

After she'd poured him some water and held the cup

for him, he thanked her, and she settled back down on the chair arm.

"I believe I owe you an apology, Jacob. I've not been the best father to you kids."

A rock-hard lump filled Jake's throat.

"I…didn't have the first clue how to be a dad."

"None of us do." It was something he'd thought of constantly since learning about Allie.

"But most men figure it out. Just not me." His dad swallowed, looking pained. He struggled to find the next words. "Work was my refuge. I spent all my waking hours there. Told myself that was what my family needed the most—someone to bring home a paycheck."

An uncomfortable silence stole over the room. Jake decided it best to let the man get it all out.

"Do you guys want me to leave?" Savannah asked.

Strangely, Jake didn't. He would've expected having her here would be the most awkward thing in the world, but the idea of her leaving him alone with his father, with this conversation, made him sweat. He shook his head and touched her arm.

"You're fine," his dad said. "When you get this close to dying, you don't worry so much about the small stuff. Only the big stuff."

Savannah relaxed a couple of degrees.

"I'm sorry I ever told you to leave home," Dean said, his attention fastened back on Jake. "Sorry about so many damn things…." His voice cracked.

Jake leaned forward, resting his elbows on his knees, long-buried sadness making his head feel very heavy. He'd always thought that in the extremely unlikely case his father apologized, he'd feel somewhat righteous, but otherwise unaffected. He'd been wrong.

Savannah put her hand on his back. Her touch seemed the most normal thing in the world in this very abnormal moment.

"The fight that night," his dad began again, "wasn't so much about you staying out all hours. Oh, sure, I was ticked off you weren't there when Emily got in trouble. Mad as hell I had to truck back from the conference in Kansas City to handle things. But you were nineteen. I knew we were lucky you were still hanging around. *I* was lucky you were still taking care of Emily when she was younger. You always did. Always knew what to do for her and for yourself."

He stared out the window toward the lights in the parking lot. When he turned to Jake again, Dean's eyes were moist. "You were more of a father to that girl when you were a teenager than I've ever been."

"I just did what it seemed I needed to do. I didn't know the first thing about it, either." Jake's throat felt thick with myriad emotions—sorrow, regret. Maybe even empathy.

His dad smiled sadly. "You got the dad instinct that I've never had. You'll do just fine when you have kids of your own."

Jake straightened and met Savannah's gaze. They were both thinking that he *did* have a kid. Her eyes widened and she nodded subtly, as if to encourage him to tell his father.

He wasn't ready to do that.

Jake couldn't wait to tell the world that Allie was his daughter, but...not his dad.

He appreciated the old man's apology. It was a start,

never mind that it was darn near too late. Saying he was sorry didn't come easily for Dean Barnes. Yet the father-son closeness that would have been nice his whole life was still missing.

Savannah continued to eye him expectantly, but he directed his attention back to his dad.

"I appreciate the apology. I have to tell you I have a lot of years of anger to get over. Ever since Mom died, at least."

His dad flinched at the words. He gazed at the ceiling for several seconds, then finally nodded, looking defeated. "I imagine you do."

They talked about nothing significant for a few more minutes—mostly Dean and Savannah discussing college football. Jake noticed she was getting antsy, and shot her a questioning look.

"I have to get the kids soon," she said.

He jumped up, relieved at an excuse to depart. Some of his resentment toward his father had lessened with their conversation tonight, but they could only get so far in an hour.

"We have to drive back to Lone Oak," he said.

"You planning to leave town soon?" Dean queried.

"This weekend."

"What day is it?"

"Today's Monday. I fly out on Sunday."

His dad made eye contact then, and Jake could see apprehension in his gaze. Dean wasn't sure he would make it until Sunday.

"I'll be back in Lone Oak the following weekend, though." Again, emotion balled up in Jake's throat, surprising him with its intensity. "I'll try to visit again before I go."

His dad nodded, seeming too fatigued to say another word.

CHAPTER TEN

SAVANNAH AND JAKE DIDN'T speak until they were on the highway from Layton to Lone Oak.

"I don't get it," she finally said. "You can't wait to tell Allie you're her dad, but you wouldn't breathe a word of it to *your* dad."

"It doesn't concern him."

"What do you mean it doesn't concern him? He won't be here much longer, Jake. Allie's his granddaughter. I would've thought that after he apologized to you, you might give something in return."

"You've got the give-and-take element right, but my giving was visiting him in the first place. You don't know our history, so how can you lecture me on what I should and shouldn't tell my dad before he dies?"

"I have an idea of a lot of your history. At least the part from the night we were together."

That one night... So many aspects of their lives had been hugely affected by their decisions and actions of less than twelve hours. She couldn't regret any part of conceiving Allie, but what about Jake's estrangement from his family?

"I'm sorry, Jake. I realize tonight wasn't easy for you."

"Yeah. Can we not talk about this anymore? It'll just piss me off again."

Savannah nodded, ready to be done with this crazy night and the spectrum of feelings it had evoked. The first half of the evening had triggered fear and humiliation, all twisted together. The second... If she'd known walking into Mr. Barnes's hospital room would throw her so deep into the middle of a family war, she would've waited in the car, never mind the hall. The visit had been heart-wrenching, from seeing how frail and weak Jake's dad was, to witnessing Jake's internal battle between anger and forgiveness. She could only imagine the thoughts going through his head, the emotions pulling him in different directions.

She didn't want to be so involved with Jake and his family or their problems. Didn't want to care how any of it affected him. But she couldn't deny that she *was* involved and she *did* care.

NORMALLY SAVANNAH GOT the kids to bed around nine, tidied up the house, then retreated to her bed and a book until she fell asleep around midnight. Tonight was anything but normal, though.

The children were keyed up from the break in their routine, her hand throbbed in spite of the pain meds and her head spun in a non-pain-meds way. She suspected the latter was from being with Jake too much.

She could either lie here and make herself crazy remembering everything, from how she'd embarrassed herself over a few drops of blood to the scene between Jake and his dad, or she could collapse and block it all out.

Denial got her vote.

She'd just turned out the lamp on her nightstand and glanced at the clock—it was 9:37—when her door squeaked open.

"Mom?"

"What's up, Logan?" As tired as she was, the interruption might've bothered her, but tonight she was glad to have another living being in the room with her. Especially one as cuddly as her son.

"I can't sleep."

"Jump in," she said, holding the blankets up for him on the far side of the bed. He crawled to the very center of the mattress, not quite huddled up to her but close enough that she could feel his body heat. "Is something bothering you?"

"Nope."

She believed him. He'd never been the type to hold anything back from her. She listened to the quiet sounds of him—soft breaths and little fidgets—and shut her eyes, savoring the closeness. One day too soon, he'd stop curling up with her, even if he never became as antagonistic as Allie.

"Mom?"

She turned on her side to face him. "Yeah?"

"Why is Jake around us a lot?"

Savannah was momentarily stumped. That was a question she couldn't answer honestly.

"Does he like you or something?"

She hesitated and thought fast. "He likes all of us, honey."

"But I mean *like you* like you. Are you his girlfriend?"

"No."

Logan was quiet while he considered her curt answer. "I think he might," he finally said.

"He's just a friend." She nearly choked then, because *friend* had never been a word she'd use to describe her relationship with Jake.

"But he took care of you when you hurt yourself."

"He was just doing what he had to do, Logan. If Zach had still been in the office, he would've done the same thing."

Logan was quiet again, and she hoped she'd satisfied his questions and that he was drifting off. But no.

"I like Jake." Logan was wide awake and his voice was full of conviction.

"Shh," Savannah said, damning herself for attempting to avoid the topic. "Go to sleep."

She wished she could fall asleep herself, but now *she* was wide awake, and worried about Jake spending too much time with her and the kids. She had to put a stop to that before they asked any more questions.

SAVANNAH SPOTTED HIM the second she got out of the van. Didn't matter that they'd had to park halfway across the school parking lot or that he sat on a shaded bench near the entrance. She'd recognize that relaxed, almost smug pose anywhere. Neither she nor Jake had said a word about the art fair when they'd been together Monday evening, but she wasn't surprised he'd remembered.

"Jake's here!" Allie hollered, and both kids ran toward him.

Savannah swore to herself and glanced around to see if

anyone was paying attention to them. No one appeared to care or even notice, but her heart raced anyway. She knew being so concerned about someone else figuring out Jake's role in their lives was dumb, but her body didn't appear to get the message.

She walked slowly toward them, using every step to reel in her temper. He was going to stick out in the crowd. He didn't belong to anyone else with ties to the school. Savannah would bet he'd get plenty of attention because there weren't many thirty-something men in this town who looked as tempting as he did. He'd have mothers craning their necks wherever he went.

"Can you believe it, Mom? Jake came for our art fair!" Logan high-fived Jake and bounced around as Savannah approached.

"No. I can't." She eyed Jake pointedly, but he just smiled.

"Couldn't pass up such an offer, could I?" He spoke to the kids. "Let's go see your stuff."

They were supposed to meet Lindsey and Zach and their boys, Owen and Billy, to view all four kids' artwork together. Michael was supposed to show up at some point, as well. This had the potential to turn into one giant uncomfortable moment.

"Can we go now, Mom?"

The decision was simple. She nodded. "Let's get started. We'll find Owen and Billy soon. They probably aren't here yet."

Allie and Logan hurried through the double doors to the main hall. Jake put an arm around Savannah to guide her in.

"What do you think you're doing?" She said the words softly enough that no one else could hear.

"You're uncomfortable."

"That surprises you?"

"I figure we can either make it seem that I'm here because I'm interested in you, or because I'm interested in your children."

"Why *are* you here?"

"Why wouldn't I be? Allie invited me." He opened the door for Savannah. "I notice Moser isn't."

"He'll be here sometime." Unfortunately. All she needed was for him to find out Jake was in town, if he didn't already know.

They headed for the second grade halls first, and were treated to a narrated tour by Logan. Savannah hung back with Jake for the very reason he'd mentioned. He'd taken his arm off her, thankfully, because she could have easily gotten used to the way it felt, his fingers caressing her periodically, his heat enveloping her.

She put an extra foot of space between them as she oohed and aahed over Logan's last picture, an acrylic painting of a boat on the ocean. He hadn't been gifted with Allie's talent, but the piece made Savannah smile proudly and hug her boy. Clearly, he'd worked hard on it, from the stripes on the sail to the smiley face on the sun.

They finished praising Logan and moved out of the way of another family. So far so good. They were halfway done, with no sign of her sister's family or Michael yet.

"On to fifth grade," Savannah said, and assumed the lead at a quick pace.

At the beginning of the fifth grade hallway, Savannah

stopped to wait for the others. When she glanced back, she froze. Allie was walking next to Jake, her expression full of excitement. She was talking nonstop…with her talented, dainty hand encased in his large, work-roughened one.

"Allie, lead the way," Savannah said, motioning for her daughter to precede her. She stepped in front of Jake to separate them as Logan followed his sister. Yet the image of Allie with Jake was burned into Savannah's mind and she had trouble concentrating on her daughter's explanation of the undersea drawing before them. Some long-buried part of her heart warmed to the sight of father and daughter together—something she'd never thought she would witness.

Reality crashed in on her a few minutes later just as Allie led them to her last picture. Michael was heading down the hallway, straight for them. He glanced at Jake and she could tell the instant her ex recognized him. His step faltered slightly, and his face revealed the sock to the gut he must be feeling. He gaped at them, his eyes moving between Jake and Savannah, as if trying to gauge how close they were.

"Dad!" Logan ran to Michael, and though Allie was more subtle, she stood in front of her horse head drawing, beaming at him.

After hugging both kids, Michael focused on Savannah.

"Hi," she said. "You remember Jake Barnes." She gestured to him and met Jake's gaze. She couldn't read his expression but was relieved it wasn't smug.

Jake offered a hand and Michael shook it.

"What brings you back to town?" her ex asked. His tone was uneasy and not particularly friendly.

"Family business."

"How long have you been back?"

"Longer than I'd intended."

"You were with Savannah at the hospital," Michael said, as if just figuring it out. "The kids said you drove her to the E.R., but I didn't make the connection until now."

He wasn't happy with the connection. That much was evident. Savannah just hoped Jake didn't notice and exacerbate Michael's displeasure. She felt pretty certain her ex wouldn't make a scene here…unless provoked.

"I was lucky someone was around to help me out," Savannah said, not mentioning that if Jake hadn't shown up and scared the daylights out of her, she probably wouldn't have cut herself in the first place. "We've already seen the displays of both kids, so why don't you go back through with Logan and Allie? We can wait outside."

Michael barely had a chance to answer before Logan was dragging him down the hall.

"He hasn't changed much," Jake said.

"Come on." Savannah led him to the doors. "We have to talk about something." Preferably before the rest of the Salinger-Rundle clan arrived.

"Sounds like I'm in trouble." She didn't have to turn around to know he was smiling. "Are you going to punish me?"

He made the words suggestive, and a chill ran down her spine. She didn't let her reaction show, though, just ignored him.

Once they were outdoors, she walked down the sidewalk, away from the main entrance so they could have some privacy. Jake followed her as she'd hoped.

"First of all," she said as she faced him, "thank you for last night." She rushed through the words.

Jake chuckled. "It's been awhile since I've had a pretty woman tell me that."

She punched him with her uninjured hand. "I was a mess. I don't do well with—"

"Your own blood," he finished for her.

"You noticed."

"Yes, and felt reassured to find out you do have a weak side."

She looked up at him, prepared to lay into him for giving her a hard time, but the sincerity on his face stopped her short.

"I have lots of weak sides."

He nodded. "If you say so."

She sure as heck wasn't going to list them for him. "Second of all…"

"Here it comes," Jake muttered, still more amused than concerned.

"This is serious. Last night, Logan asked why you're around so much. He thought maybe it was because you liked me."

Jake smiled at that.

"It's not funny, Jake. What am I supposed to tell him?"

"What *did* you tell him?"

"That you liked the whole family."

He struggled—unsuccessfully—to erase his grin, and Savannah stomped her foot.

"Cut it out, Jake! This isn't a joke. We're talking about my children. You think you've seen my bad side, but you haven't seen anything until you hurt my kids."

"I'm not hurting anybody, Savannah." He clasped her upper arms gently and forced eye contact. "Relax. Strange as it may sound, I care about those kids. Both of them."

She didn't fight him physically—she was too wiped out to struggle—but she met his gaze full force. "If you care about them, then back off."

"Can't."

She'd suspected he would say that. She sighed as a heavy wave of fatigue and worry and all the emotions from the past twenty-four hours engulfed her. "You can't visit them again before you leave. This is it."

"And when I return?"

"Savannah!" Her sister Katie called from down the sidewalk, and Savannah pulled away from Jake.

She moved around him and watched as her entire everloving family headed toward them. Katie and her fiancé, Noah. Lindsey, Zach and the boys. And to top it all off, her dad and stepmom.

Shoot me now.

Automatically, she tried to distance herself from Jake but he stuck right with her.

"It's a banner day," she told him quietly. "The whole family."

Zach greeted Jake first and shook his hand. Savannah introduced her sisters, Noah and the kids next, Billy and Owen, the nine-year-olds he and Lindsey had adopted. Then her dad and Claudia.

"Jake is…an old friend. We went to high school together."

"Ooh," Katie said, as if she just made the connection that this was *the* Jake.

Savannah shot her a subtle evil eye.

"Pleasure to meet you," their dad, Wendell Salinger, said. "You still live around these parts?"

Jake explained his log home business in Montana and his current work with Zach, and the men gravitated together to discuss Heartland's development project.

"Boys," Lindsey hollered at her sons, who were racing to the playground farther down the school yard.

"I'll watch them," Claudia offered. "Let 'em run some energy off before we herd them inside."

"If you don't mind," Lindsey said.

"Rough job, taking care of my grandboys." Claudia grinned and hurried after them.

"So…" Katie said quietly. "Jake, huh?"

"Don't get all coy and speculative on me," Savannah murmured. "You know who he is and what role he plays."

"Uh-huh. What I didn't realize is that he looks like *that*."

Lindsey surreptitiously glanced at him and nodded. "He's grown up quite nicely."

"It's not like that, and you guys know it. Can't be."

"Crying shame," Katie said.

"Now my evening is complete," Savannah groaned as she noticed Michael and the kids coming out of the school.

"You were supposed to wait for us to go inside," Lindsey said.

"I'd planned to, until we found Jake waiting for us at the door. Plan B was to get him out of here before you guys—and Michael—showed up."

"You should bring him to the wedding as your date," Katie said, not paying any attention to their discussion.

"Katie. The point is to keep him *out* of my life. I'm going to drag him away from Dad and Zach now, shove him toward his motorcycle and drive my kids home."

"That doesn't sound nearly as fun as the alternative." Katie laughed, but when Savannah didn't, she said, "Okay. Touchy subject. I get it. Let's go look at some kid art, shall we?"

Savannah didn't get much of a chance to talk to Jake alone again before they left. He walked them to the van and the kids got in and buckled up. Savannah waited outside the driver's door.

"What we talked about before…"

"I'm leaving Sunday, Savannah."

"Good."

"But I'll be back the week after. I'll get in touch with you then because I do intend to…" he peered in the window at the kids, then back at her "…be around them."

He sauntered off, and Savannah got into her van and slammed the door.

CHAPTER ELEVEN

YEARS AGO, Savannah wouldn't have been caught dead at home on a Friday night. Funny how life, two kids and a divorce changed things. Now Fridays were her refuge, her favorite night of the week, whether the kids were home or not. She loved the solitude and the time that she didn't allow herself to do any work of any kind. It was her Friday rule. She could only do things she wanted to do, whether that meant watching television, renting a movie or curling up with a book.

Tonight, Logan was at a sleepover with one of his friends from school. She'd convinced Allie to play a game of Sorry! with her before her daughter had gone off to the room she and Logan shared to be alone. It wasn't much, but it was a step. Savannah knew she could only fight Jake off for so long. Eventually, Allie would learn the truth about him, and then who knew how it would affect their mother-daughter relationship. Savannah hoped to build it up as much as possible before that happened.

After Allie's retreat, Savannah caught most of a movie on TV. Halfway through, it hit her that she'd seen that film with Jake, as part of a large group of kids in high school. He'd made a point of sitting next to her to drive her crazy, and she realized tonight how much of the plot she'd missed because of his nearness back then.

She shrugged and got up off the couch. The movie was mediocre, anyway.

It was almost eleven. She'd told Allie good-night an hour ago, and now the place seemed quieter than usual. She headed into her bathroom, shed her clothes and turned on the shower.

Once under the hot spray, she allowed her mind to wander, urged her body to relax. The heated water steamed up around her, cutting out the chill of the day and warming her to the core.

As the shower slowly loosened her muscles, she tried to stop the rat race of her thoughts. Her brain sometimes exhausted her, but it was just part of who she was. Always analyzing, worrying, planning or figuring. She'd started making an effort to step away from thinking lately just to protect her sanity.

An image appeared in her mind's eye, a face with a sharp brown-eyed gaze and a slight smile. Almost a smirk. Jake's face. And the rest of him. She fully realized that allowing her brain to go in this direction was a bad idea, but she was tired. Lonely. Weak.So she let herself imagine what it would be like if she did let loose and said to hell with doing the right thing. What if she gave in to the desire she couldn't deny Jake made her feel?

Her eyes closed and her head rolled back slightly as she imagined what having Jake's naked body up against hers under the hot, steamy water would feel like. A heavy ache settled between her legs and the pounding of the water on her nipples put every nerve on alert, waiting for his touch.

Savannah opened her eyes suddenly when she realized her breathing was shallow and full of need. Not want. *Need.*

Jeez.

What was she thinking? She didn't *need* anyone, especially not Jake Barnes. She turned the faucet to cold, gritting her teeth against the shock to her system. Tension slid right back into every inch of her. But that was better than arousal.

Seconds later, she turned the water off, not bothering to shampoo her hair, even though she had wet it. She climbed out of the shower and grabbed her oversize bath towel, then wrapped herself in its warmth and illusion of security. Lowering herself to the bath mat, she sat there for several minutes, wrapped in her towel, scolding herself for letting Jake invade her mind.

Finally, Savannah rose and finished drying off, reminding herself that she was in control of her life and Jake wasn't part of it. At least not much. He definitely wouldn't be part of her showers.

After drying her hair most of the way, she went into her bedroom and pulled on her favorite pajamas—flannel bottoms with multicolored polar bears on them, and a long-sleeved thermal top. She slipped her feet into worn, fuzzy slippers and headed to the kitchen for a bedtime snack. As she switched on the kitchen light, a knock sounded on the door.

Her landlord definitely needed to spring for a damn peephole, she thought as she stood face-to-face with the subject of her shower fantasies. His hair was windblown. He wore a brown leather jacket that looked soft enough to sleep on, and dark jeans that hugged muscular thighs. His eyes were so intensely focused on her that she shivered.

In spite of everything she'd told herself in the past half hour, she couldn't deny the excitement that zipped through her at the sight of his smile. Couldn't deny it, but she *could* tamp it down and refuse to hang on to it.

"What are you doing here?" she asked, feeling exposed in her thin pajamas. She knew the top left nothing to the imagination.

Jake pushed the door open all the way and sauntered past her. "It's cold out there. Winter's close."

"October's like that in Kansas." She shut the door. "Keep your voice low. Allie's asleep."

He had the audacity to remove his jacket and lay it on the easy chair in the corner of the living room.

"I don't recall inviting you in," she said, stepping away from the door and the breeze that always seemed to penetrate the outer hallway. "Much less asking you to stay."

Jake slowly raked his eyes over her body, from embarrassing fuzzy slippers to frizzy damp hair and everything in between. Savannah crossed her arms over her chest as she felt her nipples coming to attention.

"About when I return from Montana…"

Savannah glanced toward Allie's bedroom door, but there was no sign of movement.

"The community center's having a party for kids on Halloween night. Tuesday that week," Jake said. "I'd like to take Allie and Logan."

Her mind spun as she tried to find a viable excuse to keep them away from him. Unfortunately, they had no specific plans for Halloween night, just a party at her sister's the weekend before. In fact, Savannah had already considered taking the kids to the community center.

Forgetting her attire, she uncrossed her arms and paced to the back of the couch. "It's too much. You've visited with them almost every day this week. Why can't you just be happy with that?"

"Why would I be? I've missed Allie's entire life because you didn't see fit to tell me about her. I intend to be part of it now."

"When it's convenient for you. When you happen to be in town. How do you suggest we explain your presence to the kids?" she inquired.

"Why do we have to explain anything?"

"Because they're asking. They don't understand what you're doing here, why you stop by and invite us to dinner."

"Why not just, 'Jake's a really nice guy'?"

"I make an effort to avoid lying to my kids whenever possible."

He advanced on her and Savannah stood her ground, but she immediately acknowledged the error of her ways when Jake's body pressed against hers, forcing her into the back of the couch. She raised her arms and placed her hands on his chest—which also turned out to be a mistake, because, wow, those pecs…

He smelled like worn leather and Jake, and her head swam with the familiarity. She knew full well her hands were there to provide a barrier, but she couldn't bring herself to push him away. She was caught in the spell of his closeness, their discussion forgotten.

His palms landed on her hips and his heat made her skin sizzle through the thin material of her pajama bottoms.

Their mouths were two inches apart, tops, and she felt his warm breath, mirrored his shallow, uneven breathing. His lids lowered and she knew he was staring at her mouth, knew it even as her eyes zeroed in on his mouth.

He leaned down and kissed her with lips that were demanding, lacking any gentleness, and Savannah met his urgency with her own. Their tongues touched and their hands grasped for each other, exploring. She ran the fingers of her uninjured hand over the muscles of his upper back, on top of his shirt, itching to feel his flesh.

He still had it—the power to turn her inside out with just a kiss. Judging by the moans that escaped from deep in his throat and the hardness that imposed on her lower abdomen, she could still make him dizzy with need, as well. Which just made the rush more intoxicating. Her mind ceased to function, her focus fixed on every sensation, every tingle and spark that seemed to shoot directly from her lips to her very core. She arched into him, slipping her hands under his shirt and clinging to his strong back, digging in her nails to pull him nearer.

He broke the kiss suddenly and tipped his head back, breathing hard, chin toward the ceiling. "Damn, woman."

Instantly incensed, ashamed and...*horrified,* she pushed him away. "I didn't start it..."

The corners of his lips quirked. "It wasn't that kind of 'Damn, woman.'"

"Oh." From the lustful look he was giving her, she realized he was saying, "*That was hot.*"

Which was an understatement.

But Savannah had been slammed back to earth when she'd read blame into his comment, and now she wasn't playing anymore. Instead, she was beating herself up, the heated flush and the lack of oxygen caused by this man still plaguing her, making her ache in places that had been numb for more than a year.

She moved a few paces to the right and stood with her back to him, hugging herself. "You think that if you kiss me, I'll let you take the kids on Halloween?"

"I think that if I kiss you, you *won't* let me take them. Why do you figure I stopped?"

She whirled to face him and stared at him in astonishment. *Common freaking sense, maybe?* She just shook her head.

Savannah made a beeline for the kitchen, hoping a glass of ice water would shock her system back into working order. How could she have lost her mind completely in two seconds flat?

Hoping for some space, she didn't bother to switch on the kitchen light. The big dense man followed her in. Savannah was holding her glass under the faucet when he came up behind her, gently lifted her hair and kissed her neck.

"Some women get boring when they get older, but you…" His whisper on her neck made her shiver. "You've got it all backward, honey. You're even sexier than you used to be."

The husky words heated her clear through. Just a simple statement, and an innocent kiss— No, scratch that thought. There was nothing innocent about that kiss. And the memory was all it took for desire to flare inside her again like a flame that kept a hot air balloon floating above the ground. She bit down hard and tightened her jaw, talking herself down.

"So." He'd helped himself to a glass and was filling it

with ice. His voice was perfectly normal. No sign of the throw-me-up-against-the-fridge-and-do-me passion it had dripped with just seconds earlier. "I'm pretty certain Michael figured out I know about Allie."

Savannah closed her eyes against the whiplash of not only the change in subject, but also the fact that he was fully recovered from their kisses and she was standing there wishing for a chair before her legs collapsed.

Bastard.

Focus, girl. Don't allow him any hint about what he does to you. You. Are. In. Control.

She absently cracked a knuckle as she shut the tap, took a long drink and turned toward him.

Now, what had he said? Ah, *Michael knows*. Yeah, that.

"What makes you believe he knows?" She was proud of her control when her voice emerged strong and normal instead of all...*needy*.

"A look he gave me. And a...vibe I got."

"A vibe." Okay. If he was unaffected, so was she. "A look and a vibe. You sound like a woman."

"You didn't seem to think that five minutes ago."

She felt the heat rise. "What do you think I should do about it?"

"You could kiss me again."

She set her glass down. "*About Michael*. What should I do about Michael?"

"That's your call, I'd say."

"Got that right. And I decide to do absolutely nothing."

"You don't think he'd get bent out of shape if I knew your secret?" Jake asked.

"He doesn't suspect. If he did, he would've said something." Savannah leaned against the stove, as far away from Jake as she could get in the small space. "Why does it matter if he knows that you know?"

Jake flashed that cocky grin. "It doesn't. Just thought you might want the heads-up." He hoisted himself onto the counter across from her. "What happened between you two, anyway?"

"Who two?"

"You never used to play dumb," he said, shaking his head. "Hubby dearest."

"*Ex*-hubby dearest." Savannah studied her fingernails. "He left me because I was too controlling."

Jake actually chuckled. "His words, I gather."

"Well, yeah, but it's true. In case you haven't noticed, that's the kind of person I am. I made him miserable."

Jake poured out the remaining water and ice and set his glass in the sink. "All these years I've known you and I had no idea you were controlling." He said it with a smirk.

"Why are you here again?"

"We were discussing Tuesday night. Halloween. Kids."

"No."

"You can go, too."

Spending more time with him was on her to-do list right after tearing off her fingernails one by one. "No."

"We agreed I could get to know Allie."

"You know her."

"Bullshit. Don't push me on this, Savannah."

She narrowed her eyes. He had just enough of a threat in his voice, and she was just enough worried that he would follow through on it that after a long while, she nodded. Barely. "Fine. Halloween."

"You'll have fun."

"I seriously doubt it."

"Lighten up."

"What *are* we going to tell the kids, Jake? Why are you hanging around us like a hungry puppy who got a bone once?"

Jake gazed at the ceiling, exasperated. He didn't get what the big deal was. Why everything had to be explained. Chances were Logan had forgotten the question as soon as he'd asked it.

"Tell them we're getting married," he said.

It was the wrong thing to say. That was clear from the frown on Savannah's face.

"I am never getting married again." She emphasized every word to make sure he got the point.

He got it.

"Joke. Down, girl. You think I want to wake up next to you every morning for the rest of my life?"

The image that flooded his mind as soon as he uttered the words was...alluring as hell, actually. Savannah in some drapey see-through lingerie, waking up slowly as he lay next to her, watching. Waiting. Ready to sate them both.

Every day.

For the rest of his life.

The idea didn't really suck. For a guy who'd never planned to get married himself, and who had a boatload of other problems to work out, that was saying something. Something he didn't care to ponder.

"And why aren't you getting married again?" Not that he was honestly considering marrying her.

"I'm too controlling."

Her reply was a cross between flippant and threatening, although Jake didn't feel the least bit threatened.

"Nah," he said. He and Savannah would never have the problems she and Michael had had because Jake would never lie down and take it.

No. He and Savannah would never have the problems she and Michael had *because they would never get married*.

CHAPTER TWELVE

JAKE WASN'T SURE WHAT to expect when he laid eyes on his dad today. Dean had gone noticeably downhill between Jake's first visit and the night he and Savannah had stopped by. There had only been a week between those occasions.

Jake didn't slow down as he got to the door of his father's room. He'd done plenty of hesitating earlier, but Emily had convinced him this might be his last chance to talk to their dad. Jake was going back to Montana tomorrow and wouldn't return to Lone Oak until Friday, when he would finalize the deal with Zach. His grandma had insisted on putting Jake's name on the agreement, as well, in case anything happened to her.

"Jake," his dad said in a steady, strong voice when he entered the room.

"Dad." He pulled up a chair near the head of the bed, relieved to see him so alert. "How you doing today?"

"Not too bad. Haven't had to have as much morphine." He looked better than he had on Monday, just five days earlier. He seemed more alert. His eyes focused better, his coloring was not so pale, and his speech was clearer, more confident.

Jake nodded. He leaned his elbows on his knees and

tried to think of something to talk about. What, exactly, did you say to your father during possibly your last conversation ever? Pressure built in Jake's head.

"Been doing a lot of thinking lately," his dad said. "Guess that's normal when you're in the position I'm in."

"I suppose it is. What have you been thinking about?"

Dean turned toward the window and stared out at the changing leaves. The trees were showing off yellows, oranges and reds bright enough to rival any sunset.

Jake watched as his dad's expression saddened, couldn't ignore his almost translucent skin. Once again he found it hard to believe this was the hearty man who used to let nothing slow him down, let nothing get in the way of his work.

"Rennie."

The single word, his mother's name, made Jake's head pound even more, and something in his chest catch. They had never really discussed her and what she'd done. Jake wasn't altogether sure he wanted to now. But he waited for his dad to say more. If a dying man wanted to talk about something, the least Jake could do was listen.

Dean relaxed his neck and rested his head back against the raised mattress. He finally spoke.

"I've never forgiven her. All the years since she swallowed too many pills, and I've held on to the anger." He shook his head slowly, then met Jake's gaze with watery eyes. "I've let it eat me up, become a part of me."

"I was mad at her, too."

"Tough not to be. But I should've gotten over it. Should've forgiven her. Instead, I became fixated on how her suicide affected me, what it did to make my life worse.

Hell, I didn't know what to do with you kids. I didn't know how to manage the home. Your mother handled all that."

"She did everything." She'd done it to a fault, too. The house had always been spotless. Meals cooked every evening, kept warm on the nights when his dad worked late. Jake had sometimes wondered if the complete lack of support from her husband had contributed to his mother's inability to keep on living.

"And I let you handle everything after she was gone, because I was too busy being mad." Dean was quiet for a long moment, gazing at the ceiling, looking pained. "I told you the other day that I'm sorry, but that doesn't really scratch the surface."

Jake nodded. "I understand."

"I don't believe you do, Jake. I've never been one to focus on regret, but this is tearing me up." He paused again, fighting to maintain his composure. "I've wasted my life on being angry. I wonder…" He swallowed, then closed his eyes. "I wonder how things could've been different if I'd just forgiven her and moved on."

Jake regarded him as the words hit home. Pondering his youth, he wouldn't have to stretch his imagination to see his dad had been pissed at the world. Or rather, at his late wife. "Regret won't do anything for you."

"I know, but that doesn't stop me from thinking about your mother day and night."

"So have you forgiven her now?" Jake asked quietly.

His dad made eye contact. "I have. At last."

"How do you suddenly forgive someone you've been mad at for almost twenty years?"

The older man attempted a smile, but his face seemed out of practice. "Part of it is just making up your mind to do it. To let the issue go. I finally figured I couldn't do a damn thing about my wife taking her own life."

"Just like that?"

"It wasn't just like that, necessarily. I talked a lot with your sister. She told me how she got through it over the years, how she tried to understand what it must've been like to feel the way your mom did. Emily's the most for-giving of all of us, without a doubt. Maybe it's a female thing."

"Could be."

"Speaking of females, tell me about the one you had with you the other night."

"There's nothing to tell."

His dad stared him down. "I don't believe that for a minute. There was an awful lot of tension between you two."

Tension. Yeah, there was that. Always had been. "We've known each other forever."

Dean nodded, still watching him. "And?"

"I don't know what to say. That's about it."

"I could tell you two like each other."

Jake chuckled. "I don't know that *like* is the right word."

"No, there was more than that. You two have a fight before you came in?"

When didn't they? "We have kind of an ongoing disagreement."

"That's a shame."

"Probably, but that's the way it is."

"Maybe you could work through it."

"You don't know anything about it," Jake said with irritation.

"That's because you're not telling me about it."

"None of it matters, because ultimately I'll be going
back to Montana and Savannah is staying here."

With our child.

Damn, leaving Allie after he'd just found her was going
to be hard. He'd have to make a point of e-mailing and
calling regularly. They had to tell her the truth before then,
though; otherwise she would wonder why he paid her so
much attention from across the country.

"You have a decent life out there?" his dad asked.

"I like it. I have a nice piece of land and I'm building
my company up."

His dad looked at him tiredly, concern in his eyes.

"What?" Jake asked.

Dean shook his head. "Just don't want you to be as
unhappy as I've been. I hope I haven't made you that way."

"What's to be unhappy about? I told you my life is good."

"I've told myself that same thing countless times."

He was *not* like his father. Would never let himself be.

Jake stood abruptly, then checked himself. He couldn't
rush out of here, not tonight. He inhaled slowly. "Dad. I'm
glad we talked. I'm...glad I came home."

"Me, too." Dean blinked, then smiled wanly. "Take care
of yourself, Jacob."

Jake couldn't speak around the lump in his throat, so
he put his hand over his father's bony one and squeezed
gently. "I'll be back in less than a week."

His dad nodded, though neither of them could voice
their fears that he wouldn't make it that long.

THE VIEW FROM JAKE'S DECK was killer. Mountains in the distance, green rolling hills in every direction, a picturesque stream in the valley. This was what had made him fall in love with Montana.

He leaned on the railing for a few minutes as he got his morning caffeine fix. He probably couldn't afford these few minutes—they were pushing hard this week, working overtime to get Clayton's house finished before their deadline. Weather predictions were for frequent, deep snows during the upcoming winter and Jake intended to have everything done before they had to break for the weather. Fortunately, snow hadn't slowed them down yet. His crew had done a hell of a job while he'd been gone, and that was thanks to his right-hand man, Scott Turgeon. Jake would give him a healthy bonus once this project was pulled off.

He finished his coffee and took the mug into the kitchen. The room was currently cramped and closed off from the main living areas, but Jake had plans to remodel just as soon as his finances loosened up a bit. They'd loosen up nicely with the completion of Clayton's home, but until he landed more big projects, he'd have to pace himself.

Ten minutes later he was in his truck on the way to the job site. Fortunately, it was only about thirty miles from his own property, so he was able to stay at his place. As he turned onto the main road, his cell phone rang. He pulled over because the signal in those parts often faded in and out.

When he clicked off the phone less than three minutes later, he had to stifle the urge to get out of the truck and dance for joy. *Holy shit.* It was the call he'd been waiting for, for what had seemed like forever. Tony Clayton had been pleased with their work so far and had passed on Jake's name to his rich friends. Martin Fredericks, an in-demand movie producer, would like to meet.

Jake couldn't wipe the grin off his face. This was it, the beginning of what he'd wanted to accomplish. All he had to do was sit down with Fredericks one on one and show him some of the plans they could modify for him. The guy was presold, thanks to Clayton, and was ready to move ahead. He'd mentioned hoping to break ground as early as possible in the spring.

Things were definitely improving. Jake's goals were within reach.

Once on the gravel road that led to the job site, he noticed four horses in a meadow to his left. Allie would get a kick out of them. One was almost identical to the horse in the drawing she'd given him the day he'd found out he was her father.

Suddenly, the twelve hundred miles between them made her seem a world away. He missed her and her brother. Sure, Jake was returning to Lone Oak this weekend—in fact, he'd left his motorcycle there and flown to Montana because he couldn't afford to waste the two days of driving each way—but that was only temporary. He was a long distance from his little girl. He thought about how much his sister had changed since he'd seen her, even though she was an adult. At her age, Allie would change even more rapidly, and he didn't want to miss a minute of it.

He glanced in his rearview mirror at the horses again. Allie would absolutely love it out here. He had enough land that he could get a horse. There was a barn on his property that was currently unused. It would just require some minor work.

His heart pounded faster as he thought about the possibilities. He'd been joking when he'd suggested marriage to Savannah, but maybe that wasn't such a bad idea. In fact, it sounded like a beneficial option for everyone. He'd have his daughter close, Savannah could work for his company if she wanted to, her kids could have horses and the whole outdoors as their playground. Montana was an excellent place to live, to raise a family.

He swallowed hard. Did he really think that? *Raise a family?*

He might not be used to the idea, but he *was* a dad. He was determined to be an involved dad, and that was hard from twelve hundred miles away.

As he drove into the job site, he knew exactly what he planned to do. He planned to convince Savannah to marry him and move to Montana. For certain, he had his work cut out for him, but he couldn't abandon his company now, and he couldn't stand to be so far away from Allie.

CHAPTER THIRTEEN

SAVANNAH KNEW JAKE WAS in the conference room. Zach had told her they were signing the final paperwork for their deal today. Savannah had been picking up her kids when he would've arrived. Now she was hyperaware of the voices that carried out to the main office. Every once in a while she heard Jake's laugh, and she tried to ignore it.

The truth was she'd thought about him too much during the week he'd been in Montana. The kiss they'd shared the weekend before had done a number on her, even though she'd reminded herself repeatedly that it had been nothing but an accident. Chemistry did not make a relationship. Nor did she want it to.

The laughs were louder and nonstop now, as if the group was finishing up the meeting. Savannah glanced at the kids, who were on the floor between the desks, then busied herself and pretended she couldn't care less that Jake was there. The conference room door opened and her traitorous eyes zoned in on it.

Zach, the lawyer who'd drawn up the agreement, Mrs. Levine and Jake emerged, all of them smiling and joking, clearly happy with the deal they'd just sealed. Jake's gaze sought out Savannah, and she had trouble looking away.

Those brown eyes of his crinkled at the corners, drawing her in, and his smile was the real one, the one that could knock her flat.

She forced her attention to the bills she was paying on her computer.

"It's official," Zach said to her. "The Colonial Acres development is on its way."

Her brother-in-law beamed, appearing happier than he had since his wedding day. Savannah couldn't resist standing and giving him a hug of congratulations. This was big for him, for Heartland. He'd had other projects since he'd opened the company, but this was the largest by far.

As she released Zach, she caught Jake watching her with a certain expression in his eyes, as though he wanted *his* chance to wrap his arms around her. She shivered and turned her focus to Odessa Levine.

"Congratulations to you," she told the older woman. "It sounds like you have some unique ideas for the development."

Mrs. Levine grasped her hand and smiled. "Thank you. I certainly hope everything will work out. Jake and I have put a lot of thought into the plans. I can hardly wait to see the finished neighborhood."

"Did I hear you're going with a colonial style for all the houses and buildings?"

"You did. I think it'll go nicely with my little house. I sure am happy we could build around it."

Savannah smiled, then accidentally glanced at Jake again, who smirked as if sensing her discomfort.

"Where're my congrats?" he asked.

"Congratulations." She offered her hand instead of a hug.

When he accepted it, the contact had just as much of an impact on her as if he'd drawn her into his arms. He held on longer than necessary. Savannah became conscious that Zach was paying too much attention to them, and pulled away.

"We're heading to the Lazy Goat for a celebratory drink. I'd ask you to join us, but…" Zach nodded toward Allie and Logan, who were involved in a drawing and a video game, respectively.

"That's okay. I've got a stack of things I'm trying to finish here, anyway. Have a drink for me."

"We'll catch you tomorrow night at the party, then," Zach said.

She nodded, and couldn't help noting how patiently Jake helped his grandmother out the door. There was something about a man as sexy as him doing something so caring and attentive. He'd be a lot easier to dislike if he were mean to old ladies.

It was still early enough on Friday afternoon that the Goat was dead. When Zach, Jake and his grandma walked in, only two tables were occupied.

"You're supposed to be working, Zach," the short, blond bartender called out. The woman was maybe a few years older than Jake and had a toughness about her, although she was perfectly at home here and could handle whatever came up, be it a bar brawl or a drunken four-hundred pounder.

"Work related," he said. "Tough job. Kind of like standing around pouring beer for a living."

"Hey, don't mess with the woman in charge of the alcohol."

Jake accompanied his grandma to the first booth against the wall. "This okay?" he asked.

"As long as I don't have to slide far," she answered.

He helped her lower herself onto the bench seat. When he'd invited her to join them, he'd been shocked she'd said yes. He was glad she had, though. She didn't get out nearly enough to satisfy her active mind, and he knew the isolation would be worse once he left again. Emily tried to visit her weekly, but that still meant Odessa was alone most days.

"What's your poison?" he inquired.

"I think some champagne is in order, don't you?"

Jake glanced doubtfully at the bar. "We'll see what they have. I'll be back."

He went up to the bar next to Zach, who was still trading insults with the bartender. "The lady would like some champagne."

"What do you have, Heather?" Zach asked.

"I happen to have some very decent bubbly in the back. How much you want to spend?"

"As long as the stuff doesn't taste like toilet water, I don't care. Within reason," he said, as she headed to the back room.

Zach sat on a stool to wait. "Your grandmother is a hell of a woman."

Jake chuckled. "More so than I realized." He glanced over at their table. "She's getting into the trivia."

TVs hung throughout the bar, and some of them were set to the trivia channel. His grandma had found the control box on the table and was attempting to figure out how to operate it. He stifled his grin and went to help her.

Zach returned to their table a few minutes later. "We don't get the table service here but she did manage to locate some decent stuff." He set down three champagne flutes and filled each one. "Here's to a successful, prosperous partnership and to making Colonial Acres the best place to live in Lone Oak."

They clinked their glasses and sipped.

"You're right about this. It's not bad champagne." Jake's grandma took another sip and edged her glass aside. "Now I'm going to figure out how to use this machine, because I happen to be a trivia queen."

"I'm sure that's due to reading so many books," Jake said.

"Got that right. I'd challenge you any day."

Zach moved around the table to stand next to her, and explained which buttons to hit and how the game worked.

"It said I could play against people in other places. Is that correct?" she asked.

"It is."

She nodded intently. "You boys go play pool or something. I've got a game to win."

Jake struggled not to laugh. "We'll be at the pool table." He swallowed a large sip of champagne, grimaced involuntarily and stood.

They stopped at the bar and Jake ordered a beer. "Never acquired a taste for champagne," he admitted.

"Wager?" Zach inquired on the way to the pool table.

"Why not? Twenty bucks." Jake selected a cue from the rack on the wall.

Zach racked and Jake broke in silence. He shot three stripes in and then missed.

Zach stepped up to the table and aimed. "So tell me something," he said as soon as he hit the one ball into the far corner. "What's going on between you and my sister-in-law?"

Jake was glad he wasn't shooting when Zach asked, because he would've missed. "What makes you think something's going on?"

Zach went for the three ball and then straightened. "I know Savannah pretty well. You send her into all kinds of strangeness."

Jake grinned at that. "Ya figure she likes me?" he questioned in a joking tone.

"Haven't decided between that and hate." Zach finally missed a shot and Jake walked forward to catch up.

"You've pretty much summed up our relationship right there." He smacked the thirteen just right and watched it roll toward the corner pocket.

"Relationship," Zach repeated. "Interesting choice of words."

Jake missed his next shot.

"Not sure what to call it." Jake studied Zach, getting a little of the older-brother, don't-mess-with-my-sister vibe. "I've known her since kindergarten." He moved toward Zach and glanced around to make certain no one could hear. "You're going to find this out eventually, anyway. Allie is my child."

Zach had just taken a drink, and choked on the champagne. "If that's your strategy to win the twenty bucks, it's a damn good one."

Jake grinned. "Afraid not. *That* is the strangeness you sense between me and Savannah."

"Is this something her family is aware of?"

Jake guessed that Zach was wondering if Lindsey had kept Savannah's secret from him.

"She just told her sisters. Her ex is in on it, of course. But that's it."

"How long have you known?"

"Less than a month."

"Man, that's rough." Zach hit balls in on his next two shots. "So I wasn't imagining the buzz between you two."

"Buzz?"

"Attraction. Chemistry. Whatever you want to call it, it's pretty noticeable. Now what do you plan to do?"

"Thought I'd set myself up for some rejection and ask her to marry me."

Zach shot in the eight ball to win the game. He straightened and returned to where Jake stood, a grin on his face. "Sounds like a hell of an idea. Savannah could use someone like you in her life."

"Tell *her* that."

"I don't tell that woman anything."

"You do know her well."

"You figure she'll say yes?"

Jake replaced his cue on the wall and pulled out his wallet to give Zach his money. "Not without a lot of convincing. I can be very persuasive, though."

"I wish you all the luck in the world."

They headed back toward Jake's grandma, who was still engrossed in her game.

"Thanks. I'll need it."

CHAPTER FOURTEEN

"Wowza!" Lindsey stopped in the doorway of her bedroom on Saturday evening, decked out in her pregnant nun costume. "You are one hot mama, Savannah."

"Hell makes a girl hot." Savannah turned her attention from the mirror and her chest that was so…out there, thanks to the low-cut devil costume with the built-in push-up bra, and frowned at her sister. "It's a good thing you're with child."

"Why's that?" Lindsey fluttered into the room with exaggerated innocence.

"Because I would hurt you if you weren't. What were you thinking when you got me this costume?"

Lindsey put her hands on her protruding belly. "If I had the choice between looking like you in that costume or looking like me in mine tonight, I'd be all over the slinky red pants and camisole. I feel like an elephant."

Savannah stood back and evaluated Lindsey. She picked up the nun's veil, which Lindsey had left on the bed while she handled last-minute preparations for her and Zach's Halloween party, and arranged it on her sister's head. And laughed.

"It's perfect! You'll be the comic queen of the party. I still think Zach should've gone as God."

"He didn't want to give Gram a heart attack."

"What kind of a day is she having?"

"Fairly lucid compared with the past week. She won't wear a costume, though. Annie got her Little Red Riding Hood, but she refused. Adamantly."

Savannah smiled, imagining the scene between Zach's grandma and her caretaker. Grandma Rundle was a lot mellower than she used to be, but the woman could still be stubborn and feisty.

Glancing back at the mirror, Savannah instantly forgot her amusement. "Lindsey, seriously, I can't go downstairs with this much of me showing."

"Don't be such a prude. You look fantastic. The dark red with your hair and coloring, your long legs and that cleavage…" Lindsey whistled. "You're a single woman and it's okay to act like one."

"I'm a thirty-one-year-old mom, not a hooker."

"Tonight, you're a devil." Lindsey gave her a smug, devil-may-care grin and spun to check her own appearance in the mirror. She frowned. "And I'm a dowdy woman of God."

"Maybe I could tempt you to come over to the dark side." Savannah stared pointedly at her sister's tummy. "Oops. You already have." She cracked up as she grabbed her cape, horns and pitchfork and hurried from the room, out of the pregnant woman's reach.

Lindsey caught up to her on the stairs.

"Are the kids okay?" Savannah asked.

"They're in the basement, playing haunted house. They have the lights off and are taking turns scaring one another. The babysitter will be here any minute."

"Going to have to tip her well tonight."

Once in Lindsey's kitchen, Savannah drew her thin, sparkly cape around her shoulders and attached it with the single snap. She wished it covered more than her back.

Grandma Rundle sat at the kitchen table, tapping a finger. She regarded Savannah for the longest time, assimilating the whole getup. Savannah braced herself for a too-honest remark. Now that the Alzheimer's had moved in on the woman's brain, she held her tongue even less than she used to.

"Pretty," she said instead.

Savannah gazed at her in surprise. "Don't you mean trampy?"

She shook her head. "You've got the figure for it, missy. Enjoy it while you can. One day you'll be begging for one of these jobs." She motioned to the sack-like pink-and-violet muumuu she wore, and grimaced.

"You never know. You might catch yourself a bachelor tonight with that 'job.'"

"I certainly hope not. Where's your man, young lady?"

"He's missing out."

Some days Grandma remembered Savannah was divorced now, but those were fewer and further between. She glanced at Annie, who nodded slightly, reassuring her it was okay not to go into the whole explanation again.

"What remains to be done?" Savannah asked Lindsey.

Her sister launched into a detailed list, ticking each item off on her fingers. She stopped midsentence and laughed.

"What's so funny?" Savannah inquired.

"The horns." Lindsey pointed at her headband. "They're absolutely perfect. The whole costume is."

Savannah pivoted to the counter and reached for the closest bottle of red wine, which Zach had opened earlier. "I'll just have a nice refreshing glass of wine. Would you like some— Oh, wait. You can't have any." Savannah shot Lindsey a grin worthy of the devil costume.

"Witch."

"Not tonight." She cackled evilly and began arranging the relish tray.

"Whoa." Zach, decked out in a hooded brown monk costume, gasped when he entered the kitchen. "You look like a woman on the prowl."

Savannah sighed. "I'm a woman at the mercy of your wife. I may still go change into a ghost with blue jeans."

"Don't you dare," Zach said. "Gram, Annie, can I get you ladies a drink?"

They both declined, but Grandma Rundle requested some of the sweets she'd seen Lindsey carry to the dining room earlier.

Savannah studied Zach, still puzzled by his comment. "Since when do you care what I wear?"

He shrugged guiltily and Savannah glanced at Lindsey. "What did you guys do?" Then she knew. Or at least suspected strongly. "You invited your new partner, of course."

"Of course. I couldn't *not* invite him."

"And Lindsey told you everything…." She kept her voice down to avoid having the other women overhear.

"Not Lindsey," Zach answered. "I pried it out of the man himself. But as far as you and Jake needing to jump in the—" he broke off, eyeing his grandma "—needing to get together, I don't have to be up on any history to deduce that the jumping is overdue."

"You know he makes me crazy, right?"

"A little crazy never hurt anybody." Zach grinned.

Savannah felt her face start to flush, and not from embarrassment. "You guys don't understand. I can't go there." People acted as if she shouldn't think twice about finding another husband. How could she ever do that when her first marriage had done so much damage? She was not cut out for life sharing.

She took a large gulp of wine, made a face, then carried the relish tray to the table in the dining room, where the food was being laid out.

So Jake would be here. Great. She decided then and there to have a fun evening in spite of his presence.

Kelly, the babysitter, arrived, and Savannah escorted her down to the kids. The four of them were already wound up, as though they'd had nothing but sugar for a week. She kissed her children and told them all to behave themselves.

When she went back upstairs, guests were already arriving. Her instinct was to hang out in the kitchen with Gram and Annie.

Criminy. She'd never been afraid of people or mingling. Had never been a wallflower. She tried telling herself her reticence was due to the costume's neckline, which really had nothing to do with her neck at all it was so low.

"Better go find your man," Gram said, as if Savannah's thoughts were written all over her face.

Of course Gram had no idea what she was wishing on her.

The back door opened then and Katie and Noah walked in. Their home was next door and they'd only had to cross the backyards.

Savannah went over and hugged her sister. "Thank goodness you're here."

Katie tilted her head in confusion. "How much have you had to drink? You're never affectionate."

Savannah ignored her and stood back to admire their costumes. Noah wore a white jacket and carried a black bag. Katie had on a ski jacket, a stocking cap pulled down over her long hair, and fuzzy mittens. "Slip out of your coat so I can see what you are."

"My coat's part of the costume. I'm a mountain climber." A goofy grin stole over Katie's face as she grasped her fiancé's hand. "Noah's a medic, so he can save my butt when I fall off the side of a mountain."

"It doesn't count when you dress as your profession," Savannah said to him.

Noah stepped forward and kissed her on the cheek. "I'm a doctor. It's different. Besides, she needs to be saved."

"You already did that, honey." Katie wrapped her arms around his neck, a big grin on her face.

"You two make me nauseous," Savannah said, laughing.

"Who's here?" Katie asked, leaning down to hug Zach's grandma. "Where are my sweet niece and nephews?"

"In the basement. Though I'm not so sure about the sweet part."

Katie hollered down to the four and received overenthusiastic hellos back.

Lindsey arrived to get a round of drinks, and shooed them out of the kitchen.

"Sorry, Linds, not going to allow the preggo lady to do all the work. You promised you'd let us help," Savannah said.

"Fine." She fished out two beers and handed them to Savannah. "These go to the cowboy and the Hell's Angel in the living room."

"Cowboy and Hell's Angel," Savannah repeated.

As soon as Savannah reached the doorway, it became apparent Lindsey was inherently evil, in spite of her nun's costume. Jake was the Hell's Angel and Doug, one of the crew at work, was the cowboy.

Jake's lustful grin as she approached him incited chills. Absolutely annoying chills.

"If this is what the devil looks like, then line me up for hell," he said when she handed him one of the beers.

"As if you have any choice at this point," Savannah replied.

"Oh, she got you there, man," Doug said.

"Your costume is fitting," Savannah told Jake, checking him out from head to toe. Fitting very nicely, she might've added if it wouldn't have pained her to admit it.

Heat rushed through her at the sight of the black leather hugging those thighs. She'd never had a leather fetish, but he could give her reason to start. He wore what appeared to be a genuine Hell's Angels black jacket, with the words and a graphic on the back.

"Where'd you get that?" Savannah queried. "Tell me you're not…"

"I'm not. It's a long-lost uncle's. Emily found it when we were going through our dad's closets the other day."

Savannah nodded. "I better go help my sister with drinks."

Jake raised his beer can in salute.

When she pivoted around, Katie was in her face with a

cat-ate-the-canary grin. "He looks mighty fine tonight, doesn't he?" she whispered.

Savannah snarled at her and walked by, taking a couple of drink orders on her way to the kitchen.

JAKE WASN'T MUCH OF A party guy anymore, but the Rundles' Halloween bash was decent. That had nothing to do with the amusing costumes or the tables crowded with food or the free-flowing drinks, and everything to do with being able to watch Savannah in that devil suit.

When she waltzed through the room in the sparkly low-cut top, snug pants and black heels that made her legs seem a mile longer than usual, his mind ceased functioning altogether. She'd been doing her best to ignore him ever since bringing that first beer out, yet whenever she entered the room, her eyes sought his. They'd dart away at once, as if she'd never tried to find him, but he spotted her looking every time. And every time, his blood pounded harder.

Jake had been shooting the breeze with some of the guys from Heartland, since he didn't know many others. But now he'd had enough tiptoeing around what he wanted. He headed to the kitchen, where he'd seen Savannah disappear again.

The room was deserted, but the rear door was open a crack. He went to it and squinted out into the darkness. Sure enough, she sat on the top step by herself, rubbing her bare arms with her hands. Her breath made clouds of white mist as she exhaled, and Jake imagined the warmth of it on his skin.

Enough imagining.

"Hey," he said, walking out and sitting next to her. "Cold much?"

"I wanted some fresh air."

"This is pretty fresh." He removed his jacket and draped it around her shoulders, on top of her cape. "I see your horniness has disappeared," he said, eyeing her hair where the devil headband used to be.

Savannah pulled the jacket tightly around her. "Don't worry. I'm still bad on the inside."

"And very good on the outside. Just the way I like 'em."

Instead of laughing, she sighed. "Jake, why did you come out here?"

He rested his elbows on his knees and gazed straight ahead at the mother-in-law quarters in the backyard. "You want honesty or some more lines?"

"What do you think?"

He took several breaths of cold air before speaking. "You're making me crazy, woman. I can't stop watching you, remembering us. I want…"

"You want what?" Her voice was hard, lacking any encouragement.

Jake was through waiting for encouragement, anyway. "This."

He put his hand on the back of her neck and drew her mouth to his, the warmth of her breath making him shudder with desire. She stiffened and didn't respond…for all of five seconds. When his tongue slid over her lips, she yielded to him and leaned closer. Jake trailed his hands up under the jacket, over the thin material of her top, then reached under it at her waist to touch her silky skin. Savannah made a soft, approving sound deep in her throat.

The noise of the party faded away and there was nothing except the two of them and the connection of their bodies, their mouths. Savannah worked her way up onto his lap and straddled him, and their hands were all over each other, grasping at clothing, exploring greedily.

Jake ran his palms under the silky material, up both sides of her rib cage, and rubbed his thumbs over the swells of her breasts. As he worked higher and made contact with her nipples, Savannah arched into him, exposing her neck. He pressed light kisses along her jaw. The little sounds she made nearly drove him mad. He dropped his hands to her backside and pulled her into his—

"Mom?"

Savannah shot to attention and stiffened. She instantly moved off him to return to her spot on the step, and tried to act as if she hadn't been busted in the middle of one extremely hot moment. It was a good thing they'd been interrupted when they had, Jake thought, because he'd been on the verge of losing the last thread of control.

"What's up, Allie? Is Kelly okay?"

"Were you kissing him?"

Savannah's head dropped. "Apparently so."

Tension filled the silence. Jake closed his eyes, aware that Allie wasn't okay with what she'd witnessed.

"Allie? Was there a problem in the basement?" Savannah asked.

A petulant sigh came from behind him. "The boys keep making us watch boy movies."

"I thought you would each get to choose a show."

"But mine was a long time ago."

"Whose show is on now?" Savannah asked.

"Billy's. He's making us watch Power Rangers. They're stupid."

"Can you go to the other side of the room and work on a new drawing?"

"It's dark. They're playing 'movie theater.' Creeps."

Savannah sighed, and Jake could practically feel her digging deep for more patience. "Tell Kelly I said to let you turn on a light so you can draw."

"'Kay." Allie paused. "Are you going to kiss him again?"

"No." Savannah's tone said she meant it…or wanted to.

The girl stepped back into the house, letting the door slam.

SAVANNAH BLEW OUT A LONG breath of air and ran her hands through her hair. Clearly, Allie was upset about Jake. And because Savannah had had no intention of kissing him tonight, let alone getting caught by her daughter, she was completely unprepared to deal with this problem. Why had she succumbed?

She chuckled. She had succumbed because the attraction between Jake and her had the gravitational force of a small planet. Or something. She wasn't really up on science, and she definitely wasn't up on attractions.

"She'll be all right," Jake said.

He was either full of crap or clueless, but Savannah said, "Yeah."

"So I thought of a solution for the whole parent thing with the kids and you and me."

"And that would be?"

"Let's get married. You guys could move to Montana with me. Allie could have a horse."

Savannah closed her eyes and wondered if this day could get any worse, because so far she was still upright and maybe it would feel better if she wasn't. "You can't be serious, Jake."

"Serious as a heart attack."

Her eyes widened and she slowly turned her head toward him. "How much did you drink?"

"I'm sober. Promise."

"You're off your rocker."

"Why is my idea so crazy? We're her parents. We want the same thing—what's best for Allie."

"I don't grasp how me marrying you could possibly be beneficial for Allie."

"She gets a live-in dad, you get a co-parent, Logan gets a role model."

"What do you get, Jake?"

He stared straight ahead. "Come on, Savannah. It's the practical thing to do."

She suddenly started laughing, her shoulders shaking uncontrollably. She didn't even know what was funny, or if anything was. Yet all she could do was sit there and laugh until tears filled her eyes. Then it struck her that these were not tears of joy. They were the real McCoy.

She wiped her eyes with the Hell's Angel sleeve and inhaled a steadying breath, except it turned out anything but. "Jake."

"Savannah."

"Why would I marry someone who holds a grudge against me?"

"What grudge is that?"

"The one about missing out on eleven years."

Jake seemed to give that some thought. "Might take me awhile to get over it, but I will."

"Marriage is not practical, grudge or no grudge. It's anything *but* practical." She lay back on the concrete landing outside the door, gazing at the stars, feeling so darn tired.

Jake bent toward her and whispered, "Totally...practical."

He kissed the sensitive spot beneath her ear, then stood and went inside, letting the door slam just as Allie had. Like father, like daughter.

The tears instantly reappeared in Savannah's eyes, and now she let them fall.

CHAPTER FIFTEEN

"Guys, I'm pregnant, not dying," Lindsey said when everyone but her sisters had left the party. "And I'm not letting you ruin my kitchen." She got up from the ladder-back chair Zach had banished her to, and walked over to the counter. "These go in the dining room hutch." She took the crystal serving dishes Savannah had just dried, and headed for the front of the house.

"Zach's going to blow a gasket when he sees her cleaning up again," Katie said.

"She's a big girl. She can handle it and him." Savannah rubbed another piece of pain-in-the-butt, non-dishwasher-safe china dry with a now-damp towel.

"I noticed you disappeared from the party for a while," Katie said.

"Wanted some air."

"Uh-huh. For as long as you were gone, you must've nearly frozen with just the devil costume."

Savannah eyed her sideways and could tell Katie knew Jake had joined her outside. She didn't rise to the bait.

"Imagine my surprise," Katie continued, "when soon after, I saw Jake without his jacket."

"Yeah? He joined me. So?"

"Did he *join you* join you?"

Savannah could play games with her sister all night, but who had the energy?

"He asked me to marry him."

The heavy pan Katie had been scrubbing sloshed back into the water and clunked on the sink bottom. She slapped the spigot off and stared at Savannah. "I'm going to assume this is another one of those things you wouldn't joke about."

Savannah couldn't help laughing. Not the same hysterical shakes of earlier, but an evil, I've-succeeded-in-wigging-out-my-sister howl. She nodded her head in response to Katie's statement.

"And you said?"

"You have to ask? Really?" Savannah turned the water back on to rinse a serving bowl. "Well, I never really answered, if you want to get technical. But I'm pretty sure he got the implied 'Hell no.'"

"Linds!" Katie called to the other room. "Get in here. *Now.*"

"I can handle myself when Zach explodes," Lindsey said as she made her way back into the kitchen.

"We know you can. Sit down." Katie led her by the elbow to a chair.

"You people are making me crazy, you realize that?"

"Jake asked Van to marry him."

Lindsey's eyebrows shot up and her eyes got as big as quarters. She looked at Savannah, then back at Katie, seemingly waiting for the punch line.

"We're going to Vegas next weekend," Savannah said.

If Lindsey's eyes could get bigger, they did. Katie hit Savannah lightly and said, "No way."

Savannah struggled to keep a serious face, but couldn't for long. "Apparently, *that* is something I will joke about," she finally said. "Are you guys nuts?"

"If I go into premature labor, it is totally your fault," Lindsey said. "You're serious about the proposal part? Jake really asked you to marry him?"

"My advice?" Noah said as he and Zach strolled in from the living room. They'd been out front talking to the last stragglers. "Elope."

"The sexy getup worked then, huh," Zach said.

"I'm not marrying him. Not marrying anyone, but thanks for the thoughts, guys."

"Pleasure." Noah bent over and kissed Katie on the lips, lingering until the rest of them told them to stop.

"Boys, go away," Lindsey said. "This is girl talk."

"Gladly," Zach said. "We're going to return the folding table we borrowed next door."

The men retraced their steps and Katie removed the dish Savannah was drying, placed it gently on the counter and led her to the table, then sat between her sisters.

"So you said no. How come?" she asked.

Savannah sighed. "It's so true what they say about once you fall in love you want *everyone* to be in love. Let's see. First reason, I'm not going to remarry. Second reason, *ever.* Third reason, marrying for the sake of a kid is the dumbest thing I've ever tried and failed at. That's just the beginning of the list. Care for more?"

Lindsey rested her hands on her nun tummy. "I hear you. But I don't agree."

"You think I should marry him? Are you high?"

"Not necessarily. I have no idea if Jake's the guy for

you, because I don't really know him. What I don't agree with is that you won't marry again ever. I don't get that."

"Me, neither," Katie said, leaning her chin on her hand and staring at Savannah as if she were a feature article in the making.

Savannah shrugged. "I'm not cut out for it."

"For marriage? That's ridiculous," Lindsey said. "Just because one failed doesn't mean you're not cut out for it."

"I'm not. Remember me? Ms. Controlling?" She shook her head. "I have no desire to give up any control, girls. I love control."

"At last she admits it," Katie said.

"I've always admitted it. What I never realized before was that it wouldn't work in a marriage." Savannah planted both elbows on the table. "Michael had every reason to take off. There was no partnership in anything. It was all me, all the time."

"You may have controlled everything, but you also handled everything. House, kids, life," Lindsey said. "He didn't have a bad gig, Savannah."

"Having someone wash your clothes and care for your children does not make a marriage."

Lindsey apparently had no reply to that.

"So…" Katie began. "Can we back up for a second? Was Jake serious about this proposal?"

Savannah slowly nodded. "He was. I keep going over the conversation, searching for a smirk or something I missed, but I believe that if I'd said yes, he would've gone ahead."

"And how did he take the rejection?"

"The way Jake takes everything. He walked away."

"Marrying him would solve a lot of problems," Lindsey mused.

"Linds. Shut up. He wants us to move to Montana." Savannah jumped up. "I have to pay Kelly and tell her she can leave." At the basement door, she glanced back at her sisters. "Not a word of any of this to Dad."

"Does he know about Jake yet?" Lindsey asked.

Savannah shook her head. "Nothing."

"You really have to tell him. If he finds out any other way…"

"I'm going to tell him. Soon," she promised over her shoulder, and then descended into the mostly quiet basement to kiss her children good-night for their sleep-over, and rescue the babysitter.

She'd tell him, just as soon as she could get up the courage, she mused. Confessing to her dad that she'd made some serious mistakes didn't top her list of Fun Things To Do Before She Died.

JAKE HEARD THE KIDS laughing and thumping around inside before he knocked on the door. Theoretically, they hadn't even begun the Halloween festivities yet. Just wait until he got them full of sugar at the community center party.

"Jake!" Logan was the one to open Savannah's door and drag him in, as if the party were there instead of on Main Street. He was covered from head to toe in black, including a hood and a belt full of plastic weapons.

"Hey, Mr. Ninja. Excited?"

Allie skipped over to him, her eyes shining. She wore her hair in two braids under a straw cowboy hat with a pink ribbon. A pink-and-gray-plaid shirt, jeans, and pink cowboy boots completed the costume.

"What have we here?" Jake asked. "Wait, let me guess. You're a scarecrow."

"No-o," Allie said with a laugh.

"She's a cowgirl!" Logan hollered.

"Ahh. I can tell now. You just need a horse."

"I asked for one for my birthday, but I didn't get it. Not a real one, anyway."

Savannah breezed in from her bedroom then, and Jake was momentarily disappointed she wasn't wearing the devil costume from the other night. She wasn't wearing any costume at all. Just dark jeans that hugged those long legs, and a fuzzy cream sweater. Her shoes were brown, bootlike things with heels that made her only a few inches shorter than him.

"I was hoping you'd have your costume on," he told her.

"This *is* my costume. I'm a single mom with her act together." She moved around the room, gathering up a couple of random toys and her purse as she spoke. "Notice I don't have a hair out of place," she said, pointing to her locks, which were straighter than he'd ever seen them and pulled back at her nape. "My outfit doesn't clash, I have matching socks, even though you can't see them..."

"And her underwear and bra match, too!" Logan said in his usual "outdoor" voice.

Jake laughed and Savannah looked like she might wring her son's neck.

"That's private," she scolded.

"Sorry," Logan said, slightly abashed.

"See?" Savannah addressed Jake. "Note that a frazzled single mom would've lost her cool there. I've got it together."

"Gotcha." The outfit was clever, but had nothing on the devil's cleavage. "Let's get going. Trunk-or-treating started ten minutes ago."

"Where's my pumpkin?" Allie asked, wandering in circles, searching for it.

"Your pumpkin?" Savannah queried.

"For her candy." Logan held up his big round Spider-man version of a candy toter.

Savannah frowned. "I haven't a clue. You had it before dinner. You were swinging it."

A full five minutes passed before they found it on the bathroom floor. Savannah was rushing around now, hunting for coats to throw over the kids' costumes as she tugged her own coat around her.

"So much for your costume," Jake said quietly as they followed the children out the door.

She sent him a phony grin. "We hadn't left the house yet. Doesn't count."

She led him to the garage below and lifted the old door by hand.

"I hope you don't mind driving," Jake said. "Didn't figure we'd all fit on the Harley."

"Mom always drives," Allie told him.

"Duh. She's the only one who's old enough," Logan said.

"She even drove when Daddy lived with us," Allie remarked authoritatively.

"I'm a better driver," Savannah stated.

Jake thought she might be partially joking, but he couldn't be certain. "I have a truck back in Montana," he said.

"Cool," Logan called from the middle of the van. "Is it one with a backseat for kids?"

"It is. Lots of room there."

He turned around from the passenger seat to find Logan nodding. "So me and Allie can fit in if you ever bring your truck here," the boy said.

Savannah eyed Jake before backing out. Instead of the killer glare he'd half expected, he got kind of a nervous, secret-sharing look. Was she reconsidering his proposal? Jake checked the urge to touch her hand reassuringly. Savannah was the last person who usually needed reassurance.

Two minutes later they entered the fray known as trunk-or-treating. The community center parking lot was packed with cars in every space, each with the trunk or rear doors open. People handed out treats to kids as they made their way from vehicle to vehicle.

Jake and Savannah walked behind Allie and Logan, keeping just out of the rush of children but close enough to stay in sight. When they hit the end of the first row and rounded to the next aisle, Jake slipped his hand around Savannah's.

"What are you doing?" she asked so no one else could hear. She didn't remove her hand, though.

"Excellent question," he said. "It could be answered a couple different ways."

"Such as?" Her eyes twinkled, even though she tried to act annoyed.

"Well, first you get the practical argument. I'm keeping your hand warm."

Her eyebrows rose skeptically and she fought a grin. "Or I could whip out a pair of thick mittens."

"You could. If you were really a single mom with her act together and had some with you."

"Touché. What's the other argument?"

"The nonpractical one."

"Which is?"

"Because I want to."

Savannah rolled her eyes.

"Some people would say that's not reason enough to hold hands, but clearly, it is. Because you want to, too."

"I do, huh?"

Jake nodded. "When two people want the same thing, it's often a good idea to go ahead with it." He craned his neck to locate the kids again, letting the words hang between them.

Allie spotted him watching her and ran over. When she noticed how close Savannah and Jake stood, and saw their interlocked hands, she glared at her mother and yanked Jake's other hand.

"Hey, Jake. Come with us to the next van. It's decorated all spooky."

He caught the frustration on Savannah's face before he was drawn more deeply into the crowd with Allie.

SAVANNAH WOULD *NOT* LET the absence of Jake's warmth bother her. She wouldn't get upset by her daughter's snub or chilly reception. Tonight was all about the kids, she reminded herself.

She hadn't meant to keep holding on to him, but the roughness of his skin in contact with hers, the way he'd gently caressed her with his callused thumb, had intrigued her, made her respond to him, made her cherish the touch. Made her want those hands to keep touching her. Everywhere.

Which put her in a quandary. Two quandaries, really.

When Allie so openly disapproved, Savannah was torn. Her instinct was to avoid letting her children interfere with her personal decisions. Her life was her own and she wasn't going to let an eleven-year-old run it. Unfortunately, things weren't so cut and dried. The eleven-year-old was one of the people Savannah loved most in the world, and whom she was on the verge of losing all semblance of a relationship with.

And then there was the whole gray issue of whether she wanted to fight for the right to hold Jake's hand. His smugness when he'd sidled up so close and wound his warm, strong fingers around hers had made her want to push him away and observe his reaction. But another part of her, the trouble-causing part, reveled in his aggressiveness, his confidence.

Allie would dislike her no matter what Savannah did. Regarding Michael, regarding Jake, regarding breathing. She couldn't please her daughter, couldn't do anything to win her back. She'd tried. Even expensive art classes had failed to give them something to talk about.

But somehow Savannah resisted letting Jake in on any aspect of her private life. That went so much deeper than her current volatile relationship with her daughter. It wasn't even that he'd proposed, because she felt confident she could refuse the marriage suggestion till the cows came home. The feelings were what she didn't like to handle. Or maybe couldn't. Because if she could fight them off, she would've swatted Jake's hand aside like a pesky West Nile-infected mosquito.

There it was again—that lack of control that always swept her away in Jake's presence. She stifled a growl, searching for Logan, whom she didn't immediately spot with Jake and Allie. There was his little clad-in-black head. She moved toward him.

As for control, she had to do better than she'd done so far tonight. For her kids to pick up her mixed messages to Jake wasn't fair. Because no matter how tempted she was, she would never have a permanent relationship with him or any man.

BY NO FAULT OF Jake's, he and Allie became a team. Savannah and Logan made their way around the indoor party activities separately. He would've loved that his daughter had chosen him and wanted to be with him, if it hadn't meant Savannah's being shafted by her own kid.

He figured that when they rejoined, Savannah would have words for him because he'd been alone with their child. But the crowd and Allie had taken him away, and he'd let them, not realizing how long they'd be apart.

Now Allie was throwing pumpkin beanbags at plastic vases, trying to win a prize. When her three bags were gone, she turned to Jake. "Next, the Plinko game," she said excitedly.

They stood in line for a few minutes, then she dropped a disk at the top of the board and watched it fall to determine her prize. Luck was on her side tonight; she won the top prize, a stuffed black cat.

"I have to go to the bathroom," she said as they moved away from the Plinko crowd.

Jake glanced toward the throng outside the main restrooms, then checked the other way, down a side hall. Spotting another bathroom, he held his hand out to Allie, then he wondered if she would take it or if she thought she was too old to hold a grown-up's hand. She hesitated, then grasped his fingers.

As he waited for her to come out of the otherwise deserted restroom, Jake skimmed the notices on a nearby bulletin board. When he saw the handwritten flyer about horses for sale, he smiled, and wished for once he was rolling in cash. Maybe one of these days. Money would likely be less of an obstacle than Savannah.

Allie appeared, grinning up at him and holding on to her stuffed cat.

"Why don't we go find your mom and brother."

The grin morphed into a frown. "How 'bout we try some more games?" she said.

He gently pulled her to the side of the hallway. "What's up with you and your mom tonight? I noticed the look you gave her outside…."

Allie crossed her arms and dropped her gaze.

Jake leaned down a bit to make eye contact, but attempted not to appear the bad guy. He was concerned about Allie's treatment of Savannah, yet his own relationship with the young girl was so new he didn't want to alienate her if he could help it.

"I gathered you didn't like me being with your mom the other night at the party."

"Or tonight," she offered.

"Your mom and I are friends. What's wrong with that?"

"Friends don't kiss."

She did have a point, but not one he would concede.

"I didn't kiss her tonight." Jake nudged her chin up a little with his thumb. "I like both of you, Allie. The three of you. Can't I be friends with all of you?"

Her brows knitted and she lowered her gaze again. "I'd like you to be *my* friend. I don't want my mom making you go away."

"What do you mean, honey?"

"She made my dad go away. I don't want her to do that to you."

Ah, hell. Jake stood up as he wondered how in the world to handle this. He'd like to reassure his little girl he wouldn't go away, but Savannah was a wild card and he couldn't be certain she'd let him continue to get closer. Yes, he would maintain ties with his daughter at all costs, regardless of what happened between him and Savannah, but as far as being a regular in the family's life…who knew what would happen. The one thing he couldn't do was promise Allie he and Savannah would always be on amiable terms.

He bent down again. "I'm not going anywhere. Even when I return to Montana in a few days, we can keep in touch. If you and I are friends, we'll continue to be friends, no matter what happens with your mom."

Allie shook her head. "She won't let us stay friends if she makes you go away."

"You still get to see your father, right?"

She chewed that over for a few seconds. "Yeah, but he's my dad. I have to see him."

Jake closed his eyes and bit his tongue to keep from telling her he was her dad, too, and that there would be no problem. How to convince her everything would be okay without telling her the truth?

"Allie, do you trust me?"

"I dunno. I guess so."

"Then try hard to believe it when I say everything will be okay. You are one cool kid. I like you and won't just disappear."

She sized him up in a way similar to her mother, and with a lot of effort, Jake maintained a straight face. Finally, she nodded.

"I still don't want to go find my mom, though."

Jake couldn't help smiling briefly. "Sorry, kiddo. She's your mom." He held out his hand. "But I'll be there, too."

CHAPTER SIXTEEN

JAKE FOLLOWED SAVANNAH to the kitchen after they'd put both children to bed.

"Don't go getting too comfortable, Barnes."

"Now I'm Barnes? I help tuck your kids in and we revert to last names?" He came up behind her, so close she felt his heat all along her back, from her thighs to her shoulders. "I figured that'd make you nervous." He reached in front of her and grabbed a handful of peanuts from the open can on the counter, then backed away. She cursed herself for missing his closeness.

She turned and glared at him, acting fiercer than she felt, and he grinned.

"I never said you could have some of my nuts, either," she said.

"I'll buy you new nuts, sweetheart."

Savannah dug out her own handful and faced him. "You and Allie sure disappeared tonight."

"Yeah." Jake dusted the leftover salt off his hands. "I wanted to talk to you about that."

A rock of dread filled her stomach and she pushed the peanut can away. Jake, typical man-who-could-eat-through-anything, took it from her and plucked more nuts out to pop in his mouth. She waited tensely until he finished chewing and got to his point.

"We have to tell her, Savannah."

She shut her eyes and resisted the urge to scream. "Jake. We've gone over it a hundred times. We're not telling her now."

"She needs to know. She's convinced you're going to make me go away."

"She's a wise little girl with a good idea," Savannah said dryly.

"Glad you can joke about the reason your daughter scowls at you more often than she breathes."

Savannah fought to swallow the hurt that rushed up her throat like bile. "You think telling her will make her run into my arms?" Her voice was a vicious whisper, kept in check by her stark fear of Allie learning the truth.

"She'll be angry, hurt—of course she will. But are you saying she's not both those things right now? You're deluded if you think offering her a chance to forgive you for the divorce, and then dropping yet another bomb on her, will work in your favor."

"So now you're an expert on family relations. How's it going with your dad?"

Jake flinched, as if she'd struck him physically. "I'm not an expert on family anything." His eyes met hers and held.

Dammit, why did she have to feel bad? Why, in the midst of his attacking her and threatening to throw her life so far off-kilter she didn't believe she could ever recover, did sympathy overcome her at his humble concession? She drew closer to him.

"He's still…alive?" she asked quietly, dropping their argument for now.

Jake nodded and straightened. "Wasn't sure he'd make it till I got back in town, but apparently, he rallied."

"Apparently? You haven't been to the hospital?"

"I saw him before I left."

"You have to go visit. Even if he rallied, he doesn't have much time."

"You sound like my sister."

"Wise woman."

"Something like that. Can we get back to Allie?"

"Go see your dad."

"If she learns the truth, she won't worry so much about losing me. About you making me go away."

"And tell him about his granddaughter. That'll show him you care."

"So now *you're* an expert on family relations?" Jake asked her pointedly.

Her shoulders sagged. "Touché."

Neither of them spoke for a long while. The refrigerator motor started up, filling the room with a comfortable buzz, but they just stood there, against the cabinets on the same side of the kitchen, inches apart, at an impasse. Or was it a temporary truce?

"Do you want to tell her before or after we tie the knot?" Jake inquired.

Definitely not a truce.

"You've been hallucinating if you think we're getting married."

Jake took hold of her hand and gently wove their fingers together. She couldn't seem to move away from his touch. His heat. The tenderness that she knew flowed through him.

She expected him to plead his case again, to argue with her why getting married was such a *practical* idea. Instead, his lids lowered halfway with barely controlled passion and his eyes zeroed in on her lips.

But he didn't kiss her right away. With his free hand, he brushed her hair behind her ear, tenderly, just a whisper of contact. Then he trailed his fingers along her jaw, making her crave more of his touch. Savannah leaned into his hand and, without conscious thought, kissed his palm, eliciting a sound from deep in his throat.

She ached for him to kiss her with all the desire she saw in his eyes, but still resisted. Pressing tiny kisses on his skin, she worked her way up his little finger, bit by bit. When her lips reached the tip, she caressed it with her tongue and drew it into her mouth to suckle briefly. Then she entwined their hands and pulled him flush against her body. Her lips parted, but, dammit, he still didn't make the final move to kiss her. Her breath caught in her throat as, winding her arms around the back of his neck, she inclined his head to hers, then finally touched that infuriatingly sexy mouth of his.

For all his refusal to initiate the kiss, Jake responded now and took over, his tongue roving, seeking hers, exploring frantically as if he expected her to retreat at any second.

Savannah wasn't stupid. The house could burn down around them before she'd end this soul-scorching, demanding kiss. Their hands roamed, discovered, found bare, hot skin beneath clothing.

He picked her up, never breaking the contact of their

lips, and Savannah wrapped her legs around him, wanting more of him, pressing her body against the unmistakable hardness in his jeans. Needy, breathy sounds filled the kitchen and she wasn't sure whether they were from her, him or both of them.

Jake eased her onto the counter. There, he unfastened her bra and cupped her breasts beneath her sweater, sending a pulse of electricity and desire even deeper to the center of her. She arched into him, gasping for air and release. His fingers worked magic over her nipples, making her crazy with need. She grabbed at his shirt and yanked it up, ready to strip him bare and have her way with him; in the kitchen, on the counter, on the floor—she didn't care.

"Damn," she said between hitched breaths, sliding his shirt back down.

"What?" His voice was ragged.

"Kids. Sleeping. Other room." She nibbled at his lips, lightly, attempting to separate herself from him and regain her sanity.

"Damn!" He breathed out shakily. "Crazy."

He kept kissing her with playful nips as well, as if he couldn't stop.

Savannah closed her eyes and struggled to pull in a full breath. Jake rested his forehead on hers and she could feel his heart pounding, or maybe it was hers. They were silent as they sought to regain their composure.

"If we got married, we could do this every night," Jake said huskily. "And more."

The thought of "and more" made Savannah shiver. She felt Jake smile, but she was still too jellylike to move. Or speak. And she really wished he'd stop ruining things by speaking, too.

"I felt that," he whispered. "You want me. You want to be with me. Why are you fighting it?"

There it was—the right motivation to snap her back to attention and quit with the clinging.

"Tell me you don't want me, Savannah. Tell me you're not still shaking from…*that*. Because I am."

She leveled her eyes at him and nodded. "Yeah. Got me there, Jake. I want you. Our chemistry has never been lacking." She stepped away from him. "But how can you possibly consider that enough for a marriage?"

He studied her, his eyes dark with heat. "You're still running, aren't you?"

"I've been here the whole eleven years you were gone."

Jake shook his head. "Eleven years ago *you* ran. You may have stayed in Kansas, but you pushed me away because you couldn't handle the way I make you feel. It scares the hell out of you."

"You should go, Jake. I don't have energy to fight this battle with you anymore. I'm not marrying you. I'm not marrying anyone."

She headed to the living room and opened the front door, but Jake didn't follow. She angrily retraced her steps to the kitchen.

"Leave. Please."

He gazed at her with eyes that seemed to see deep inside her, with an assumption that he'd been right on. He thought he understood her hesitancy. But she wasn't afraid of him. She just hated the way he made her common sense spiral completely out of her grasp.

The look he gave her before walking out was smug and knowing. Insulting and maddening.

She trailed him and, reining in every bit of control she could muster, closed the heavy door behind him. Softly, because she was *not* going to lose control this time.

SAVANNAH KEPT CRAZILY BUSY the next few days, helping Katie with last-minute wedding details. It was a way to avoid Jake and get her hormones under control.

Saturday finally arrived. Wedding day. Insane day. The three Salinger sisters had been running since eight that morning, and for Katie, the eternal night owl, that was quite a feat. Their dad and stepmom had been helping by watching Allie, Logan, Billy and Owen for most of the day, and getting them ready for the ceremony.

"Crap. Only an hour left," Katie said, rushing around in her wedding gown and bare feet.

"You're doing fine," Lindsey said. "Your hair and makeup are done. Gown is on. All you have left is your hose and shoes."

"Do you understand how long it'll take to get panty hose on in this thing?" Katie asked.

"That's what we're here for," Eve, Katie's friend and Noah's receptionist, said. "I got you thigh-highs. Much easier."

"And Noah can remove them with his teeth," Lindsey said. "Pictures don't start for another fifteen minutes. Why don't you sit down and relax while we finish getting beautiful."

"I can't sit in this dress," Katie said, and Savannah laughed.

The door opened and Allie sneaked in, wearing her junior bridesmaid dress that matched the coral of the rest of the others. Each of the dresses had a different style, necessitated by Lindsey's pregnant middle. Savannah's floor-length dress had a halter neckline, and wrapped to the side just under her bodice. Her daughter's had a similar neckline and was full-length, as well. Realizing how grown-up Allie was getting made Savannah's heart swell with a bittersweet mix of pride, sadness and amazement.

"You're gorgeous, honey," she declared.

"Thanks." The single word was said almost shyly, with no venom. After a day filled with stress and arguments, Savannah would accept that happily.

"Everyone decent?" Their dad was at the door, clad in his tux.

"We're dressed," Katie said. "Don't know if all of us would qualify as decent."

He regarded her with a grin on his face. "My little girl. You're beautiful." He went to her and hugged her carefully in order not to crush her dress, or the flower pinned to his lapel.

"Thanks, Daddy." Katie wiped the corner of her eye. "No more. I refuse to cry, so you have to stop the mushy stuff."

Wendell turned to the rest of them. "Wow. All of you. Gorgeous."

"Especially this girl." Katie came over to admire Allie, and Lindsey and Eve joined in. Allie's smile grew. "Nice purse, too. Whatcha got in there?"

"Drawing paper. Pencils."

"Of course," Lindsey said. "Just what every young artist has in her purse."

"You're pretty," Allie told Katie.

"It's the makeup," her aunt said, laughing.

"Can I wear some lipstick?" Allie looked around at them and everyone peered at Savannah.

"Aren't you a bit young?"

"Just this once won't hurt her," their dad said.

Savannah stared at her daughter, wondering when she'd changed from little girl to young lady who asked for makeup. "Anyone have a subtle color?" she inquired.

Lindsey went to her purse for a leather pouch, and dumped out a pile of cosmetics. Sorting through them, she picked up one lipstick and checked the bottom. "Sea coral. This will be perfect."

Their dad went to find his wife, the head babysitter. The four attendants and the bride finished getting ready, then made their way to the sanctuary for Katie's big event.

An hour later, the wedding party and all the guests made their way to the church hall, a building across the parking lot. Thankfully, the facility permitted alcohol. Savannah needed a drink or three before she delivered a toast to the bride. She'd been surprised when Katie had asked her to be maid of honor, but they'd grown a lot closer in the past year. Her sister had been staying at Savannah's when Savannah and Michael had separated, and also when Katie was struggling not to fall in love with Noah. They'd been through a lot together in a few months.

Toast time arrived before Savannah was ready. The best man, Brian from Noah's med school, went first, and kept the crowd laughing. Savannah missed most of his speech because she kept going over what she would say. Then they were all looking at her, waiting for her to join Brian at the microphone. She pulled in a deep breath, got up and took the mic from him.

"To my little sister, the baby of the family. The one who always had to prove she was more daring than the rest of us. She's always been the wild child, so when it seemed she might be falling for this guy—" Savannah pointed at Noah "—we sat back and watched what the crazy single girl would do. And she didn't disappoint. She ran like hell."

Everyone laughed and Savannah drew in another deep breath, trying to get past the lump in her throat.

"We're so excited that Katie met this wonderful man. Now *he* has to live with her, not us." Savannah smiled as everyone laughed again. She motioned to her sister to stand next to her. "All kidding aside, I'm so happy for you, Katie. You've always been our risk taker, but in this you went with the sure thing. You and Noah are perfect for each other. Here's to many, many years of happiness and wild adventures."

Savannah raised her glass and clinked it with Katie's, then the two sisters embraced.

"Thank you," Katie said in her ear.

Savannah nodded. As she opened her eyes, still hugging Katie, she spotted him.

Jake sat at a table across the room, staring at her. The expression on his face was… Hard to say what it was, but he wore a slight grin, and a cross somewhere between smug and…lustful?

"Katie," Savannah whispered. "What is *he* doing here?"

The bride pivoted to see who she was asking about. "Oh." Her smile got too big. "Noah and I wanted him to feel welcome. He doesn't know many people in town anymore…."

"You are so full of it. You think you can set us up, don't you?" Savannah fought to keep the pleasure off her face. God, he looked good.

"Dance with him and I'll leave you alone. Promise," Katie said as she flitted off to talk to more well-wishers.

The deejay was getting ready to begin the dance part of the reception. The kids' table was suddenly empty, so Savannah went in search of her children. In the opposite direction of Jake.

The music started, and the bride and groom shared their first dance as husband and wife. Savannah stopped to watch them. She joined the crowd surrounding the dance floor as Katie danced with their dad and Noah with his mom. Then others joined them, thanks to challenges thrown out by the disc jockey.

Savannah was circling around to the wedding party's empty table when she spotted Logan heading for her.

"Mom, you have to come here," he said, and he grabbed her hand.

"Where are we going?" she asked, bending down to be heard over the music. Her heart beat faster as she wondered what could be wrong.

"You'll find out."

She scanned her son's face and decided he wasn't acting as though something was wrong. Then she figured out where her traitorous child was taking her. Straight to Jake.

Jake, who was damn tempting in a black suit. His shoulders seemed even broader than usual. His hair was as neat as she'd ever seen it, though still a tad tousled on top, and his eyes caught her every move.

"Jake wants to dance with you, Mom."

CHAPTER SEVENTEEN

SAVANNAH GLANCED AT Logan. "You're grounded for life. Now, go find Billy and Owen and your sister, and stay together, in this room."

Logan took off and Jake stood up.

"Coward," Savannah said, having to bend close to him to be heard over the music. Her heart continued to race, but now it was in anticipation instead of fear.

"I like to think of it as strategic." He touched her waist as he spoke into her ear.

The softness of his breath on her jaw and neck sent a shiver through her. She'd hoped avoiding him for the past few days would strengthen her resistance. Apparently, it hadn't.

"Will you dance with me?" he invited. "They're playing our song."

"We don't have a song."

"I know. That was a line," he said, grinning.

She couldn't resist. Not when he looked like *that* and smelled like that and focused all that male attention on *her.*

Savannah accepted his proffered hand, and couldn't help noticing anew how warm and strong it was, how gentle his grasp. She followed him to the dance floor, determined not to let anyone detect how vulnerable she was to this man.

He stopped and faced her, still holding her hand, and their eyes met. He didn't bother to hide the thoughts going through his head—naughty thoughts that involved her and him. Alone.

His hands slipped around her waist and she moved close, so that their bodies touched from chest to thigh. Her dress was cut low in the back and she felt the heat of his hands directly on her skin.

The way she fell into him, closed her eyes and rested her head on his shoulder, soaking in his familiar scent, was almost involuntary.

Realizing how she must appear to everyone around them, hanging on Jake, she straightened a little and glanced up at him.

"You're the sexiest woman here, Savannah."

"Sweet-talking me won't help your case, Jake. Still not marrying you."

He chuckled.

"In fact, consider this a good-bye dance," she said. "After this, we just share a construction project."

"And a child," he said softly.

She avoided his gaze, focusing on everyone else, trying not to think about how right it seemed to be in his arms.

She felt someone watching them from one of the tables. Michael. She'd almost forgotten he was here. Ignoring him, she eased away from Jake as the music faded.

"Do you mind if I ask Allie to dance?" he said before she could escape.

Habitual fear made her chest tighten momentarily. She

followed his line of sight to their daughter, who was laughing with her cousins. Jake wouldn't tell her the truth while they danced, she reminded herself. Allie would love being led around the dance floor by him.

"Just make sure you keep the secret to yourself."

He nodded, one corner of his mouth crooked up smugly.

While Allie was occupied and Logan was busy with Owen and Billy, making fun of his sister from the edge of the dance floor, Savannah escaped the noisy room for a few minutes.

Once she was away from the music, she could hear how her ears were ringing. She kept walking to the outside doors, hoping to cool off and get some fresh air. Her heart still hadn't returned to its normal rate.

Outside, she wrapped her arms around herself and walked a few feet down the side of the building. She leaned against the brick wall, inhaling the brisk, November air, struggling to regain her balance. After about two minutes, the door opened. Michael walked out and stood there, regarding her. Something intangible told her he wouldn't utter a friendly hello.

"I thought you told me nothing was going on between you and Barnes," he began without preamble.

Savannah exhaled tiredly. So much for fresh air and getting away. "Nothing is going on, Michael."

"Looked like quite a bit was between you when you danced."

"We have a history. That's all it is."

Michael chewed on the inside of his cheek as he decided whether he could believe her or not. She straightened, and was about to go back inside when he spoke again.

"He's dancing with our daughter, Savannah."

"He asked me if it was okay."

"Why don't I get a say in that?" Michael asked.

"I didn't feel it was anything to make a federal case out of. Jake cares about her and isn't going to hurt her."

"Oh, so now you're starting to trust him?" Michael's voice rose.

"Calm down," she told him.

"I'm not going to calm down, Savannah. I'm suddenly the outsider and I don't like it. So help me God, if that man breathes a word to her about being her father, I will make him wish he'd never come back to town."

"She's going to find out who he is eventually. You might as well start accepting that. It's no longer just you and me who know the truth."

"That was never part of the deal."

"In case you haven't noticed, the deal changed when we split up. I'm going back inside."

As she walked past him, she realized Michael was right about one thing. She was starting to trust Jake.

CHAPTER EIGHTEEN

"I'M HOLDING YOU UP." Jake's grandma took another dainty bite of her frosted cinnamon roll as she sat next to Jake at the bakery.

"No rush, Grandma. I'm not in a hurry," Jake said. He'd already downed a chocolate-frosted long john and a bear claw and was now finishing his coffee.

He was probably exhausting his grandmother with all the outings the past couple of days, but he was leaving on Monday and wanted her to get out of the house plenty now.

"I'm so glad you stayed an extra week. It's been wonderful having you around."

"My pleasure. I'll miss you and Em when I go back."

A surprise snowstorm had hit his part of Montana last weekend, and very little work was going on at the Clayton job site. His meeting with the movie producer wasn't until next Wednesday, so he'd decided to stick around Lone Oak to attend some additional planning meetings with his grandma and Zach, and to spend more time with his own family. He and Emily had put in hours together, sorting through their dad's house. The only ones he hadn't seen enough of were Savannah and her kids. And his dad. He'd been putting off that final visit.

"Please tell me you won't stay away so long," Odessa said between bites.

"I won't. I'll be back much more often." What with the building project, which he was getting really involved in despite himself, and his daughter, there'd be no keeping him away for long. He'd already decided he'd fly back for the holidays.

Activity right outside the window caught Jake's eye. His pulse sped up when he recognized Savannah, Allie and Logan skipping toward the front door. Even Allie was smiling. They all stopped and laughed at something Logan said, and Jake found himself smiling, too.

"What is it?" his grandma asked. She craned her neck to find out what had caught his attention.

Jake glanced around to discern if anyone could hear him. The other two tables of customers were involved in their own loud conversations.

"That's Allie out there. And her mother and brother." He'd told his grandma all about her great-granddaughter this week. He couldn't wait for the day when the two could meet and acknowledge their relation.

The trio entered the bakery but didn't notice Jake and his grandma sitting on the opposite side by the wall. They were still laughing and carrying on and having fun just ordering doughnuts.

As Jake watched the threesome, something happened inside him. He realized nothing made him happier than those three. Not just Allie; Logan and Savannah, too. He'd fallen hard for the kids early on. As he watched Savannah now, her hands resting protectively on each of her children as they ordered, he knew at once that he loved her.

He hadn't had many chances to see her so relaxed with the kids. Obviously, she was a wonderful mom to them. The best mom they could have.

He'd held a grudge against her for not telling him about Allie earlier, true. But that was gone now. All he could feel was gratitude that she was so good to their child. Admiration, respect…and, yes, love. That was what he felt. God, he loved her.

"She's precious, Jake."

"Yeah. She is. I want to marry her."

His grandma stared at him. "I was talking about the girl."

Jake laughed. "That, too. Sorry. I was lost in my thoughts. I'm going to go talk to them. Remember, Allie doesn't know who I am yet."

His grandma nodded and turned back to her cinnamon roll.

"Hey," Jake said as he came up behind Savannah. The kids were down a ways, crawling up on spinning stools at the counter.

"Hi. What are you doing here?"

"Doughnuts with Grandma. I thought it was Michael's weekend with the kids."

"It is, but he had a business trip and isn't getting back until today. They're going over this afternoon."

"Perfect. Would you like to have dinner?"

She gave the short old man behind the counter a ten, seeming flustered by Jake's question.

"I can't, actually," she said once she'd gotten her change.

"Do you have a date?" The question was supposed to be in jest, but the thought made him edgy.

"I've told you repeatedly I don't date." She opened her wallet to put away the change. "I have to go to my dad's." Her brow furrowed and she acted nervous.

"Have to? Is it dinner?"

Savannah checked on the kids, then faced him. "I have to tell him. About you. Us."

"Ahh. Will it cause problems?"

"I don't know. But I'm dreading it."

"I'd like to come with you, Savannah."

Her head shot back in surprise and, if he wasn't mistaken, suspicion. "Why would you want to do that?"

"I wasn't able to be there for you eleven years ago or anytime since." He shrugged, trying to make light of his offer, because if she knew how much he wanted to go, she'd turn him down. "I'd like to be now."

She considered his words, still not convinced. "It won't be fun. I have no idea how he'll react, but it won't be the typical telling-Dad-we're-expecting scene."

Jake attempted to stifle a grin. "I realize that. I'm not saying you can't handle this alone. There's no doubt in my mind you'll be fine by yourself, as you always are. It's just…I missed out on everything, Savannah. Good and bad. I want to be involved."

"This doesn't mean we're telling anyone else." She glanced pointedly at Allie.

"We can argue about that a different night. Right now, all I want to do is go with you to talk to your dad."

Savannah finally nodded wearily. "Okay. Fine."

"Really? No she-woman stuff?"

"Not right now. Maybe later," she said, almost grinning. "I'll pick you up at six and we can go get it over with."

"HOLY TOLEDO, SAVANNAH. You're just telling me *now?*" Wendell Salinger leaned back on the new mocha leather sofa in the living room of the house he and Claudia had moved into last year. His wrinkled face showed every one of his years—and maybe some extra ones tonight.

Savannah stole a glance at his wife, who removed her glasses to gawk back in disbelief. Her stepmother appeared to be even more shocked than he was. Darn. Usually, Claudia helped her dad come around to his daughters' ways of thinking. He was bowled over by the confession, but she seemed absolutely flattened.

Jake, who sat next to Savannah on the love seat, wrapped his hand around hers and squeezed. Thank God he'd accompanied her. Though she wouldn't say so to him, having him next to her, at her side, was reassuring. An accomplice of sorts. Not that her dad had said anything bad…yet. He hadn't said much at all. She checked to make sure she hadn't sent him into cardiac arrest.

"So you were involved with my daughter back then?" Wendell inquired of Jake.

"Yes, sir." Jake appeared much more relaxed than she felt. He glanced at her, one corner of his mouth curving up. "Then and now."

Savannah's eyes widened. Was he insinuating they were sleeping together again? Because that had been the heart of the matter back then….

"I found out about Allie when I returned to town a few weeks ago. I've been getting to know her ever since."

"Why on earth didn't you tell Jake you were having his baby, Savannah?" her dad asked, sitting forward again.

"In all fairness, I was incommunicado," Jake interjected. "She made an effort to find me, but I didn't want to be found."

Savannah squeezed his hand in gratitude. "Michael helped me. We spent several weeks searching for Jake."

"When do you plan to tell Allie?" her dad asked.

"Soon," Jake said.

"Later," Savannah insisted.

"Do your sisters know?" Wendell asked.

"They do now. They didn't back then," Savannah said. "I'm sorry I didn't tell you, Dad. It's just that…"

"It's okay, Savannah. I'm not sure how helpful I would've been. I still wasn't handling things very well then."

She nodded, aware now he continued to feel guilty for all the time he'd spent in a fog of grief over losing his wife. It'd taken him years to start living again, and Claudia was a big part of that.

Savannah focused on her stepmom again, and her dad followed her gaze.

"You okay, honey?" he inquired.

Claudia nodded and put her glasses back on. "Surprised is all. You've hidden it for a long time."

"I'm sorry," Savannah said. "Not that I didn't trust you guys. Just that I had to make things work with Michael. I had to protect Allie."

"Interesting you say that," her dad said. "I like Michael. Accepted him as a son-in-law and all. But there was something about him… I never did feel he was the right man for you."

Savannah rolled her eyes. "There isn't a right one for me, Dad."

"I don't know about that," he said. "This one here doesn't seem so bad." The two men exchanged a smile, and Savannah wanted to yank Jake out of there before they got too cozy.

"Pardon me for prying, but *are* you two involved again?" Claudia asked, reaching for her husband's hand.

"No." Savannah didn't hesitate for a second.

"I'm trying to convince her to marry me," Jake countered.

She was going to kill him. Slowly.

Both her dad and stepmom turned their full attention to her, as if she needed to justify herself.

"What?" she asked. "I'm not getting married to anyone. Tried it. It didn't work out. End of discussion."

"Michael wasn't your type. Your dad just said so," Jake stated. "Of course it didn't work with him."

"We are not having this conversation here, now or ever." She stood.

"She's a tough nut to crack," Wendell told Jake.

"Dad! Whose side are you on?"

"I want what's best for you, honey. You and Allie, and Logan, too."

"We're doing great, Dad. This is the twenty-first century. Women don't have to be married to have a happy life."

"Can I ask you something, Jake?" Claudia's voice was quiet compared with the two Salingers. "Are you wanting to marry Savannah to be in Allie's life?"

"Claudia…" Wendell's tone was scolding.

"No, it's okay," Jake said. "Fair enough question. I can't wait to be more a part of Allie's life. She's an amazing girl.

But…" He stared at Savannah now, though she avoided eye contact. "I want to marry Savannah because I love her."

She froze and closed her eyes. He'd said that *here?* In front of her *dad?*

A soft, almost dreamy sigh issued from Claudia, which made Savannah's eyes pop open. "We have to go," she announced, and reached for her purse on the coffee table.

Wendell stood then and walked toward her. He wrapped his arms around her and she automatically did the same.

"I love you, honey." He stepped back. "Thank you for telling us. We're here for you. Whatever you need us to do. If that means babysitting so you and Jake can go out and get reacquainted…"

Savannah glared down at Jake and her dad chuckled.

"Appears to me you're getting under her skin, Jake. In my book, that's a move in the right direction."

Jake stood and shook Wendell's hand. "Thank you, sir. She's a stubborn woman."

"I can tell you know her well."

Claudia joined them, putting her hand on Savannah's arm. "Just don't go eloping on us, please, kids. Doesn't have to be a big ceremony, but I'd like to be invited."

Savannah pressed a quick kiss to Claudia's cheek, then pivoted to leave, pulling Jake with her and muttering, "I can't believe this."

"THAT DIDN'T GO SO BADLY," Jake said as he backed her van out of her dad's driveway. Why she'd let him drive over here from his grandmother's house she still wasn't sure. He refused to give the keys up now. He'd gotten in the driver's side and started the engine. Savannah had no doubt he would leave her there just to be ornery, so she'd climbed in the passenger side.

She didn't respond to his assessment. Barely even heard it because the blood was rushing through her head so loudly. Her heart raced and her jaw locked.

Instead of driving to his grandmother's house, he went directly to hers, and that didn't help her temper any.

Once the van had stopped in the garage, she bailed out and hurried up the front steps to the door. Jake caught up with her as she fought with the stupid, antiquated, stubborn lock.

"You think they didn't take it well?" he asked.

Finally, the key twisted and she headed inside. She would've slammed the door in his face had he given her the chance, but he was too close behind her.

Jake had the nerve to remove his jacket and toss it on the chair in the corner.

"I didn't invite you in," she said evenly, in a tightly re-strained voice.

"I'm used to it." He followed her into the bedroom, where she set her purse on the dresser. "You're pissed that I told them I wanted to marry you."

"You think?"

He blocked her way out of the room, and instead of fighting him, she crossed her arms and stared him down.

"What's bugging you even more is that I said I loved you."

"What the hell *was* that?" Savannah demanded.

"The truth."

She fought not to get flustered, fought not to miss a beat, but she couldn't help it. Eighty percent of the fight flowed right out of her. As tough as she wanted to be, as much as she needed to be by herself, declarations of love from this man could apparently bring her to her knees. Because she knew, deep down, he wouldn't lie. Would never say he loved her if he didn't mean it.

He leaned one shoulder against the door frame and caressed her cheek until she met his eyes. "That whole thing about my grudge? I told you I'd get over it. I'm over it. You're an awesome mom, and a hell of a woman. I love you, Savannah. And I think you love me, too."

She was weak. At this moment she knew it, but she ceased to care. The kids were gone for the weekend. The truth was out to most of her family. She was worn out from battling her attraction continuously, and this once, she was going to stop fighting and grab what she wanted.

Savannah stepped toward him and ran her hands up his abdomen to his chest, feeling the strength beneath his shirt. God, he had muscles, and she needed to feel them. See them. Taste every last bit of him.

But first she needed to drive him crazy. As crazy as he made her.

The only illumination in the bedroom was from the dim lamp in the living room. She kept it that way and pulled him farther into the room.

She tugged his shirt out of his jeans and started to unbutton it from the top, unhurriedly, trailing her fingertips along his skin between each button. He watched her without speaking, never losing eye contact. That gaze made her heart race. Aroused a longing deep within her that made her ache.

When all the buttons were unfastened, she dragged the

sleeves down his arms and couldn't help admiring those biceps, the pecs. Some guys softened up as they hit their thirties, but not Jake. He'd been in great shape as a teenager years ago, and he'd only improved. Filled out, broadened in all the right places, hardened. She whisked her tongue over one of his nipples and he sucked in his breath. But he didn't touch her. Maybe he sensed that this was her moment and she was going to play it her way. He seemed just fine with that, if the groan that escaped his throat when she swirled her tongue around his other nipple was any sign.

Savannah explored every ridge and dip of his chest, working her way down to his waist, leisurely, following the sparse hair. She unbuttoned his jeans and drew the zipper down painfully slowly. She glanced up at Jake's face, and the look there heated her blood even more. His eyes were half-closed, his lips parted, his breathing uneven.

Good.

She wanted him begging before she could beg herself.

On her knees now, she untied his shoes with shaky fingers. She removed them and tugged his jeans down his legs, then helped him step out of them. Savannah stood, admiring the fit of the navy-blue boxer briefs, and moving so close she could feel his warm breath on her forehead. She longed to devour those lips that were so near, but held back. Instead, she inched her fingers into the elastic band at his hips and slid the shorts down without touching anything but his outer thighs. He moaned as he became naked in front of her, fully revealed while she remained clothed. Not touching him was absolutely killing her.

He stepped out of his briefs and his gaze bored into hers.

She took in the sight of him, every masculine, solid inch and felt a response deep within her body.

"Now what are you going to do with me?" His voice was ragged, husky, so sexy.

She stood on her toes and placed light kisses on his lips, still without touching the rest of him. "Whatever…I…want."

His arms closed around her and he forced her up against his length, pressing his hardness into her. Jake ran his palms over her back, and settled his mouth on hers, kissing her until she was dizzy. She nearly forgot that this was *her* deal. She was the boss for the next half hour, hour, night, however long necessary to make him crazy and to stop this insane craving inside herself.

She pulled away and shook her head, her lips hinting at a smile. Taking his hand, she led him to the end of the bed and gently pushed him onto it. She stood between his knees and drew her sweater up inch by inch, then over her head. Jake moaned again when he saw the red lace she wore underneath. He reached out and cupped one of her breasts, but she took his wrist.

"No touching. Not yet," she said, hardly recognizing her own voice.

She kicked her shoes off, unbuttoned her jeans and wriggled out of them, revealing more red lace, which met with more approval. She smiled, feeling the power of his desire, knowing she could have just about anything from him right now. Knowing she would give him almost anything.

She prolonged the striptease, her hands shaking even more, her knees threatening to give out. She undid her bra and let it slide down her arms to the floor. Then she hooked her fingers into the strings at her hips and eased them downward. In the dim light, she saw Jake swallow as his eyes followed. She inched out of her panties, and the predatory, barely restrained look he sent her made her shiver. And step forward to touch him at last.

CHAPTER NINETEEN

JAKE'S PATIENCE WITH being passive for Savannah's sake was running mighty low. He'd never been this turned on in his life, and seeing as how he remembered in exquisite detail the only other night he'd shared with her, that was saying a lot.

He lay back on her bed now, completely still except for his heart, which slammed against his chest, and his lungs which fought for oxygen. She slid over him teasingly, hovering just above him, not quite making contact. And he waited. Biding his time.

Savannah finally moved in and kissed him, hard, and Jake would have wept with joy if he hadn't been so swept away by the taste of her, the feel of her lips on his. It was as if they'd never kissed, and yet the kiss was so perfect and familiar.

Her body fit between his legs, her breasts pressed against his chest, and that was just about all Jake could stand of lying there under her. He wrapped his arms around her and with one fast move had her beneath him. Surprisingly, she didn't complain. In fact, she became more frantic for him, grabbing his ass, making sexy little noises in her throat.

He needed every bit of willpower to pull back six inches and break the contact of their mouths.

"One thing," he said, sounding out of breath.

"Don't even say it…."

"I'd like to think we're older and wiser, but…birth control? Apparently, we're pretty fertile together."

"Oh. It's okay. I'm on the pill."

"That'll take care of pregnancy."

"Jake, I haven't had sex for almost two years. I'm clean. You're the only one we need to worry about."

"Same for me," he said, secretly thrilled she'd had no one since her divorce. He kissed her again.

"Same for you what?" she asked, inching to the side.

"I'm clean."

"Has it been two years for you? Is that what you mean?"

He went back to kissing her, hoping to distract her.

"Jake."

"What?"

"Tell me."

He drew away and stared down at her. "Not two years. Not quite one year. But I've had a physical. I'm clean. Now…if my recent history checks out okay, can I get back to what I was doing?"

She pulled his head down and got back to it for him, which worked just fine for Jake. When she somehow rolled back on top and straddled him, it was still fine. More than fine. She eased herself down on him, taking him inside her.

This was the closeness he'd ached for ever since he'd first experienced it. For nearly twelve long years, she'd been in his dreams, and still the reality of her blew his mind—which was nothing compared with what she was doing to the rest of him.

Having her on top gave him the erotic show of a lifetime. Her languid sexy movements were driving him mad. Jake reached up for her breasts and ran his thumbs over her pebbled nipples, played with them, pinched them lightly. Savannah threw her head back and arched even more, moaning his name and a jumble of other words that nearly made him lose it.

Their slow pace became more frantic quickly, until Jake knew that if he didn't hold her back he'd lose control too early. To get her to this point had taken him long enough; he was not going to ruin it for her. Grasping her beautiful backside, he again switched their positions and slowed things down a little. A very little, because no matter who was in control, it was too good between them. Her hips rose to meet him at every thrust. He became oblivious to any intention to send her over the edge first, as the need in him built to a fevered pitch, burning through him, making him lose his mind.

Savannah called out his name and dug her nails into his back, and there was no hope for him any longer. He plunged over right after her, losing awareness of everything except the exquisite woman in his arms and the way she made him feel.

Their hearts pounded in unison and they both gasped for air in the aftermath. When Jake could muster the strength, he rolled to his side, Savannah along with him.

"Holy…"

"Yeah," she said with a lazy, satisfied grin. "We're good at that."

"*Good* doesn't seem like the right word."

"I know, but my brain doesn't have enough oxygen to locate a better one."

She trailed her fingertip over his jaw, down his shoulder and onto his upper arm. There, she stopped at a tattoo, which appeared to be healing.

"Is this new?"

He nodded and moved so she could see it. "You might recognize it."

Savannah flipped on the lamp on the nightstand. He feasted his eyes on her nakedness as she inspected his tattoo.

"It's one of Allie's designs." She traced it tenderly.

"You got it. My sister did the tattooing for me. She was very impressed with it."

"I can't believe you did that." Savannah grinned sentimentally. "You're a total softie."

"No way. Softies don't get tattoos." He pulled her closer and ran his fingers lightly up and down her back, thinking he'd like to stay this way for the rest of the weekend. Or longer.

JAKE OPENED ONE EYE, momentarily confused until he recognized Savannah's bedroom. The sun had risen, though the day must be gloomy and overcast, judging by the dimness of the room.

Savannah was tucked up against him, her naked body partly on top of his, her back toward him. He touched her stomach gently, not wanting to wake her but unable to resist the silky feel of her. He stirred just enough to see over her to the clock on the nightstand. Eight-thirteen. Perfect. Still some time to wake her in the most erotic way he could conjure and linger in bed with her.

He inched away, and Savannah's body shifted so she was flat on her back. She made no sign that he'd awakened her yet, but he would change that.

Jake leaned over her and trailed his fingers over her nipple, teasing it and pinching it. He could tell she was aware of his touch, though now pretending to still be asleep. That was okay. Two could play that game. He smiled to himself, anticipating the challenge of arousing Savannah.

He took her nipple into his mouth and circled it with his tongue. Savannah tensed a fraction but still didn't open her eyes. He dragged his tongue from her breast to her navel, giving every inch of her skin close attention. She was very obviously awake, breathing unevenly, but still she kept her eyes closed, as if she could fool him.

His kisses moved lower, then lower still, to the place between her legs that was hot and moist, anticipating his touch. At the first caress of his tongue, her body jolted to life, arching toward him as a needy moan escaped her throat.

"Oh, you're awake," he said innocently, grinning up at her.

Her lids were only half-open. "*Awake* is one word for it," she said breathlessly.

"What's another word?" he asked, after suckling and teasing her body some more.

"About to crawl out of my freaking skin," she gasped, arching again.

"You sound like you're having a hard time breathing," he taunted.

"Can't…imagine…why…" She was tunneling her hands through his hair, trying to pull him closer.

"Maybe you should consult a doctor."

He brought her nearly to the edge with his tongue, then crawled up her body, bestowing kisses and nibbling her skin, until he reached her lips.

"You," she said, wrapping her legs around him, "are such a tease."

"You could send me home." He rubbed his hardness against her and she moaned again.

Savannah took control then, directing his shaft exactly where she wanted it to go, then thrusting her hips against him, making him just as wild and hot as she was. Damn, this woman knew how to work magic.

Holding on longer than Savannah demanded a gargantuan effort. The witch was making him crazy. She met every thrust and gradually drove their tempo to a frenzied rush. They rolled over several times and nearly fell off the bed, kicking blankets out of their way, laughing together. When she finally climaxed and called out his name, he let himself go and fell with her.

They lay quietly, still joined intimately, slowly returning to reality.

"Not a bad way to wake up," she said at last, running her fingers over the stubble on his cheek.

Jake couldn't help smiling in agreement. "I could stand to wake up like that for the rest of my days."

Her fingers stopped moving. She dropped her hand to her side and didn't meet his eyes. There was nothing overt, but the expression on her face told him very clearly she had a problem with what he'd just said. A problem with them having a future together.

He was an idiot for believing her seduction last night had any meaning.

He sat up and swung his feet over the side of the bed to the floor, rubbing his face with his hands. Savannah stood on the opposite side and, from the sound of it, drew on her robe.

"So now you're backing out," he said.

"We shouldn't have slept together."

"I don't know," he said, standing and searching for his underwear. "I think it was inevitable."

Savannah shook her head. "I was weak. I'm sorry if you interpreted it—last night—to mean more."

He stared at her, feeling tired. God, so tired. Defeated. "You're doing this again." There was no question in his voice, because obviously, she was running away from him once more. He yanked on his underwear, then shoved his legs into his jeans, his jaw set. "I would've thought that in all these years you'd have grown up enough to handle the intensity. To handle us. Not pull the same thing as before."

"This isn't the same." She wrapped her white robe more tightly around her and crossed her arms in front of her chest.

"Oh? We sleep together and a few hours later you change your mind. I'm not seeing how it's any different."

"The difference," she began, her voice shaky, "is that before, I was scared and might have even made a mistake. This time?" She inhaled deeply and tilted her chin to gaze up at the ceiling. "I know what I'm doing. I let this happen because I wanted it. Wanted to spend the night with you."

He slipped his shirt on with a grimace, then stepped toward her. The expression on his face must have given his anger away, because she edged back.

"You can't have it both ways, Savannah. I won't play that game with you."

"I'm not playing a game…."

"The hell you aren't. You want me enough to have me spend the night when the kids aren't here, but you're too scared to make a commitment and have me in your life full-time. It doesn't work that way. If you want me, you get all of me. You let me into your life and your kids'."

Savannah walked past him. "Is this an ultimatum, Jake? Your way or the highway?"

She kept her back to him, so she didn't catch his nod.

"Yes." He'd never been so sure about anything in his life. "I can't play around with you whenever the opportunity arises, when the kids are at Michael's for the weekend, and then walk away when it's time for you to return to your real life. You can't ask that of me."

She turned around. "I'm not sure I was asking that."

"Then what?"

She shook her head slowly, shoulders sagging. "I still can't marry you, Jake. Not now, not a year from now. We'll just get hurt in the end."

"*Who* will get hurt?"

"You." She met his gaze, her eyes shining with emotion. "Me." She sat on the edge of the bed. "Allie and Logan, too, eventually."

She hadn't changed a bit, he thought angrily, stifling the urge to punch something. "Let me see if I can figure out your theory, here. We get married. Because you went through one bad marriage that ended in divorce, you and I would most certainly end up divorced, too, thereby hurting everyone in the family. The kids would lose another dad, you'd lose another husband…."

"That," she said, springing up, "is exactly what would

happen if I made the humongous mistake of marrying you."

Jake pressed closer to her, his temper raging. "You have feelings for me, Savannah. I know you do or I wouldn't be here. It *is* just like before. You're afraid of what you feel, so you're running away again."

Clenching her jaw, she shook her head. "You're wrong."

"You don't have feelings for me? You expect me to believe that?"

"I do have feelings for you, Jake. I love you." She spat the words at him as if they were a curse, and he stood there, stunned, for several long, confusing seconds.

"You love me." His voice was much quieter. She'd taken all the force out of his anger with that one little admission. Now his heart pounded with cautious hope.

"I love you," she repeated. "Whether I think that's the best idea or not, I freaking love you. Is that what you want from me?"

Jake's mouth flirted with a grin. Not only did she love him, but she'd *admitted it.* "That's a decent start."

"Well, that's all you get. Because sometimes love isn't enough to make things work."

The hope died with her words and the determined look on her face. She marched off to the kitchen and began viciously scrubbing a dirty pan soaking in the sink. Jake followed her and leaned against the wall, watching her.

"I don't understand you, Savannah. I've known you for almost as long as I've been alive, and after all these years, I just don't get you."

"You're not supposed to," she said. "It doesn't concern you."

"You love me, but say we won't work." He straightened and advanced on her. "Yeah, I'd say it concerns me."

He wrested the pan from her and calmly set it in the sink. Her hands were dripping, but he took both of them in his anyway, and turned her toward him.

"Don't do this," she said.

"Do what?"

"Reason with me."

Jake chuckled. "Excellent advice."

He grabbed the towel hanging on the oven handle and dried their hands. Then he looked hard into her eyes and tried like crazy to get through to her.

"Savannah, we've got something between us, a hell of a something. I know you're scared of having another failed relationship, but what if we could make it work?"

She shook her head and broke eye contact. "I'm not scared. I'm just not up for it." She moved a couple of steps away from him. "I don't want to change the way I am. I'm impossible to live with."

"I'm certain you are," he said, and meant it.

"I control everything."

"You controlled everything with Michael."

"Yes. And I would with you, too. It's the way I am."

"Do you really believe our relationship would be anything like yours and Michael's?"

"It's not about the relationship. It's about me, Jake."

He rested against the cabinets.

"What?" Savannah asked.

"Do you remember when you went on your very first date with Michael? It was the summer after we graduated."

"Of course I remember."

"I told you then that he was all wrong for you. You two would never work."

"Right. You know it all, Jake." She threw her hands up as she spoke.

"That's not my point."

"Could you maybe cut to your point? Because we're not getting anywhere and it's just about time for you to go."

"My point is that Moser is a doormat. He was back in high school, and still is today. He's not like you and me, Savannah."

"And what, exactly, are we?"

"Strong-willed. Controlling, yes. Sure of ourselves, sure of what we want. Willing to fight for it."

"A recipe for disaster."

Reasoning with this woman was impossible.

"Michael left you because you were too controlling."

"I know. I was there."

"You could never control me so much that I'd leave."

She actually laughed. "Is that a challenge? Is that your plan? You're going to lure me into marriage by tempting me to prove you wrong?"

"Would it work?"

She stared at him, flushed and flustered. Sexy. "No. My kids' well-being is on the line here. I won't screw with that."

Jake smacked his hand on the counter. "Dammit, Savannah."

"Maybe I shouldn't have let you come over, but it's not as if I've led you on or made you think we had any future together."

But they could if she wasn't so hung up on her twisted logic. Her hard head was standing in the way of their having a life together.

He stared at her for a moment longer, then had to get out of there before he lost it. And God knew this woman could definitely cause him to lose it several times over.

"What are you doing?" she asked, following him as he steamed out of the kitchen.

"Leaving." At the door, he stopped and glanced back at her. "I'll be in touch with you about Allie. I intend to stay in regular contact with her."

Then he left.

CHAPTER TWENTY

THAT WAS IT. Jake was gone. Out of her life.

It was what she'd wanted. What she'd been fighting for since the day he'd first walked into Heartland Construction. Leaving was the right thing to do, because she'd meant every word she'd said to him.

Then why did it feel as if her heart had turned to a rock and stopped beating as he closed the door behind him?

Yes, she *had* meant every word, including the admission that she loved him. She probably always had.

But she truly believed love wouldn't get them through all the fights that would arise from their knocking heads, from her extreme need to be in charge of everything in her life and her kids'.

On the other hand, what would be wrong with being together whenever the kids were gone? Why couldn't they have something casual they squeezed in among everything else? Something fun. Spontaneous. Obligation-free.

Savannah ran her hands through her messy hair and paced. She knew, of course. A relationship between her and Jake could never be casual. Even if she was the type for halfway, there would always be Allie, always that unfinished business.

She shuffled to the living room couch and absently sat

down. The house was so suffocatingly quiet she wanted to scream to shatter the silence. Her throat throbbed with sadness, but her eyes remained dry. After all, this was her doing. This was how she'd wanted it.

She was not going to break down. She'd gotten her way, as lonely as it was. Time to put on her big-girl panties and deal with it.

The kids would be home in a few hours. She had until then to overcome her mixed emotions, to remind herself repeatedly why Jake's leaving was for the best.

SAVANNAH HAD FULLY intended to tackle cleaning the place before the kids got back, but instead, she'd fallen into a deep sleep on the couch. She woke up just minutes before the knock sounded.

The kids bounced in as she opened the door, and for once, she embraced the commotion.

"Hey, guys, how are you?"

Logan rushed into her arms as he usually did, hugging her and jumping into a play-by-play of the day he'd been away. Savannah only half listened as she eyed Michael. He'd been tense every time she'd seen him lately, ever since Jake had come to town.

"Hi, Allie," Savannah said as her daughter walked past her. Her silence was becoming as normal as Logan's noise. "Go get your bags unpacked, kids. Then we can work on homework before dinner."

The children disappeared and she faced Michael, expecting him to move toward the door. Instead he focused on the easy chair in the corner. Savannah followed his gaze and instantly realized the problem.

"Had company this weekend, did you?" He strolled over to the chair and held up Jake's jacket.

"That's my business." She took the coat from him and placed it over the back of the couch, as if she had nothing to hide. It was too late for hiding.

"When my kids are involved, it's not just your business."

"The kids were with you. What I do when they're gone doesn't concern you."

"I disagree."

She eyed him in disbelief. Who did he think he was?

"You can do whatever you want with any man out there, Savannah…any man but him."

She stepped closer, cracking her knuckle. "You have no say in the matter."

"Jake will do irreparable damage to this family, and you know it."

"He's not doing anything to the family. Have you really become this paranoid, Michael?"

"Don't act like I'm being ridiculous, Savannah. He knows the truth and he'll use it to get past you to Allie. He'll tear her world apart."

"He cares about Allie." That, she knew with every fiber of her being.

"What's happened to you? I thought you were in favor of not telling her the truth."

"Telling me what truth?" Allie said quietly from the bedroom doorway.

Savannah's heart stopped and she thought her legs might give out. She braced herself against the wall and closed her eyes.

"Nothing for you to worry about, honey," Michael said, going to her.

The young girl sidestepped and marched into the living room, and the look of determination and stubbornness on her face struck Savannah like a physical blow. And she knew there would be no more hiding. Not if she ever wanted her daughter to trust her again.

"Allie," she said, straightening her spine and trying to garner some strength. "We have to talk. There are things you should know. But give me a few minutes, because there's one other person who must be in on this conversation."

"You're calling… Savannah, what do you think you're doing?" Michael asked.

"I'm going to get everything out in the open," she replied, forcing herself to sound confident. In truth, she dreaded having Jake here again after the way they'd left things. How ironic that Allie had overheard her and Michael when it would be far easier for Savannah to let Jake catch his plane tomorrow and not have to see him for weeks.

JAKE'S GUT CHURNED as he made his way to Savannah's. The scene ahead of him couldn't be pleasant for anyone, but especially not Savannah. Her voice on the phone had been heavy with bottled-up emotion, and though she hid the fear well, he knew she was scared to death of Allie drifting even further from her. That was the last thing Jake wanted. In fact, if he could find a way to get Allie to treat her mother better, he'd do it.

Still, a nervous anticipation buzzed through his veins,

because at long last the secret would be out. He'd be free to tell the world about his daughter and, if he was fortunate, be a father to her at times. He didn't expect miracles, and guessed that Allie would be mad at him, as well, but hope beat stronger in his chest.

The door opened almost immediately when he knocked. Savannah didn't smile, didn't meet his eyes, just stood aside. Her hair was pulled back loosely and her face was pale. Fear radiated off her and he had to check himself to keep from drawing her near. Had to remind himself she'd chosen to handle the rest of her life without him next to her.

One look at Michael told Jake that this meeting wasn't his idea and he thought telling Allie the truth was a mistake. Jake couldn't disagree more. The sooner they told her, the sooner she and Savannah could work through the new reality and rebuild their relationship. Not that that would be simple. It could take months. Maybe longer.

Savannah brushed past him to the hall. "Kids, come on out. Jake's here."

"Logan doesn't need to be in on this," Michael said, alarmed.

"He should know, too. It's time for everyone to know." Savannah met his eyes with a determined stare, and Jake understood how their marriage had gone wrong. Michael was no match for this woman when she made her mind up about something. Which was usually.

Allie arrived then, appearing like a mini Savannah, her face etched in resolve, but with a hint of trepidation. She was doing her best to be tough, though. Jake had to work hard not to grin. A smile wasn't appropriate, yet he was so damn proud of that little girl.

"Why don't we all sit down," Savannah said stiffly.

They filed around the couch. Allie took the love seat. Savannah and Jake both ended up on the sofa and Logan crawled up into Savannah's lap. She invited Michael to sit, but he shook his head and burned a path in the carpet behind the couch.

"Are you going to tell me the truth now?" Allie asked.

"Tell her what truth?" Logan had no idea what was going on. Heck, he still might not comprehend once they explained everything.

"Honey," Savannah began, addressing Allie. "what you overheard your dad and I arguing about…"

"About lying to me."

Savannah inhaled deeply, quickly. "There is something we haven't told you before because the time wasn't right. You weren't old enough to understand."

Jake tensed as he watched his daughter, unable to fully process the significance of this moment and how it would change everything. His heart was thudding painfully. What if she never accepted him? What if, as soon as she found out the truth, she started hating him?

Savannah squeezed Logan absently, wondering exactly how to get through this conversation without losing it.

"You know that a man and a woman make a baby, right?" she finally said.

Allie rolled her eyes in response. "We're not going to talk about *that,* are we?"

"The people who make a baby are called biological parents. I'm your biological mother." Savannah hesitated.

"Jake…" She put her hand on the cushion between them and felt the warmth of Jake's hand settle over hers. "…is your biological father."

The incessant tick of the wall clock in the dining area was the only sound as Allie took in that information.

"You mean Dad…isn't my dad?" Her bravado was gone and her voice was all little girl as she struggled to make sense of Savannah's words.

"He's…your dad in a lot of senses of the word. He's the dad who raised you."

At last Michael came around the couch to kneel in front of her. "I love you very much, Allie. Always have and always will."

She glared at him and curled up in a ball on the cushion. Michael moved back, helpless and shaken.

"Allie, your mom and I met each other years ago," Jake interjected. "We've known each other all our lives. We cared about one another a lot and went on dates."

"I know about doing it." Allie spat the words out. "You and Mom did it."

"Jake wasn't aware he made me pregnant, and he left town. I couldn't find him, and that's when Daddy—" Savannah pointed to Michael to show *which* daddy she referred to. "He helped me. When we couldn't find Jake, he asked me to marry him."

Allie continued to glare, and Logan sat stock-still.

"What about Logan?" Allie asked.

"I'm his father," Michael said.

Logan nodded once, as if he was reassured. God, he was going to be in therapy before he hit adolescence. Allie, too. What had they done to these children?

Savannah switched to the love seat next to Allie, carrying Logan with her. The last thing she wanted was for him to feel unwanted or unimportant because this was all about his sister.

She reached out to put her arm around her, but Allie ducked under it and moved away.

"You have two dads who love you, Allie. And one mom."

"And a brother," Logan added helpfully.

"I don't want two dads," Allie said. She pierced Savannah with a hateful stare. "I knew you would mess it up!"

Jake knelt in front of Allie now. "Kiddo, I realize this is all hard to understand. We grown-ups have made some mistakes and it's all a little confusing. But I love you."

Allie regarded him, tears beginning to fall. "You only liked me because you're my dad. I thought…"

Her sobs filled the room and Savannah's heart shattered. She moved toward Allie again, and this time her daughter didn't brush her off. She just ignored her as she buckled over, shoulders heaving.

"Allie, I like you because you're an amazing person. You're one heck of an artist, you're sweet and you're fun to talk to. I loved you right away because you're my daughter, but that has nothing to do with why I like you."

"Allie," Savannah said, but the girl made no sign she heard her. "Honey, come here."

Allie leaped off the love seat then. "No! Leave me alone. I don't want to talk to you. Any of you!"

She rushed to the bedroom and slammed the door.

Savannah stood and cracked a knuckle, wanting to

punch something. She'd known this was how Allie would take the news, and she hadn't been able to find a way to soothe her daughter or make things easier for her to understand. Hot tears welled, but she was not going to cry in front of these men.

"You two might as well go now. She won't talk tonight. All we can do is be there for her when she's ready."

"I'll go check on her, Mom," Logan said earnestly. Savannah nodded as he went to their bedroom, love for both of her children choking her up more.

Jake walked over to her. "I can stay for a bit. Make sure she's okay."

Savannah shook her head. "I've got it covered."

He didn't look as though he'd back down soon, and that raised Savannah's ire.

"What about you?" Jake asked.

"What *about* me?"

"This is hard on you."

"Yes, it's hard on me. But that didn't concern you when you were so bent on telling her."

"I didn't do this tonight, Savannah. You can't lay it all on me."

"Go, Jake." She grabbed his arm and directed him toward the door. "You, too, Michael."

"Call me when she wakes up in the morning, please. I'll drive over," her ex said.

"It's going to take a while," Savannah replied. "I'll let you know."

Michael glared at Jake and then left.

"Savannah, I'm sorry this hurts so much," Jake said.

She eyed him, her vision blurring from the damn tears.

He had to get out of there, because she wasn't sure how much longer she could keep the sobs in. She tried to nod once, then just bowed her head instead, hoping to hide how close to losing it she was. She held the door open and silently begged him to leave.

"I'll talk to you tomorrow. I can postpone my flight if necessary," Jake said. He found a scrap of paper on the end table and scribbled his number. "Phone me if you need me before then." He hesitated, then walked out the door.

JAKE MADE HIS WAY DOWN the busy hospital halls after leaving Savannah's. This was an overdue visit, one he'd put off until the very last minute.

His dad was asleep when he walked in. Jake settled into a chair against the wall, prepared to wait as long as it took for him to wake up.

Their previous conversation about Jake's mom and Dean's inability to forgive her had weighed heavily on him. Why his dad had been so unforgiving and distracted for all those years made total sense now. That didn't excuse him, by any means—it just made the matter easier to understand.

Recognizing the similarities between his dad and him had been rough, but they existed. Jake struggled with forgiveness, too. He'd thought about little else lately. The last thing he wanted was to end up like his father—unhappy, mostly alone, full of regrets.

Maybe all this thinking had spurred on his realization of how he felt about Savannah, or maybe he'd just been thick-skulled enough not to recognize he'd loved her for years. But whatever had changed, he felt a weight lifted from his shoulders by letting go of the past and no longer worrying about what he'd missed out on with Allie.

Instead of looking back, Jake was looking forward now. Not quite as enthusiastically as he had been twenty-four hours earlier. He slumped in the chair and closed his eyes, seeing Savannah's face in his mind's eye. He still didn't accept her decision, but he wasn't certain what his next move should be.

"Jacob? That you?" The voice was a mere echo of what it'd been two weeks ago.

He opened his eyes and stood. "Yeah, Dad, it's me."

The old man looked terrible, the worst Jake had seen yet. Emily was right—it wouldn't be long now. His dad blinked repeatedly, as if trying to clear his vision, then lifted a bony hand to wipe his eyes. His arm shook with the effort and Jake felt something inside him sink. This really was the last visit.

He located a box of tissues and handed one to his dad. Then he sat on the edge of the bed and gently helped him wipe his eyes.

"Thank you."

"I didn't wake you, did I?"

Dean attempted to smile. "All I do anymore is sleep. I'm glad you're here."

"Me, too. I have some things to say."

"Oh?"

His dad licked his lips repeatedly, and Jake retrieved the pitcher of water, pouring some into a large hospital mug.

"Let's prop you up." He wasn't sure his dad could hold his head up otherwise. He hit the button to raise the bed, then held a straw so his dad could drink.

"All that stuff you told me about Mom the last time I was in…" He sat on the side of the bed again; there was plenty of room because his father occupied so little space. "It made a lot of sense. Hit home pretty hard, in fact. It seems Barnes men aren't good with forgiveness. I just wanted to let you know…I've struggled with forgiving you."

His dad nodded, the movement slight but unmistakable.

"When you apologized to me, I wasn't ready to let go of my anger, but now I am. It's in the past, Dad."

Dean raised a shaky hand and gripped Jake's weakly. Tears filled the older man's eyes and Jake knew he understood. For the first time in years and years, the air was clearing between them.

"You're a better man than me," his dad said.

Jake studied him and saw he really believed that. "Nah. I just got some good advice."

They sat there, not speaking but feeling more peaceful than they probably ever had together.

"I've got something else to tell you," Jake said after several minutes. He checked to make certain his dad was still awake. Surprisingly, he was. "I have a daughter. An eleven-year-old little girl I never knew about until I returned to town. You're a grandfather, Dad."

His dad's lips moved as if he was trying to speak, but nothing came out.

"Her name is Allie and she's amazing." He told him all about her and his dad paid rapt attention, a rusty chuckle emerging from him every once in a while.

"I wish you could meet her, but she kind of hates me right now."

"Sounds pretty par for the course."

"She found out tonight that I'm her father. It pretty much turned her whole life upside down, but I think we'll be able to work through it."

His dad nodded and they fell silent again for a long while.

"I'm considering moving back to town," Jake finally said, amazing himself, since he hadn't ever put words to the idea. "I want to be in her life, and that won't be easy from twelve hundred miles away."

Dean nodded. "If you move, you could see her every week." His voice was more animated now than when Jake had first arrived, though still very weak.

"My company in Montana is just taking off, though." Jake explained about his two Hollywood clients and how he hoped to build a name for himself with that crowd. He went on for longer than he'd intended, his excitement about his career fueled.

"So you're torn," his dad said when he'd finished.

Jake nodded. "That's one word for it."

"I can give you my opinion, if you'd like."

Jake gestured for him to continue. "Shoot. Please."

"You're trying to choose between your family and your job, in essence. I had the same dilemma, though the circumstances weren't so dramatic. I chose my job." He shook his head sadly. "These past few years have been lonely, but the loneliness really hits home when you lie in a hospital bed for weeks, spending most of your time by yourself. Without family."

Jake's chest ached with sorrow for this man.

"None of that is your doing, son. All mine. I made a

choice, and I feel confident telling you now it was the wrong one."

He fell silent and closed his eyes. Jake didn't move, suddenly afraid that this was it, that his father was going to take his last breath as he sat there on his bed. He covered the old man's hand with his and sighed with relief when those eyes opened again.

"A job won't keep you company on cold nights and holidays," Dean said, and shut his eyes again.

Emotion roiled inside Jake. He sat there for several more minutes, watching his dad, thinking about his words, knowing what he had to do.

Then he stood and bent over his sleeping father. "I have to go."

The old man's eyes opened once more and he struggled to focus on Jake.

"Thanks, Dad. I love you," Jake said in nearly a whisper.

"Love you, too, son."

Jake brushed his hand over his dad's wispy hair, then walked out of the hospital room.

CHAPTER TWENTY-ONE

SAVANNAH WOKE UP before her alarm went off the next morning. Her head throbbed and her mouth was dry, as if she'd gone on one heck of a bender the previous night. She groaned as the evening came back to her.

Heart heavy, she jumped out of bed, grabbed her robe and dragged it on as she made her way across the hall to the kids' room. The door was closed. All was silent and she instinctively knew no one was stirring.

Savannah quietly pushed open the door, needing to reassure herself that everything was okay for now, knowing when Allie got up the day would be one of the most trying of her life.

Logan, whose bed was opposite the door, sprawled diagonally across his twin mattress, blankets twisted at his feet. A sleeping child always brought a certain calmness to Savannah.

She glanced over to Allie, her lips still hinting at a smile—and her heart stopped.

Allie wasn't in her bed. The covers were pulled up semi-neatly, free of child-size lumps. Not breathing, Savannah backed out of the room and did a frantic search through the other rooms of the house, her own included.

Finding no sign of Allie, she raced back to the kids' bedroom and whipped the closet door open, hoping…

To no avail.

Fear clogged her throat and threatened to choke her. An inability to accept the worst had her searching through the house again, this time checking under furniture and in all the other closets. When she passed the cordless phone in its cradle, she grabbed it, then held it as she continued her search.

Her baby girl. Where was her baby girl? God, please let her be okay.

Staring at the phone, she considered whether dialing 911 was the right thing to do. Her head felt as if it were full of molasses. Finally, Savannah acknowledged to herself this really was happening and that it was an emergency. She hit Talk and dialed.

"Nine-one-one, what is your emergency?"

Savannah swallowed hard. "My girl…my little girl is missing. I think she ran away."

"How old is your daughter, ma'am?"

"Eleven." Savannah was on autopilot.

"Did something upsetting happen?"

Savannah nodded; as if the woman could hear her. She couldn't speak, couldn't get enough air.

The dispatcher asked her several more questions and said a car was on its way.

Hanging up to face the too-quiet house triggered the tears, and her shoulders shook with her wrenching sobs.

Allie had to be okay.

Savannah couldn't handle anything bad happening. *Could not handle it.*

Without thought, she hit the talk button again and dialed the number Jake had left for her last night. She told him Allie was missing. He inquired if she'd talked to Michael yet, then said he'd take care of calling him. In less than two minutes, Jake was off the phone and on his way over.

Savannah blindly dug a long-sleeved T-shirt out of her drawer and threw it on, then found sweatpants and socks. Standing in the center of her bedroom, she couldn't seem to think where she kept her shoes. She turned in a slow circle to find them, trying to hold in the sobs. Her old tennis shoes in the corner by the closet door finally registered in her brain, and she stuffed her feet into them.

Without stopping for a jacket, she barreled out the front door to see if, by some chance, Allie hadn't gone far. But no one hid behind the bushes or around the corner of the duplex. There weren't any other places to hide in their yard, and Savannah couldn't go any farther and leave Logan alone.

Helplessly, she went back, still scanning the area as she walked to the front door. Nothing was moving. It was a cold day and no birds or squirrels or rabbits had dared to venture forth to forage.

Where would Allie have gone?

Savannah dialed Lindsey, feeling dumb for not trying her earlier. But her sister hadn't heard from Allie. She promised to drive over right away.

Logan rounded the corner from his bedroom then and Savannah hugged him to her, unable to speak.

"What's wrong, Mom? Where's Allie?"

That made Savannah's breath catch on a sob.

"I'm not sure, sweetie. The police are coming to help us search for her."

"Will they have their sirens on?" he queried somberly.

"I don't think so." Savannah fought down her panic and bent to her son. "Did you hear Allie make any noises in the night?"

Logan considered, then shook his head.

Within minutes, a policeman—Kurt Humphrey, whom Savannah had been a couple of years behind in school—was at the door to get information and start a search.

Savannah wished his presence made her feel better, but it was all she could do to sit and answer his questions, while her daughter was out there…somewhere. Possibly by herself. She refused to entertain any other possibilities because anything else would be even worse.

JAKE AND MICHAEL ARRIVED at Savannah's at the same time. Judging by the cars in the driveway, they weren't the only ones who'd rushed over as soon as they'd heard.

"Thanks for calling me," Michael said as the two men went up the stairs.

Lindsey answered the door as soon as they knocked, and practically yanked them inside. Mr. and Mrs. Salinger sat at the dining room table, worrying. Katie and Noah were on the love seat.

Jake sought out Savannah, who was curled up in the corner easy chair. Her hair was a mess, her eyes looked as though she hadn't slept and the worry etched into her face instantly made her seem five years older.

Instinct propelled him over to her. Ignoring her vibes, which said stay the hell away, he pulled her into his arms. He was shocked when she didn't belt him or push him back. Instead, she buried her face against him and stood there, not crying, not moving. Not putting her arms around him—but that was okay. That she accepted his comfort was enough.

"It's going to be all right," he whispered. "We'll find her, get her home and start helping her cope."

Savannah hesitated, then nodded. He had the feeling she was fighting to keep from crying. He pulled her even tighter and kissed her forehead. Then he released her.

"Let's get busy hunting for her. What's the plan?"

"The police are out searching for her, but…"

"The rest of us will get out there and help," he said. "You stay here in case she returns home."

Savannah nodded again. Jake took charge, splitting up the town between Michael, himself, Noah and Katie and the elder Salingers. Lindsey would stay with Savannah and Logan. Apparently, Zach was already out searching, with the kids in tow.

"I'm going to borrow your van," Jake said. Savannah handed him the keys without blinking. He held up his cell phone. "Call me when you hear something."

She didn't reply, and the terror in her eyes grabbed him. He went back to her and clasped her hands as the others left.

"We'll get through this and everything will be okay. This is the worst part. Just hang in there. Allie's going to need you."

"I doubt she'll let me in."

"Eleven-year-olds get confused sometimes." He gave her a brief smile, the words *I love you* on the tip of his tongue. But he kept them to himself. That was his problem—one he would reckon with later, after they'd found their daughter.

THE NEXT HOUR LASTED an eternity. Savannah paced, cleaned, answered Lindsey when necessary and made promise after promise to God if he'd only let her child return home safely.

"More coffee?" Lindsey asked her, carrying in a full pot.

Savannah picked up her mug from an end table so Lindsey could fill it.

"Sit down," Savannah told her. "Your back has to be aching by now."

"My back is always aching. If I sat down whenever it hurt, I'd never get up." But Lindsey lowered herself to the couch next to where Savannah had collapsed yet again.

"I've never felt so helpless in my life," Savannah said numbly.

"I know. It's horrible just sitting here. But if she happens to come home…"

Savannah stood and opened the front door to the main hallway, then went outside on the front step. She shivered as the wind blew through her thin T-shirt. Seeing no sign of Allie, she went back inside.

She picked up the cordless phone and pressed the talk button, then turned the phone back off. If anyone knew anything, she would've gotten a call. She paced to the kids' bedroom and checked on Logan, who was busy drawing a card for his sister. Lindsey, bless her heart, had convinced Logan that Allie would be home very soon and that she would require some extra love and care for a while.

Savannah just wished she believed that as wholeheartedly as her son did.

The phone rang in her hand, making her jump out of her skin.

"Hello?"

"We've found her," Jake said. "She's okay."

Savannah's entire skeletal system failed her and she slid to the floor in relief. "Where?"

"She went to my grandma's house to see me. Grandma phoned and I'm on my way there. She says Allie's fine, a little cold and scared, but okay. We'll be over as soon as I pick her up. Call Michael and tell him to get to your place, too."

"Oh, thank you, God." Savannah closed her eyes. Allie had walked to Odessa Levine's? "How did she know where your grandma lives?"

"Phone book, apparently. Smart kid."

Savannah nodded, unable to speak as tears rolled down her face. Lindsey moved toward her, her eyes questioning. She nodded and mouthed, "They've found her."

Lindsey carefully sat on the floor next to her and threw her arms around her.

"Savannah?" Jake said. "You still there?"

"Yeah," she squeaked.

"We'll be over in ten minutes." He hung up, and Savannah let out the sobs.

When her crying slowed down, she jumped up and went to the door to wait for them, asking Lindsey to call Michael.

Savannah watched her van whip around the corner a few minutes later and pull into the driveway. She ran down the concrete steps to meet Allie.

Wordlessly, she wrapped her arms around her daughter, and again tears fell. She'd never cried so much in her life, and right now she didn't care.

"Thank God you're all right, Allie," she finally said, after a long look at her. "Let's get you inside and warm you up."

Allie started crying then, too, but she allowed Savannah to hold her hand. When Jake reached them, he lifted Allie, kissed her and carried her inside.

Lindsey opened the door for them. "I've phoned Michael, Dad, Katie, Zach and the police. Everyone will give you guys some privacy now, some breathing room for Allie. I'm going to take Logan with me, let him play with the boys."

Savannah hugged her sister. "Thank you. I've got to go figure out what the heck to do next, after duct-taping Allie to my wrist."

A FEW MINUTES LATER, it was clear all was not well. Allie refused to speak to Savannah or Michael, and only answered questions when Jake asked them.

Allie said she'd wanted to talk to Jake about staying with him, and that was why she'd walked to his grandma's house. He promised that he would have her out for a sleepover the next time he was back in town. The promise seemed to calm her down a little.

Jake made her swear she wouldn't disappear again, no matter what happened.

"The sleepover's off if you try any funny stuff before then," he told her. "Deal?"

Allie nodded.

"Allie, we all love you very much," Savannah insisted. "I know you probably don't understand everything that's going on...."

"I get it, okay?" Allie said.

"Well, great. Then you're ahead of me," Savannah replied. "This will take awhile for all of us to get used to. But there's one thing you should know. The reason we didn't tell you about Jake earlier is that we didn't want to hurt you."

"You hurt me."

"We knew it would upset you," Michael said. "None of us wanted you to go through this."

Allie crossed her arms. "Can I go to my room now?"

She appeared absolutely exhausted, and Savannah wondered exactly when she'd left the house. "Go rest. Tell everyone goodbye for now. And why don't you write down Jake's cell phone number in your notebook. I bet he would like it if you called him when he's in Montana."

Savannah glanced at Jake and he nodded.

Grudgingly, Allie found her pad of paper for him to write his number on.

Jake hugged her, told her again how much he loved her, then kissed her forehead.

Allie glared at Michael, ignored Savannah and went to her room.

Michael stood. "I guess that's all for now. Let me know what's next. I have to check in at work, but I can come back if you need me."

He walked out the door, leaving Savannah and Jake alone.

"I have to go now, too. I rescheduled my flight for tonight. Call me if there are any Allie emergencies, please."

Savannah didn't want him to leave, but they'd already been down that road. So when he went to the door and said goodbye, she didn't move, just sat there on the couch, wishing she knew where she'd gone so absolutely wrong with everything in her life.

CHAPTER TWENTY-TWO

SAVANNAH DID HER BEST to act as though everything was normal, but obviously, it was anything but.

She'd put fish sticks and Tater Tots on the table half an hour ago. Logan, who'd chattered nonstop since Lindsey had dropped him off, had eaten more than his share. Savannah herself had picked at a few of each. Allie had reported to the table when Savannah had forced the issue, had even put two fish sticks on her plate, but she had yet to have a bite of anything. And if Savannah knew her stubborn child at all, she wouldn't eat a thing.

Which of course worried Savannah like crazy. Throughout the day, she'd tried gentle urging, reasoning, then all-out ordering, to get Allie to eat, but the girl had refused.

Savannah knew when she couldn't win, and this was one of those times. Allie was hurting badly and needed to lash out. No matter how often Savannah reminded her she was only hurting herself by not eating, her daughter ignored her. So…Savannah decided to let her daughter get really good and hungry if she so chose.

But she wasn't going to sit there and watch.

"Logan, you may be excused whenever you're finished

eating. Then you can play quietly in your room for a while. I'll be outside getting some air."

Allie met her gaze with one of anger. Savannah didn't return the sentiment, though. All she felt was a deep sorrow that she couldn't help her child. That and utter helplessness.

After grabbing her jacket, she went out to the front and sat on the top step. The bulb had burned out, and there were no streetlights close, which suited her perfectly.

She leaned her elbows on her knees and bent over, out of tears and out of ideas to aid her daughter or herself.

She'd made a royal mess out of the situation. Not just today or this week or this month. She'd been trying so hard to control things, from her children to her emotions to every little aspect of her life, that everything had gotten screwed up.

So much for trying to control her daughter. Allie had found a way around that by refusing to eat. She hadn't had a thing to eat, the one thing Savannah couldn't force. The joke was on her.

And controlling her own emotions? God. She was a basket case. Not just about Allie. Look how well she'd stood up to her feelings for Jake.

What she wouldn't give to have him here now.

She raised her head from where she'd buried it in her arms. Had she really just thought that? He was gone, as he was supposed to be. Sure, she'd hear from him regarding Allie, but that was it.

She didn't begrudge him time with Allie. Now that the truth was out, she was as willing to have her be with Jake as with Michael. No, visitation wasn't the problem. The problem was that Jake would be no more than her daughter's father, someone who would call her or pick her up to visit him whenever he was in town. When Michael collected the kids for the weekend, she felt no emotion for him. He was merely a fact of their lives. But she knew she would never feel so indifferent toward Jake, not in a dozen years or more.

There again, her need for control was messing things up. If she could just get over her fear... Yes, she was scared. Control and fear of losing had been wrapped up together for her ever since her mom had died. Her mother's sudden death, caused by a drunk driver, had affected Savannah profoundly. The loss had been so great that she'd made up her mind then, even at age fourteen, barely a teenager, that she would never leave herself vulnerable to loss again. She had run from strong feelings ever since.

It was true, though she'd never really realized it before now.

She stood and walked slowly, absently, down the steps.

With her sisters, she'd always put up barriers. Did what she could to keep them from knowing her too well, and vice versa. Only in the past couple of years had she and Katie gotten better acquainted, and then just because they'd both gone through tough times.

Years ago, Michael had felt like a haven compared with Jake. She laughed humorlessly. He'd been safe because she'd never been in love with him. He'd never made her feel she was falling helplessly without a net to catch her. Nothing like Jake, who could merely look at her and make her feel to her very soul.

Her kids—well, she'd fallen in love with them the day

they were born, probably even before. They were her Achilles' heel, she imagined. She'd spent all these years trying to control things in order to protect them from any pain.

And here they were. In a world of hurt and confusion.

Savannah jammed her hands into her jacket pockets and strolled around the double-wide driveway, shaking her head and at the same time feeling a spark of hope.

Obviously, clinging to control so desperately was getting her nowhere except crazy. Control had helped to distance her daughter from her, and had cost her the man she loved.

Could she learn to lighten up? Be less frantic about having everything go as she wanted it to?

She'd open herself up to a whole new brand of hurt, without a doubt. But right now, her heart was in so much pain she didn't see how it could hurt worse. In fact, the more she considered having Jake in her life permanently, every day, at her side, the more she felt her life could be a whole lot better.

She rested against the closed garage door and thought about him. Remembered how it had felt when, amid all her fear and worry about Allie, he'd pulled her close. He hadn't been able to fix things, but his touch had made them…not quite as bad. Being held by him had centered her, calmed her somewhat.

She realized now that he'd taken control. And she'd needed him to do that. Suddenly, what he'd been trying to get her to see about the two of them made sense. As he had said, she could never control him so much that he'd leave, because he wouldn't allow her that power. He was nothing like Michael, and that would make all the difference in the world between them.

She could lean on him when she needed to—something she'd never been able to do with her ex-husband. When she'd been alone, pregnant and terrified, yes, Michael had been there for her, but in a passive way. He'd never once taken control. She likely hadn't wanted him to.

She shook her head. There was no sense wasting any more time out here. She knew what she had to do.

"WHY ARE YOU LETTING ME stay up late?" Allie asked suspiciously, as Savannah tiptoed out of the kids' room.

"We have some girl stuff to talk about."

Allie groaned. "I'd rather go to bed."

"Not that kind of girl stuff. I have things to tell you, discuss with you. Come on." She held her hand out, and when Allie still hesitated, Savannah said, "You're not in trouble. I am."

That got her daughter's attention. They went to the couch and stretched out on opposite ends.

"I've made a bunch of mistakes, Allie. For years and years."

Her daughter sat up and stared at her, speechless.

Savannah told her about how her mother had been killed when she was just three years older than Allie, how awful that had been and how much it had hurt her. She tried to explain how she'd felt—that she never wanted to experience pain like that again.

"I knew it hurt so badly because I loved her so much."

Tears glistened in Allie's eyes.

"And that's when I decided that loving people was too painful."

Her daughter frowned. "You always say you love me and Logan."

"I love you two more than you'll ever know. Maybe when you have your own kids you'll find out. I couldn't fight that if I wanted to. But everyone else... I've tried really hard not to care so much."

"That doesn't sound very smart," Allie said.

"Why is that so easy for an eleven-year-old to figure out, but so hard for a thirty-one-year-old?" She sat up in the middle of the couch to make eye contact with Allie. "I've decided that was dumb and that it might be better to do things differently. And I'd like to tell you my plans."

Allie looked confused but interested.

"The man I love, the one I've probably always loved?"

Allie sat up straighter. "It's Jake. I know it is."

"You are so smart." Savannah reached out and hugged her. "I was thinking that if I'm going to start being smarter and not scared of caring, I should probably see if Jake will marry me. What would you think about that?"

"What would happen to Daddy?"

"Daddy will be in your lives as much as you want him to be. Living with Jake might mean moving to Montana, but we'd make sure that was all right with your dad first. And if it's okay, you could e-mail Daddy, call him, visit him. Could you live in Montana? They have lots of horses there."

Allie pondered awhile. "Maybe. If there're horses, and you and Jake and Logan are there."

"That's my girl."

"And you won't make Jake go away?"

"I hope he'll never ever go away. So I'm going to go for it."

Allie nodded very seriously. "I hope he'll never go away, either, Mom."

That her daughter still wasn't smiling didn't escape Savannah. The happiness would come eventually, she hoped.

CHAPTER TWENTY-THREE

SAVANNAH LEANED BACK in the driver's seat of the rental car and closed her eyes for a moment.

She was really doing this.

Opening her eyes, she reassured herself that the directions were on the passenger seat beside her, her cell phone was in the center console and the heat was blasting full force.

The Butte airport was nearly deserted when she'd arrived after 9:00 p.m. The weather was cold, and she crossed her fingers before taking the car out of park. Not a good night to get lost.

Jake had no idea she was on her way. Her entire family had united behind her when she'd approached them with her idea, bringing her to tears. Lindsey and Zach had invited Allie and Logan to stay with them, and her dad had volunteered to pay for her plane ticket. She'd promised to reimburse him when she could, but he'd waved away the idea, hugged her and wished her luck. Katie had cheered her on and thrown in a couple "I told you so's." Just thinking about them all and their undying support brought fresh tears. She wiped her coat sleeve across her eyes and decided to get on with her mission. They'd all be pissed if she sat here and froze to death in the airport parking lot.

The roads in Montana sucked. She followed a highway for a few miles, but the directions called for her to turn off onto a frighteningly narrow gravel road. About five or six gravel roads later, Savannah had no earthly clue where she was. There was no light to speak of, except for her dome light, and it was barely bright enough to read the map.

This was crazy. She had no idea what to expect when she found Jake. Maybe he'd changed his mind about getting married, especially after he'd gotten a flavor of the Salinger children's drama. Or maybe she'd convinced him she was too controlling, and he would send her away.

She hoped for his sake he hadn't, because she would *not* accept no for an answer. Not after switching flights twice and riding that dinky little plane all the way from Salt Lake City. Not after having her dad pay the equivalent of two weeks' of her wages to get her here. Not after she'd told Allie she would do everything in her power to keep Jake around.

She'd been on this road for too long. She pulled off to the side—not that there was any other traffic, anyway— and consulted the map again. Dammit, she was no longer certain where she was or where she was supposed to be. The more she studied the map, though, the more she thought she was still on track. The drive to the ranch just wasn't supposed to take this long.

Refolding the map, she drew in a deep breath. "Almost there. Have to be close now," she told herself.

Before starting up again, she peered in every direction, hoping to see the lights of a house or a barn. Even if it wasn't Jake's, at least she'd know she wasn't all alone out here. She felt like the only human for miles and miles.

But half an hour later, she became convinced she'd made a wrong turn or missed one. Panic began creeping in as she imagined running out of gas and freezing by the side of the road. So close to finding the man of her dreams, but…

She shook her head and admonished herself that she was losing it. Then she spotted the cell phone and reached for it. She would ruin the surprise by calling Jake and asking for help, but at least she'd show up alive.

She waited for a signal. Nothing. No bars. She swore a long stream of the most colorful words she could come up with, and decided to drive farther to see if she could pick up a signal. Finally, about a mile and a half down the road, she got one blip on the signal bar. She hit the brakes and stopped right in the middle of the road.

Her fingers shook as she pressed the numbers to Jake's cell, but when she was almost finished dialing, it hit her that he probably didn't have a signal, either. She held the phone to her ear, crossing her fingers.

He answered after two rings, and it was all she could do not to whoop and holler and scare the crap out of him.

"Hello?" he said again.

"Jake, where *are* you?" she asked, tears blurring her vision.

"I'm in Montana. Savannah, what's wrong?"

"Where in Montana are you?"

"At my house."

"Where in the name of God is your house in Montana, because I've been driving around for two hours now, trying to find it, and if I don't reach it soon, I'll be eaten by bears or wolves."

"Savannah…" He laughed happily. "Wolves don't eat people, but you should probably be worried about bears. What in the world are you doing here?"

She made a frustrated sound. "Surprising you."

"Where are you exactly?"

"If I knew, I wouldn't be lost." She told him where she'd last known she was.

"That road isn't far from me at all. Any idea where on it you are?"

"No, Jake."

"Stay put. Don't move, and don't open the door to any bears. I'll be there soon."

Savannah disconnected and began laughing hysterically. Instead of grandly surprising Jake, she had to be rescued by him.

In less than ten minutes, a vehicle approached from behind her and slowly drove past. She couldn't see the interior of the dark-colored truck, but the vehicle pulled over in front of her and stopped. She waited, a billion different emotions swirling within her, until Jake climbed out of the driver's side.

Savannah was out the door, racing to him, as soon as she recognized him. She ran right into him and threw her arms around him. He embraced her for several seconds, then gazed into her tear-filled eyes.

"Wow. You're really happy I'm here," he said.

"I'm scared of bears," she said through her laughter. She tugged him to her again, unable to get enough of him, the outdoorsy scent of him, the roughness of his stubble on her cheeks, the feel of his arms wrapped around her.

She breathed him in and attempted to get control of

herself. Then she laughed again, remembering her vow not to worry so much about control.

"Marry me, Jake. Please?"

The smile that came over his face was worth every single obstacle she'd encountered that day, from the layovers and transfers, to the toy plane, to the endless gravel roads. Her heart felt as if it would explode with the power of his smile.

Then he shook his head and her heart sank.

"That won't work, honey."

Savannah froze. "What do you mean?"

"You can't ask me to marry you. I asked you first. It's *my* proposal."

Her eyes fluttered shut and she almost collapsed with relief. But she straightened, recovering quickly. "You may recall," she said, struggling not to smile, "that I rejected you. Several times."

He lifted her and carried her to his truck. "Ah, yes, how could I forget? You've kept me guessing about when that thick skull of yours would allow you to see the light."

"Put me down for a second," she said, and he set her on the uneven gravel. "You gave me this whole song and dance about the two of us having a partnership, being equal, sharing control, blah, blah, blah. So why don't we just agree that getting engaged is the thing to do."

Jake stared at her, looking very serious, then a grin crept back across his face. "That sounds like an excellent idea."

"The kids and I can move here as long as you give us a few weeks to prepare…."

His grin got bigger. "Actually, that won't be necessary.

I put my house on the market yesterday. I'd decided to move to Lone Oak with or without your blessing. I want to be with my family. My grandma, my sister, my daughter."

"What about your company? Your dream?"

"I'm making my right-hand man a partner. He'll run it. I trust him. The company will be here if we ever want to return. You and the kids have become more important to me."

She wrapped her arms around him. "If you're sure, Jake, then that's okay with me."

"I'm sure. And you know what's even better?"

"What?"

"A very short engagement."

"We have to have a ceremony or Claudia will disown me."

He paused, considering it. "All right," he said, "I'll make you a deal. We'll let Claudia have her ceremony… if you come to my house and start pretending you're my wife right now."

Savannah laughed. "Seems like a tempting deal."

"It can be our little secret," he said, setting her inside his truck.

"What about my car? My bag is in it."

"What's in your bag?"

"My clothes…"

"Honey, where we're going, you won't have any need for those."

She laughed and moved over enough for him to climb in and start them off on the rest of their lives together.

* * * * *

A KISS TO REMEMBER

BY
KIMBERLY VAN METER

Kimberly Van Meter started her writing career at sixteen when she finished her first novel, typing late nights and early mornings on her mother's old portable typewriter. Although that first novel was nothing short of literary mud, with each successive piece of work her writing improved to the point of reaching that coveted published status.

Kimberly, now a journalist, and her husband and three kids make their home in Oakdale. She enjoys writing, reading, photography and drinking hot chocolate by the windowsill when it rains.

To my three most perfect creations –
Sebastian, Jaidyn and Eryleigh. I am so blessed
the universe chose me as your mother.
You make me proud every day.

To my growing list of loyal readers.
Without you, I'd be no one.

To my publisher and editor for believing in me.
I'm forever grateful.

And to my agent, Pam,
for her patience and vision.

CHAPTER ONE

NORA SIMMONS DROVE past the old Victorian that sat on the outskirts of Emmett's Mill as she went on her way to Sonora to meet with a prospective client, and what she saw made her stomp on the brakes and nearly eat her steering wheel.

A sleek, shiny black import convertible sports car sat in the driveway, completely out of place for the aging home with its chrome wheels and leather interior, parked as if it had a right to be there when it certainly did not.

Sonofabitch trespassers. She made a quick U-turn, kicking up dirt and gravel as her truck chewed up some of the shoulder and barreled toward the house. Whoever it was, they weren't local. Nora was willing to bet her eyeteeth on that score. No one in Emmett's Mill drove a BMW roadster, as far as she knew—a car like that would stick out in the little community. Driving such a hot little number around town was likely to drop jaws and send a lot of die-hard American-manufacturer purists shaking their heads in disgust. For a town in California, Emmett's Mill had a peculiar attitude at times.

She hopped from her truck with her cell phone in

case the sheriff was needed and prowled for the trespasser, caution at approaching a stranger barely registered. She was sick of tourists thinking that just because the town was small and quaint, the locals enjoyed having their privacy invaded. Well, B.J. and Corrinda might be dead, but Nora was not about to let a stranger wander all over their place.

She rounded the side of the expansive house and found an incredibly tall man with fashionably cut blue-black hair, with an air about him that reeked of money and privilege, examining what had at one time been Corrinda Hollister's prized roses.

Nora often found herself looking up at the opposite sex, but the breadth of his frame complemented this man's height, creating a strong, powerful build that immediately made her feel distinctly feminine. She scowled and silenced the breathless prattle in her head as she stomped toward him, purpose blotting out anything other than her own ire at his trespassing on private property.

"Can I help you?"

He turned, surprised that he wasn't alone, and no doubt the frost in her voice and the annoyed arch of one brow said volumes, as if she were the one who didn't belong on the property. "Excuse me?" he said, giving her a hard look from eyes so green they almost looked fake.

The breath caught in her throat as she met his gaze. Swallowing against the very real sensation of déjà vu, she continued in a strident tone that betrayed little of what she felt inside. "I said, can I help you? In case you weren't aware, most people don't take kindly to strangers parking in their driveway and trespassing." His perturbed expression egged her on and she launched into him with fresh vengeance. "I happen to know the people who used to live here so don't try to say something like they were friends of yours or some other kind of bull puckey. I'll tell you what…if you just get back in your fancy car and get off the property I won't call the sheriff. Fair enough?"

"Your Mayberry Neighborhood Watch routine is cute but not necessary. I own this house."

What nerve. "Nice try, but I happen to know different," she retorted, ignoring the faint glimmer of something at the back of her brain and continuing indignantly. "This house belonged to—"

"B.J. and Corrinda Hollister, up until six months ago when they both died in an unfortunate car accident, leaving the house to their only grandson. Me."

The air left her lungs. Ben? She stared a little harder and although she didn't want to see it, that niggling glimmer crystallized in her memory and the image of a boy she'd kissed one summer changed into the strong facial planes of the man watching her sternly.

Oh shiza. "You're Ben Hollister?"

"It's the name on my birth certificate."

She took in the shoulders that filled his dark Henley and hinted at the solid swell of muscle hidden underneath, and the spit dried in her mouth. Where was the skinny twelve-year-old kid with braces and his hair falling over one eye? Who was this *man?*

He turned away, dismissing her again and all she could think to say was a lame "No, you're not."

He did an annoyed double take. "I am and this is becoming irritating. Who the hell are *you?*"

She was about to jog his memory, but something—pride mainly—made her stop. She didn't consider herself a great beauty—not that she didn't catch her fair share of men looking her way—but most people said her personality made her hard to forget.

She sent him a suspicious look, but his only response was an increasingly testy glare. Either he truly didn't recognize her or he was a fabulous actor. To be fair, she looked as different as he did when they were kids. Too bad Nora wasn't in a gracious mood.

"Well, are you going to tell me who you are or not? If not, you know your way out."

Temptation to spin on her heel and do exactly that had her toes twitching but she wanted to see his reaction when she revealed her identity. Surely, her name—if not her appearance—would strike a chord, and when that burst of recognition went off like a paparazzi camera flash, she'd unleash the windstorm he'd earned for neglecting his grandparents over the years. For God's sake, the man skipped out on their funeral and now he was here surveying the property as if it were a spoil of war? What an asshole.

"Listen, I—"

"Nora Simmons," she cut in, waiting for that delicious reaction to cue her next comment, which after years of practice, had become rather scathing. But he offered very little for her to grab on to. The momentary glimmer in his eyes didn't blossom into full-blown acknowledgment as she'd hoped, but winked out in a blink and his next question was like a lawn mower over her ego.

"You're the landscape architect who did the gardens at Senator Wilkinson's lakeside estate? Near Bass Lake?" He accepted her slow nod with a smug grin that showcased each of his pearly-white, braces-free teeth, and she could only stare warily. He continued, completely missing her confusion. "How synchronistic. I was planning to call you later in the week. I never imagined you might come charging in like the Neighborhood Watch brigade, but it saves me the time of tracking you down."

Uh. What? "I…" *Twilight Zone* episode? *Punk'd?* Something wasn't right. "Wait a minute. Are you saying you don't remember me?"

"Should I?" He gave her a blank expression that looked a little too earnest to be believable and her brain started to bubble.

What game was he playing? She eyed him guardedly, deciding to see where he was going with this. "Uh, never mind. Yes, I worked on Jerry's lake house. Fun project. So, you were saying?"

"Right. I would like to hire you to fix up this place."

It was the way he said *this place* that almost ruined her ability to keep her temper in check, but her curiosity was greater than her desire to pummel him into the ground for his insensitivity, so she made an effort to cast a quick look around the craggy ridge on which the house was perched.

She took in the tall grass, star thistle and twisted

branches of manzanita of the surrounding scenery and asked, "What do you mean? What's wrong with it?"

"What's wrong with it?" he repeated incredulously. He pointed at the dead roses and the withered dry grass flanking the house that looked nothing like the beautiful oasis Corrinda had created despite the notoriously hard topsoil that, during the summer, turned to stone without constant tending. In this area of Emmett's Mill it took some skill to grow anything aside from poison oak and manzanita, but Corrinda had coaxed roses and daffodils from the difficult earth.

"Are you kidding me? It's a mess," he said. He turned a speculative eye toward her and she bristled. "Aren't you the best in the area?"

"Some seem to think so." She all but growled. Thank goodness the Hollisters never saw how their grandson had turned into such a haughty jerk. It would've broken their tender hearts. As it was, the fact that he never returned to Emmett's Mill after that one summer told Nora volumes. Her sister Natalie liked to drone on about not judging people too quickly, but frankly, in Nora's book, if it walks like a duck and quacks like a duck it ain't a giraffe. And right about now, she was thinking Ben Hollister was a jerk. If he wanted to be obtuse, she could be obtuse, too. "What do you want me to fix?"

He gestured toward everything in the yard, from the grass to the bone-dry fountain that looked older than the house itself. "Everything on the outside. Now that I've seen it again, I'll bet the inside isn't much better, but I'll obviously have to hire someone else for that. It's no wonder it hasn't sold. In four months there hasn't been

FREE BOOKS OFFER

To get you started, we'll send you
2 FREE books and a FREE gift

There's no catch, everything is **FREE**

Accepting your 2 **FREE** books and **FREE** mystery gift
places you under no obligation to buy anything.

Be part of the Mills & Boon® Book Club™ and receive your favourite
Series books up to 2 months before they are in the shops and delivered
straight to your door. Plus, enjoy a wide range of **EXCLUSIVE** benefits!

- Best new women's fiction – delivered right to
  your door with FREE P&P

- Avoid disappointment – get your books up to
  2 months before they are in the shops

- No contract – no obligation to buy

We hope that after receiving your free books you'll
want to remain a member. But the choice is yours.
So why not give us a go? You'll be glad you did!

Visit **millsandboon.co.uk** to stay up to date
with offers and to sign-up for our newsletter

2 **FREE** books
and a
FREE gift

S0AIA

Mrs/Miss/Ms/Mr   Initials

BLOCK CAPITALS PLEASE

Surname _____

Address _____

_____

Postcode _____

Email _____

MILLS & BOON®

NO STAMP
NEEDED!

Ⓡ MILLS & BOON®
Book Club

FREE BOOK OFFER
FREEPOST NAT 10298
RICHMOND
TW9 1BR

NO STAMP
NECESSARY
IF POSTED IN
THE U.K. OR N.I.

one call. I figured I better come and take a look myself and this is what I find. A broken-down old house with more weeds than dirt that screams 'fixer-upper.'" He turned away and muttered, "I'm going to kill my Realtor for not telling me what I was dealing with."

"You're selling the house?"

He glanced around the yard with a frown. "It seems the For Sale sign has disappeared. When I call to berate my Realtor about these other issues, I'll be sure to remind her to get another sign out here right away." He looked up to see her staring at him. "Something wrong, Ms. Simmons? You look a little pale."

"You're *selling?*"

"That's what I said. The sign must've disappeared after I had it listed. Some kid probably used it to play mailbox baseball." Nora's continued stare prompted him to ask with a short sigh, "Ms. Simmons…are you hard of hearing? You've been echoing everything I say."

She jerked at his question and the implication that she might be hearing impaired. "No," she answered indignantly. "I'm just surprised, is all."

"Why is that?"

"Because it's your grandparents' house. I would've thought you might like to hang on to it," she said, taking great effort not to clench her teeth.

His black brows furrowed with irritation and her blood pressure peaked as he asked, "Why?"

Why indeed? She refrained from letting sarcasm drip from her voice. "Never mind. My mistake. You were saying? No, I take that back. Why wouldn't you want to keep this beautiful house?"

"Not that it's any of your business, Ms. Simmons, but I plan to use the proceeds from the sale to open my own law practice in the Bay Area. I have no need of a house in the country. I rarely vacation."

He turned away and Nora was struck by a fleeting moment of sadness for a man who never took the time to enjoy what life had to offer. A flash of the boy she'd known for one summer made her wonder where that natural curiosity had gone and why—until she realized she was sympathizing with the enemy and stiffened.

He turned to her, more annoyance on his face. "Are you always so full of questions for your potential clients? I can't say I agree it's a good business practice."

"I don't need business advice from you, thank you," she said, chafing openly at his criticism. "And no, I don't usually care."

Keen interest flared in his eyes but it was gone a heartbeat later. "Why do you care with me?"

"I don't," she answered, not quite convinced she hadn't seen what she'd seen. "I'm just trying to figure out why you'd want to sell the only possession your grandparents owned. Now I know." Subtlety was not her forte, but she was pleased to see her comment rubbed him the wrong way. "Most people I know tend to cherish gifts, especially one with such value."

He'd have to be an idiot not to catch the insult couched inside that seemingly benign statement, but he didn't take the bait as she'd hoped. Instead, he cast a long look around the property, saying, "Well, I can't say much for the Realtor I've listed the house with. I'd have thought as her client she would've told me what I was getting into."

"Who's your Realtor?" she asked for appearances' sake. There were two in Emmett's Mill and only one was female.

"Janelle—" he paused, searching his memory for her name "—Grafton, failed to tell me what a hard sell this was going to be. I figure by hiring you, a local landscape architect, I might create some goodwill and perhaps word of mouth will help move this giant money pit."

"Do you think just because I've grown up in this town once people hear I've done the work on the landscaping the house will sell faster than it would otherwise?"

His mouth twisted. "Of course I do. Two reasons. First, small towns are all about supporting the locals. Second, as I've said, I'm familiar with your work and I know it's good."

"And how is that?"

"How is what?"

"How do you know my work? You mentioned Jerry's lake house and that house is not on my Web site."

He offered a small smile. "I know the right people."

"Yeah? Me, too. I know the sheriff's home number by heart. How'd you know about that job?"

He raised his hands and his mouth tightened. "Calm down. The firm I work for travels in certain political circles. Jerry was bragging about the work you'd done and I was curious, so I started asking around. If it's any consolation, my snooping uncovered only favorable results. Like I said, you do good work. Don't get me wrong. I shopped around and checked other landscape architects, but I kept coming back to you. Your work speaks for itself."

Nora tried not to soften under his praise because, in all honesty, although the words were complimentary, she got the distinct impression they had been delivered with a hint of cynicism. She met his stare. "This isn't Stars Hollow or Pleasantville or any other fictitious town where everyone is nice and the neighbors bring apple pie when you move to town and the mayor owns a soda shop and holds town meetings in a community garage. You know, it really drives me crazy when people come to a rural area and assume just because we're not choking on smog or rushing to the nearest gourmet coffee shop for some overpriced whipped mocha soy latte with nonfat foam and an organic blueberry muffin, that we're stuck in a time warp. My working on the house won't make a bit of difference. For a lawyer, I gotta tell you, you're A game leaves much to be desired."

"Do you always insult potential clients?"

She smiled. "Not usually. But ordinarily I don't deal with people who have their head up their ass yet have the gall to try to tell me what color the sky is."

The tips of his ears reddened and his gaze hardened. "That will be sufficient, Ms. Simmons. Just because I admire your work doesn't mean I will allow you to continually insult me without provocation."

Nora eyed him with open disdain. "Mr. Hollister, I think we've already established that you need me and not the other way around," she said. "It's no skin off my nose to walk away from this job. Maybe that's what I ought to do. It's obvious you and I don't suit."

A spark flashed in his eyes and a muscle in his jaw twitched, but otherwise there was little to betray what was going on inside his head, which Nora was willing to bet was a maelstrom of pissed-off retaliatory statements. She hadn't meant to say so much, but his arrogance poked at her already roused temper. She was half tempted to tell him exactly why the house wouldn't sell no matter what he did to it, but she wasn't about to give him any kind of advantage.

"Are you finished?"

She hesitated, his civil tone made her leery. Ben struck her as the silent but deadly type. The quieter he got, the more dangerous. "Yeah," she answered.

"Good." He advanced toward her, and for the first time in her life she felt she'd just surrendered the upper hand without even realizing they were in a power struggle. She couldn't take a step back without seeming to be intimidated, but if she didn't put more space between them, she'd be forced to stare up at him, which only made her feel vulnerable and short. Damn her sisters for getting all the height. He was too close; she could smell his expensive cologne and it made her want to lean in for a deeper whiff.

She glared up at him but that was no help, either. In this position she could see the unique flecks of brown woven into the green of his eyes, like freshly turned soil on a grassy hilltop interspersed with flares of gold. She hadn't remembered his eyes being so…gorgeous.

What she did remember was his… Her gaze dropped

to his full lips and the slumbering voice of her feminine core whispered in her ear as if awakening from a deep sleep, offering all kinds of torrid suggestions that would make her grandmother blush if not her conscious self. *Ridiculous*, Nora wanted to say. They had been kids, not even old enough to know what they were doing. Why it made such an impression then, and why being so close to him now made her insides quiver and shake was a mystery—one she concluded that was best left unsolved.

His words cut into her thoughts, and although she didn't like what she was hearing, she was immensely grateful for what he said. "You're right. It does seem you and I are not the best fit, but you're the one I want for the job. Your manners stink and you've the professionalism of a hillbilly, but no one can argue that you can create miracles with plants and whatnot. And I think I'm going to need a goddamn miracle to move this house. So, the only thing I want to hear from you is whether or not you'll take the job."

Nora balked and sputtered. Nobody talked to her like that. She had half a mind to sweep his ankle and watch him crash to the ground, but she didn't relish the idea of going to jail for battery.

Her teeth ached as she held back the urge to tell him where he could stick the job, but within the short amount of time she'd been with him, an indescribable lunacy had taken hold of her and she struggled to find stable ground within her own mind. *Think of B.J. and Corrinda,* a desperate voice said, and she clung to it and the accompanying ire. She'd given him the opportunity to exonerate himself from the wretched picture he'd created by bailing on his grandparents, but he'd failed that test miserably. His only motivation for coming here was to sell the one thing his grandparents had owned and left to him with love and hope in their hearts.

The thought burned, but what could she do? She really didn't want someone else to take the job, despite what she may tell Ben. Her gaze threatened to roam the courtyard as her imagination plucked new and exciting ideas from her mental cache, but she held firm. She may tremble with anticipation at getting her hands on this property, but she sure as hell wasn't going to admit it.

Round one, you namby-pamby, fancy-dressing, loafer-wearing city boy.

She put her index finger against his chest and gave him a small push to indicate she was back in charge. "I'll take the job, but only if you stay out of my way while I'm doing it."

"I'm your employer. I'll do no such thing. You'll do what I tell you. That's what I'm paying you for."

"You're paying me to fix this house so it will sell. Unless you want to hire someone else, listen to my suggestions."

"God, you're impossible. Has anyone ever told you you're not easy to work with?"

"Nope. All my clients love me."

"I find that hard to believe," he retorted.

"I don't care what you believe. All I care is that your check clears." She turned and deliberately walked away, allowing herself a small victorious smile. He'd learn she wasn't easily bossed, intimidated or impressed. Not even by or with men who were too attractive for their own good. "Meet me here tomorrow. Nineish. We'll discuss details."

He called out to her and she turned but didn't stop walking. "Tomorrow's no good. How about—"

"How about tomorrow?" she interjected, ready to get the hell away from Ben before she did something stupid. She needed to regroup. "Tomorrow's all I got. Take it or leave it."

"You're not the only person in the area I could hire," he snapped, but she simply shrugged as if he could take his chances. She jerked open her truck door and climbed inside. When she looked back at him, he was holding some sort of phone/PDA and moving the stylus in an agitated manner, quickly rescheduling what she assumed were his prior appointments. "Fine, 9:00 a.m. Don't be late," he said, but she was already gunning her engine, loving that the sound drowned out his voice and forced him to yell. "Wait a minute! Do you have a business card or something with a contact phone number?"

"Yep, I sure do." She waved from the truck. "See you tomorrow. Nineish!"

BEN COUGHED as a cloud of dust followed Nora's departure. Ah, hell. He brushed at his fine linen trousers and shirt but still felt the dirt clinging to him. He should've just hired someone else. Someone less difficult. Someone who didn't send odd snaps and sparks arcing through his body when anger caused a dark and dangerous light to flare behind her gray eyes. But someone else wouldn't be the best and that's what he needed. He didn't care what Nora said—he was convinced she was the ticket to selling this house. Her online portfolio was impressive despite the relative obscurity of Emmett's Mill. She had clients all over California. Big, high-profile clients. Her work would move this house faster than some no-name landscape architect who wouldn't argue with him or call him names.

She wasn't the kid he once knew. Except for the name-calling part. That was familiar.

Yeah, he'd lied through his teeth about remembering her but she was far from the kid in his memory. He remembered a honey-haired hoyden with more tangles than curls and a really cute gap-toothed grin that made goofy look cool. She'd been swimming in the creek, her hair had been plastered to her head as if she'd just popped from the water to climb onto the granite slab of rock that descended into the watering hole. When he'd announced his presence, she might've looked guilty for trespassing on private property if it wasn't for the blackberry-juice stain on her lips. If there was ever a picture of a tomboy, she'd fit the bill.

"Who are you?" she'd asked without hesitation, tossing a blackberry into her mouth as if it were a peanut.

"Who are you?" he'd countered, not quite sure what to make of the girl with the wild nest of hair spilling around her bare shoulders. She wore a red string bikini top that covered an area of skin that was as flat as a board and would've taken the imagination of a skilled storyteller to fill and a frayed pair of jean shorts that looked like hand-me-downs from an older sister. His mouth went strangely dry.

"I asked you first."

"I asked you second."

She shrugged and popped the final blackberry in her mouth before hopping to her feet to find more. He had no choice but to follow. She began picking the plump berries, ignoring him completely.

He eyed the tangle of blackberry bushes with fear. "Aren't there snakes?"

She paused and tossed a look over her shoulder. "Probably."

"You're not afraid?"

"My dad says they're more afraid of us than we are of them. As long as I leave them alone, they'll leave me alone. Besides, the only one you gotta worry about is the rattler and they make lots of noise before they bite you."

"What kind of noise?" he asked, straining to listen.

"A *rattling* noise. Duh." She turned and tossed a berry at him. "Here."

"How do you know it's not poisonous?"

The look she gave made him feel as if he was the dumbest person on the planet and he ate it if only to get her to stop looking at him like that. The berry was sweet and juicy and the best thing he'd ever tasted. "I didn't know you could just eat them straight from the bush," he admitted, coming to stand cautiously beside her so he could pick his own.

"Where'd you think they came from?" she asked incredulously.

He shrugged defensively. "I dunno."

"Boy, you're real dumb, you know that?"

"Am not!"

"Anyone who doesn't know where blackberries come from is pretty dumb in my book. You must be a city kid."

The all-knowing tone in her young voice was all the more degrading because she was right.

"Yeah, so?"

"So, only city kids don't know where their own food comes from. My dad says that you shouldn't be able to eat it if you don't know where it's coming from."

That was a horrifying idea. If that were the case, Ben would most likely starve.

"So who are you?" she asked.

"Ben Hollister," he answered without thought, too focused on the humiliating realization he'd been shown up by some girl. He jerked his head toward the large house on the hill above them. "That's my grandparents' house."

Tinkling laughter followed. "Now I know you're not only dumb but a liar, too. The Hollisters ain't got a grandson."

"Do, too!"

"Do not. I've never seen you before. If you're their grandson, where you been all this time?"

"New England." He lifted his chin, answering with as much disdain as he'd grown up hearing in his father's voice. "You probably don't even know where that's at."

"Wherever it's at, apparently there ain't any blackberry bushes!"

With that, she jumped down from the brambles and skipped toward a bike lying on its side at the water's edge. He scrambled after her.

"Wait! What's your name?" he called after her, intrigued as any twelve-year-old who was alone in a strange town and desperate to make friends—even sass-mouthed girls who made his stomach feel weird—would be. She giggled and pedaled away. "Tell me your name!"

Her answer floated on the wind. "Nora!"

BEN DECIDED to get a hotel room rather than drive all the way back to the Bay Area where he owned a small apartment. Seeing as Nora had effectively made him rearrange his schedule, he didn't see the point in making the three-hour drive when he was just going to turn right around in a few hours' time.

Nora was blind if she thought Emmett's Mill wasn't in a time warp. Driving through the sleepy town, he'd wondered how the place had managed to defy the touch of time. Everything was as he remembered as a kid, with the exception of the old Frosty. The ice-cream shop was gone and in its place was a razed spot with a sign that proclaimed the new offices of Grafton Realty were soon to come. His grandmother had taken him to the Frosty for vanilla soft-serve ice cream that summer he'd come to visit. His mouth twisted wryly. Visit—that's what his parents had called it. Ben had known, even at twelve, what it really was—an opportunity for Ben to get out of his parents' hair while they finalized their acrimonious divorce. As an adult he realized it had been a blessing; being at home while they tore each other to bits over every little detail would've been hell, but as a kid he'd just felt discarded.

Sighing, he moved away from his hotel window and went to the bed. An odd phantom sadness drifted over him when he thought of his grandparents. Aside from that one summer, he hadn't really known them. They sent cards on his birthday, but he had never been allowed to call. Their relationship with his father had soured for reasons unknown to him and he'd only been able to visit once. After he moved out and went to college, Ben managed to call a couple of times during odd moments of nostalgia but he hadn't really known what to say to them. They were nice but virtual strangers.

When he'd heard that they'd left the house to him instead of his father, he'd been stunned and his father had been pissed. His father's anger made no sense to him, but he'd long since stopped trying to decipher the man's mercurial moods. In fact, they rarely spoke. That was the advantage to living in separate states. His mother—Ben suppressed a weary groan—was another matter. Fortunately, for the moment she was too busy with the new love of her life to bother too much with Ben. He only hoped this one lasted. Penny Hollister-Ulacher-McDonald-Schlitz had a tendency to fall for the worst of men—his father included.

Without conscious thought, his mind drifted to Nora. He should've said something, revealed that he remembered her, but she'd taken him by surprise and he hadn't been prepared. Plus, the storm shooting from her gray eyes was alternately arousing and disconcerting. Her body had changed but her temperament certainly hadn't. He figured if she wasn't going to say anything, neither would he. It was probably easier this way, pretending neither knew the other. Kept the awkwardness—and the memories—at bay.

The last part wasn't quite true, but Ben had grown adept at ignoring even the most insistent inner voice. As a family law attorney for one of the most exclusive firms in the Bay Area, such talent was a requirement.

His BlackBerry chirped and he picked it up. His contemplative mood evaporated as he read a text message from the firm secretary, Celina, flashing on the small screen. He wasted no time in opening it, though his guts were roiling as he suspected what it would say.

Franklin says no go. You're on the Wallace case. Sorry.

Shit. Wallace versus Wallace. Classic case of love gone wrong with one kid as collateral damage. He tossed his BlackBerry to the bed and tried not to dwell, but this was one case he didn't want anything to do with. Ed Wallace was a despicable son of a bitch with loads of cash—and he wasn't willing to give one red cent of it to his wife despite her giving up her career to put him through college. Now she was in the same position many women found themselves in once their breadwinner husbands decided to trade them in for younger models. One with bigger, perkier boobs and a willingness to take a lot of crap for the perks that came with a loaded husband or boyfriend. And Franklin, the senior partner of Franklin, Mills & Donovan, wanted Ben on the case for reasons he was beginning to realize weren't something he'd want to announce at business meetings. *Ben Hollister, ruthless bastard. Nice to meet you.*

Ben shoved his hand through his hair. He couldn't stand to stay at Franklin, Mills & Donovan. He didn't want to enable one more scumbag to cheat his spouse out of her fair share just because he had more money than she did. Ben was beginning to feel soulless after each victory, as if he was destroying his humanity with each sweaty palm he shook in congratulations. But until he collected enough capital to open his own firm, he was stuck. Franklin, Mills & Donovan was the top of the food chain. When he made his move, it wouldn't be a step backward with a smaller or lesser firm; that's why he needed to open his own. His gaze drifted to the car parked outside his window. If it was his, he'd sell it in a heartbeat. Unfortunately it was simply on loan from his father, Dale. He allowed Ben to drive it when he was on the East Coast, which was where his father was most of the time, but the three or four times a year that he visited the West Coast, he liked to drive in style.

And although his mother was wealthy at the moment, thanks to Husband No. 4, Ben would rather crawl through raw sewage than ask her for money. Besides, even if he managed to swallow his pride and ask, there was no guarantee she'd give it. Her money was usually tied to the husband du jour, and the amount he'd need wouldn't go unnoticed. He sighed, scrubbing his hands across his face. His future, or more specifically, his sanity rested on selling his grandparents' house.

CHAPTER TWO

"THESE AZALEAS are going to look lovely, Mrs. Pruitt," Nora exclaimed, leaning back to admire her own work as the elderly woman watched from her gardening chair while Nora did the actual planting. "I think the color really dresses up the yard, don't you think?"

"Oh, yes," Mrs. Pruitt breathed, a happy smile wreathing her aged face. Nora caught her expression falter ever so slightly as she added, "I just wish I was the one doing all the work. I do so miss my gardening. But you do a fantastic job for me."

"Well, thank you, Mrs. Pruitt. I take that as a high compliment coming from you. Now." She got up and dusted her knees, though the effort only removed some of the dirt ground into her worn jeans. "Let's take a look at that sprinkler system I set up for you. I've made it so easy, you don't even have to remember to turn it on. See this? This is a timer that will do all the work for you."

"Bless your heart." Mrs. Pruitt's face wrinkled in a grin as they headed toward the house, her gait slow due to the walker. "You think of everything, don't you?"

"Well, not everything," she answered. Truthfully she should've installed the sprinkler the first time so the last batch of azaleas hadn't died. Mrs. Pruitt hadn't been able to get around as easily and the bright, colorful blooms had been one of the casualties. As if sensing her thoughts, Mrs. Pruitt's expression saddened.

"They were so beautiful. It plumb made me sick when I couldn't get to them. This old body just isn't the same anymore."

"Don't worry about it," Nora assured her, gesturing to the new plants. "Besides, I think that stock was weak. These ones are much hardier. I bought them from a new nursery."

She'd done no such thing, but the small fib was worth the relieved look Mrs. Pruitt gave her. "Well, if you say so, then I believe you," the elderly lady said, moving to the front door. "Are you coming in for some iced tea today?" she asked hopefully.

"Not today," she answered regretfully, noting the time. Nine o'clock—she was officially late. "I have another client. But I'll take a rain check, if that's all right with you."

Mrs. Pruitt nodded. "Of course, dear. I'll see you at the senior center, won't I?"

Nora made a show of looking scandalized. "Me? Miss Bingo? Surely you jest? Of course I'll be there. I'm determined to win that microwave or die shouting *Bingo* while trying."

Mrs. Pruitt tittered. "All right then, see you Wednesday."

Nora waited until Mrs. Pruitt disappeared into the house before clearing her garden space and packing away her tools. A quick glance at her clothes made her wonder if she should run home to change but on the heels of that thought she questioned why. It wasn't as if she were going out on a date. She was meeting a client—a coldhearted snake of a client with a deplorable memory but a client nonetheless. And since, basically, she worked with dirt in her chosen trade, it served to reason that she might have a bit of it on her clothes. And in her hair. How'd that get there? She shook her short hair free of the odd assortment of soil clumps that had somehow managed to station themselves there. She probably looked like Pigpen.

Good.

She hoped his aristocratic mouth pinched at the sight of her soiled and rumpled condition. It would probably go a long way toward quelling the ridiculous quiver that kept shivering her insides every time she thought of Ben Hollister.

She hauled her garden box into the back of her beat-up truck and headed out to the Hollister house. It was probably too much to ask for the man to have a paunchy belly and a balding pate, but it didn't stop her imagination from bloating the memory of a twelve-year-old Ben in a three-piece suit, trying to comb over the last remaining strands of his black hair. He was destined to lose his hair, she reasoned. B. J. Hollister had been as bald as Jean-Luc Picard, but he'd carried it nearly as well. She doubted Ben had the same poise—his character was much too weak.

Sliding from her seat, she paused long enough to lean over and grab her client notebook and then strode toward the house. She hadn't had time yesterday to truly note the house's flagging spirit, but now that she was in job mode it was hard not to see how quickly the old house had succumbed to the weather and vandals. The broken entry gate hung limply on its hinges by a single screw and looked as if a stiff wind would take it down. She had little time to bemoan the home's sad, victimized state as Ben suddenly appeared in the doorway and commanded her attention with his completely unbald and disgustingly fit state.

"You're late." His flat statement brooked no argument so she didn't try. Besides, there was no point in arguing fact—she was seven minutes late. His gaze swept her mussed appearance but he didn't comment. Disappointment washed over her as she realized she wanted him to disapprove. *Nora, you're gunning for a fight,* she chastised herself with a rueful grin. It wasn't like her to act childish but something about Ben brought out the worst in her. That didn't bode well for their working relationship.

"My other client ran long." She wanted to add that she was *only* seven minutes late, but judging by his stiff appearance, seven minutes might as well be an hour in his book. She mentally shrugged. Who cares? It wasn't as if they were dating. "Shall we begin?" she asked, pleased to hear her own voice resembling the professional she usually was under normal circumstances, even if she hadn't quite managed it thus far.

"Ah, right. So, as I told you yesterday, the place is a little run-down," he said, moving into the yard, kicking at the dead crabgrass with a disgusted motion that immediately set her blood percolating. Perhaps if he'd made more of an effort to see how his grandparents had been faring, the house might've been less derelict looking. "I talked with my Realtor yesterday after we spoke and she assured me a nice landscaping overhaul is sure to sweeten the offers, which at this point are non-existent."

She ignored him and bent down to pull a dandelion from the ground, tossing it out of the yard and into the dirt driveway. The price was too high for the blue-collar residents of Emmett's Mill. Before B.J. and Corrinda bought the place, it had sat empty for close to ten years. And, although it was certainly a beautiful old home, it came with typical old-home problems. In other words, it was simply—as Ben called it—a money pit. But—she slid her gaze over to the sleek sports car and back to Ben—he looked as if he could afford what Nora wanted to do to this place. Honestly, she would've done it free of charge before the Hollisters died, but the old couple was proud and had waved away her offer every time. Now she could do something nice for them, even if it was under the guise of doing a job for their grandson.

She glanced up in time to see him tug at a lone, straggly rose, the petals floating to the ground to scatter in the slight breeze. "These'll be the first to go," he announced, and Nora looked at him sharply. He shrugged. "I hate roses."

"Why?"

"They're clichéd."

She blinked at his dismissive tone. "How is a flower clichéd?"

"It's not so much the flower but rather what they're used for."

"Enlighten me."

He crooked a cool grin, completely missing the sarcasm in her tone, and said, "Roses take little to no imagination on the part of the person sending them. What's the go-to flower for the new boyfriend? Long-stemmed roses. What's the first flower of choice for a husband who has cheated on his wife and is seeking to get back in her good graces? What's the flower of choice for heartbroken schmucks writing terrible poetry in the name of their loved ones? Roses. Red roses to be specific. And I'm not interested in seeing a bunch of rosebushes everywhere."

"Roses evoke a sense of culture and beauty that would complement this house," she said.

Something flitted across his face that almost qualified as pain, but it was gone before she had a chance to find out more, and in the next moment, he fixed her with a hard stare as he declared, "No roses."

Obviously he'd never seen a hybrid tea rose, such as the Gemini or the Condessa de Sastago, otherwise he would never make such an ignorant statement. She returned to her notes and bit her tongue in an attempt to keep her mouth from running away from her, but she was never good at keeping her mouth shut even when it was paramount.

"So if roses are so passé and clichéd, as you put it, what flowers would you send to your…girlfriend or significant other?"

"I don't send flowers."

"At all?"

"No."

"I bet the women cross crowded traffic to get to you," she snorted, suddenly feeling sorry for the women in his past who'd been suckered by his beautiful face only to find a heart of stone. "You sound like a *great* boyfriend. And when I say great, I mean crappy, in case you were confused."

Although she certainly hadn't meant the retort to be amusing, he reacted with a low and throaty chuckle that bordered on smug and made her want to smack him over the head with her clipboard.

"Haven't had any complaints yet," he said, sealing the coffin on her low opinion of him despite his looking like a Greek god masquerading as an Ivy-League-educated businessman. The man could benefit from being taken down a peg or two.

She graced him with a tight, completely saccharine smile. "That you know of. For all you know, your past lovers could be meeting once a month to compare your deficiencies—of which I'm sure there are many—over raspberry margaritas and tortilla chips." Her smile brightened at the thought. "You never know."

The superiority left his eyes, but his voice retained its infuriating confidence. "I doubt it but it's an entertaining thought."

Didn't the man recognize when he'd been slammed? She'd practically shot an arrow straight through an area most men were incredibly sensitive about, but he'd taken the hit as easily as if it had glanced off his shoulder. She'd have to try harder.

Back to business. "You know, Corrinda loved her roses," she said, unable to keep her thoughts on the subject completely professional. "She didn't seem to think they were clichéd at all. In fact, before her arthritis got really bad, her roses were some of the best. Everyone said so," she added for additional weight, though she wasn't sure why.

"Really?" His expression was contemplative as he reluctantly said, "I suppose it doesn't matter. It's not like I'll have to look at them every day. So you're saying the house will have a better chance at selling if we keep the rosebushes?"

Silently counting to ten, Nora continued, "I have no idea whether or not it would help the house sell. I just thought that you might want to keep them in deference to your *dead* grandmother." He gave her a blank look and she nearly bit her tongue in half.

Insensitive lout. Scratching out *American Beauty* from her notes, she gave him a terse, "Never mind" and moved on. "So, are there any other verboten flowers on your list?"

"Why does there need to be flowers at all?"

Oh, c'mon! "Because they're bright and pretty and always look nice when well tended." The man was a clod and had no sense of what makes a house a home.

"Your answer illustrates my point."

"Which is?"

"Who's going to tend them? My plans do not include moving here to ensure the flowers stay pretty and bright, as you say. Likely, if the house doesn't sell right away they'll end up looking exactly as they do now."

"That's what automatic sprinkler systems are for," she countered, dismissing his comment. "Now—"

"Automatic anything sounds expensive. I was thinking of a rock or gravel garden with some cactus."

She made a face. "That sounds awful."

"Awful? Why?"

"Because it's a travesty to surround this gorgeous house with gravel and cacti. Besides, it would completely clash with the surroundings."

"But it would eliminate the need for constant care. I could hire a person to come out and weed now and then and it wouldn't run up a water bill."

Cheapskate. "Do you want the house to sell or not?"

His gaze narrowed. "That's a dumb question."

"Then let me do my job."

"I don't like your tone."

"What a coincidence. I don't like your attitude," she said, and they both stared at each other in hard-edged annoyance. Nora tucked her clipboard under her arm. "Listen, if you trust me, I'll do my best to make this house shine. I promise."

He looked ready to disagree or argue but didn't. Instead, he nodded grudgingly. Feeling she'd won the first of many battles, Nora kept her chortling to herself and focused on the next issue—money.

"I should tell you I require a ten-thousand-dollar deposit on jobs this extensive."

His eyes widened at the sum. "That seems a little high."

"That will cover any expenses and ensures that I get paid whether or not you change your mind."

"I'm not going to change my mind," he assured her.

Nora shrugged. "Doesn't matter. One bad experience has a way of making you gun shy. Ten-thousand—take it or leave it."

"Fine, but any other expenses that exceed that amount must be cleared by me before you proceed."

"Fair enough," she agreed. "Will that be personal check or credit card?"

"You'll take a check?"

She smiled. "As long as it's good."

"My checks are always good," he muttered as he reached into his back pocket and pulled out a slim checkbook. *It must be nice to be able to write a check for that kind of money*, Nora thought abstractedly. She did well on her own but she wasn't a millionaire. Ben had the look of privilege and wealth, but B.J. and Corrinda had been practically broke when they died. In essence, the only thing of value had been the house, and even if the market had been favorable, they wouldn't have sold.

He handed her an executive draft and after she folded it in half, she stuck the check in her back pocket. "When will you start the work?" he asked.

"Soon. I'm going to take some soil samples, test the pH balance to see what I'm working with and then draw up some plans. When are you coming back into town so we can talk about the overall design?"

"Why don't you just fax them to my office—"

"No can do. No fax line. Besides, I prefer to do the walk-through in person." As much as she'd like to see less of Ben Hollister, she made a point never to start a job before explaining what she hoped to do with the property with the client. And she really didn't own a fax machine. She could probably find one but she wasn't interested in expending that kind of effort for him.

"Ms. Simmons, I'm sure you can appreciate how difficult it was for me to come up here. I'm an attorney with a full caseload. I can't just pop up here whenever you snap your fingers."

Laughter tickled her insides at the idea of Ben popping anywhere but she prickled at the implication that his time was more valuable than hers. "Why do you want to open your own firm if you're already so busy?" she asked, noting quickly how his demeanor changed at the innocent question. Sore spot. Good to know. "What kind of law do you practice? Corporate? Personal injury? Or something completely dry and boring like contract law?"

His mouth tightened and he all but gritted his teeth when he answered. "Family law. Divorces, mainly."

How perfect. Nora imagined Ben was a shark in court. She could sense a ruthlessness in him that made goose bumps riot across her exposed skin in what should've been a warning sign, but Nora never ran from a challenge.

"Family law? So you went into the family business, huh?"

Ben stiffened and his eyes became wary and she wondered if the attitude came with the law degree or if it was something he came by naturally.

"Normally I don't like lawyers, but B.J. managed to bend my opinion a little. He always had lollipops for the little kids who came into his office and a joke up his sleeve." She slid her gaze to Ben. "Are you sure you're related?"

It came out as a joke, but a part of her wasn't kidding. It didn't seem natural that Ben, a man who would be the last person to offer a kid a sucker for fear of a choking liability, would share genes with someone as gentle and funny as B. J. Hollister.

Ben ignored her question. "I'll see what I can do with my schedule. I might be able to squeeze out one day next week."

"Great."

"Anything else?"

Tell me why you never came back. "Nope. That's it."

"Good. I'll leave you to come back to me with a plan and we'll go from there. Remember, we agreed no roses."

We didn't agree. I got frustrated and dropped the subject, she wanted to yell but didn't.

She tapped her head. "It's all up here. Don't worry, I won't steer you wrong."

"I know."

For a split second she thought she saw truth reflected through his gaze, as if he trusted her despite her sharp tongue and blatant attempts to goad him, and the fleeting glimpse left her off-kilter.

"All right then," she said, moving slowly toward the front gate, a bit concerned by her sudden desire to stick around. They weren't friends. They weren't anything but client and employee. "I'll be in touch." She started for the gate then doubled back, realizing she ought to give him a business card this time.

"Thank you." He accepted the card and their fingers brushed. The contact was minute, but it was enough to send an electric zap down the length of her arm and end with little pops and gasps at the pit of her stomach. She yanked her hand back and the corner of his mouth lifted in subtle acknowledgment. She eyed him suspiciously. Had he felt it, too?

But he offered nothing, saying, "I look forward to hearing your ideas," before ascending the front steps and disappearing into the house.

Nora's mouth dried conspicuously and she stared down at her offending fingers, all too aware of the physical reaction to Ben's brief touch. Grimacing, she wiped her hand on the back of her jeans and stalked to her truck. She'd never been the type to act all fluttery and girlie over a guy. Wasn't her style. She would much rather hang out with the guys than the girls any day.

She was a tomboy in a woman's body. Nora glowered at the house, more specifically at Ben inside, and jerked the truck into gear. Not gonna happen.

CHAPTER THREE

BEN LET THE DOOR close behind him and listened as Nora's truck rumbled down the weed-choked driveway to the highway until the sound faded to nothing.

The card in his hand still felt warm, as if it had sat in the sun all day, and he could almost imagine the heat was from Nora herself.

There was something about her that drew him without conscious thought. Something unguarded and free. The same quality she'd exuded as a kid. Life might've leached it out of someone else but not Nora. He wondered how some people managed to hold on to that quality yet others lost it. Stepping from the foyer into the expansive hallway that dissected the house into separate rooms, he drew a deep breath and pushed Nora out of his mind.

The house was utterly still; the walls were covered with antique clocks, mostly of the cuckoo variety, but without someone to reset their chains, they hung silent. Ben remembered the constant ticktock—and cuckoos—from his summer visit years ago, and how he had found the noise distracting the first night. But by the end of the week, the odd cacophony was soothing and he'd slept like a baby.

In the absence of such sounds, the silence was un-natural.

He wandered to the nearest Black Forest clock, enticed by old memories, and gently pulled the pine weights, the mechanism inside moving smoothly despite its age, and then he pushed the tiny hands into their proper place. Finally, he gave the small pendulum bob a light tap to set it swinging.

The soft, distinct ticking replaced the disquieting stillness and he inhaled against the tight feeling in his chest. He hadn't known the man long, but he remembered how much his grandfather had loved these clocks. A slow turn around the room revealed countless in pristine shape. Every available wall was crammed with them. Ben leaned in to take a better look at the clock he'd just reset and even though he wasn't an expert, he could guess they were worth something to the right person.

And the house was filled with them.

He could sell the clocks at auction. As quickly as the thought came, he discarded it. He didn't know what to do with them, but the thought of selling them left him cold. But Ben couldn't very well tote around hundreds of clocks. It wasn't practical. Selling most of them was probably what he'd end up doing.

Moving through the first floor, he took careful note of the worn spots in the faded sofa set where sunlight had bleached the once-vibrant fabric and shone through moth-eaten areas in the drapes over the cobwebbed bay window. The wood floor was dull and scratched in many places and would need a complete overhaul if he wanted to use it as a selling point.

A shadow of regret settled on his thoughts as he looked around the house. After that one summer, his father had refused to allow him to return, and as the years went by, the desire to visit faded. Now, standing in his grandparents' home, surrounded by their possessions, he realized he should've made more of an effort. He could've helped out monetarily if nothing else. Judging by the house's appearance, it seemed they'd had little to spare. That in itself puzzled him more than he wanted to admit. His grandfather had been an attorney here—surely there were enough clients, even in a town as small as Emmett's Mill, to support one little old couple? Without saying it aloud, he resolved to ask around if he found time.

He grimaced. The repairs were bound to be expensive. He'd have to tap his trust, though it wasn't something he wanted to do. He didn't have millions, just a little over one hundred grand. He'd have to be careful—home repairs, especially on places this old, could get ridiculous.

Ben made a cursory tour of the rest of the house and found it in similar condition.

Moving to the large window that looked out behind the house and down the hill, he saw the winding creek below, the water shimmering in the light, catching the sun rays and tossing them back in a glorious dance of sunshine and sky.

He glanced down at his shoes. Brown dress loafers stared back at him. Not the least bit appropriate for going hiking. There used to be a path from the house to Nora's favorite swimming hole, the one where he'd first found her that summer. He wondered if anyone went there anymore. The path was probably overgrown by now.

Dismissing the idea before it had the chance to germinate, he walked away from the window.

He didn't have time to wind clocks or think about traipsing around the creek where he'd no doubt trudge right through poison oak because, as Nora so aptly put at the tender age of ten, he was no country boy. A sound of annoyance escaped him as he left the house and he quickly locked up. He had to get back to the city. Back to his life.

"YOU'RE UNUSUALLY QUIET tonight," Natalie observed later that night while at their father's for dinner. Since their mom died last year of pancreatic cancer, Natalie made it her job to ensure their dad was okay, as if the man were going to slowly die of starvation. Nora looked up from her plate and realized she'd been staring at her carrots, her thoughts stuck in a direction they shouldn't be. Natalie's comment drew Tasha's attention and now both her older sisters were staring at her, their husbands joining them seconds later. "Is everything okay?"

She squirmed under everyone's gaze. "Everything's fine," Nora told Natalie, but it wasn't entirely true. She was replaying her earlier meeting with Ben in her head, looking for some clue that he hadn't really forgotten her. Of course, she had the misfortune to remember every single nuance of their acquaintance because it wasn't every day a girl got her first kiss. She could admit it, her ego was bruised. She'd just come to the conclusion that Ben had to have remembered her, when Natalie drew her attention again.

"Janelle came into the bookstore a few weeks ago and mentioned that the Hollister house is on the market and has been for the past four months," Natalie said, making conversation. "I think she was dropping a hint that Evan and I ought to look into buying it but I told her we were happy with our little place. I wonder who will buy it."

Gerald Simmons appeared mildly interested at the subject change. "Don't imagine it's going to sell anytime soon."

Nora agreed with her dad.

Natalie placed her wiggling one-year-old son, Justin Cole, into her husband's arms so she could help their three-year-old, Colton Jeremiah, with his hamburger. "It's a beautiful house, but I don't know who could afford it. I didn't tell Janelle that, though. I didn't want to seem pessimistic."

"Before the Hollisters bought it, it sat empty for years. There was talk of donating it to the historical society, but no one had the money to relocate it into town, so the owners just let it sit. Damn shame," Gerald said, excusing himself from the table. Natalie rose to see if he needed anything but he waved her away.

"Will you stop mothering him, for crying out loud?" Nora muttered in annoyance. "He's fine. You're driving him crazy."

"I am not," Natalie retorted indignantly. "He's still not recovered from Mom's death. I worry about him."

Tasha intervened, motioning to Nora. "Down, girl. I think Natalie's right, though. Something's got you all preoccupied. Care to share?"

Nora thought about it, then answered, "No, not really."

"Oh, I see how it is. You get to pry into our business, but when it comes to yours, it's off-limits?" Tasha teased.

"You're a smart woman," Nora said, sparing a glance at her sister.

Natalie's husband, Evan, and Tasha's husband, Josh, took that as a cue to leave the women to their discussion and Nora was half tempted to follow their lead. She didn't feel ready to discuss Ben. *Why not?* a voice demanded, her inner psyche realizing Nora was squirming. It wasn't as if he meant anything to her. So they'd kissed years ago. Big deal. If Nora lined up all the men she'd kissed in her lifetime, they'd probably reach from here to Coldwater. Well, that was exaggerating, but there were a few. And none of them made her think twice or dwell on it.

Natalie recovered from Nora's earlier remark to ask, "Didn't you know the Hollisters?"

"Yes. They were the cutest couple. Totally in love even after fifty-some odd years of marriage. I met them at the senior center at a bingo night." She glanced at her sister. "Why?"

"The name rang a bell. I seem to remember one

summer when a certain boy…Ben, I believe his name was…"

Natalie was baiting her and it was working. Nora looked away. Tasha leaned in, interest etched on her face, while Natalie continued with a playful gleam in her eye.

"When Nora was little…she used to go swimming in the creek behind that big house, even though she wasn't supposed to ride her bike that far down the road."

"Such a rebel," Tasha said, clucking her tongue like an old lady.

Nora snorted. "I wasn't the one to run off and join the Peace Corps. I believe that was you. We've got the postcards to prove it."

"Touché," Tasha said, but her green eyes danced with mirth at how Nora was obviously trying to deflect the conversation.

Natalie continued, enjoying herself. "And, I remember a certain someone coming home one day looking like she'd just gotten her first taste of chocolate cheesecake with an extra dollop of fresh whipped cream."

"Are you pregnant again?" Nora asked. "Last time you started to use food analogies you were knocked up."

"I'm not pregnant," Natalie assured her, sending a conspiratorial look Tasha's way. "The question is, did you kiss the Hollisters' grandson, little sister?"

Tasha broke out in a peal of laughter when Nora's cheeks reddened in answer, and Natalie nearly jumped out of her chair in victory. "I knew it! I always wondered but never asked. How old were you? Nine? Ten?"

"Ten," Nora grumbled, wishing she'd left the room when she'd had the chance. She speared Tasha with a dirty look. "It's all your fault, you know."

Tasha sobered with difficulty. "How is it my fault?" she choked out.

"If I hadn't seen you kissing Josh all the time I wouldn't have been so curious. I wanted to know what all the fuss was about."

Tasha and Josh had been high-school sweethearts, and like most teenagers, whenever they thought they were alone, they couldn't keep their hands off each other.

"You were watching? You little perv," Tasha said, grinning.

"Well, what do you expect? It was kind of hard to miss. You guys kept stealing all my good hiding places."

Tasha's eyes turned misty as she reminisced, then as her husband walked by, the look turned primal.

"Ugh, it's my childhood all over again. Get a room." Nora grabbed her plate and walked to the adjoining kitchen.

Sisters, she grumbled to the sink as she rinsed her plate, were a pain in the ass because they saw way too much when you didn't want to share. But, even as she shied away from sharing her recent experience with Ben, a part of her needed their perspective. Sighing, she returned to the dining room.

"Here's the deal," Nora said, ignoring their knowing expressions. "The Hollisters left the house to their grandson, Ben, who has now hired me to overhaul the outside landscaping so that he can sell it."

"Why does he want to sell?" Natalie asked.

"He wants to open his own law practice in the Bay Area. Noble cause, I know. Personally, I think it's pretty cold but it doesn't matter. I think he'll have trouble selling it."

"Why?" Tasha returned, puzzled. "After you're finished with the place, it'll look like a *Better Homes and Gardens* special."

"It's too expensive," both Nora and Natalie said in unison.

"Like Dad said, that house sat for years before the Hollisters bought it," Nora added. "It's too much house for the older, retired set who might be able to afford it and way too expensive for the young families who might actually put it to good use. Plus, it's on the outskirts of town and when it snows, the driveway virtually disappears. Since it's private property it doesn't get plowed by the county."

"Did you tell Ben this?" Tasha asked.

She turned to Tasha. "No. And I don't plan to."

"Why not?" Tasha's expression turned speculative. "Seems like pertinent information for your client."

Nora lifted her chin. "I don't care. He doesn't deserve to know."

Natalie looked puzzled, then concerned. "I don't understand. Why doesn't he deserve to know?"

"Do you realize he only visited his grandparents once in his lifetime? What kind of person is that? Frankly, I don't want to reward that kind of behavior."

"You're not his mother, you're his employee. I think you're making a mistake," Natalie said.

"Maybe I'll buy it," Nora said, although the idea had only just popped into her head. "I've always liked the house and I'll take care of it far better than Ben."

"Can you afford it?" Tasha asked tentatively and Nora shifted in her chair under her scrutiny.

"Umm…well, not yet but maybe by the time I finish the job." And a few others, she thought with a private wince.

"Nora…" Natalie's tone had a warning to it that Nora hated. She always had a way of making Nora feel like the baby even though she was thirty-two. "What are you doing? I've never seen you act like this… Well, I take that back, there was one other time…"

Nora stiffened, knowing exactly what time Natalie was referring to and she shot her a dark look. "It's nothing like that."

"Like what?" Tasha asked. "I hate being out of the loop. What happened before?"

"Thanks a lot, Nat. You know, you don't like everyone to know you got pregnant from a one-night stand with your river guide, maybe I don't like everyone to know I slept with a client who turned out to be married."

"I married my river guide, thank you very much," Natalie retorted. "And don't get on your high horse. When it comes to secrets it isn't like you're the locked box. You can't wait to butt your nose into everyone's business." She turned to Tasha. "Why do you think she hangs out with all those seniors? They love to gossip as much as she does."

"I hang out with them because they're good people and they're far more interesting than everyone else. You included these days."

"Little sister, you've got juicy secrets," Tasha teased, plainly happy to be included even if Nora's mood was bordering dangerously on annoyed. "A married man. Details, please."

"No." Nora got up and walked back into the kitchen to grab a beer from the fridge, but it was empty. She leaned out and hollered to Natalie because she was in charge of the groceries for Dad. "Where's the Bud Light?"

"Dad doesn't need that stuff. I stopped buying it," Natalie hollered back.

She ground her teeth and made a note to buy some for Dad tomorrow. The man lost his wife, the least Natalie could do is let him have his beer.

She returned to see Tasha and Natalie in a hushed conversation that they immediately stopped the moment she reentered the room. Nora wasn't stupid; they were talking about Griffin. A girl couldn't make a mistake without having it broadcasted in this family. She glared at Natalie. "He didn't tell me he was married and he never wore a ring. How was I supposed to know?"

Griffin was a subject she hated to visit. It served to remind her why she didn't let people get under her skin. She'd fallen hard and he'd let her fall face-first in a big pile of humiliation. The scene with the wife had been particularly mortifying.

Tasha sensed Nora withdraw and changed the subject, or rather returned to their original discussion—not that Nora was relieved. She didn't want to talk about that, either. Frankly, she was ready to go home. In her present frame of mind, it'd been a mistake to come tonight, but Natalie was adamant they come to these dinners for Dad. Nora liked to say she went so Natalie would stop hounding but she enjoyed seeing her nephews. They were the cutest little suckers and Nora couldn't get enough of them.

"So tell me again why you can't stand this guy?"

Nora considered her answer, looking for the most succinct way to convey her feelings when they were in a tumbled mess inside her head. "The Hollisters were good people and they adored him. Always talked about how much they hoped he'd come to visit when he was older. They were so proud of him for going to Harvard Law and becoming an attorney. But he couldn't come to visit a handful of times to make his grandparents feel loved instead of forgotten?" she said, making what she thought was a serious point in her favor until Natalie fixed her with a "big sister" look that she'd perfected while Tasha was away at college and then the Peace Corps. Nora sighed. Sometimes she didn't even know why she opened her mouth.

"Do you want my opinion?" Natalie asked.

"No."

"Too bad. I think you should find someone else to do the job. It's obvious you're not acting in the best interests of your client."

Nora glowered at Natalie. Why did she have to be

such a Dudley Do-Right? Would it kill her to just go with the moment?

"There's no rule that says I have to like someone I work for. I'll do the job, collect the cash and be gone."

"If it's that simple, why are you acting like something's bit you in the ass tonight?" Natalie asked. "I think it bothers you that you have feelings of some sort for this guy and you're doing everything you can to fight them."

"That's ridiculous," Nora said, but her cheeks flared. "This isn't the fourth grade, Natalie. Besides, if you met the guy you'd agree with me that he's an arrogant jerk." With an amazing set of eyes and a physique that could make a nun sit up and take notice. "A class-A jerk with an Ivy-League pedigree. *So* not my type."

Natalie offered a smug smile and Nora wanted to groan, but Tasha distracted her.

"Nat is right. I think you should pull out. There's no way you can be objective here and whether you realize it or not, you're sabotaging your client with your animosity. You need to think rationally, not emotionally in this situation. This involves your career. Besides, you're better than that."

"Who says?"

"We do," her sisters answered in unison.

"Oh, kiss my butt," Nora grumbled, but she was wavering. If the job were for anyone else, she wouldn't care. But it was Ben. The truth of the matter was, she'd harbored a secret crush for years after that one kiss. She'd spent each summer hoping he'd come back but he hadn't. After each disappointment, her crush had turned to resentment. It was irrational, which was why she'd never shared her feelings with her sisters, but it didn't change the way she felt.

"B.J. and Corrinda were good people. They deserve better than what their grandson gave them," she said stubbornly, ignoring her sisters' advice. "I'm doing this for them."

"Well, that might be true, but just be careful about judging others when you don't know their circumstances," Tasha said. "It could change your perspective. What did Ben say when he realized it was you?"

Her cheeks heated. "Nothing. He didn't remember."

Natalie's eyes widened but there was laughter in them. "He didn't remember you? That's hard to believe. Your personality is…well, either people like you or hate you. There's no gray area."

Nora agreed but didn't feel the need to say so. She shrugged. "He didn't say anything so I didn't, either. No point in rubbing it in my face that I'm nothing in his memory." *When for years I used to replay that one brief moment over and over in my mind, making it bigger and more wonderful in my head with each passing day.* What an idiot. "Besides, it's better this way. It's not like either one of us is hoping for a reunion tour. I can't stand him and I think the feeling is mutual."

"So why'd he hire you?" Natalie asked.

"Because I'm the best."

Natalie sighed. "At least he's not dumb."

Tasha's speculative look had Nora staring at her in suspicion. "What?"

"What if he does remember you and just isn't saying anything?" Tasha wondered aloud.

"You know, for a second I wondered that, too. I thought it seemed a little weird, but if on the off chance he was being genuine, I wasn't about to embarrass myself," Nora said.

Tasha laughed. "Maybe he thought saying something might make things awkward between you. He probably didn't want there to be any kind of barrier between you as employer and client. Makes sense to me, especially if neither of you is interested in reliving the past."

"Whatever." Nora tapped her fingers against the tabletop in a rapid, agitated movement. Damn. Tasha's theory made sense to her, too, but that made it worse. If he really remembered her, he should've said something. Somehow his omission seemed fraudulent. "I'll tell him tomorrow," she said glumly, hating that her sisters had talked her out of avenging her childish disappointment. She must be getting old.

BEN KEPT HIS PEN still while Ed Wallace, as pompous as he was self-centered, rejected the latest offer presented by his soon-to-be ex-wife's camp.

"Forget it. If I agree to that I'll be paying her for the rest of my life, plus I'll have to sell my new yacht to meet the settlement."

Ben drew a measured breath while his patience for the man fluctuated between barely there and nonexistent. "It's not a bad offer. Probably better than you'll get if we go to court. You're paying me for my counsel. Take the deal."

"I'm paying you to get me out of giving my ex-wife everything I've worked for for the past twenty years to achieve," Ed growled. "Or have you forgotten that?"

Ben met the man's hard stare with one of his own. Ginny Wallace was being much more lenient than she could afford to be in Ben's opinion, but Ed couldn't see past his own greed to take the offer before she came to her senses. "You're worth ten million today. Twenty years ago, when you were a busboy at some small restaurant in Oakland and met a young waitress named Ginny, you were worth zip. You probably had twenty dollars in your pocket on payday. She quit college so you could get your business degree and later your master's. If we go to court, you'll lose. And that yacht will be the first thing to go."

"She's no saint," Ed retorted, his gaze darting away from Ben.

"No, but if this goes to court, she's got a pretty good case. Even in a no-fault state like California, judges tend to turn a jaundiced eye toward men who look like they're just trading up when the old model no longer shines. Let's face it, Ed, you've been seen all around town with a busty blonde half your age. You and I know the only reason she's on your arm is your money. If you go to court, you'll have a whole lot less of it."

Ed's face turned an ugly shade of red and he shifted in his chair before adjusting his tie with slow, deliberate movements. "It's a good thing I have you then, isn't it? I know you got Harold Crimshaw off and his ex-wife was a cripple. Last I heard she was living on disability with a small supplement from her settlement. How much did she end up with? Barely fifty thousand from what I remember…" His expression turned mildly generous, though on his hard facial planes it still held an edge of malice. "I'm not asking for a miracle. Just something fair. I don't want to pay more than one million. Not a penny more. Got it?"

Ben withheld his snarl. The man deserved no less than a kick to the groin. He was half tempted to sabotage the case and offer some pointers to the other side. The image of Sherry Crimshaw's stricken face was with him every time he walked into a courtroom with another scumbag millionaire looking to get off scot-free after discarding the wives that stood behind them when they had nothing.

Ed was right. Ben had enabled Harold to bilk his wife out of her rightful share by twisting the facts. Harold had claimed Sherry was an alcoholic and the accident that put her into a wheelchair had been her fault. With Harold's help, Ben managed to convince the judge that Harold was the poor husband who could no longer allow his drunken wife to drag him down. A piece of Ben's humanity broke off that day.

The worst part? The look of pride on his father's face. He'd flown in just to watch Ben in action. It was that much more awful because for years he'd yearned for that look and never received it; but the day he had, the reasons made him ill. He didn't want to be like his father and the fact that he seemed to have inherited his father's skill for decimating innocent witnesses wasn't something Ben wanted to crow about.

Now, each case too close in circumstance to Sherry's

made him realize how much of a bastard he was to help these people. He wasn't kidding himself; he wasn't a saint, either. Ben had no visions of opening a free clinic, but he wanted the choice to decline a client. Right now, he was at the beck and call of the firm. And the firm catered to assholes like Ed Wallace and Harold Crimshaw.

It was moments like this that made him wonder how he ended up in a place like Franklin, Mills & Donovan.

CHAPTER FOUR

NORA SAT on her front porch with her best friend, Sammy Halvorsen, sharing a beer and watching the sun sink in the horizon. She tried to derail her annoying train of thought, but wasn't doing such a bang-up job. Despite her attempts to enjoy Sammy's company and the visual pleasure of a brilliant burnt-orange sunset, she couldn't stop thinking—no, obsessing—on one thing.

She turned to Sammy. "Can I ask you something?"

Sammy paused, Corona bottle halfway to his lips, at Nora's pensive question. "Sure."

The call of a red-shouldered hawk split the air from atop the forested skyline and echoed against Bald Rock. Nora waited until the sound faded, replaced by the crickets' night song. "Do guys forget their first kiss?"

Sammy lifted the bottle to his mouth. "Nope."

"I didn't think so," she said. "I'd be willing to bet my right foot he remembers perfectly clear."

"Who remembers?"

"Ben Hollister."

"Who's that? I don't recall the name from school. He a client or something?"

"Sort of."

Sammy reached for a fresh Corona from his small

cooler and cracked it. "We gonna play Twenty Questions or are you going to start making sense?"

Nora drew a deep breath, but her mouth retained its tightness.

"You okay?"

"It's stupid," she admitted. "I can't believe I'm even letting my brain think about it, but for some reason I can't let it go and it's driving me crazy." She swigged her own beer before continuing, needing the alcohol to give her courage. If it were anyone but Sammy sitting beside her she wouldn't divulge anything, but she trusted him with her secrets and he'd never let her down. Plus, he had the right chromosomal makeup to answer her question. She might feel comfortable acting like a guy in many ways, but her brain was still decidedly female. "He's pretending not to remember me. I find that hard to believe. Who was the first girl you ever kissed?"

"Connie Villiandi," he answered without hesitation. "Mmm. All puckered lips and strawberry-flavored lip gloss."

"Connie?" Nora repeated, distracted by his revelation and his lazy grin. She snorted in something akin to disgust and his cheeks flared with heat. "The girl couldn't catch a pitch to save her life and acted like the prom queen at twelve. Geez, Sammy, my respect level for you just took a nosedive."

"Yeah, well, that girl turned into a very smart woman. Last I heard, she was working some government job with top-secret clearance. Not everyone is a jock like you, Nora."

"You're right. I'm sorry. I'm all jacked up because of this thing with Ben."

"Which is?"

Nora sighed and shook her head. Curiosity thoroughly pricked, he gestured impatiently for her to get on with it.

"I'm not getting any younger, Simmons. Out with it. Wait…is this something I'm going to feel obligated to kick this guy's ass over?"

She chuckled in amusement. "I've got a meaner left hook than you."

Sammy worked his jaw in memory. "You got that right. So what is it?"

"Ben Hollister is my new client. His grandparents owned the big Victorian just outside of town."

"Are they that old couple who died in that bad accident on Highway 41?"

"Yes, and they left the house to their only grandson. He's hired me to fix up the landscaping so the house will sell. The thing is…I've met him before."

Sammy gave her a blank stare. "Yeah, so?"

"He came to Emmett's Mill one summer when we were kids and, well, we kissed."

He grinned. "Was it weird between you?"

She looked at him sharply. "When?"

He gestured. "Today, now, whenever you saw him again."

Her shoulders relinquished some of their stiffness but her jaw still felt tense. She blew a hard breath and shrugged. "Yes, I mean no. He didn't seem to remember me and I didn't know how to bring it up without looking like a complete idiot. What was I supposed to say? 'Hey, good to see you, Ben. You've sure changed a lot from the boy I kissed down at the swimming hole.'"

"You could start there but I'd finesse it a little more," Sammy offered before breaking into a wide smile. "How old were you?"

"Ten."

"Ten! I can't believe you beat me to it! And to a kid who was just passing through. Un-freaking-believable."

"Oh, get over it. Stay on topic, please. So now my sisters are saying that I should just come out and tell him, because it wasn't right for me to go on pretending that we're strangers, but why should I when he seems perfectly content to go on pretending?"

"From a guy's standpoint, I'd say he didn't want to be embarrassed if you didn't remember him. It goes both ways, you know."

Nora made a sound of disbelief and rose to grab another Corona from Sammy's cooler. She returned to the old rocker and propped her feet on the porch railing, rocking the chair as she lifted the bottle to her lips. "So you're saying that it's possible he didn't say anything because *he* was afraid I might not remember him?"

"What can I say? We men have fragile egos."

"Not this guy," she mumbled, leaning down to place her beer on the weathered wooden planks of the porch. "He's got confidence oozing out his pores like cheap cologne. It's called eau de conceit. Somehow I doubt he's sitting at home wondering if I remember him." She barked a laugh. "The thought is ludicrous."

"So just ask him."

"Like it's that simple."

"Uh…it is. Open your mouth and just ask. You've never seemed to have a problem with asking anyone anything in the past. I still remember Rocky Slonik's expression when you asked him point-blank why one of his ears was bigger than the other. Poor kid blushed five different shades of red you embarrassed him so bad."

Nora grimaced, picturing that long-ago scene only too well. "Yeah, I'm an expert at shoving my foot in my mouth. Sometimes I wish I were more like Natalie. She's always doing the right thing. Even Tasha knows when to shut the hell up and take the high road. Maybe I'm the defective sister."

"Maybe."

She grinned. "You're an asshole."

He lifted his beer in thanks. "Card-carrying member from what I've heard."

"That's probably why we've been friends for so long. We're both defective. Peas in a messed-up pod. Aren't we the lucky ones?"

"Amen, sistah."

Nora laughed and retrieved her beer. "So who you seeing this week?" she asked, her heart much lighter than earlier in the evening. It was hard to stay in a bad mood with Sammy around, the guy's sense of humor was infectious. She shot him a curious look when he failed to answer right away.

"Holding out on me, Halvorsen?"

He grinned but his eyes didn't follow. Nora sat straighter. "Now it's my turn, I see. What's going on?"

"Nothing. Just been a long day."

"Tell me about it. I got nothing but the rest of the night to burn and we've got a few more Coronas to kill. I'm all ears, pretty boy."

He shrugged, the motion nonchalant enough, but he began playing with his beer bottle, focusing on his hands rather than the conversation. Nora should've seen something was eating at him when he showed up with beer but she'd been too concerned with what was going on in her own head. Some best friend she was. She made a point to try harder. "C'mon, am I going to have to play Twenty Questions or what?" she teased, using his own words against him.

He smiled but it was followed by a difficult sigh. "I think I'm getting old. I've been worried about things that never bothered me before."

"Such as?"

"I started thinking about where I'm going to be in a few years and I didn't like what I saw."

"What are you talking about? You've got it made. You work with your brothers in a successful family business, you make decent money and you're not in debt. What's the problem?"

"Nothing, I guess."

Unconvinced by his tone, she pressed harder. If there was one thing she excelled at, it was getting information out of someone. "Sam, what's eating at you?"

His gaze left his beer bottle and traveled out toward the darkening sky. The automatic porch light switched on, followed by the bug lamp. Soon the air would be filled with the sound of insects meeting their doom in one loud electric zap. She considered moving their powwow inside, but didn't want to disrupt what he was working up to share. The decision turned out to be wise, for Sammy turned to her a moment later, his hazel eyes troubled. "I'm just starting to wonder if I'm looking for love in all the wrong places."

"I didn't know you were looking for love at all." For as long as Sammy had been noticing the opposite sex, he'd never been one for commitment. He was a genuine player in the field of serial dating.

"Yeah, me neither," he admitted. "I guess I figured I'm not a kid anymore. The idea of being alone doesn't sound very appealing."

"So don't be alone," she suggested. "You're never at a loss for finding willing and eager women to share your time."

He nodded but Nora got the impression she'd hadn't been much help. Something turbulent remained trapped behind his eyes, but he didn't give her a chance to try again.

"Thanks for the company, but I gotta get going." He rose from the battered wicker chair and scooped up his six-pack Igloo cooler. "Dean's got a big job for us tomorrow and he ain't big on sympathy when you're dragging your butt 'cause you stayed up too late."

"Gotta love older brothers."

"Yeah. Something like that."

He headed down the stairs until her voice stopped him.

"Sammy, if you need to talk I'm here."

He lifted his cooler in acknowledgment. "Thanks."

THE SPORTS CAR PURRED along the country back road, eating up the miles between the bay and Emmett's Mill as the sun crested the east, slanting bright yellow morning sun through Ben's window. The brisk California air reminded him that it was too early to take the top down, but Ben had wanted to feel something other than the damp fog of the bay. The sunshine, though not exactly warm yet, was a welcome change.

He and Nora were meeting today to discuss her plans for the landscaping and that's all he wanted to think about.

He didn't want to consider this an escape, but there was no mistaking that he was humming and actually smiling.

A change of scenery was always good.

His good mood didn't have anything to do with Nora.

He geared down to take a sharp turn; the high-performance vehicle responded with a low, throaty growl as he accelerated out of the turn. If nothing else, the ride was enjoyable.

Miles of road stretched ahead of him and he relaxed. Before long a memory floated out of his mental lockbox and startled him with the feelings it aroused.

The kiss.

A brief smile ghosted his lips.

It was so easy to see the scene in his mind, hear the water gurgling over stone slabs and smell the faint odor of algae and moss that collected in the areas where the water didn't run freely. He could also smell the coconut suntan lotion on her golden skin, see the white-gold of her hair spilling in a wild nest around her shoulders.

"It's really an experiment," she'd said primly one day. "I need to see what all the fuss is about when it comes to this kissing stuff. Tasha does it *every time* she sees her boyfriend, Josh, and I want to see why she likes to do it."

"Why don't you just ask her?" he suggested, not entirely sure he should be kissing a ten-year-old. But she was kind of cute and persistent and, honestly, he was curious to see if she would truly go through with it.

Nora's young face screwed into a scowl. "She says I'm too young to understand, but I'm not. I'm the smartest in my class and I want to know. Are you going to help me out or what?"

He took a moment to think about it. Truth was, he'd never kissed anyone either.

She put her hands on her hips. "Well?"

"Well…I guess. What do you want to do?"

Nora came to him with a stern expression. "You have to put your arms around me like this," she instructed, nodding in approval once Ben's arms closed around her small frame. "Okay, now I'll put my arms around your waist and then you'll bend down and I'll reach on my tippy-toes and we'll meet in the middle with our lips. Got it?"

"Sounds simple enough," he said, hoping no one happened to walk by this particular stretch of creek when he placed a soft kiss on her baby lips, catching the lingering scent of bubble gum on her breath. He pulled away. Her eyelids were closed and he could've sworn he felt her heart racing. Faint blue veins ran a course over her lids and her cheeks had pinked despite her golden summer tan. She was probably the prettiest girl he'd ever seen. Her eyes popped open and in a surprising motion, she jerked away with a halting nod.

"Experiment concluded! Bye!"

And then she was gone.

He'd hoped to catch her around town, but even as small as Emmett's Mill was, they hadn't managed to bump into each other again. A few days later he returned to New England, his life unrecognizable from what it'd been.

The enjoyable feelings of that long-ago kiss faded with what followed that summer. He hated that this particular memory still had the power to make him feel small and vulnerable.

Ben breathed deep the clean air and pushed away the dark feelings crawling around in his chest. Divorce was a fact of life. This was something he dealt with every day. Irreconcilable differences. He read that on the paperwork that came across his desk so many times, he once spent some idle time trying to figure out how to spell it phonetically on a personalized license plate for his car. As a family law attorney who specialized in ugly divorces, he thought the idea was darkly tongue-in-cheek. His girlfriend at the time hadn't agreed. As he recalled, she'd said that such a cynical view was pessimistic about love in general. That's when he'd blithely dropped the bomb—he didn't believe in love. She wasn't around anymore.

He'd yet to meet someone who wasn't hung up on the idea of true love and all that crap. Personally he was sick of playing the game. The next woman he invited into his life would be one who shared the same sentiment toward love. He didn't have the time to deal with someone who was looking for their soul mate.

What about someone who commands kisses in the name of science…?

No time for that either, but he had to admit, the thought was intriguing.

CHAPTER FIVE

"ARE YOU *ever* on time?"

Nora strode toward Ben and ignored his tone. Despite the stuffiness of his earthy-brown slacks and cream dress shirt, he still looked like something out of an Abercrombie & Fitch commercial. He had a butt you could bounce quarters off and not even those preppy pants could hide that. She glanced down at his brown loafers and smirked. The man didn't know how to dress for the country. "Depends."

He followed her gaze and frowned. "Depends on what?"

"On how I'm feeling that day. Sometimes it's an on-time day and sometimes it just isn't. You can guess what kind of day today is."

"What were you smiling at?"

"I wasn't smiling, I was smirking."

"Fine. What were you *smirking* about? Is there something wrong with my shoes?"

She cocked her head at him. "Just an odd choice for someone who's going to tromp through thistles and ragweed. I prefer good old-fashioned hiking boots." She lifted her foot and modeled her worn shoe. "But that's just me. City folks tend to do things differently I'm told."

"Oh, I get it. You're playing the wise country local while I'm playing the part of idiot city guy who wouldn't know a poison-oak branch from a manzanita bush."

She arched her brow. "Do you?"

"Of course I do," he retorted, but she caught his eyes darting to the side a bit nervously. "Poison oak has bright green leaves and manzanita has sticky red berries attached."

"Not bad, professor, but what about in the winter? What does poison oak look like then?" He faltered and she grinned, affecting a country-bumpkin stereotype voice. "Well, mister, when it's winter time pois'n oak looks like plain ole sticks, but if'n you touch 'em, you're still gonna be in a world of hurt 'cuz it still has the oils that cause the 'llergic reaction."

"Cute."

"I thought so."

"Thanks for the botany lesson. Can we get to work now?"

"You're the boss." She pulled a rolled-up chunk of paper from her back pocket and handed it to him. She supposed she could've finessed the presentation, but she liked to keep her work with her at all times and packing around a clipboard wasn't always convenient to the way her mind operated. He unfurled the papers with an air of exasperation and her mouth itched to smile. How anyone could be so uptight was beyond her but it was fun watching him loosen up.

While he studied her plans, her imagination ran a little wild wondering what he'd look like in a pair of faded jeans, no shirt and nicely mussed bed-head. Her toes curled and her fingers tingled in anticipation of an event that she'd never allow to happen. She shook her hands, annoyed at herself and the sensation.

"What's wrong?" he asked.

"Nothing," she said too quickly, shuddering at the idea of sharing that crazy thought. "What do you think of the plans?"

His gaze returned reluctantly to the papers in his hand. "Aside from the proliferation of flowers everywhere, they look suitable for what I'm going for."

"Well, I told you I wasn't going for the desert look. Flowers sell houses, makes them look homey and welcoming."

He made a noncommittal noise but otherwise didn't protest, and after rolling the papers in a column, he tucked them under his arm. "Shall we commence the walk-through?"

"Are you sure? In those shoes?"

"Just lead the way."

"Fine, but if you end up with poison oak in an unmentionable place, don't go blaming me. If I have to drag you out of a patch my rate's going to go up exponentially."

He grimaced. "Duly noted. I'll do my best to stay on my feet."

"Good."

BEN FELL IN STEP with Nora. Irritation at her attitude fueled his stride until he happened to catch the view of her backside. Plump and pert and clad lovingly in khaki cargo pants, it was all he could do not to stare. He stumbled on a rock partially hidden by overgrown weeds and she slowed.

"You okay?"

"Fine," he answered, his cheeks flaring. "I'm right behind you. Where are we going by the way?"

She high stepped the tall grass as she talked, the movement of her legs sending his imagination into overdrive. His frustration returned, only this time it was directed at himself. Her voice jerked him to attention.

"I'm not sure if you saw it in my plans, but I'd like to define the trail that leads down to the creek. Right now it's just a deer path, but I think it would add to the ambience if there was a lighted stairway. People love to know they have their own little spot on the creek. Of course, since the river feeds this part of the creek, the water runs all year, which is another draw."

"Good to know." He glanced down at his slacks. They were covered in an assortment of sticky weeds. The pungent odor from the crushed foliage was oddly enjoyable, though he wasn't sure his slacks would ever recover. "This hill is pretty steep. You sure that's a good idea?"

She spared him an indulgent look. "Of course I do."

The sight of the lazily winding creek glistening below brought up treasured memories, ones he kept under lock and key because they weren't tainted by his parents. His time with Nora seemed unreal, as if he'd dreamed it in an attempt to escape the sound of his mother crying and his father beating her down with his words as much as his hands. It was part of the reason

Ben hadn't said anything to Nora, but keeping the secret weighed on him in a way he hadn't anticipated. It needed to be out in the open so they could move on. Sounded simple enough, but the only problem was that he hadn't a clue how to tell her. The purest opportunity passed him by days ago. Deciding to try a casual approach, he gestured to the creek. "You ever go down there anymore?"

In hindsight, he realized casual hadn't been the right choice. Though if he really gave it some thought, sinking to his knees in apology probably wouldn't have worked either.

She sucked in a sharp breath and swore softly as a storm built behind her eyes.

"Hold on…" He started in alarm at how quickly her temper kindled. "Let's not make a mountain out of a molehill."

"You haven't seen the half of it," she said, her eyes flashing. "You pretended that you didn't remember me but I knew it!" She swore again and bracketed her hips with her hands, drawing his gaze to her nicely spanned waist until he realized he was enjoying the view a little too much. "Why? Why would you do that? Do you have any idea how long I've been stressed out over this stupid thing? My God, I can't believe I let myself get sucked into your little game."

"I wasn't playing a game," he tried assuring her. Apologize. It was the right thing to do, his mind instructed, but his mouth didn't obey. "I just didn't feel it was relevant to the job."

She sputtered. "Not relevant? Perhaps not, but it

would've been decent of you to admit that you remembered me instead of acting like you'd never laid eyes on me before. That was mean, if you ask me."

"Well I didn't ask you, and judging by your reaction it's a damn good thing I didn't. I don't have time for drama, Ms. Simmons. I hired you because you're the best in the area. I was impressed with your portfolio and despite your oddities, I'm amenable to continuing this relationship if you'll agree to stop with the histrionics."

"Spare me your benevolence. You can take your double-sided compliments and shove them, Benjamin Scott Hollister III." He startled at her use of his full name but she continued, snatching the plans from his hands and shoving them into her back pocket again. "Your opinion of my work means nothing to me. I agreed to take the job because I thought highly of your grandparents, but not even my regard for B.J. and Corrinda can change the fact that you're a jerk. Find yourself someone else to fix the yard. I quit."

Caught off guard at her unexpected announcement, he realized things had gone too far. His brain screamed for damage control and he caught her arm before she managed to stomp away. "Where are you going? We need to talk this out," he said, striving for calm.

She yanked her arm, but he held it firm. "Let go."

"Not until you agree to talk rationally about this."

"I said let go!"

She gave a savage jerk of her arm, ripping it out of his grasp, the violence of the movement sending him off balance and teetering dangerously on the rocky terrain.

"Nora!" he managed to gasp, and she turned just in

time to watch in wide-eyed surprise as he went tumbling down the steep embankment. He tried to protect his body, but his side connected with a half-buried rock and a damp crack sent stars bursting behind his eyes.

SECONDS MAY HAVE PASSED before Nora sprang into horrified action, but it felt as if time had slowed to a crawl as she watched Ben's body tumble and flop down the embankment, gathering momentum as he headed toward the creek that was swollen with the winter-snow runoff until he finally stopped a hairbreadth away from smacking his head on a slab of granite.

"Oh God, Ben," she breathed, scrambling down the hillside to reach him, her heart thudding painfully as she cursed her temper and her mouth. "Please don't be dead. *Please* don't be dead!"

Her stomach pitched dangerously at the sight of Ben's cuts and contusions. Blood seeped from a deep gash in his forehead. She fought the dizziness that never failed to come whenever she was faced with the sight of blood and closed her eyes to clear her vision. Now was not the time to faint. The wave passed and she opened her eyes, moving closer to Ben in search of some kind of sign that she hadn't just killed him with her temper.

She dropped to her knees and gently pressed her fingers to his wrist. A steady heartbeat thumped softly and she exhaled in relief. He wasn't dead, but judging by his obvious injuries, when he woke up he might want to be.

Ben groaned and she winced at the pain couched inside the sound.

"Don't move," she whispered, pulling her cell phone from her back pocket to dial 911. He groaned again and she slipped her hand into his and gave it a gentle squeeze to let him know he wasn't alone while she waited impatiently for the operator. His eyes remained shut but the moaning stopped. An operator came on the line and Nora wasted little time in telling the man what had happened.

"We're down at the creek below the Hollister house. Hurry, he's hurt pretty bad. I think he may have broken something." *Or everything*, she thought worriedly, wincing at the mess Ben had become during his trip down the hill. His previously beautiful shirt was ripped and torn, the fine fabric completely trashed, and he was missing one shoe. "Please hurry."

"They're on their way," the dispatcher assured her as the line clicked off.

Nora bit her lip, never before faced with a situation like this. "Stupid shoes. Who wears loafers in the mountains?" she grumbled, but fear overrode her pique. Why did she jerk her arm like that? She'd known they were too close to the edge but her temper got the best of her. No, a voice reprimanded sternly, not temper—mostly pride. She'd been humiliated by his omission.

Ben's eyes fluttered open, pain darkening the soft green until he squeezed them shut again. "Damn," he muttered from between clenched teeth. "Nora?"

"I'm here. Try not to move around. An ambulance is coming," she said, her guilt tripling when he grunted against the pain, his chest moving in short, stilted motions. "You lost your shoe somewhere," she said, searching for something to say. "I'll buy you a new one."

"Screw the shoe," he said. "Where's that ambulance?"

"Be patient, they're on their way. We're not in the city, so it's not like they're just around the corner. Besides, if you hadn't been so damn pushy this wouldn't have happened. For future reference, I don't like to be—" The sound of the ambulance cut her off, which was probably a good thing because her nerves had taken hold of her mouth. Paramedics appeared at the top of the small ridge and hollered down to them.

"Who's the victim?" a tall, curvy woman questioned in a clear voice. Nora gestured to Ben and the woman disappeared only to reappear with reinforcements in the way of firefighters carrying an orange stretcher.

The woman called out. "Do you need help, too?"

"No, *I* wore appropriate shoes for the day," she answered, but the woman only stared. Nora waved her away. "I'll sit with him until the firefighters get down here."

"Fine."

Moments later, two firefighters were roped and anchored to the top while they were lowered to Ben and Nora's position. Nora scooted carefully out of the way and, while they loaded him onto the stretcher, she made the climb back up, huffing a little with the exertion by the time she got to the top.

The firefighters pulled Ben over the edge of the ridge and the paramedics took over. The woman who'd first called out to them wasn't anyone Nora knew, but she seemed to know her job.

"At least one broken rib, possibly bruised lung and a fractured ankle." She turned to Nora. "What happened?"

"He fell."

The woman made a sound of annoyance. "I gathered that. How did he fall?"

The woman was just doing her job, but explaining what happened only served to make Nora feel worse. She glared. "The usual way. He went ass over teakettle until he stopped at the edge of that big rock. What difference does it make to his treatment how he fell exactly?"

A sheriff cruiser appeared on the scene and the woman smiled thinly. "It makes a big difference to them. I'd say it's the difference between attempted murder and an accident."

Nora gaped. Who would think that she'd try to purposefully hurt someone like that? It wasn't as if she had a history of pushing people down mountains. Mike Curtis, an older deputy who'd gone to school with her dad, approached them.

"What happened here?" he asked, taking a moment to spit a stream of chewing-tobacco juice on the dusty ground. "Heard on the radio someone took a spill."

"Mike," Nora said, glad someone was here who'd show this newcomer how things were done in Emmett's Mill. "Thank God you're here. My friend Ben fell and this woman is acting like I pushed him or something."

"Now, Dana, that's no way to make friends," he admonished, and the woman snorted and climbed into the back of the ambulance just before it took off, siren blaring. He chuckled. "She's a live one. Gotta love her, though. How you doing, Little Gerry?"

Nora gave him a stony look for calling her the nickname he'd picked for her years ago because, according to him, she was just like her father, Gerald. In other words, stubborn, obstinate and ornery on the best of days. "I was fine until Ben decided to go off-roading with his face. Who is that woman anyway?"

"Dana Collins. New to the area. Just got hired on a few weeks ago. She has a relative here or something housed over at Laurel Manor Senior Center. I only know about her because I heard Samuel Halvorsen had dated her for a spell."

Nora forgot all about Ben and stared at Mike. "What? No. Sammy would've told me. We're pretty close. He's never not shared who he's seeing."

"Be that as it may, I have it on pretty good authority that Sammy and Dana were sweet on each other…at least for a while. Don't know what happened, but I suspect the same thing that always happens with that boy." He shook his head as he walked away. "He's in love with the *idea* of being in love."

She wanted to defend her best friend but there was some truth to Mike's statement. Sammy loved the hunt, not the prize. But the bigger question was, why hadn't he told her about this Dana woman? As Nora headed for her truck to go to the hospital, she answered her own question—Sammy must've been trying to tell her the other night, but she'd been too wrapped up in her own troubles to pay attention. What had he said? She jumped into the truck and started the engine. She sat up straighter. He'd said something about wanting more out of a relationship. Oh, Sammy, she wanted to moan, peeling out of the driveway. You really know how to pick 'em.

CHAPTER SIX

NORA WALKED INTO the emergency room of the small hospital and went straight to the only closed curtain. She could hear her family physician, his voice low and gravelly and oddly soothing, and knew he was talking about Ben to the nurse.

She pushed aside the curtain and slipped inside, ignoring Dr. Hessle's expression as the nurse left them alone. "Did you have something to do with this, young lady?" he asked gravely.

Nora avoided his stare and squirmed a little. Doc Hessle had had an ability to see into her conscience that he'd honed over the many years filled with cuts, broken bones and contusions. They weren't always her own injuries, but she was most certainly involved in some way or another.

"Who wears loafers in the mountains?" she retorted, and a subtle smile crept onto his aged face, and she knew no matter what she said, he wouldn't hold it against her. Nora was Doc Hessle's favorite patient. Nora's mom, Missy, used to joke that he liked Nora the best because she helped pay for his second home with all her hospital visits. "Is he going to be okay?" she asked in all seriousness.

"Eventually," he replied with a nod. "Pretty banged up. You didn't push him down that hill, did you?"

Nora gasped. "Doc! You know me better than that. You must've been talking to that new paramedic, Dana something or another. She and I are going to have words real soon, I promise you that."

"Leave her alone, she's our best paramedic. I don't want you scaring her off. Besides, I know you better than most and I know you've got a wicked temper." He grinned. "It's the best part of your personality. But this boy is hurt bad. It's just as Dana said—broken rib, bruised lung and a fractured ankle. Who is he?"

"Ben Hollister," Nora answered, her gaze skittering away from the puffy gash on his head. "Remember B.J. and Corrinda? He's their grandson. He inherited the house."

Doc Hessle nodded. "That explains him, what about you?"

Nora groaned. "Doc, let's just say I'm not completely innocent and I feel really bad about it, so please drop it."

He chuckled and Ben stirred, his eyes opening slowly. "How you feeling, son? Those pain meds kick in yet?"

Ben paused as if checking for any aches and nodded carefully. "No pain, just tired," he said, his voice husky and very sexy, which she realized was incredibly inappropriate given the situation, but since it was in the privacy of her own mind, she simply enjoyed the guilty pleasure. "What's the prognosis?" he asked, his perfectly set hair askew.

"Your rib and lung will heal on their own in a few weeks, provided you don't do anything strenuous. The ankle is another matter. It's a rather bad break. I'm going to have to recommend that you stay off it for at least six weeks."

The medicine-induced haze cleared from his eyes as he shook his head. "That's going to be hard to do, Doctor. I don't live in Emmett's Mill and the only person I know here is Nora." He met Nora's gaze briefly before going back to the doctor. "I'm an attorney in the Bay Area and I have a job to return to."

"Fine by me, but do you have someone who can drive you, help around the house and ensure that you don't put pressure on that foot?"

"Is that really necessary?"

"Do you want to walk again?"

He blanched. "Of course I do."

"Then you'll find a way to stay off that foot." Doc Hessle gathered his clipboard in front of his stomach and gestured toward Nora. "I heard you inherited your grandparents' house, so you have a place you could hole up in while you recuperate. Nora here could help out I'm sure."

Nora caught Doc Hessle's last statement and nearly swallowed her tongue as she protested his suggestion. "I have clients…lots of them Doc. I can't take time off to play nursemaid. Sorry. Not really my forte."

Doc Hessle raised an assessing eyebrow at them both and then turned to Nora. "This boy needs help and you're the only person he knows. Don't make your mama turn over in her grave, young lady. Where's your manners?"

"He's not a boy," Nora muttered, shooting Ben a mutinous look. "And he has a life to get back to." Chagrined by Doc Hessle's disappointed expression, she looked to Ben for backup. Surely he didn't want her for a nursemaid, either. As she'd already proven, she wasn't the caregiving type—that was Natalie's area of expertise. Nora was more of the get-mad-push-a-guy-off-a-cliff type.

Ben drew a deep breath and thanked the doctor for patching him up but Nora read more than irritation in his eyes. She caught a moment of bleakness that immediately poked at the soft spot in her heart, which she did her damnedest to cover most of the time, and she realized how alone he felt. If the situation were reversed, Nora couldn't imagine being without her family in a town full of strangers. "Maybe you should call your parents," she said, fishing for information as much as making a helpful suggestion.

"I'm a little old to be running home to Mommy, don't you think?" he said.

"No one's too old for the love and care of their parents—especially from their mommy, as you put it. I'd give anything to have my mom here with me again, but I don't have that option. She died last year." Ben's expression faltered and he mumbled an apology, which she waved away. "You didn't kill her, cancer did. But what I'm getting from your comment is that your parents aren't exactly the kind you can turn to. Am I right?"

He gave a grudging jerk of his head, then shifted uncomfortably in the small hospital bed to say a bit snappishly, "Not everyone has the Walton house to grow up in."

"More's the pity," Doc Hessle interjected with a sad sigh, eyeing Ben speculatively before looking at Nora with expectation. "Well? What's it going to be, young lady?"

Nora ignored the doc and turned to Ben in earnest. "So, who can you get to care for you in the Bay Area? A friend, perhaps. Maybe a girlfriend?"

His eyes shut. "No girlfriend and no one I'd consider calling in this particular instance." He opened his eyes again but chose to stare past Nora. The disconcerting way he refused to meet her gaze made her wonder what kind of sterile life he was living. "I have a maid but she doesn't speak English," he said. "The firm pays for her services."

"You don't have any friends?" Nora asked curiously. "No one? Who do you hang out with when you're not working? What about weekends? Holidays?"

He glared as if angry at her for pointing out how sad that sounded and then looked at Doc Hessle who'd been watching the exchange with an expression of mild amusement. For the life of her, Nora couldn't see anything remotely amusing about the situation, and asked, "When can Ben get out of here?"

"His discharge paperwork will be ready in a few minutes I suspect," he answered, handing Ben a prescription for more pain meds.

Ben nodded in grim satisfaction and closed his eyes

again, giving Nora the distinct impression he'd just dismissed both her and Doc Hessle. A frown replaced the doc's amusement and he narrowed his bushy-browed gaze at Ben much as he would at a surly teen. Nora had been on the receiving end of that look more times than she wanted to count and didn't envy Ben.

"Being as I knew your grandparents to be fine folk, I'll only say this one thing and then get out of your hair," Doc Hessle began, the authority in his tone jerking Ben to attention. "You're seriously injured and you need someone to help you out. I suggest you look at the blessings, odd as they may seem, that are right in front of your damn nose." Ben opened his mouth to offer a rebuttal no doubt, but Doc Hessle didn't give him the chance. This time it was Ben who was dismissed as Doc Hessle walked away grousing under his breath.

"Way to go." Nora smirked. "Now I know why you don't have any friends."

"I said I don't have friends in the Bay Area," he snapped.

"Fine, then you'd better get on the horn and call up those long-distance friends of yours so they can care for your sorry ass, or else you're going to have to learn a second language so that you can communicate your needs to your maid."

Ben looked ready to throw out another scathing remark, but apparently thought better of it, closing his mouth and shaking his head. "This is great timing," he muttered. "Ah, hell."

Guilt crept up and tapped her on the shoulder, and despite her efforts to shrug it off, she was reminded of the part she'd played in Ben's injuries. He couldn't—or wouldn't—call his parents. No friends. A foreign maid who didn't speak a lick of English. And he was basically crippled for the next six weeks.

He could afford to hire someone, the rational side of her brain reminded her, but it didn't matter, the crazy side had already won control and her mouth was moving before she realized what she was saying.

"Alright, here's the deal. You hired me to do the landscaping, I suppose since I'll already be there, I can help out a bit if you decide to stay for a while."

Ben stared at her, not quite sure he heard correctly.

"Well, don't look at me like I lost my mind or something," she grumbled, "because it already feels like I did and I don't need you to rub it in."

It must be the pain meds. They were messing with his brain. Surely Nora hadn't just suggested he stay here while she cared for him. A ripple passed through his numbed body and he jerked against the implications. "No," he stated flatly. "I can't let you do that."

"Why not?"

Because of all the dumb things he could possibly do, letting a woman he was clearly attracted to—in the most baffling way possible—care for him begged for trouble he didn't want to invite into his life. "Because it's ridiculous for one, and two, it would be unprofessional."

After a moment of consideration, she countered, "Not if you paid me."

"Paid you?"

"Yeah, paid me. You're going to end up paying someone to care for you anyway, why not me? That should take care of any weird interpersonal issues. Besides, I'll be working on the house and coming in and out, so I can easily pop in wherever you're sitting and check on you. As much as I was against it in the beginning, now I see the sense in it."

At least one of us can, he wanted to grouse. Her suggestion made sense on paper but when put into practice fell apart because certain emotions, in this case, inappropriate curiosity, mucked things up. But she did make a valuable point. He was still muddling through the logistics of such an arrangement when Dr. Hessle returned and gave the two of them an assessing look that Nora capitalized on.

"I've agreed to look after Ben while he's recuperating," she told him, although Ben hadn't actually accepted her offer.

"Good. Glad you came to your senses," the doctor said, though Ben wasn't sure whom he was addressing. "A nurse will come in a few moments to put a cast on that ankle, and once it's set Nora can take you home but I would like you to come back in about two weeks so I can check that rib. Remember, off your feet."

The doctor left the curtained area and Ben was left with Nora. "You don't have to drive me," he started, feeling more awkward than he'd ever felt in his life. "I can get a taxi or something."

"Sure, and while you're at it, why don't you order up some Thai food to go." His blank stare prompted her to explain in annoyance, "We don't have a taxi service or a Thai-food restaurant. You can't walk to your grandparents' house, so I'll take you."

"I don't want you to go out of your way," he said glumly. "I'll figure something out."

"Don't be stupid. I'll drive you."

A smiling nurse entered, pushing a cart filled with casting materials and Ben swallowed the retort on his tongue. It was probably better he hadn't let his mouth take over at this point. While he wasn't keen on climbing into a car with the same woman who'd nearly killed him even if it was by accident, she made a good point. Without any transportation and an inability to drive, he was stuck.

The nurse gestured to the material with an apologetic expression. "Pink or blue? We seem to be out of the plain white we usually use for adults," she said, and out of the corner of his eye, Ben caught Nora grinning.

"Blue," he sighed.

"Oh, I don't know, they say real men wear pink," Nora joked.

Ben cut Nora a short look. "This man doesn't."

She shrugged, but she was practically vibrating from the laughter she was holding back. "Suit yourself," she said.

"Blue it is, then," the nurse said, settling beside Ben to start the process.

Fifteen minutes later, Ben's ankle was cast in blue plaster gauze, and another ten minutes later, it was hard as a rock. He could already feel an itch in a place he wouldn't be able to reach for the next six weeks and he wanted to curse the situation up one side and down the other, but he settled for getting the hell out of there. The nurse left and Ben swung his leg over the side of the bed.

"Let me at least give you some gas money," he offered gruffly, hating how helpless he felt.

"Fine. I'll go get someone so we can wheel you out of here. I'm starving."

Moments later Nora returned with a surly-looking male nurse who looked ready to stuff him in the wheelchair he was pushing just for the sake of doing it. Nora must've pulled him away from a break.

"Paul is going to wheel you out front, and I'll meet you there with my truck." Nora didn't wait for him to agree or disagree and was gone in a blink.

Ben eyed Paul. "Did she interrupt something?"

"My dinner."

He grimaced. "Not my idea. Try not to take it out on me."

Paul's expression didn't change and Ben was thankful he was still doped up on pain meds. Instinct told him Paul wasn't in the mood to be gentle.

THE AWKWARD SILENCE was nearly unbearable, but Nora suffered through it, telling herself penance was never a picnic. Several times the nippy draft coming from the outside caused Ben to shiver, reminding her that he was made from different stock and accustomed to different things—such as vehicles that didn't require a wrench to roll up the passenger-side window—and wondered if her sanity was on permanent hiatus, or if it was bound to return before she did something really stupid.

She slid a surreptitious glance his way, taking in the strong angles of his silhouette in the darkened cab, and realized a part of her—that ridiculously breathy and girlie part—was curious to see what kind of mischief they could make together.

Keep it together, Simmons. She'd caused enough damage for one day.

She pulled into Ben's driveway and hopped from her side to help him out. His clenched jaw could've been from the pain meds wearing off or that she was snugged up to him as she helped him from the truck so they could manage an odd hop and lean to the front door.

"This is ridiculous," he grunted, breathing hard against the exertion. "We should've waited until I could've found some crutches."

"I already told you, I asked around when I went to get the truck. The medical-supply closet at the hospital was locked and the guy with the key had already gone home. So suck it up and get to hopping—you're killing my shoulder!"

Nora focused on getting him up the short steps to the front door and not on the mix of scents assaulting her nostrils, scents that if pressed, she'd have to admit were annoyingly arousing. Fresh dirt, the faint cling of crushed grass and the tease of some expensive cologne played with her senses, and she gritted her teeth against the desire to bury her nose in the crook of his neck…or somewhere else on his hard body. If all lawyers were built like Ben, she might've adjusted her opinion about them a long time ago.

"Can you hop any faster?" she grunted, irritation with herself making her surly.

"Sorry my hopping skills aren't up to your standards," he retorted as they both wobbled on the last step. "Can you hold steady before you break my other ankle?"

Nora stiffened, tempted to drop him for that comment, but swallowed her impulse. She was trying to do a good thing and she wasn't going to let his attitude derail her. Ben pulled away and struggled to hop on his own to the front door. She watched in sardonic amusement as he tried to keep his balance without her. Nora's mom used to say you couldn't help someone who didn't want your help, but she didn't say anything about not being able to laugh at their dumb ass when they fell on it.

Ben stopped and steadied himself with his right arm against the doorjamb and fished in his pocket for the key, but Nora saw that the strength in the leg holding up his ankle was flagging. Stupid pride, she thought with exasperation, knowing he was seconds away from losing that battle. But pride was something she understood and even as she was tempted just to take the key and open the door to save him from himself, she waited.

Nora recognized Ben's need to be self-sufficient despite his obvious need for help. She'd fought that battle her entire childhood. Carving an identity for herself against two older sisters and an overbearing father had left its share of battle wounds. Seeing something similar in Ben made her appreciate there was more to the man than what she'd been ready to believe.

He finally managed to get the key in the lock and once the door was open, she slipped under his arm and he let her help him inside.

CHAPTER SEVEN

THE NEXT MORNING Ben lay in the double bed where he'd spent a restless night, and despite the sunlight streaming through the window of the master suite, he felt panic at his predicament.

Nora had been right—he had no one to call upon for help. He was alone in this world, surrounded by people who'd love to watch him fall, simply for the entertainment value of seeing him break into a million pieces.

Ben hadn't made friends at the firm purposefully. He didn't want to give anyone the power to stab him in the back later. He kept to himself and made work his life. Crossing his forearms across his eyes, he blocked out the sunlight and the fear that smothered his confidence and reminded him that, in hindsight, his choices were to blame for his loneliness.

No, Nora was to blame for this. The insidious voice whispered in his head, and while it was easier to accept that counsel, he knew it wasn't entirely true. He shouldn't have grabbed her. He'd acted like a self-righteous prig with a woman who had a flash-burn temper, and now he was paying her to help him out. The irony was disturbing.

He winced as his side pulled, but when he tried to

suck a deep breath against the burn, his bruised lung protested and he rolled onto his undamaged side and concentrated on taking slow, shallow breaths until the stars spinning around his head faded and disappeared. What was he going to tell the firm? What about the Wallace case? He needed the case files, needed to make contact with Ed and let him know of the situation, not that the bastard would give a damn. From what Ben had seen, Ed Wallace had turned in his heart in exchange for lots of money. Ben bounced his head against the flat pillow in frustration and growled. He had to find a way to fix this before he ended up without a job and nowhere to go.

NORA ARRIVED at Ben's place around 9:00 a.m. with a brown bag filled with groceries, well, edible foodstuff like packaged doughnuts and coffee packets just in case Ben was the type who needed a pick-me-up in the morning, and bounded the stairs to the front door.

She was in good spirits despite getting up earlier than she preferred and detoured to the kitchen before heading into the bedroom, where she knocked twice and entered without thinking.

Boy, there was a reason her mom always said to wait for permission before opening a closed door. Ben stood haphazardly clutching a towel much too small for his wide frame across his lean hips, his hair wet and dripping. She gaped at the six-pack of muscle cording his stomach and daring her to follow the happy trail of dark hair that disappeared behind the towel and teased her with the promise of what lay beneath. Not even the motley bruising around his injured rib did much to ruin the view and she was mortified to note if she stared any harder, her pointed gaze might pierce his skin and pop out the other side.

"Oh!" She spun around, her cheeks hot enough to catch the drapes on fire, and mentally counted to ten to give her heart a chance to begin beating again. "I... I...didn't think...well, of course, I should've waited... oh, God!"

Nora heard his labored breathing and the springs on the bed creak as it absorbed Ben's weight. Showering must've been terribly difficult, she realized. A shadow of concern managed to override her embarrassment long enough for her to ask tentatively, "Hey, are you okay?"

There was a long pause and then, "Yeah, uh, I'm fine, just a little winded. And exposed," he added unnecessarily. She bit her lip and cursed silently for not thinking before she opened that door. But, oh goodness, the man was hot. Thanks to that tantalizing snapshot her dreams were bound to be bothersome.

He exhaled softly then ground out, "I think I need your help."

"What kind of help?" she asked warily, not sure she trusted herself not to pet him like an exotic animal if she got too close.

"I can't get my pants on," he admitted, and by his tone she could almost see his own cheeks reddening. "I guess I didn't think this through, but I had dirt in my hair and grass stains on my palms and had to wash up."

"How'd you manage to shower with your cast?" she asked, careful to keep her eyes focused straight ahead and nowhere near where she might catch another glimpse of his naked skin.

"I wrapped it in a plastic bag and taped it off. It's not perfect, but I couldn't stand going to bed another night covered in dirt and sweat."

She nodded. That made sense, even if it wasn't the smartest thing to do. He could've fallen in the shower or something. She looked around as she asked, "What happened to the loose hospital trousers you were wearing last night?"

"Uh, they ripped when I was trying to get them off." He added defensively, "They were made of very thin cotton."

Nora drew a deep breath and slowly turned, hoping he was covered with a blanket so she didn't humiliate herself further by drooling. A mixture of relief and chagrin washed over her when she saw the lower half of his body was hidden from view by the faded quilt on the bed.

"Is that it?" As if that wasn't enough, she wanted to snap. "Help you get dressed?"

"No, I have one more thing to ask," he admitted.

"Which is?"

He adjusted his body with slow, deliberate movements and she caught his wince but didn't comment. She didn't think he would appreciate coddling, which was fine by Nora—coddling didn't come naturally to her anyway. Ben settled into his new position carefully then met her wary gaze.

"I need you to drive me to my place in San Francisco

so I can make arrangements, get clothes and forward my mail for the next six weeks."

HE KNEW HIS REQUEST wouldn't go over well, but honestly, how was he supposed to hole up in Emmett's Mill without provisions? At least he had to pick up his work files and some clothes.

Her face screwed into an annoyed frown but she didn't protest. "I suppose that's reasonable," she said. "But I'm not sure if my truck is up to driving to the city. Usually when I have trips farther than Coldwater or Sonora, I borrow a friend's truck. It's newer and doesn't threaten to die after a few miles. I guess I can ask to borrow it for this trip."

"You can drive my car," he said.

"Your car?" she repeated, her expression pensive. "You'd trust me to drive that fancy sports car?"

"Is there some reason why I shouldn't? Can you drive stick?"

"Of course."

"All right then. I don't see a problem."

Nora worried her bottom lip, taking a long moment to mull over his offer and then reluctantly agreed.

Her hesitation surprised him. So Nora Simmons *wasn't* fearless. He understood her apprehension. There was something heady about slipping behind the wheel of a seventy-five-thousand-dollar vehicle. He didn't have long to savor the moment, though, as her demeanor changed as she gestured toward him.

"Okay, so that's settled, but what are we going to do about your pants? Your old ones are ripped and ruined, and as far as I know you don't have a spare pair in the closet. I'm sure as hell not driving you into the city wearing just your underwear."

"I have a pair of sweats in the trunk of the car." He picked up the keys from the nightstand and tossed them to her. She caught them neatly and he further instructed, "Just bring the entire gym bag. I keep spare toiletries in there, as well."

"Of course you do," she muttered. "Late-night gym visits? Or rather early-morning emergency supplies for that *all-nighter?*"

"A little of both," he admitted with a discomfited chuckle before she spun on her heel and left him. The odd spurt of jealousy flashing in her gray eyes made his groin tighten. There wasn't a word in the English dictionary to describe that woman, but his body didn't care. Those were matters of the brain; his body reacted to something else entirely.

The next six weeks could be hell—or one wild ride.

CHAPTER EIGHT

SAMMY POUNDED BACK another beer, trying to tune out the sound of Dana's laughter. She was having a good time with her ambulance buddies in the corner of the bar, and he'd been miserable since she left him.

What was wrong with him? He'd only known her a handful of months since she'd come to town but she was unlike any woman with whom he'd ever shared a bed. Just thinking about those golden moments made his guts twist and roll at the knowledge he'd screwed it all up with one idiotic move.

What was so special about her? he thought bitterly, hating this new development in his brain, wishing and waiting for the familiar feeling of ambivalence to return when a relationship came to an end. He was Sammy Halvorsen, an infamous player in the love game. His dad used to joke Sammy could charm the good sense out of any woman faster than a few cocktails. The ladies didn't seem to mind. He was upfront and honest with them and everyone had a good time.

Until now.

He stole a glance her way, his heart aching for what he couldn't have. She wasn't what usually turned his head. Too tall, too skinny and brunette. Did he mention smart? Yeah, she was that, too. Too smart to put up with his crap, apparently.

The bar was loud, but he could still pick out the sound of her voice from the crowded table. Her laugh was full of the confidence she exuded from every pore, and while at first glance she wasn't the kind of girl who turned heads, one look from her sultry brown eyes and Sammy's head had nearly swiveled off his shoulders.

He tipped his beer in a sullen motion, finishing it in one loud swallow, and decided he didn't want to listen anymore, didn't want to drink himself into a stupor to numb the pain, and damn well didn't want to pretend he was the same as he ever was.

Slanting a look her way, willing her to see him yet trying to be invisible, his blood heated when he saw one of the guys at her table sling an arm casually around the back of her chair. Sammy swallowed a snarl and forced himself to look away.

As much as he wanted to act the same as always, he'd changed and he blamed her. He hated the foreign feelings crowding his thoughts and making him surly and hard to be around. Even his older brother, Dean, a man not known for his verbosity had a few choice words for him the other day when Sammy had snapped at another worker on the job site. All he could think of was her and how cold his bed seemed without her—and by the looks of it, she could really care less.

Screw this.

He rose from the stool on stiff legs and headed for the door.

NORA HELD OPEN the apartment door for Ben so that he could maneuver his crutches through, and then followed him inside the tidy residence.

"Make yourself comfortable," he said, moving slowly into what she assumed was his bedroom. "I'll just be a minute."

"Make it a Manhattan minute," she grumbled, not quite sure why she'd agreed to this little excursion. It was bad enough she was his makeshift nurse, now she was his chauffeur? Nora harrumphed, and let her gaze wander the living room, taking immediate note of how bare and spartan the place looked. Every countertop shone as if it'd been buffed and waxed and the brushed stainless-steel refrigerator matched the fixtures. Perfectly contrasting throw pillows in no-nonsense materials sat at attention on the luxurious soft black microfiber sofa as if they were glued to the surface, and the floor was immaculate. Not a speck of dust, an errant lint ball, not even a dead plant leaf anywhere in sight.

"Your maid may not speak English, but she keeps your house like a mortuary," she observed out loud, then clarified silently that it was more like a museum. A museum dedicated to the barren corporate existence of a man who never actually lived.

She glanced at the smooth, clutter-free surfaces in the living room and frowned. Not a single photo to liven up the place.

"Are you sure you live here?" she asked.

"What?" he hollered from the back.

"Nothing. What are you doing back there?"

"Packing a few essentials. Take a load off. Have a seat."

Where? Nothing looked as if it was made for sitting. The place looked more like a designer showroom than an area where you could pop a squat and relax. Just being there made her shoulders tense. For a moment she tried hard to imagine Ben kicking back on a Sunday morning, newspaper in hand, hair all rumpled, in anything less somber than a three-piece suit, but her imagination went a little overboard and stripped him down to boxers, a silk robe and a wicked, sexy-as-hell, come-hither grin before she put an immediate stop to her mental wandering with an annoyed growl. Who she was growling at—her or him—she couldn't be sure. All she knew was that seeing him trying to shield himself from her view with a worn piece of fabric that looked more like a hand towel had whipped her brain into a frenzy of inappropriate and irritating mental imagery. Spending an entire car ride in such proximity had only made things worse.

Thirsty, Nora stalked to the fridge and peered inside, shocked to see it full of food. She half expected it to be devoid of anything more substantial than a box of baking soda, much like the apartment itself. An image of Ben in the kitchen, cooking gourmet meals—judging by the ingredients stocked—popped into her head and she batted her hand as if that alone could dislodge the direction of her thoughts. Things had been a lot less complicated a week ago. Hell, one morning ago, she amended before eyeing a Corona and grabbing it.

She opened it and looked for a trash can but couldn't

find one. Ben hobbled into the room and found her searching. He pointed to a small machine built into the counter. Ah, of course—trash compactor. She pulled out the tray and dropped the top inside.

"Got some fancy stuff here," she commented as he moved past her into the living room to sit down. "Did you buy out the IKEA catalog when you furnished your apartment?"

"I like clean lines and uncluttered space," he said by way of explanation. "I find it hard to concentrate when things are a mess."

He'd probably lose his mind at her place. Not that she'd ever invite him. "Do you consider pictures clutter?" she asked.

"No, I just never got around to hanging some. Unlike you, I'm an only child. A bunch of pictures of me on the walls seemed a little odd."

The barest hint of a smile edged his mouth and she reacted with one of her own. "So you do have a sense of humor buried under that three-piece-suit demeanor of yours. I was beginning to worry."

"You? Worry about me? I wouldn't hear of it."

"Have you always been such a smart-ass or is this something you save just for me?"

His grin widened into something bordering on playful and Nora was struck by how it changed his face from aloof to warm and engaging. He should do that more often. *No, he shouldn't,* a part of her snapped. More smiles like that could land her in a bad position— like horizontal. "What about your parents?" she blurted, panicked by the feelings erupting in her body and the possibilities that abounded in her unbridled imagination.

All signs of jocularity left his expression. "They're divorced. I rarely see either. We have our own lives and we don't cross the same paths."

Ouch. There was a sore spot. "Why?" she asked, deciding to poke at it a bit to see what oozed out. "What's up with your parents?"

"Nothing."

"Don't want to talk about it, huh?"

"How very astute of you," he said dryly. "And here I thought country folk tended to be a little slow."

"Watch it, city boy, or you'll be hobbling back to Emmett's Mill," she warned, but there was no rancor in it. She was enjoying herself. "Seriously, what happened in your family that was so bad that you don't like to talk about it?"

"You don't give up, do you?" He arched one dark slash of brow at her in a weary fashion.

Nora smiled. "You don't know the half of it. Please continue. I'm all ears." She settled into the uncomfortable sofa as best she could and tipped her beer, waiting to see if he'd budge. She didn't really expect him to, but he couldn't fault a girl for trying.

"Nothing out of the ordinary, Nora," he answered, surprising her. "We don't have holiday dinners and get-togethers unless we can't avoid it and when we can't, there's copious amounts of single-malt scotch to get us through the rough patches." He quirked a wry but entirely sad grin at her. "Does that sound like something you'd want to commemorate with pictures and video?

Well, I for one, didn't think so. I learned at a very young age that the only person you can depend upon is yourself. And thus far, the principle has served me well."

Nora lost the grip on her cavalier attitude. She knew at times she took her family for granted, which was something she realized when her mother died. But even at her worst—and she could claim some doozies—Nora had always known her family would be there for her. Learning that Ben didn't have that same assurance made something in her chest ache. She rubbed absently at her chest as if she could reach the undefined pain under her skin and massage it out, but it remained. "Where's that leave you now when you need to depend upon a virtual stranger?"

Ben answered honestly. "Uncomfortable."

"I'll bet," she said softly and swigged her beer, her thoughts in a jumbled mess. She wanted to press, to delve deeper into the private cave of his life, but something held her back. Maybe it was the silence that hung between them, filled with questions he didn't want to answer and she was dying to know; maybe it was the latent sense that if he didn't want to share, she shouldn't push. Nora couldn't say. All she knew was that she understood his feelings and felt bad that she'd put him in this situation.

Not just me! His shoes—

She closed her eyes against the sound of her own defensive voice and effectively silenced it. Her mom used to say Nora was the worst for taking responsibility for her actions. Well, Nora decided, not today.

"You got what you need?" she asked, rising to throw

away the bottle. As she entered the kitchen, an idea came to her. "You have a paper bag or two?"

"Bottom drawer, left of the stove. Why?"

She opened the fridge. "It's a waste to leave all this food when you're not going to be here. Besides, it'll save me a trip to the grocery store."

"Right," he said, struggling to rise, the exertion giving his skin a rosy tint that complemented his tan. "Let me help you with that."

She waved him away. "I got it. Besides, not to be rude or anything, but you can't really carry much when your hands are handling crutches. Why don't you make sure you have everything you need and I'll load that ridiculously small space you call a trunk."

"It's a sports car, not a minivan. It's not made for hauling stuff," he said defensively as she headed past him with a loaded brown bag. "And try not to let anything spill back there."

"I'll give it my utmost attention," she said with a fake smile. With any luck the milk would topple and soak the damn thing.

CHAPTER NINE

THE FOLLOWING DAY Nora took the steps to her father's home two at a time and went inside.

"Dad, I got something for you," she hollered, heading for the kitchen. "Ice-cold beer." She smiled as he appeared from his hobby room and checked down the hallway to make sure his other daughter wasn't around. "Coast is clear, Dad. Come and get some liquid refreshment."

Gerald accepted the beer from Nora and she put the rest of the six-pack into the fridge. She jerked her thumb. "Tell Nat if she throws these out, she's going to have to answer to me, 'cause they're mine. I don't know what she's thinking lately but it's annoying. I'm about ready to whack her over the head with a stick."

Gerald chuckled despite the promise of violence in Nora's comment and gestured they sit out on the porch where the sun was warm but not overly so.

Outside, Nora hopped onto the railing and settled against the support post while her father eased into the old swing. After a long, satisfying swallow of beer, he sighed and said, "Your sister means well. You shouldn't be so hard on her. She's got a full plate with those babies and now me. A daughter shouldn't have to shoulder so much."

Nora waved away his concern. "Nah, Nat is in her element. She wouldn't know what to do with herself if she wasn't mothering everyone. I just wish she'd lighten up a bit. I mean, what's the deal with her deciding what you can and can't eat or drink? She's your daughter, not your warden," she continued, affronted by the very idea. "It's not like you're an alcoholic or something."

Gerald sighed and took a slow slug. "Yeah, well, with your mom gone she's probably just trying to fill in the gaps. Missy used to get after me for having a beer or two. She'd complain and I'd bluster." He shrugged, a momentary sadness creeping into the warm air. "It was our thing, I guess."

"I never saw Mom argue with you," Nora countered with a soft snort. "When did this happen? Behind closed doors?"

Gerald slanted his gaze at her. "Maybe you didn't pay close enough attention to what was going on around you. Your mom got her point across without having to make a scene. It's a talent you didn't seem to inherit," he added.

"Hey! Who brought you beer?" she retorted, only slightly offended at his comment because it was true. He lifted his bottle in acknowledgment and her chuckle ended with a difficult realization. "I think I might've missed out on a lot with Mom. I spent way too much time fighting with her. There's a lot of things I never got to tell her."

"She knows."

"How do you know? You got a landline to heaven or something?" she joked. She then sighed and added, "If so, put her on speakerphone, I've got a few questions of my own."

He smiled. "I pity the man who decides to marry you. All piss and vinegar with only a sprinkle of sugar to make it all go down."

"Yeah, a spitting image of *you,* from what I hear," Nora said wryly. It felt good to banter; it'd been a long time since she'd felt the urge to do so. The easy silence between them allowed her mind to wander, and her thoughts went to Ben and his unusual circumstances. "Dad…" she began, feeling the need for a little parental advice but not entirely sure she wanted to hear it. "There was an accident and my client, Ben, got hurt. He's paying me to help him out, in addition to the landscaping job. We don't really get along that well but there's something about him that—" she shrugged in confusion "—I don't know, is interesting. There's something intriguing about him, I guess."

"You like him?"

She reacted with an immediate scoff. "Dad, I just said we don't get along. He's arrogant, snobby and completely at a loss without his Starbucks and art house theaters. He's the complete opposite of me. And he's irritating."

"So why are you helping him out?"

"Because it seemed like the right thing to do. He's all alone, his family is scattered and I guess I felt bad for him for a split second. Unfortunately my mouth reacted before my brain could stop it and I volunteered.

And Doc Hessle didn't help either. He practically guilted me into taking the job. When's that man going to retire, for crying out loud?"

"You could've asked Rhonda's daughter, Kelly, to look after him for a while," he suggested, to which Nora scowled.

Kelly Crawston? A leggy redhead with fake boobs and an equally fake tan who was on the prowl for husband No. 2? "I said I don't like him, but I don't want to make his life miserable, Dad."

"Fair enough. But I'm sure there's plenty of people you could've rustled up to help the guy out."

"Well, I already offered, so it would be rude to back out now," she said. Plus, she hated the idea of some woman no doubt fawning over Ben once she caught a glimpse of those tightly muscled abs and devastating green eyes. If he managed to affect her in such a disturbing manner, what defenses could a single woman in Emmett's Mill possibly mount against the man? Given a chance, he could ruin every eligible female from here to Coldwater. In a way, Nora was sacrificing herself to protect the masses. Oh, whatever! *Sell that to someone who's buying.* Nora shut out the voice and realized her father was watching her speculatively.

"What?"

"Did I ever tell you how I met your mother?"

"No. Why?"

He swirled the remainder of his beer. "Let me tell you a story. I think you'll find it a good one."

"Dad, I don't want to hear how crazy you were over Mom. I already know that," she said plaintively, the idea of her parents being young and in love was nice, but learning any further details didn't appeal. She liked to think her parents had sex three times and that was the extent of it.

"Shut up and listen for once in your life," he growled, and she sighed, resigning herself to the story. "It was the summer of '66 and it was a hot, blistering son of a bitch. The grass was dry as tinder and the winds had finished off the low-lying shrubbery and trees. All it took to start a raging wildfire was one idiot tossing his lit cigarette out his car window and everything was ablaze for miles. At one point even Emmett's Mill was on the verge of evacuation.

"Well, I was on the CDF crew, working the summer like I'd been doing since I graduated from high school and was put on sandwich detail."

"Sandwich detail?" Nora arched her brow. Her big, brawny dad pulling the lunch wagon? "Who'd you piss off?"

"Doesn't much matter at this point," he countered with a mild glare, shifting his weight in the swing. "Suffice it to say it was me who went into Darlin's for the pickup."

"Darlin's?"

"Little sandwich shop that used to be where the gym is now. Owned by Darlin Amensted before it changed a few hands and then finally closed down completely in the mid-1970s. Great place. Anyway, your mother happened to be working there for the summer and the minute I walked through that swinging door I—"

"Fell in love," Nora supplied in a half-bored voice.

"No, I thought she was the snippiest, snootiest, sassiest-mouthed thing I'd ever encountered."

Nora did a double take. "What?"

"See? You don't know so much after all. Now stop interrupting."

Chastised and more than a little surprised, she did exactly that. Mollified, Gerald began again, only as he spoke, his smile grew and Nora could feel the love he still felt as he told a story of two people who couldn't seem to stand each other at first blush.

"She had a temper to match my own, only hers was more dangerous because it was silent. Of course, I thought I was hot shit on a cold stick and was more than happy to show her who was boss, until I bit into my sandwich—how she knew it was mine, I'll never figure out—and instead of egg salad there were two thick slabs of pimento loaf and tons of mustard smeared all over it." He shuddered at the memory. "She got me good. I hate mustard, and pimento loaf ain't fit for criminals."

"You probably deserved it," Nora said, smiling at the picture in her head. "But I can't believe Mom did something like that. In my whole life I never heard her raise her voice to you. It used to drive me crazy."

"You don't know what she had to say in private. That woman could scald the insides of a person's ear without ever having to shout. She was quite a woman." He seemed lost in his reverie for a moment until his eyes cleared and he was back on track. "The point is, love hits us square in the forehead when we're not looking. Maybe you ought to give this Ben guy a second glance. Who knows? Maybe he's the only guy who can put up with your sass. God knows Missy knew how to handle my bluster."

Nora suppressed a shiver and sent her father a wry look. "Dad…I loved your story, but that's not how things are between me and Ben. It's my fault he's hurt. I hardly think that will make him want to marry me. Ugh. The very thought is disturbing."

Gerald chuckled. "Nora Marie, take it from someone who knows—you can run but you can't hide. If this man's under your skin, he's there for a reason. I guarantee it."

A FEW HOURS LATER Nora pulled into the driveway at Ben's and was puzzled to see another beat-up truck full of squawking, caged chickens and smelling like cow manure parked outside.

She grabbed the bag of supplies she'd bought at the hardware store and headed inside.

"Yes, I'm B.J.'s grandson but I'm only here temporarily, Mr.—"

"Buster's the name."

"Mr. Buster—"

"No, just Buster. I ain't one to stand on ceremony."

She set the bag in the kitchen and then moved toward the voices.

"Listen here, son. B.J. was a good man even though he was a lawyer. He and I worked out a deal for some work he did for my family and since he's not here I aim to fulfill my debt with you."

Ben saw Nora standing in the doorway and the look in his eyes begged for help.

The man identified as Buster turned and tipped his worn and dirty hat to Nora and then returned to Ben. "We's good folk and we honor our debt. So you and the missus here is gonna get fresh eggs delivered once a week and that's just how it is. Got a few chickens to spare, too. But seeing as you're just getting settled, we'll bring those later." He headed for the door and stopped short. "I was right sorry to hear of your grandparents passing the way they did. God must've needed himself two more angels up there but it's a right shame for us down here."

Ben struggled out of the faded armchair, trying to hop after the man but Buster was already outside. Nora pointed to the chair and indicated he put his butt back in it and went to the front door herself just in time to receive a pretty basket with a red gingham napkin folded over what she assumed were fresh eggs.

Buster gestured to the gingham. "That's the missus's idea. She likes to pretty things up. I'll be back next week same time, if it's all the same to you."

"Thanks, Buster. The eggs are great," she said, suppressing a giggle at the circumstances. "See you next week."

Buster waved and climbed into his truck, and once it rumbled down the driveway, she walked inside and returned to the living room where Ben sat with a confounded expression.

She set the basket on the end table and said, "Just so we're clear, I prefer cash—not eggs—as payment for services rendered."

"That makes two of us," he returned, raking a hand

through his hair and leaving it ruffled and tantalizingly mussed.

Why'd he have to do that? Her good mood vanished, replaced with a need for something she couldn't put her finger on but needed badly enough to notice. She grabbed the eggs. "I'll put these in the fridge," she said, exhaling loudly. She wanted to regroup. She returned a few moments later with an interesting thought.

"You know, your grandfather used to work out of his home. I suspect you might have more people showing up on your doorstep once they find out you're here."

He looked horrified. "Why do you say that?"

She shrugged. "Just a guess, but judging by Buster's surprise visit I'd say if B.J. worked deals with anyone else, you might find yourself up to your elbows in bartered goods."

"You're not kidding, are you." His flat statement was rhetorical. "You've got to put a stop to this right now."

"Me?" Not on your life. "This is your problem. Not mine. You fix it."

"You know these people. You can finesse it."

She shot him a sardonic look. "I'm sorry. Have you met me? I don't finesse anything. Besides, just because I live here doesn't mean I know *everyone*. You're the lawyer. Talk your way out of it."

"You know, I'm getting tired of your insults. Can you say something without being rude or slanderous?"

She gave a show of thinking about it, then lifted her hands. "Nope. Seems not. And you're still in the same situation you were ten minutes ago. Fix it yourself, city boy."

"Fine, I will." He glared.

"Good." She grabbed the cordless phone and tossed it to him. "I've got a small backhoe coming in to tear up the old lawn and if there's an emergency you can call my cell."

"Wait a minute," he called out, causing her to pause and wait impatiently. "Did you leave me anything to eat? I'm paying you to take care of those types of details."

"Right." She pulled a candy bar from her back pocket and pitched it to him with a smarmy grin. "My favorite— Snickers. Enjoy."

BEN CAUGHT the candy bar and as his hand curled around it, he was tempted to hit Nora upside the head with it. He must've been out of his mind when he asked her to help him out. He'd liked to say it had sounded like a good idea at the time but that was a lie. He'd known it smacked of disaster. Well, he was paying for it now.

He ripped open the candy bar and devoured it in two bites. The chocolate hit a good spot and it tasted better than he'd anticipated. Perhaps it was the sugar high or the odd events of the morning that had thrown him off kilter, but he grabbed his crutches and hobbled his way carefully to the study area where his grandfather had apparently held court with the motley group he called clients.

His responsible nature demanded he focus on the Wallace case, but his curiosity effectively silenced that demand as he settled into the soft leather chair at the desk that seemed the only indulgence on his grandfather's part and started going through the piles of paperwork.

What he found created a bigger puzzle in his mind.

It was no wonder his grandparents were practically destitute when they died. Most of his grandfather's clients paid exactly in the manner Ben feared—the barter system.

Chickens. Heirloom tomato seeds. A purebred hound dog?

How'd they survive? And if the community was as poor as this—that the only way they could pay their bills was to bring odd items for trade—why did his grandparents stay?

Leaning back in the chair, he listened as it groaned softly with his weight and thought of the reasons his father had refused to let Ben visit his grandparents again the following summer.

His father had been reading the *Wall Street Journal* and had barely looked up when Ben had made his request. The answer had been a simple no.

"Why not?" he'd retorted, his young voice cracking with adolescent angst and hormonal change. "You let me go last year."

"That was your mother's idea."

"And?"

The paper dipped slightly to reveal his father's hard gaze. "And if it'd been up to me, you wouldn't have spent a moment with those people."

"They were nice," he said under his breath, but his father caught it.

"Nice?" he sneered. "What do you know about anything? You're just a kid. *Nice* people don't screw you out of your inheritance and claim it's for your own good."

"What inheritance?"

"What does it matter? It's gone. Given away to some nonprofit hospice for sick kids, but that was my money."

"How do you know it was yours?" Ben asked. "Maybe they didn't remember that they were going to give it to you."

"They knew. But since I'd already made my own fortune before that particular account matured, they said those sick kids needed it more. I had plans for that money and they didn't have the right. Stupid old geezers," his father muttered and returned to his paper.

Ben had sat stunned, unsure of what to say. He didn't like to hear his father talk of his parents like that and neither did he like seeing his father act so uncharitably toward those less fortunate. But his father was a hard and bitter man, and Ben had learned long ago not to try to change him. Dropping the subject, he never asked to visit his grandparents again.

Looking back, he realized he might've gone to his mother for answers, but Penny had been too busy securing her future with someone else to notice and even if she hadn't been distracted, she wasn't about to upset the gravy train with her ex-husband. Ben's father could be tightfisted when it pleased him and Penny had expensive tastes.

And, in all honesty, Ben had eventually lost interest in finding out the intricate details of what happened or even going to see the grandparents he'd known one summer. He sighed and let the paperwork drop to the desk and wondered what was going to show up on his doorstep next.

CHAPTER TEN

SAMMY DROPPED down from the mini backhoe and accepted the bottled water from Nora, leaving a smear of mud where he wiped a bead of sweat from his dirt-speckled forehead.

"For April, it's damn hot out here," Sammy said after downing nearly half the bottle. "Well, you've been waiting to get your hands on this place for years. What are you going to do with it?"

"It's going to look gorgeous when I'm finished," Nora said with a huge grin. "I'm going to plant a few cedars over there as wind breakers and fresh grass all through here. A bower of English ivy creeping along an arched doorway to the herb garden—"

"Herb garden? Who'd you say your client was?" Sammy interrupted incredulously.

She scowled. "Stop being such a Neanderthal, Sammy. They're aromatic for one and useful for another. Remember when I used to make you that drink that soothed your stomach after a wild night of drinking? It was made from herbs, and I didn't hear you complaining. It was more like, 'Ooh, Nora, please make me some of that stuff, please!' That's how I remember it."

Sammy's ears reddened, but he didn't deny it. "Yeah well, that's you. You're a woman. I don't know of any *man* who grows a herb garden, so there."

"You should broaden your circle of acquaintances to include more than just beer buddies and bobble-headed bleached blondes with the IQ of a dish towel."

"Who pissed in your cornflakes today?" Sammy asked, only slightly ruffled by her comment. "You're not your usual sunny self."

A grin pulled at the corners of her mouth. She was never what anyone could call *sunny*. She shrugged, but her eyes strayed to the house and her thoughts went straight to Ben. She wasn't ready to share what was happening on that score—mostly because she didn't have a clue—and focused on something else. "So who's this Dana chick?"

Sammy faltered. "Dana..."

"Yeah, tall brunette paramedic who likes to pick fights with total strangers and make them feel like they've done something wrong when whatever happened was *clearly* an accident. Ring any bells?"

"Uh, she's new to town. Only been here about a year..."

"Yeah, I already got that much information. I'm interested in the part where my best friend was dating her and failed to mention this small detail."

Sammy looked away and hooked his thumbs on his jean pockets. "Aw, c'mon, Nora. Contrary to what you believe, I don't tell you everything in my personal life. Yeah, we were dating. And now we're not. Simple as that. Why? Where'd you see Dana?" he asked, staring keenly enough to destroy the nonchalance he was trying to project.

"She responded to Ben's accident."

"Ben? That's your client, right?"

"Yeah. He's inside. Fell down the ridge and nearly landed in the creek. He's pretty busted up. Anyway, she came and started acting like I pushed him or something."

"Did you?"

She shot him a dark look. "No."

"Just asking. You do have a temper. Need I remind you how I got this?" He pulled up his pant leg and revealed a faint scar that ran down his right shin.

"Someday you're going to need to find new material. I no longer feel guilty about that," she lied with great aplomb. "Besides, I told you not to jump. You're the one who had something to prove."

"You goaded me into jumping. I'm lucky to have limped away with a gash instead of a concussion."

She chewed the side of her cheek. Honestly, they had been fifteen and sixteen. A woman shouldn't have to pay for her mistakes her entire life. "It's not my fault you didn't clear the rock, and I hereby declare that incident inadmissible in future arguments."

"How so?"

"Ever hear of double jeopardy?" she asked.

He nodded warily, not quite sure where she was going with this. "Yeah, what of it?"

"I was punished pretty good for that little escapade down at the river. I'll have you know I spent the rest of my summer cleaning toilets up at my dad's CDF station, and let me tell you that was punishment enough."

Sammy burst into laughter. "You're right—you've paid your due. I promise not to use that one anymore. I've got plenty of others."

Of that she didn't doubt. As often as Sammy had been her partner in crime, he'd also been her guinea pig on numerous adventures. It was a miracle they were both still alive.

They sobered and Sammy started clearing his gear. "I'll be back tomorrow around 9:00 a.m. to start tearing up the side yard. I've got something to do or else I'd finish it now."

"Yeah? Hot date?"

He grinned but it was pained around the edges. "Not really. Just need to clear something up."

"Does this have anything to do with that paramedic?"

"She has a name."

"Touchy. All right, does this have anything to do with *Dana?*"

"Maybe."

Nora eyed Sammy. This tight-lipped routine wasn't like him. She accepted the empty water bottle, but she wasn't finished with the conversation. She didn't like being on the outside—yet another reason she didn't care for this interloper. She wanted her Sammy back. "You want to go get a beer after your thing?"

"Uh, aren't you busy with Ben?"

Yes. Damn. She shrugged. "He's not paying me to be his beck-and-call girl. I'll leave him with a bowl of water and some kibble."

Sammy grinned knowingly as he climbed into his truck. "Knowing you and your cooking skills, it most likely will be kibble. I pity the poor guy. He doesn't know what he's taken on."

That was true in more ways than one. Nora would rather spend an evening listening to Sammy whine about his lost love than spend an evening alone with Ben. He made her feel uneasy. Not to mention ravenous for his naked flesh. She patted the beads of sweat from her forehead and chased after Sammy. "You sure? Hanging out with that guy makes me crazy. I can only take his attitude for so long. C'mon…me, you, a couple of rounds at Gilly's? First round's on me."

He waved her away and gunned the engine. "Rain check. I gotta take care of this and I don't know how long it'll take. See you tomorrow."

Fine. "Traitor," she mumbled, and turned on her heel and faced the house. Ben was inside, working like a busy, overworked robot bee—probably oblivious to the effect he had on her—and she was standing outside like a ninny when she ought to just tell him he'll have to find someone else to be his nurse. She trudged inside and put on a stoic—completely unaffected—face for an audience of one.

BEN WAS STILL SITTING in his grandfather's office, knee-deep in paperwork when Nora came in at the end of the day.

"Ben?"

"In the study," he called out.

She appeared in the doorway. "What are you doing?"

she asked, sounding a little alarmed at the piles of paperwork he'd spent all day separating into some semblance of order. "Isn't it illegal to go through someone's things?"

"Not when the owner is dead and the person who's going through those things inherited the estate. Have a seat. I have some questions you might be able to answer."

"Yes, Counselor?" she said, sinking into a nearby chair with an amused expression. "What can I do for you?"

"Thanks to our egg-paying friend Buster and your earlier comment, I got to thinking I better find out exactly how many clients bartered for service. Honestly, I thought it would be easy, seeing as the town's not so big, and well, how many eggs could one man possibly need?" He sighed. "But it goes beyond eggs."

"Beyond eggs? Like bartered milk? Or completely out of the dairy family?"

"I'm serious."

"Did everyone lose their sense of humor today?" she mumbled, but gave him her full attention. "What are you saying?"

"B.J. and Corrinda bartered for eighty percent of their income. From homemade casseroles to bushels of fresh apples. In this day and age, I just can't wrap my brain around the fact that they managed to turn back time and live as frugally as possible with very little money."

"That would explain why the house started to look so ramshackle."

"Yeah, apparently B.J. hadn't done any work for a carpenter or gardener before they died," he said with a healthy dose of sarcasm.

"Hey, watch it. I liked them—a lot—remember? And I for one think it's kinda cool. Very old world."

"It's not cool," he retorted, astounded at her opinion. "It's…it's ridiculous. And do these people expect me to reciprocate because my addled grandfather chose to?"

"Maybe until they meet you. One face-to-face meeting with you will probably clear up any misconceptions they might have."

"Yeah, well, I didn't have much luck in dissuading Buster, now, did I?" He pushed a hand through his hair. "What kind of hillbilly hell has my crazy old coot of a grandfather gotten me into?"

"I said watch it," she murmured low in her throat. "He wasn't addled or crazy. He was kind and generous and clearly cared about his clients. He believed everyone should have legal representation, no matter their financial situation."

"Yeah, so does the Constitution, which provides legal counsel for those who can't afford their own."

"It provides for people charged with a *crime*. It doesn't say anything about a seventy-year-old rancher facing off with the state when they threatened to withdraw the Williamson Act contract on his land, which would have tripled his property taxes and basically forced him to declare bankruptcy and move."

He stared at her sudden vehemence. "You're saying my grandfather helped someone like that?"

"Yes, that's what I'm saying," she snapped.

"Then where's the documentation?" he demanded, shaking a sheaf of paperwork. "Everything else is here. Hell, here's a paper for the barter of a purebred hound dog, which as far as I can tell, didn't come with the house. I don't care to inherit a flea-bitten mutt as well as all this junk."

Nora shot to her feet, her eyes flashing. "His name is George Brummel. He owns hundreds of acres off Highway 140. The property's been in his family for generations, and the Williamson Act contract enabled them to keep the land as long as it was designated agricultural or kept as open space. The Brummel family was once a proud, flourishing group of people who helped build Emmett's Mill. In fact, Hop Brummel— George's great-great-grandfather—has his name scratched into the mortar of one of the oldest buildings in town, built in the 1800s. George came to B.J. for help, and B.J. saved the Brummel legacy. I don't see anything *ridiculous* about that." She was almost out the door when she reconsidered and left one final comment. "As for the dog, his name was Howie the Howler, and you don't have to worry about him because he died of heartworm complications a few months before B.J. and Corrinda. And they were devastated, you prick!"

A door slammed and rattled every window in the house and Ben knew Nora was gone. Grimacing, he grabbed his crutches and hobbled from the room, an unsettled feeling in his gut to match the echo of Nora's parting comment. He *was* a prick and he wished to God he didn't come by it so naturally, but it flowed through his veins as surely as his own blood.

Perhaps it was better this way. At least Nora wouldn't mistake him for anything else.

CHAPTER ELEVEN

NORA RETURNED the following day and waved to the crew she'd hired to start preparing the ground for planting, before reluctantly heading inside. She shouldn't have left the way she did but Ben managed to push every button she had and her temper flared before she had a chance to launch a defense. Her mom had been fond of telling her to act like an adult, so in deference to that advice, Nora came with a peace offering of sorts.

"Ben?" she called out, knowing better this time than to barge into his bedroom for fear of sending her hormones into overdrive again. She hollered again. "Are you decent? I have something for you."

There was swearing coupled with a loud bang in the kitchen and Nora jumped before rushing to investigate.

"What are you doing? Remodeling the kitchen?" she asked, rounding the corner to find Ben standing over a skillet with what looked like some type of omelet on the tile floor. She clapped a hand over her mouth to keep from giggling at Ben's frustrated expression at the demise of what she assumed was going to be a delicious breakfast. "What was it?"

"Denver omelet," Ben said from between pressed

lips. "It's very hard to balance on crutches and carry a hot skillet."

Nora grabbed a few paper towels and began mopping up the mess. "Don't you think that was a little ambitious for a man in your condition?" she asked, dumping the soiled towels in the wastebasket and surveying the remains of red and green peppers, onion and fresh chives on the cutting board.

"Yes, but I wanted to do something to make amends for my behavior yesterday," he said, looking more miserable by the moment. "You were right. I was being a prick. I figured the one thing I could do was make you a nice breakfast but it seems I can't even do that right now."

"Well, good thing Buster is bringing more eggs next week. Looks like most of them are on the floor," she said, biting back a smile. It was incredibly sweet. She'd have to be made of stone not to appreciate the effort. Why he cared what she thought was baffling but it gave her a dark thrill just the same. "It's funny, because I brought you something for breakfast, although it's nothing like you were trying to whip up." She opened the small grocery bag and pulled out two muffins the size of a plate and two short coffees.

"We don't have a Starbucks, but we do have a coffee joint that's pretty close. You don't seem the type to drink fancy sugared drinks so I went with black. Is that all right?"

His face lost some of its frustration and a smile smoothed out the tension in his lips. "Perfect," he said, accepting both the coffee and a muffin.

"Seems we're both sorry for yesterday," Nora began as she peeled the wrapper from her muffin. "It's no excuse but it bothers me when you talk like that about your grandparents. I wish you could've known them better. They were good people."

"Nora, I'm not doubting they were good people…but you have to admit, my grandfather went a little over-board with the bartering. I mean, look at the house. It was practically falling down around their ears. I think that's irresponsible."

"Maybe they were trying to create a world that was more equal than the one we live in."

"There's no such thing as a utopia. Everyone has needs and my grandparents needed cold hard cash."

Nora set her muffin down. "I can see that. Why didn't your parents kick down some or, for that matter, why not you? Judging by that car, you have some to spare."

He fell silent, uncomfortable with the turn in the conversation. She didn't blame him. One wrong word and they'd end up fighting again. He drew a deep breath before continuing. "I didn't know they needed money," he said carefully. "If I'd known…well, I'd have helped as much as I could, though I should level with you, the car's not mine."

"Whose is it?"

"My dad's."

She stared but her mouth trembled with the effort not to burst out laughing. "You're telling me, at thirty-four years old you're still driving around in daddy's car?"

He scowled. "For practical reasons. I can afford to buy my own, but he rarely drives the vehicle and I don't see the logic in just letting it sit in a garage. Besides, my dad rarely visits the West Coast, so it's practically mine."

"I see." *Spoken like a true spoiled brat.* She shook her head and popped a piece of muffin in her mouth. "So what's the deal with your parents, then? Why didn't they offer to help your grandparents?"

"It seems they had a falling-out before I was born and it was never resolved," Ben said, shifting on his crutches. "And before you ask, no, I don't know exactly what happened between them, but it had something to do with money and an inheritance my father believed belonged to him."

"If that's the case, that would explain why your grandfather eschewed money for trade. Money was responsible for ruining his family."

Ben appeared thoughtful. "Yes, I suppose that's one way of looking at it."

"Do you have another theory?" Nora asked.

"Nora, I can't possibly offer any kind of educated guess or theory without all the facts. I'd have to ask my father for his view of the situation to get an idea and without my grandfather's version, it would only be one-sided."

"Still, it'd be something. I don't understand how you can live your life in complete ignorance of something so big in your family."

"There's the difference between you and me. It doesn't affect my life, so therefore I don't care to know."

Nora snorted softly. "How do you know it doesn't affect your life? Ben...if things had been different in your life, don't you think you might have sustained a relationship with your grandparents? That maybe you might have known them for more than one summer?"

Ben's demeanor changed. A long pause punctuated their conversation until he drew himself up and forced a tight smile. "Nora, it doesn't matter what I think, it won't change what happened. I grew up without them. That's how it goes. Thanks for the muffin and coffee. If you don't mind, I'm going to drag myself into the shower."

So much for making amends, Nora thought grimly.

LATER THAT DAY, head throbbing and stomach queasy from the pain medication, Ben decided to take a break from the Wallace case and found himself watching Nora from the study window.

The day couldn't have been more glorious; the blue sky gave no hint of the storm that was supposed to be coming tonight, and Nora was completely in her element—which appeared to be knee deep in dirt. Although she'd hired a small crew to tear apart the yard, she didn't slough off the tough jobs. Earlier, when his focus had wandered and fastened on Nora she was man-handling a rototiller with the ease of a seasoned laborer. Her small frame was muscled and when she'd stood to stretch her back, Ben had caught a glimpse of her near-perfect belly as her shirt had risen, teasing him with a landscape he'd never travel.

A grudging smile tugged at his lips, safe in the knowledge no one was apt to catch the unguarded moment. His gaze went to the strong line of her calf, bare to the sun thanks to an old pair of cut-off jeans that were nearly indecent the way they hugged her behind and set his imagination on fire. She was like Daisy Duke, Princess Leia and every other boyhood fantasy all wrapped up in one sassy package that was so out of his reach he'd get a cramp if he tried.

Ben didn't suffer from an inferiority complex, he just knew his limitations. He didn't have the time to deal with the complications that would come with dating someone like Nora. Logical advice. But, as he watched her high blond ponytail bounce as playfully as a child on a playground, he couldn't help but wonder what those golden strands would feel like sliding through his fingers, or better yet, brushing across his face. His hardening groin jolted him out of his idle thoughts and forced him to return to the Wallace case and all it entailed.

Even as he stared at property lists and income declarations, his mind refused to stay on track, inching again toward forbidden territory as he pondered why someone with so much to offer was still single. Her temper was surely a mark on the not-so-desirable list, he thought with a wince as his side twinged. But he'd never met anyone with such an abundance of spirit. And so beautiful, sometimes it made his teeth ache from wanting. He heard her laughter—robust and full, no hesitation—and returned to the window, wanting to know who had made her laugh so easily.

The brawny guy running the backhoe grabbed her by the neck, looking as if he was burying her in his armpit, until she twisted out of his grip and whacked him in the butt with the top of her tennis shoe. Even from a distance, Ben could sense a bond between the pair that left him struggling with the impulse to separate them. A ridiculous thought at best, he scoffed, deliberately moving away from the window. It didn't matter how she felt about him nor that she'd never shared a bit of genuine laughter with him. Scooping the files he needed, he hobbled from the room, not to escape the sound of her laughter, but to keep himself from caring.

NORA ENDED THE DAY tired but pleased with the progress they were making. The yard looked like hell—giant furrows of freshly churned soil exposed thick roots of old trees that Nora wanted to save, and the air was thick with the smell of earth, water and crushed grass, but the promise of what could be filled her with barely bridled excitement. Nora drew a deep, restorative breath, savoring the smell assaulting her senses, and wondered if anyone else enjoyed gardening as much as she did. She loved her job.

Twisting sharply to ease the kinks in her back, she smiled as a chorus of pops and snaps sounded from her spine. *Ahhh…that felt good.*

Now for her second job. She gave herself a quick mental pep talk filled with advice on how much easier life would be if she minded her own business and stopped wondering if he was a boxer or briefs kind of guy and walked into the house.

Aside from the soft ticktocking of the multitude of clocks, the house was silent. She found Ben, as she expected to, bent over his grandfather's desk, his brow furrowed, one finger pressed against his lips while he perused a sheaf of papers. She knocked on the door frame and was privately delighted by the way his eyes lit up momentarily.

"Finished for the day. I was fixin' to head out. Do you need anything before I go?"

A hungry light flared in his eyes that took her breath away but he shook his head and returned to his reading.

Wait a minute. She pursed her lips, knowing what she'd seen hadn't been a mirage. What's behind door No. 2? "I have an idea," she said, brooking his attention once more. "Let's get out of here for the night."

He blinked. "Excuse me?"

"You know, blow off some steam, get a bite to eat or just, um, I don't know, just change the scenery a bit. You look like you could use a break from whatever it is you're doing."

He chuckled in a way that told her he wasn't about to take her up on her offer and said, "Thanks, but I have more work than I can possibly handle and it wouldn't be prudent to stop."

"C'mon, Ben. Where's your sense of adventure? You need to loosen up, live a little. What's an hour or two? Surely you can swing that."

He opened his mouth to—no doubt—politely but firmly decline, but he must've sensed that she wasn't going to back down and in the interest of his sanity, agreed. "An hour? I suppose I can."

Nora clapped her hands in victory. "Great! What'll it be? Gilly's or the Grill? You feel like bad pizza, beer and peanuts or an overpriced hamburger that'll make you wonder if Reggie stole the recipe from some four-star place." She eyed him speculatively. "Actually, you don't seem like the beer-and-peanuts kind of guy. How about the Grill?"

"I like beer and pizza," he retorted, mildly offended. "Just because I don't wear flannel and tote a wrench on my belt doesn't mean I can't appreciate the simpler elements of life."

"Right. Say something like that to anyone else and you might get your butt kicked. The Grill, it is. Grab your coat. My truck is drafty, as you may remember."

He stopped short after settling his crutches under his arm, a look of distaste on his fine features. "Let's take my car."

"Are you kidding me? My dad is a card-carrying member of the I Only Buy American Made club. If I drive into town in that fancy import I'm likely to be lynched—or at the very least disowned—by my family. No thanks. Button up. It's Bettina or bust."

She left the room with Ben following close behind. When they were at the front door, she turned to find him looking at her curiously. "What?"

"Am I to believe you actually named your truck?"

"Damn straight. Cars have personality whether you believe it or not. My dad had a '73 'Cuda that I swear was a cousin to Stephen King's Christine. She only let my dad drive her." She stifled a giggle. "My sister Natalie actually stalled her when she was sixteen and learning to drive. It was an automatic!"

"How do you stall an automatic?" he asked, grabbing

his coat from the hall tree as they closed the door behind them.

Nora grinned. "I have no idea. You'd have to ask Natalie. But a word of advice if you do…be prepared to duck. She's had about twenty years of our teasing. She probably won't take too kindly to you joining in!"

"If her temper is anything like yours, I won't mention it at all," he said dryly.

Nora flashed him a teasing smile. "It appears that Ivy-League education was good for something."

He laughed and climbed into the truck, hanging his elbow casually out the window like any country boy might on an evening ride, and Nora had to stop herself from picturing him in other aspects of her life. They were from two different worlds. Sure, she was college-educated as well, but Ben wore his education like a shield, whereas Nora preferred to keep things simple and only dusted off her Cal Poly University education when needed.

They arrived at the Grill and Nora rumbled into a tight parking spot with ease, laughing at Ben's apprehension. "I've been parking Bettina in smaller places than this for years. And you should see me parallel park," she added with a confident wink before climbing out of the truck.

A smile borne of grudging admiration tilted his mouth, and Ben followed her slowly as they entered the bustling restaurant.

NORA LED BEN to a spot away from the lounge entrance where country music blared and bodies could be glimpsed shaking and grooving despite the early-evening hour. He relaxed into the chair, glad to get off the crutches for a minute. His underarms were sore from the pressure and his back felt out of whack from sitting with his foot elevated for most of the day.

"So what's good here?" Ben asked over the crowded scene.

"Everything," Nora answered smugly just as their waitress came over to them wearing big hoop earrings and a wide-mouthed grin painted with fire-engine-red lipstick.

"Who's your friend?" the waitress gestured, flashing that clown smile Ben's way. There was no mistaking her flirtatious intention. "I haven't seen you around, so you must be from out of town. I know everyone."

"Ben meet Jenny, the local 411 directory," Nora said in dry introduction.

"Nice to meet you, Jenny," Ben said politely, accepting a menu. "And, no, I'm not from around here."

"Yep, thought so. I'm pretty good with faces…and other things. What happened to your foot?" Jenny asked with sympathy.

Ben shot a look at Nora and she blushed but all he did was shrug and answer, "Wasn't watching where I was going and tripped."

"Aw, you poor thing. Need any help with anything? Anything at all?"

Nora snapped her fingers at Jenny before Ben could respond to her blatant innuendo and he was immensely grateful until she started giving the poor girl a ration. "Yo, Jenny, keep your eyes in your head and your hands to yourself. Besides, I know you're dating Timmy Landers, so don't go eyeing candy you'll never get to taste."

Ben caught his mouth before it dropped open, but Jenny retorted with only a slight pout saying, "Don't get yourself in a twist. I was just kidding. Anyway, you know I like 'em country." She sent Ben a playful look that was only slightly less lascivious than the first. "But I don't mind looking at the city lights once in a while."

"I'm flattered…I think," he added, wondering if Nora hadn't been sitting across from him if Jenny might've added him to the menu for the night. He caught Nora's narrowed gaze before she returned to her menu with a muttered expletive and ordered buffalo wings and two beers to start.

"You got it," Jenny said, throwing a wink over her shoulder for Ben's benefit.

"Was that good for your ego?" Nora asked after Jenny was out of earshot, smiling too sweetly to be trusted.

Ben chuckled with a shrug. Maybe if the woman wasn't completely off the charts from his type, but he withheld his answer, choosing to let Nora draw her own conclusion. "She seems like a nice woman."

Nora snorted. "She's nice to everyone. And when I say everyone—"

"I get it," he cut in wryly.

Her smile turned devilish. "You're a smart man."

"Thanks. Glad to hear my education hasn't gone to waste. I take it you and she aren't the best of friends?"

"Why would you say that?"

He arched his brow. "Because most people don't insinuate their friends are loose women."

"What if it's the truth? I'm not saying anything Jenny wouldn't tell you herself. I'm just saving you the trouble of finding out the hard way."

"Thanks," he said, his voice warming with the laughter he felt bubbling inside. If he didn't know better, he'd say Nora was a little jealous. Odd, given their circumstances, but he didn't deny enjoying the possibility. "I appreciate your looking out for my well-being. If you're ever in the Bay Area in the social scene frequented by attorneys and their clients, I'll be sure to point out the ones to avoid."

Like Ed Wallace, his thoughts immediately going to the paunchy older man who was, at this minute, probably engaging in all sorts of debauchery because he could pay for people's discretion.

"You know a few bad apples, huh?"

"A few."

"How bad?"

He met her gaze. "Bad enough."

Jenny arrived with their hot wings and beer and after taking their order for the main course, disappeared again without so much as batting an eyelash this time around.

Nora grabbed a wing and within seconds had sucked the meat from the bone. Her lips, wet and glossy from the hot sauce that Ben could tell the moment it hit his taste buds could probably sear the enamel off his teeth, began to swell slightly from the heat. It was all Ben could do not to choke or stare like a man who hadn't been with a woman in over a year.

He matched Nora and grabbed another wing, noting that she didn't once reach for her beer even though *he* was dying to cool the inferno in his mouth. If she could take it, so could he. An alarm sounded in his brain and his eyes watered but he reached for another, smiling through his tears as if he could do this all night.

"So tell me about these bad guys you know," Nora said, wiping the corner of her mouth with her napkin before digging into another wing and almost making Ben's eyes cross at doing the same but he did it anyway. "Just how bad are we talking? I thought you practiced only family law. I mean, it's not like you're representing murderers or anything."

He swallowed with difficulty. Had she no taste buds? This was insane. He eyed the tall draft and his mouth watered in time with the flow threatening to spill from his eyes. No. He wouldn't drink until she did. He focused on answering her question. "You'd be surprised by some of the despicable things people will do to one another in the throes of a custody battle or property dispute. One woman actually accused her husband of molesting their daughter when that wasn't even the case, but the girl—who was only five at the time—had to undergo a sexual-assault examination, which later traumatized the poor kid more so than the divorce of her parents. In the end, we found out the woman had only said that to try to keep the man from his daughter."

Nora stopped eating for a moment and the clearly disturbed expression on her face mirrored what he'd felt that day. "Let me guess…you were the woman's attorney?"

"You guessed it."

"So when it came out that he hadn't done anything to his daughter, what happened then?"

"The father got full custody and the woman was required to serve community service for perjuring herself."

"Seems kinda light for lying on the witness stand," Nora balked. "And about something so awful. I guess you can't control that part. Either way, justice was served, right? Must've felt good to see someone who deserved to win actually take home the prize."

He attempted a smile, but honestly, at this point, he couldn't feel his lips any longer and the gesture wouldn't have been genuine anyway. Losing that case had felt morally satisfying but had jeopardized his job. Layla Griggs's family had deep pockets and had paid Ben's firm handsomely to assure a win. When they hadn't…well, it wasn't pretty. "Yeah, it did."

Nora reached for her beer, and Ben nearly wept with relief on the inside but waited a whole half second before picking up his own. He crowed at this small victory until Nora gave him a wide grin, saying, "Not bad for a beginner. I was wondering how long you'd hold out."

"It wasn't that bad," he lied.

"Really? 'Cuz that's the mild sauce. We could call for a plate of the real hot stuff if you want," she teased.

"God, no!" Ben exclaimed, not knowing whether Nora was bluffing and not willing to chance it. "You win. My taste buds can't take another round of that stuff."

As she laughed and reveled in her victory, they fell into the kind of comfortable conversation that Ben realized he hadn't enjoyed in a long time. It seemed most of his social interactions of late had been client related and he never felt content to be himself in those situations. And since his last girlfriend, Olivia, left, he hadn't felt the urge to do anything beyond casual dating.

Ben studied Nora's animated expression as she spoke, watching as her gray eyes lit up with unabashed excitement as she launched into another story that Ben had lost the thread to long ago. He was more captivated by how beautiful she was and wondering why someone hadn't slapped a ring on her finger by now.

What the hell are you thinking? his brain whispered harshly, reminding him that inviting more intimate inter-action was asking for trouble and further complications to a relationship that was already rife with them. *Don't ask about her personal life. It's none of your business.* Sound advice if he ever heard any—too bad the temp-tation was too great to listen.

"So how'd you manage to get through your early twenties without getting snagged by one of the locals?" he asked casually, grabbing her attention and dimming the light in her eyes. Her reaction immediately piqued his interest even as he sensed it was a subject she didn't want to talk about.

"I never felt the urge to settle down. You?"

"Same." He washed the remainder of the hot sauce from his mouth with a swallow of beer, watching and waiting to see if she would elaborate. She didn't. Instead she turned the spotlight back on him.

"I find it hard to believe a guy like you has remained single his entire adult life. You never met anyone special?"

"I didn't say that," he equivocated. Olivia had been special but not enough in her estimation. "I've had a number of serious relationships. Your turn."

She chuckled, but the sound wasn't as light and airy as it could have been. "Let's just say I haven't had the best of luck in that department."

"How so?"

A wry look followed. "How do you think? I've managed to hook up with all the wrong guys. The last one was married." At his startled expression, she clarified, "I didn't know he was married until his wife showed up at their lakeside cabin and caught us in a compromising position."

"Ouch. Surprised you managed to get out of there alive."

"You and me both. I didn't blame her, though. Her husband duped us both. I think they're divorced now."

"And he didn't come slinking back once he didn't have his wife anymore?"

She crooked a sardonic brow. "He did, but I think I communicated my thoughts quite succinctly when I leveled a shotgun at his cheating ass. He never came around again."

He grinned at the image of a gun-toting Nora and didn't envy the poor sap who'd underestimated his bed partner. "Do you have a license for that firearm?" he asked half-seriously.

"Of course. I've been registered to own a gun since

I was eighteen. I'm a better shot than most of the guys down at the shooting range. You shoot?"

He shook his head. "No, but I can swing a mean 10-iron."

"Of course, what was I thinking? You're a lawyer, for crying out loud. Your idea of adventure is probably heading over to the bad side of town to grab a scotch."

"Hey, now you're getting mean. For your information, I can handle a bow and arrow pretty well. I used to belong to an archery club."

"Impressive…sort of." She laughed, the light slowly returning to her eyes as she relaxed. The conversation returned to safer topics and over the course of dinner, Ben realized he didn't want the evening to end. She was a lively dinner companion—funny, smart, articulate, despite her propensity for playing up her country roots, and damn attractive. How was he going to keep a professional distance when all he could think of was pulling her into his arms and tasting those lips and watching those expressive eyes go dewy and soft while her body melted into his?

As his grandmother might've said if he'd gotten to know her better…he was in a real pickle.

CHAPTER TWELVE

NORA WAS OUTSIDE Ben's house, fertilizing the soil in preparation for the rows of flowers she'd picked to rim the side yard, when Sammy tore into the driveway, kicking up dust and gravel, angry music blaring. She straightened with a frown. *What's got him all bent?*

He stalked past her and went straight to the mini backhoe, and before she could get a word in, he gunned the engine and it roared to life.

"Careful! You break it, you buy it," she yelled over the noise, reminding Sammy that he was abusing a rental with her name on the signature line.

Sammy gave a curt nod to indicate he'd heard and gentled his actions but didn't respond otherwise. Guess he wasn't up to talking about whatever was eating him. Nora wasn't worried; Sammy would spill sooner or later. Besides, Nora had other things to occupy her mind.

She hoisted another bag of fertilizer and shook it out, the pungent odor assaulting her nostrils and prompting a grimace. Perhaps if she worked herself to exhaustion each day until the job was finished she wouldn't be thinking of things she had no business thinking. Like Ben.

She groaned and grabbed a hoe to spread the odifer-ous mix. While she may have invited him out to dinner for humanitarian reasons—the guy needed to get out of the house before he went stir-crazy—the end result had been disturbing. For a short time, she caught a glimpse of a different version of Ben, one that laughed easily, had a dry sense of humor that she completely appre-ciated since it mirrored her own, and when he flashed a playful smile at her, her insides had done silly flips and flutters and she'd hungered for something far less tangible than the food on her plate.

Plain and simple…she was wildly attracted to him and keeping her hands to herself wasn't as appealing an idea as it had been before.

The final layer of fertilizer finished, she headed into the house to scrub her hands.

A quick wash later, she told herself to go right back to work, but her feet didn't listen, and she headed straight for Ben's study.

He saw her coming and for a split second his eyes lit up and that blink of time sent her to cloud nine until she realized she was grinning from ear to ear and probably looked like a lovesick puppy.

"Need anything?"

He studied her as if contemplating something, then slowly nodded. "Actually, I do."

"Thirsty? Hungry? What do you need?"

"A date."

The air escaped her lungs in a whoosh and she stiff-ened. "I doubt Jenny is available. She's dating someone. A big, burly dumb ox of a guy who'd be likely to tear your arms off and beat you with them if you came near his girl. Sorry."

He startled her with a gusty laugh. "Thanks for the warning, but no, I wasn't looking for a date with Jenny. I was hoping you were available."

Her cheeks warmed. "Me?" Geez, was that her voice that sounded so high-pitched? She cleared her throat and tried again, this time shooting for a pleasantly curious tone. "Why me?"

"Well, it seems to make the most sense. I have a business engagement in the city that I can't get out of and since I already bought the tickets and I need you to drive...it's the most practical solution."

Oh. Her hopes deflated with a hiss. Of course it was practical. His car only sat two—didn't leave much room for a chauffeur and a real date. "I'll check my schedule," she retorted, suddenly intensely aware of how filthy— and smelly—she was at that moment. "When is this business thing?"

"Tomorrow."

She looked at him in annoyance. "Tomorrow? That's a little late notice don't you think?"

"Yes, I'm sorry. I tried to get out of it, but there are certain events at my firm that require attendance. The Poppenshier Benefit is one of them.

"Poppenshier?"

"Weird name, good cause. It's a benefit for a high-profile children's center for abused youth. My firm is a major benefactor. We give a substantial gift every year and my boss likes his top attorneys there."

"And you're one of them," she surmised.

He nodded without a hint of modesty, and she couldn't help but bristle just a little. "Well, I don't know if I'm free tomorrow. You might have to find yourself someone else." She turned, intending to leave before her bruised feelings became too evident, but the sound of his voice stopped her.

"Nora…I would really like you to come with me."

"Because it's convenient."

"Because…I enjoy your company. You're not like most women and, despite your eccentricities, I find you fascinating."

She thawed just a little. "What kind of dress requirement is there for this shindig?"

"Black-tie. Do you have anything you can wear on such short notice?"

She pictured Ben in a sharp black tux and her heartbeat sped up. In answer, she nodded. "Do you have anything against red?"

His gaze sharpened and roamed her body in a hungry perusal that she felt down to her toes. He slowly shook his head. "Red sounds fine by me. Be here by four? The dinner starts at six and we don't want to hit traffic."

She noted the mundane details, but a part of her brain was still focused on the feral look Ben had given her, as if he'd somehow seen into her closet to the hot red number that clung to her curves and breasts and the pair of sassy heels that helped add height to her slight frame.

"All right, it's a date," she finished, swallowing hard as she practically flew from the room, not quite sure why she was agreeing to such madness, but reveling in the adventure and hoping it didn't end as some adventures do…with a crash and burn.

BEN SPENT most of the afternoon fighting his baser, more primal nature and tried to focus on work rather than his uncomfortably tight groin area. He adjusted himself in annoyance, feeling much like a randy teenager who couldn't control his anatomy. But one thought of Nora on his arm, dressed to the nines, sent his pulse racing and his mind moving in R-rated directions. Did she feel the same? Did she wonder what she'd feel like pressed against him? Tongues dancing together, moving in a slick tango that sent heat spiraling through their bodies until clothes were an abomination and had to be discarded before they both went up in flames? He shuddered and scrubbed his hands down his face, wondering if he'd just made a huge mistake by inviting Nora deeper into his life.

He supposed he'd find out soon enough.

THE NEXT DAY Nora stood before Ben's front door, her insides shaking and fingers tingling as she tried to relax. This was a dinner engagement, a social function, that's all. No sense in making a huge deal out of something that had all the potential to be a big fat nothing.

So why was she so hesitant to open that door?

Nora pushed the thought out of her head and propelled herself inside, gritting her teeth against the spiraling sensation in her gut that felt too much like excitement.

Ben was standing in the foyer waiting, and despite

the crutches, he looked every bit the stylish sophisticate with a polished air reminiscent of Pierce Brosnan in the *Thomas Crown Affair*. In a word: ohhhhhhh…

But even as she was ogling him shamelessly, he was doing the same.

"Beautiful," he murmured finally, warming her insides, as he did a slow perusal.

"An improvement from the usual Levi's and dirt," she said, fighting the urge to bite her lip.

"I'd say," he said, his voice drifting over her bare shoulders in a soft caress. The moment was fraught with tension that Nora knew to be dangerous, but the delicious feeling was alluring. The scrutiny in his gaze cleared and the corner of his mouth lifted in a subtle smile as he gestured toward the door. "Shall we, then?"

Moment broken, Nora lifted her chin and met his smile with a sassy one of her own. "Yeah, let's get this show on the road. I don't want to spend all night around a bunch of lawyers."

She turned and gave him a nice view of her backside, knowing the smooth lines of the dress looked fabulous, and made her way to the car.

You can look, but you can't touch. She grinned from ear to ear. Tonight she was going to make Benjamin Hollister's eyes cross.

Guaranteed.

THEY ARRIVED on time despite a traffic snarl on the 880 and when they finally entered the glittering building and moved past the woman guarding the entrance, ensuring only those with an invitation gained entry, Nora was struck by the glamour of the backdrop.

"Pretty swanky place," Nora murmured, taking in the glitzy ballroom with the crystal chandeliers and rich burgundy wall hangings rippling in the subtle bay breeze coming from the open doors. "How many times have you been to this benefit dinner?"

He shrugged. "Since my first year at the firm."

"So what can I expect tonight?"

He shifted on his crutches and grimaced as he repositioned his weight. "Well, first there's an interminable amount of mixing with the overprivileged members of San Francisco society coupled with copious amounts of alcohol to make the experience remotely palatable. Then there's the overpriced dinner of something fancy and unrecognizable, and when everyone is good and drunk, there's a live auction for items that are—"

"Overpriced," Nora interjected with a smile.

He grinned. "You get the idea. But, as I mentioned, it's all for a good cause."

She scanned the room, taking careful note of those milling around, and surmised, "These are your friends?"

"Friends? No, I wouldn't say that."

"Then what would you say?"

"I'd say some are people I work with, others are clients and the rest are unknowns."

She chuckled. "Unknowns? Sounds like a math equation."

"It's all about networking. The only reason I come to this function is because my boss asks me to and the reason he asks is so that our firm has a presence among the elite who, by the way, are always just one step shy of needing representation of some kind sooner or later."

Nora wrinkled her nose at him, not liking the way that sounded at all. "Kind of like a vulture circling in the sky, knowing that in time, something's going to croak and it'll be good eating."

"That's a disgusting analogy, but I suppose it works on a certain level. I prefer to consider it being in the right place at the right time."

She let a pause rest between them as she privately considered what he'd revealed and wondered if his life was as he'd hoped it would turn out. To her, this kind of existence seemed horribly inadequate and toxic, but as Natalie was fond of pointing out, Nora had a habit of judging everyone else's life by her own yardstick.

"If these people aren't your friends who do you hang out with on your downtime?" He gave her a sardonic look and she was reminded of their first encounter. "Wait, I remember—you don't have downtime. You don't even take time out for a vacation," she finished dryly and grabbed a glass of champagne from the smartly dressed waiter passing by.

He smirked. "You have a good memory."

She returned the smirk. "I do. Ridiculously so, it seems." Nora sipped her champagne, then asked, "So, why do you hate roses so much?"

"Excuse me?"

Nora tapped her temple lightly. "The ridiculously sharp memory strikes again. There's a reason you hate roses. What is it?"

He looked ready to change the subject, but he surprised her with an answer. "My dad. It was his flower of choice. The more exotic the better. Women thought when my dad sent them roses that they meant something to him, but the truth was, they were just one of many."

"Your dad's a player, huh?"

"The worst kind."

How sad. Nora couldn't imagine having such a man for a father. Her dad was a grump, but at least he wasn't chasing every skirt in town.

"Aren't you supposed to mingle or something?" she teased, purposefully lightening the mood.

"That I am. Thanks for reminding me." The corners of his mouth played with a full-fledged smile and she marveled at how handsome he'd become. From a gangly boy to a broad-shouldered man, she mused dangerously, sipping her champagne as Ben eased his way through the crowd to talk with an acquaintance. It didn't matter that he hobbled on crutches; his confidence was alluring.

She tore her gaze away from him, perturbed that he managed to impress her without even trying. Emmett's Mill needed someone like Ben. She jerked imperceptibly at the ludicrous direction of her thoughts and finished her champagne. This was Ben's world, not some forgotten town in the California foothills. And this was not Nora's world. The two didn't blend.

As if the universe needed to prove this point to Nora, a man in a sharp black designer tuxedo entered into her space and his presence immediately set Nora's teeth on edge. His gaze slid over Nora's figure in a way that made her feel as if she should go wash, and for all his outward polish Nora could almost see the corruption coming off him in waves. Buster, the egg deliveryman, had more character in his worn overalls than this man. Nora smiled politely but refrained from joining in the conversation and was relieved when he sauntered off to find someone else's ear to bend.

"Again…not a friend," Ben said when he returned, looking almost as relieved as Nora that the man had left.

"I know," she replied simply. Somehow she'd been certain that Ben would never call someone like that a friend. Gracing him with a warm smile, she slipped her arm through his and he drew her intimately closer as if they truly were a couple instead of what they were, which was infinitely harder to explain. Snugged against him, Nora felt she belonged there. It was a wonderful if startling feeling, and one she wasn't ready to relinquish.

THEY WERE HALFWAY to their table when Ben heard his name. He turned and swallowed a grimace when he realized who was coming at him with a speed that should've been impossible in the blue dress clinging to her body.

Nora must've felt him tense for she glanced at him inquiringly, but he didn't have time to explain that a former lover was heading straight for him, no doubt to gauge his and Nora's relationship. Elise Birkeland was a woman who loved a fair bit of competition and enjoyed considering Ben the prize. Ordinarily he didn't mind the game but tonight he wasn't interested.

"Benjamin," she purred, her native Norwegian accenting his name with a distinctly foreign flavor. She walked straight to him without sparing Nora a glance from her glacial blue eyes, though her gaze swept his injury briefly as if it were not serious enough to warrant much curiosity. "You do not call. It's impolite." She pouted even as she slipped her arms around his neck before he could thwart her intention. "I don't like to be ignored."

"What a coincidence," Nora bristled beside him, drawing both their attention. "Neither do I."

Elise lifted one perfectly arched light brown brow as if amused and allowed Ben to disengage himself from her grasp. "My apologies. I didn't realize you were together," she said with an air that was only mildly apologetic.

"We're not," Nora retorted coolly despite the fire Ben recognized burning behind her eyes. "Together, that is."

Elise angled a look at Ben, who was enjoying Nora's barely contained territorial clutch a little too much and shrugged. "Perhaps when you are not so indisposed?" she asked.

"Perhaps." He inclined his head in a noncommittal gesture, but had a feeling he should've chosen his words more wisely. Elise's beauty didn't hold the same appeal any longer. Her pale hair and light blue eyes looked washed out in comparison to the woman nearly vibrating with life beside him, drawing every set of male eyes in the room to her earthy beauty.

Elise nodded in sardonic deference to Nora and

floated away, another target in her sights, Ben completely forgotten.

"Client, acquaintance or unknown?" Nora asked, a subtle cut to her tone.

"We used to date off and on. Why? Do I sense jealousy?"

She straightened as if realizing how she sounded and scoffed at the very idea. "Get over yourself, Hollister. Where's our table? I'm starved."

He chuckled and led the way toward their seats, annoyed that his crutches prevented him from resting his hand on the small of her back as he would've liked.

Once at the table, he used one hand to pull out Nora's chair and he watched with pleasure as she slid gracefully into it, giving him a subtle smile of thanks for the gentlemanly gesture.

Franklin, Mills & Donovan had bought a table, which always sat eight, and Ben knew all the players occupying the seats. Most were benign to the point of bland, but one in particular was a shark and notorious for ass-kissing, back-stabbing and downright sleazy maneuvers in court but the guy had a winning streak that was close to Ben's and that made him an irritant if nothing else. Seconds later, the object of his irritation appeared out of the throng of people, and Ben replaced the scowl he wanted to show with a tight-lipped courtesy smile in greeting. But the moment Ted Paulsen's eyes alighted on Nora's voluptuous figure and rested a second longer than necessary on the plump swell of her breasts, it took every ounce of self-control not to send him a hard look and growl *back off*. The odd spurt of possession took

Ben by surprise and forced him to take a breath and reassess his reaction. Broadening his smile in fake welcome, he extended his hand to his colleague. "Ted, congratulations on the Wilson case. I heard it was a tough one."

"Slam dunk. Shaky prenup," Ted said, shrugging off the congratulations and taking the seat near Nora. His attention swiveled immediately to her rather than to Ben. "I don't believe we've been introduced." He accepted Nora's hand and raised it to his lips, pressing a kiss to the top in a smarmy gesture that caused an incredulous expression to appear on Nora's face.

"Ted Paulsen, Nora Simmons." *Now stop touching her, you idiot, before some of your personality rubs off on her.*

"Nora…beautiful name," he said. "Are you from around here?"

She laughed. "God, no. I can't imagine living in the city. Too many fakes and liars for my taste. How about you?"

Ben wanted to burst out laughing at Ted's stunned look and Nora's accompanying saccharine smile. It took a moment for Ted to realize Nora had seen right through his game and was playing one of her own. Moments later, Ted moved to the opposite side of the table.

"Nicely done," Ben observed lightly.

"Thank you. I hate to say this but I think I've come across every cliché of the wickedly wealthy and those who chase after them all in one night. Is there anyone here who isn't a total waste of oxygen?"

He smothered his laughter, but couldn't stop the

smile and managed to gesture discreetly toward another table where an aged woman sat surrounded by those Ben knew to be her protective family. "Over at that table sits one of the richest women in the Bay Area, but aside from this one function, she never goes to these things."

"Why not?"

"Because she hates the people. She calls them 'finks and carpetbaggers.'"

Nora giggled and angled a look. "So why does she come to this one?" she whispered.

"Because she believes in the cause. Staunchly. She's never given a reason for her stalwart support, but something tells me she can empathize with the children who seek shelter within Poppenshier House."

Nora's expression softened. "That's amazing that she shares her wealth with those less fortunate. I wish more people were like her."

He inclined his head but his forehead wrinkled as unwelcome comparisons to his grandfather surfaced. Ada Willows could give millions to help someone, but B.J. had given the only thing he had—his time. Both were noble in their own way but Ben hadn't recognized this fact. Nora had. He glanced surreptitiously her way and his pulse quickened just having her by his side. His feelings posed a significant problem, the analytical side of his brain railed, but he wasn't interested in listening. Right now he wanted to focus on Nora.

The evening passed quickly, but unlike evenings in the past where Ben kept a constant watch on the time, waiting for the first opportunity to politely bow out, an evening spent with Nora felt like time well spent and he wanted more.

"That was actually better than I thought it was going to be. Honestly, I was afraid it was going to be a ridiculous bore but I had a good time," Nora remarked as they made their way to the car. "It isn't very often I get to wear this dress and you're not a bad date. All in all, I'd say the trip was worth the gas money."

He laughed. "Glad to hear it. What now? Head back?"

"Well, I was thinking we could stop by your apartment and change because as much as I love this outfit, my feet are killing me."

"Absolutely. Did you bring a change of clothes with you?"

"Yep."

He unlocked the car. "Then to the apartment we go."

"Great."

Was that a tremor in her voice? Did she sense the difficulty he was having keeping his thoughts away from what he most wanted? God help him but he wanted to seduce the woman in the worst way and he was fast losing sight of the reasons why it was a bad idea.

CHAPTER THIRTEEN

NORA FOLLOWED Ben into his apartment and gratefully slipped out of her shoes. She groaned as she wiggled her toes and blood returned to the poor little digits that had been cramped into the fashionable little torture devices pretending to be designer heels. Rarely was Nora a subscriber to the tenet "Sacrifice your body for fashion," but tonight she'd wanted to look every inch the sophisticated woman on Ben's arm. And the fashion gods required the sacrifice of her baby toe on each foot apparently, but a covert glance at Ben revealed her sacrifice had not been in vain.

The man who prided himself on being contained and orderly in all aspects of his life was fumbling with the corkscrew on a bottle of vintage wine. Granted, he was trying to balance on crutches while trying to accomplish his goal, but Nora could almost see the tremble.

She'd most certainly made his eyes cross.

Unfortunately he wasn't the only one. Ben took her breath away each time he pinned her with those intense gazes. They rendered a woman defenseless and that was simply not fair. Sort of like declawing a cat and then throwing the poor feline outside to fend for itself against…a bear.

"Need help?" she offered, wanting to laugh but unable to because of the flutters in her belly.

"Uh, no…well, maybe," he admitted, pursing his lips in agitation as the corkscrew slipped out of his grasp to clatter on the countertop. She took the bottle and returned it to the counter, not sure alcohol was needed; she already felt intoxicated. He watched her cautiously. "What are you doing?"

"I'm not sure," she answered, running the tip of her tongue across her top lip. "But I think I need to get you out of my system and there's only one way I can think of to do that."

His eyes darkened. "Which is?"

"This." She latched her lips onto his and nearly knocked him into the sink, both crutches clattering to the floor as he wound his arms around her, crushing her to him. Coherent thought—and any counsel as to why this may be a bad idea—fled her mind, and her body took over. Despite his injuries, he managed to hoist her onto the counter and, without stopping the ravenous kiss, her legs went around his waist, drawing him ever closer to that hot heat radiating from her center and spreading to her limbs.

Ben broke the kiss with a savage groan as if the action had cost him. "I don't think this is a good idea," he whispered, but his gaze seared into hers, demanding more.

She dragged his head back down to hers, saying breathlessly, "So don't think."

"Right," he quickly agreed and claimed her mouth again, his tongue slipping inside and ruthlessly teasing her with the promise of what else he wanted to do to her. She moaned and her hands went straight to his pants, making quick work of the clasp and ripping his shirt free of his waistband, so eager she was to touch the flesh only inches away from her questing fingers. His stomach muscles clenched as her palms spread across his belly and hungrily climbed, buttons popping as she divested him of the cumbersome fabric.

"Nora?" he murmured against her mouth, his voice ragged and aroused. "Are you sure? I don't want to do anything that—"

She jerked away from him and gripped his loose lapels. "For the love of God, just shut up and kiss me!"

It was at that moment Ben decided to follow Nora's terse advice and forget about the warnings in his head blaring above the rush of erotic sensations. A wild, hot need burned and ravaged him until all he could see, hear or feel was Nora in his arms.

He didn't notice the pain in his rib or the soreness in his lungs or even the clumsiness of his cast. All he felt was Nora.

They made their way to the bedroom slowly and a bit awkwardly but neither seemed to mind. Soon Nora unzipped her red dress and let it pool at her feet before modeling the delicate black, lacy demi-cup bra-and-panties set that looked straight out of the *Victoria's Secret* catalog. Immediately his heartbeat began thumping wildly against his chest.

"God, you're something," he said as she straddled him gently, keeping most of her weight on his hips and away from his injured side.

"You're easily impressed," she said playfully, pulling her hair free from the pins so that it fell in waves around her shoulders.

"No," he clarified, anchoring his hands on her waist, loving the way the moonlight dusted her blond hair with silver highlights. "I'm not."

Nora paused, as if letting his simple statement sink in, and then she slowly smiled. "Good to know," she said, her voice low and husky. Then she added devilishly, "Neither am I."

Ben sucked in a sharp breath as she did a sensual grind against the swollen ridge in his loosened pants, and he knew if he made it through tonight he might just touch heaven.

He rolled, wincing when his side protested, and bringing Nora to rest beneath him. He loved the feel of that superior position until his heavy cast made him feel less like Casanova and more like Quasimodo with a concrete block on his foot.

"Ouch," Nora said, wiggling away from the hard plaster rubbing against her leg. She eyed him. "Let's go back to the way we were. With me on top."

He grimaced. "This isn't working out how I planned."

She arched a brow playfully. "Planned, eh? And here I thought we were being spontaneous."

Instead of answering, he dipped down and claimed her lips softly, nibbling the pouty flesh, determined to make sure he wasn't the only one drowning in sensation and enjoying every minute of it.

They rolled again, returning Nora to the top, and as

she unclasped her bra, freeing her breasts, any reservations he may have held disappeared like wisps of smoke in a stiff breeze. God, she was perfect. And for this moment, she belonged to him.

Danger whispered at the heady thought, but he was too far gone to listen. Pausing long enough to reach into his bedside drawer to grab a condom, he ripped the foil with shaking hands and tried not to think of how she affected him but all he could think, smell or see was Nora and he couldn't seem to get enough.

THE NEXT MORNING Nora awoke with a start, momentarily disoriented by her foreign surroundings. A soft snore beside her sent warmth crawling into her cheeks as she slowly turned, clutching the sheet to her naked body to stare at Ben. Heated memories of a torrid night filled her mind and she was caught between wanting more and fleeing the room.

It'd been her idea, but honestly, what had she been thinking? She rubbed her palm against one eye and sighed softly so as not to wake him, then slid out of bed carefully. She needed a shower and coffee right away to clear the cobwebs in her head that were clouding her judgment. As she padded silently to the bathroom and shut the door, a part of her was wondering why she wasn't snuggled up to the brawny man for a repeat performance.

Because this was a bad idea, her conscience screamed, kicking to life with a vengeance. This was exactly the kind of impetuous maneuver that had got her involved with a married man. She leaped before looking and ended up flat on her face because there'd been no one there to catch her.

She knew Ben wasn't married—wasn't even remotely attached—but tangling with him was worse because she knew from the get-go that he had no desire to stay. Ben fitting in with the small town of Emmett's Mill was as ludicrous and unlikely as Natalie suddenly turning into an exhibitionist and running through the town square naked as a jaybird. But last night had been…phenomenal. And she wasn't just talking about the sex, although that had been sizzling and would most likely ruin her for anyone else in the foreseeable future.

Seeing Ben in his element—confident, secure and knowledgeable—had caused an insidious change in her brain about the man. He no longer seemed arrogant and distant, but someone who was solid in his convictions and didn't care who disapproved. God, he was a man after her own heart. Scary thought, that.

Great. She had to go and ruin the image she was fostering of him. What now? Did they pretend as if nothing had happened? As if they hadn't just rocked each other's world…three times?

She stepped into the steaming shower and let the water sluice over her, content just to let her concerns wash down the drain for the moment.

Irresponsible seemed to be her middle name.

After a quick scrub, she shut off the shower and wrapped herself in a thick white towel. She was prepared to sneak back into the room to retrieve the change of clothes she'd brought last night, but as she opened the door, Ben greeted her with an appreciative grin. "If I didn't have this cast I might've joined you," he said, bending down to nuzzle her neck.

Her eyelids fluttered shut as her heartbeat leaped into her throat but good sense had her sidling out of his reach. "We have to get going. I have a crew coming at noon," she said, throwing a brief smile his way and running from the bedroom.

"Nora, wait," he called, but she'd disappeared into the spare bedroom and shut the door. Leaning against it and clutching her clothes to her chest, she squeezed her eyes shut against the pictures in her head of last night's romp. A knock sounded. "Nora? What's wrong?"

"Nothing."

A pause. "Then why are you hiding behind a door?"

"I'm not hiding. I'm getting dressed. I like a little privacy."

"O-kay," he said, clearly puzzled by her actions, and she didn't blame him. She wasn't making much sense, but that wasn't what was important at the moment. What was important was that they both returned to their senses, and she certainly couldn't do that with him unwittingly enticing her to throw him to the floor and have her wicked way with him. A shudder of delight rocked her body at the thought. *Stop that!* The point of last night was to get him out of her system, but it didn't seem as if she'd achieved her goal. If anything, he was more firmly entrenched in her mind than ever before. *Good going*.

She opened the door to find him still standing there, leaning casually against the doorjamb on his uninjured side. A pang of concern followed as she considered that perhaps sex hadn't been advisable for his recovery. Doc Hessle probably hadn't thought to mention that little bit of advice. "You okay?" She gestured to his side. "Nothing...broken?"

"No more than I started out. How are you?"

"I'm fine," she bluffed, walking past him. "But you better get dressed because we really have to get going."

He pushed off. "I have a better idea," he said, moving much too quickly for a man who was supposed to be incapacitated. He grabbed her by the waist and pulled her to him. Her breath escaped in a little girlie gasp and his eyes dilated at the sound. "Let's go back to bed."

She tried to put on a stern face, but it was hard to hold on to when she was practically nodding her head in agreement. "We shouldn't."

"I agree," he said, surprising her.

"You agree?"

"Absolutely." He started making his way back to the bedroom, pulling her with him. "This is a terrible idea but as terrible ideas go, I think it's pretty damn fantastic. We're good together, Nora. Sinfully good. And let's just say, it's my turn to get *you* out of my system."

"Oh," she said in a breathless whisper, privately delighted by his husky growl and the way his hard body responded so eagerly to her own. "I have appointments," she countered weakly, licking her lips in anticipation of the carnal promise she read in his eyes. "Lots of them."

"Cancel."

"It's not that simple," she protested even as he pushed her onto the bed, the forcefulness sending her heart racing. He silenced her last objection by pressing his mouth over hers, his tongue slipping and darting inside as his hand closed over her braless breast and squeezed possessively. Her last thought was lost on a moan as his mouth cleared a path to the sensitive skin of her neck, nipping and sucking gently while the stubble on his chin sent goose bumps chasing the waves of desire, clamping down on any sense.

She'd pay for this later but she'd savor it now.

CHAPTER FOURTEEN

BY THE TIME they returned to Emmett's Mill, the day had long since passed, but thanks to a quick phone call to Sammy, the work that had been scheduled was finished and Nora spent the day with Ben. It'd been hedonistic and wonderful, but as the sweat dried and the heated moments cooled, Nora realized she might never get enough of Ben Hollister. That smacked of trouble, she thought ominously, uncomfortable with the one-way road she was traveling. It wasn't as if Ben was staring into her eyes professing his feelings for her. Not that she wanted him to exactly. Rarely did she respect any man who fell at her feet, but she wouldn't be adverse to a little show of affection rather than simple lust.

"I guess I'll take off," she said, gathering last night's clothes from the trunk of Ben's car, not quite sure what to say after the day she'd had. They were no longer strangers, but she still felt as if she didn't know the man, and awkwardness was setting in. "Do you need anything for tomorrow?"

His gaze narrowed seductively and she had to look away, her body reacting in a primal way to that silent signal. "I can think of only one thing I need," he said.

"Well, I wasn't one of the choices," she retorted,

shouldering her overnight bag and wincing as the heel of one of her fancy shoes dug into her back. "I meant things like food, toilet paper, essentials."

"I could argue having you naked in my bed is essential but something tells me you're not in the mood."

"Perceptive."

"So I've been told."

Time to set the record straight. "Look, Ben, today was fun but I need to focus. I missed a whole day of work to…" devour your perfect body like a starving woman. She drew a deep breath and finished quickly, "You know, and that's not my style. Time to get back to reality."

The subtle flex of his jaw belied the amusement in his expression and she knew she'd just bruised his ego with her rejection. But he surprised her when he said, "Fine."

"Fine?" she repeated, watching him closely. "Your feelings aren't hurt?"

He gave her a patronizing stare. "Nora, it takes more than that to hurt my feelings. I'm a lawyer, remember?"

"Ah, right. So we're good then?"

He chuckled but the sound held a ragged edge. "We're as good as we'll ever be, I suspect. I was going to ask you to stay for dinner, but if you need to go I understand."

The feminine part of her whined and pouted at his offer, knowing she'd cave if only to get that part to shut up so she could think clearly. "You could still ask, I suppose," she said slowly.

His expression brightened momentarily, illuminating

those impossibly green eyes until she had to tear her gaze away. She reminded herself that falling for Ben was the worst thing she could do at this juncture in her life, but there was no denying the tingle in her toes at the thought of spending more time alone with him.

"Would you like to stay for dinner?"

She nodded. "I could eat."

"Glad to hear it. I've got all this food and as I've already proved, I can't cook on these crutches. I could use your help."

Oh criminy. He wasn't asking her to stay for dinner because he couldn't bear to spend a night apart—he needed a cooking assistant. She couldn't help the starch in her spine as she nodded curtly. "I suppose that fits within my job description."

"I believe it does," he agreed, further inciting her indignation until he added with quiet honesty, "But you don't *have* to stay. I was hoping you might *want* to stay…as a friend."

A friend? Her heart melted a little even as he gave her what sounded like a classic line. "Are we friends, Ben?" she asked, peering at him curiously.

He took a moment to answer and when he did, her heart disintegrated into a useless puddle. "I don't know what we are exactly, but I know you're unlike any woman I've ever met and I crave your company. I'm not just talking about your body either, in case you're wondering. Although that's high on my list of desirables. It's just not everything."

The man had talent. "Yes, I'll stay for dinner. Just dinner, though," she reminded him sternly, though her teeth ached just saying it. "I need to get my head straight and I can't do that with you touching me."

One eyebrow lifted sardonically. "You've made yourself clear, Nora. I don't need to be told twice. Just dinner."

An inexplicable sense of disappointment followed and she wanted to slap herself silly for acting like such a girl. She sure as hell couldn't say one thing and then act disappointed because she got what she wanted.

Where was the harm in a little dessert? A suspiciously female voice whispered as they walked into the house. Dessert was a complication, she told herself, but Nora couldn't help the train of her thoughts with such a nice view of Ben's behind in front of her. She knew firsthand what that flesh felt like beneath her palm and the memory made her insides tremble with need.

Lord. She must have the resolve of a drug addict. She couldn't even rein in her own thoughts on the subject. How pathetic. She inhaled a short breath and told herself all she had to remember was that Ben wasn't here to stay and she wasn't interested in looking when she couldn't buy.

Yeah right, she snorted with the delicacy of a truck driver. Tell that to her raging hormones.

"Just dinner and then I'm outta here," she reminded him. Or was it to convince herself?

NORA, BEN REALIZED, was a terrible cook.

"I never said I was handy in the kitchen," she said defensively as they stared at the rice she'd been put in charge of making. She wrinkled her nose at the gummy, gluelike gunk in the pot and shrugged. "I eat out a lot."

He chuckled as he lifted the pot from the stove and placed it in the sink. "I can see that," he said, filling the pot with water so the rice didn't stick. "How is it you grew up with two older sisters and your mom and you never learned to cook?"

"There was never a need. Natalie or my mom always did the cooking. Plus, a few incidents like this kinda helped push me out of the kitchen. Once I was in charge of making meatballs but I forgot to cook the rice and I cooked the meat too long. Anyway, well, it turned out to be meat loaf with crunchy rice inside. It was gross. No one wanted a repeat of that so I was kicked out of the kitchen." She moved to help Ben remove the casserole from the oven. Once it was safely on the counter to cool, she went to the fridge to take out a bottle of white wine that was chilling. "And once I was out on my own, I ate a lot of Ramen noodles for a while."

Ben gestured to the plates and she retrieved them. "I love cooking. Helps clear my head," he said. She held the plate while he dished out a heaping spoonful of the cheesy stuff he'd whipped up, and even though the rice was clearly inedible, the casserole looked hearty enough.

"In the dining room?" she asked and he nodded.

Nora carried the plates and silverware to the table and then returned with the wine and two glasses.

"Smells good," she admitted, spearing a piece of chicken and twirling the cheese around it as broccoli and other vegetables spilled out from under the thin crust. "But here comes the real test."

The fork disappeared into her mouth and the resulting groan of surprise sent erotic thrills down his body. Chagrined at his own lack of restraint, he focused on his own meal. "Good?" he asked, taking a bite.

"Damn good," she admitted a tad grudgingly. "Where'd you learn to cook like this?"

"College," he answered. "No one in my fraternity could cook, and I was the only one who didn't run home to my parents for a home-cooked meal. I spent a lot of holidays perfecting my methods."

She swallowed and toyed with a pea before taking another bite. The silence told him she was thinking about his last statement. Their lives were so different. Nora had never learned to cook because she was surrounded by family who did it for her; he'd learned to cook because no one else would.

"Tell me what it was like growing up with a silver spoon in your mouth," she said with a sudden smile, and he knew she was trying to keep the conversation light. He was thankful for her effort and decided to share a little. "It's not so different than most childhoods, except I didn't grow up around any blackberry bushes," he teased, referencing their first encounter all those years ago.

She blushed but managed to add, "Yeah, that was painfully obvious."

He chuckled. "You know, you looked like such a wild child that day. Almost like a pixie with your long hair tangled and knotted. I'd never seen anyone like you. Fearless even at ten."

"You probably say that to all the girls," she murmured.

"No, I don't," he said in all honesty. Her spirit demanded nothing less. "Nora, I'm not the type of man to fill a woman's head with pretty lies."

A storm built behind her eyes but she nodded. "I get that. It's honorable in a way. Is that why your last girlfriend didn't stick around?"

He sighed. "In a manner of speaking. I told her I didn't believe in marriage." Or love for that matter, but he kept that revelation behind his teeth. "And she had different goals, ones that included marriage and children. We went our separate ways."

"Why don't you believe in marriage?"

"Because evidence that it doesn't work crosses my desk every day and I get to clean up the mess they leave behind. Assets, financial declarations, custody disputes. The wreckage of a union created by a brief hormonal surge is enough proof for me that marriage is an outdated concept."

His gaze dropped to her fork as she idly played with her food. "Something wrong?"

She looked up and he saw the disappointment in her eyes, although she tried to hide it. "No. Everything's fine."

"Are you sure?"

"Yes. Tell me why you never came back to Emmett's Mill after that one summer."

He drew a short breath. "I tried. My father wouldn't let me."

"Why not?"

"Because my father hated his parents. The only reason he let me visit that one summer was because he and my mother were finalizing the divorce and didn't want me hanging around while they fought over the details. I suppose it was a blessing."

"Did you want to come back?" There was a wealth of emotion behind her question, but Ben wasn't sure where it was coming from.

"Yes."

She seemed to relax subtly as if the answer was exactly what she needed to hear. "Each summer I waited for you to return, but you never did. It was a stupid childhood crush, but I had it bad for you."

"Really?" His heart rate quickened, remembering how many times he replayed that small moment in time when, as children, their lips touched. He caressed her cheek. "How do you feel now?"

The look in her eyes gave her away but she managed a nonchalant shrug. "I feel conflicted."

He could relate. "Why?"

"Because we never should've slept together," she replied softly.

He agreed, but he couldn't get himself to say it aloud for he didn't want to acknowledge how quickly they'd complicated their relationship. All he wanted was to taste her skin, feel her body and know her mind. It was distracting and disconcerting, but the desire was there and he didn't quite know what to do with it.

"You may be right, but we can't take it back." *And I don't want to.* He shifted in his chair, striving for a cool demeanor despite feeling hot inside. "We could pretend it didn't happen and make a vow never to do it again, or we could be adults about it and recognize that we're both attracted to each other and deal with our feelings accordingly."

She leveled her stare. "And how do you suppose we deal with our feelings without making things worse?"

"Allow them to run their course."

She startled. "Excuse me?"

"As I've said before, attraction fades as does the euphoric feeling of being in love after the chemical subsides in your brain. We'll just wait it out and then peacefully go our own ways."

Her expression crystallized with cold fury and he realized she might not see things the same way. It was the same look he'd seen on his last lover's face and he knew the drill. But even though he knew what was coming and figured he was prepared, he wasn't ready for the hurt hiding behind her anger.

"Thank you for making your position perfectly clear," she said, standing. "But I'd rather not participate in your *chemical* romance, if you don't mind. From this moment forward, we're business associates. I think by the time you're able to travel and the house is finished, whatever it is I'm feeling will be completely and suffi-ciently *dead.*"

Ben struggled to go after her, but she was too quick for him. Cursing his broken ankle, he hopped to the door in time to see Nora barrel out of the driveway.

All good feelings of the day evaporated. Better now than later, he told himself, shutting the door and return-ing to the kitchen to clean up the mess. Better now than when they were more attached than they wanted to admit and a drawn-out breakup ensued.

Yes, this was infinitely better. So why did it feel as if he'd just taken a punch to the sternum from a brute with brass knuckles? The answer seemed simple but Ben refused to acknowledge it. Nora was an itch he couldn't seem to scratch because it was deep under the skin. How'd she manage to get in so quickly?

Again the answer was unnecessary. As an attorney he made his livelihood by stoically analyzing the situation between two people so that he could determine the most agreeable resolution. He'd just apply that skill to his relationship with Nora.

He wouldn't think of her golden skin and the way candlelight brought out the rosy hue along her hip bone, and he certainly wouldn't think of the tiny Chinese symbol tattooed on the curve of her left buttock that he couldn't help but nibble and kiss. He'd forgotten to ask what the character meant. Now the opportunity was gone.

Ben finished cleaning the kitchen and headed for bed. Yes, this was a blessing in disguise. He just had to convince his brain of that simple fact and everything would fall into place.

So, Counselor, closing arguments?

Just one—what the hell are you thinking? That plan is bound to fail. You've never met someone like her—and probably never will.

CHAPTER FIFTEEN

BEN WAS ENGROSSED in case files, looking for some kind of precedents that might help him win the Wallace case, when he heard a short knock at the front door. Rising from his desk, he hobbled to see who it was and saw Buster talking with Nora on the front porch.

Nora saw Ben first and gestured to the basket in Buster's hands. "Now you can give that Denver omelet a second chance," she said.

"Breakfast in bed, perhaps?" he asked, hoping to earn a smile but preparing to duck in case she hurled the garden trowel in her hand at his head. Instead she offered a generic smile that was devoid of warmth before leaving him with Buster, who was watching the exchange with avid interest.

"Good luck catching that one," Buster said with a low whistle.

Ben returned his attention to the older man and accepted the basket of eggs. "What makes you think I'm trying to catch her?" he scoffed lightly.

Buster laughed. "Boy, you've got 'the look' written plain as day all over your face. You've got it bad."

"I assure you, there's no look." Ben fought a grimace, knowing the man meant well, but Buster made it sound as if he'd caught some kind of disease. "We're just client and employer with some slightly friendly overtones," he tried to explain but even to his own ears it sounded lame.

"I call 'em as I see 'em, that's all. Enjoy them eggs. There's more where that came from."

"I appreciate that you're honoring a debt but I think you've satisfied what you owed my grandfather. Let's call it even."

Buster shook his head. "We ain't square till we're square. See you next week."

Ben tried again, but Buster was already in his truck, waving, and then he was gone.

Nora appeared from around the corner and leaned against the side of the house. "You might as well get used to it—he's not going to stop. It's just how people are around here," she said. "How much longer does Buster have on his barter contract?"

Ben groaned. "Another six months."

"That's a lot of omelets."

He skewed an annoyed look her way. "Yeah, tell me about it." What was he going to do when he sold this place? Throw in a free egg-delivery service to sweeten the deal to whomever bought it? "How's the yard coming along?"

She shrugged. "Come and see for yourself."

Ben negotiated the stairs carefully and hobbled after her. He'd been too busy with the Wallace case to spend much time staring out the window today, but it was apparent by the amount of progress she was making, she didn't waste time.

There was still work to do, but the yard was shaping up nicely. The old lawn—if that patch of crabgrass and dried weeds could be called that—had been torn out and a new sprinkler system was going in; the fountain was gone temporarily for refurbishing, and Nora was in the process of trenching for the small koi pond. Adding the fish had been a stretch, but once Nora explained that an exotic feature in the garden always caught people's attention, he agreed to it, though he was still a little uncertain about having fish in his side yard.

"It's a good thing I have a pretty solid imagination, Simmons," he said, "because this is a mess."

"It's not a mess," she retorted. "It's a work in progress. I just ordered the gazebo. It should be here in a week or two. I can't wait to put it in."

"Gazebo?" he asked, not quite remembering that detail.

She busied herself with gathering her tools. "Yeah, remember? The gazebo that overlooks the herb garden."

He stared harder, searching his memory. "I think I missed something. Did you say herb garden?"

She made a sound of impatience. "Yes, herb garden. It's all in the plans I showed you. You should pay better attention. If you had a problem with it, you should've said something before now. The supplies are already ordered."

"Why would I want a herb garden?" he asked, refusing to let the topic go. "I don't know the first thing about growing herbs, nor would I want to, and while you made a solid point with the koi pond, I don't think a herb garden is going to help sell the house."

Nora stuffed her tools in the back of her truck and glowered, muttering something highly uncomplimentary as she stalked by him. "I disagree. A herb garden that isn't tended regularly still gives the air a sweet, fresh smell even if you never use the herbs for any real purpose."

"That's ridiculous. Why would I pay for something that has no real purpose?"

"I didn't say it had *no* purpose, I said if it wasn't *tended* for any real purpose. Can't you see the difference?"

He shook his head, perplexed at her logic—or lack thereof. "No."

"Too bad for you, I guess," she said, moving past him until he grabbed her arm. She glared icily. "Remember the last time you grabbed me? It didn't end well for you."

Ben grimaced and released her. "Sorry, I didn't mean to, I just want you to slow down and talk to me. You have me at a disadvantage here." He pointed at his foot. "It's not like I can exactly keep up."

Her expression told him she didn't really care. Displeasure at how their relationship had become antagonistic again made him soften his words.

"Let's start over," he offered, but she only stared warily. "Last night ended badly. I probably could've handled our conversation with a little more tact but I didn't want to lie to you or give you false hope that I was the kind of man who wanted marriage and kids. It's just not me. But I really enjoy your company and I'd like to spend more time with you while I'm here."

"That's your idea of starting over?" she asked incredulously, her tone washing over him in strident waves. When he nodded in earnest, she slapped her thigh. "Well, that explains a lot. You. Are. An. Idiot."

He sputtered. "I am not."

"Only an idiot without a lick of sense in his head would think of telling a woman he's already slept with that he wouldn't mind hanging out and enjoying a little sex on the side while he's stuck in her Podunk town. It's no wonder you can't keep a girlfriend. You've got the social skills of a yak. To answer your proposition—so there's no room for misinterpretation—the thought of having sex with you now is as desirable as having a nail pounded into my foot. Your arrogance is only outmatched by your colossal ego and I can't imagine anyone wanting to spend more than ten minutes in your exalted company unless you were paying them—and even then, the sum would have to be pretty exorbitant. Are we clear, Benjamin Hollister?"

Perfectly. He pulled her into his chest with his free hand and claimed her sassy mouth. She gasped—and perhaps even growled, he wasn't sure, but the sound sent a zap straight to his groin—and met the thrust of his tongue with an aggressive parry as they tangled with a violence that made his knees weak. Just when he thought he was going to have to drag her to the ground, she tore her mouth away from his and gave him a savage push. His back hit the side of the house, but he was otherwise unharmed.

"Don't do that again," she said, her breath coming in short pants until she could draw a deeper lungful of air.

They stood staring at each other, but Ben refused to acquiesce to her demand. He wanted to kiss her and more. It was reckless and stupid to push the issue; she'd stated her preference—though her reaction to his kiss completely belied that statement—and he should, by all rights, back off. But he wouldn't. Something about her tied him in knots with wanting and it wasn't just her body. By God, he wished it were. It would simplify things by half.

"You can pretend you don't feel anything, Nora, but I won't buy it," he said, his heart rate finally slowing to a normal pace. "Whether you like it or not, there's something between us and I'm not afraid to see where it goes."

She swallowed as if afraid of the words she was trying to say. Finally she straightened and said with deliberate calm, "Ben, I know exactly where it will go…and where it will end. I'm choosing to end it now. I expect you to abide by my decision or I quit."

NORA SAT on the porch swing at her father's house and listened as her sisters' voices floated through the open window as Natalie and Tasha argued with their father about a subject that—by the sound of it—held neither their father's nor Nora's interest. She'd become accustomed to her sisters' squabbling since Tasha had come home a year or so ago and had usurped Natalie as the head of the siblings. Under normal circumstances Nora would have gleefully thrown in her two cents, but today, picking a side on any argument other than the one she was currently fighting didn't hold a candle.

Tucking her leg under her, she let her gaze drift over the tree line to the setting sun, comforted by the familiarity of her childhood home. A forlorn sigh escaped just in time for her sister Tasha to hear it.

"I didn't know you were here," she admonished gently. "You should've come in. I could've used your help in there."

"What's going on?" Nora asked, more out of courtesy than real interest. Her brain was elsewhere. "I heard you guys arguing."

Tasha exhaled loudly and shook her head. "Natalie thinks Dad should stop drinking, and I don't think it's a big deal. She found your beer and threw a fit."

Nora rolled her eyes, annoyance flaring bright. "She needs to stop focusing on Dad and worry more about her own life. He's fine. She needs to stop mothering him. If Mom's staring down at us right now, she's probably shaking her head and wondering how she managed to raise such a nitwit."

A small giggle from Tasha followed before she sobered, saying in Nat's defense, "She's just trying to do what's right. No doubt she felt she had to pick up the slack while I was gone. Do you think Dad should stop drinking?"

Nora leveled a look at her sister. "Only if he wants to. He's not an alcoholic. Natalie needs to relax."

Tasha nodded. "Glad to hear we're on the same page. I might need reinforcements later. Now that that's out of the way, what's up, little sis? It's not like you to hang out by yourself." Nora answered with a small shrug, but

Tasha saw right through her. "Give me some credit. I can tell something's eating at you," she said.

"Nothing I can't handle," Nora said with more confidence than she felt. "Just a little work situation. I have a client who's a little too full of himself."

"Is this the same guy you were talking about a couple of weeks ago?"

"The same."

"Is he coming on to you or something?"

Nora's cheeks heated and she mumbled, "Or something."

"Ah," Tasha murmured in understanding. "You like him, don't you?"

Nora stared morosely and thought to lie, but she needed to talk with someone and her older sister was a good start. "Yeah, you could say that, I suppose. I think I've had a crush on him since I was ten, only it took until now to realize it."

"So what's the problem?"

"Everything. He's a jerk. Of course, he didn't seem like a jerk until recently and I realized he'd always been a jerk. He just hid it well enough for me to think he was decent."

"Sounds manipulative," Tasha observed. "Did you come to this realization before or after you slept with him?"

Nora whipped her gaze to her sister's, shocked she'd been able to zero in on that particular point. "After," Nora finally answered. "And I'm really mad and achingly disappointed he's not who I wanted him to be."

"Who did you want him to be?"

A keeper. Nora swallowed the response that instantly flew to mind and shrugged. "It doesn't matter. Whatever I wanted…he wasn't."

THE SOUND OF A TRUCK rumbling into the driveway immediately had Ben shuffling to the window in the hopes that it was Nora but he was disappointed to see it was not.

Pushing open the screen door, he signaled to the man Ben recognized as Nora's backhoe buddy as he headed for the yard.

"Nora can't make it today," he explained. "Said something about not wanting to see your face. Boy, you've done put your foot in it, haven't ya?" He chuckled and Ben colored. "But don't stress, she told me what she wants done, so no worries about the job."

He wasn't worried about the job. "She's not coming at all?" he asked gruffly.

"Nope."

Great, he thought sourly. "Did she say anything else?"

The man did a show of searching his memory, then replied with great relish, "Nope."

Ben's gaze narrowed. "You don't like me much, do you?"

"No, I don't, and I'll tell you why. I've never seen Nora all tied up in knots over a guy. Whatever you did, it was enough to change the woman I've known my entire life and it wasn't for the better. So the sooner you're out of all our hair, the better, I say. Things can get back to normal around here."

"Let me guess, old boyfriend?" Ben assumed, trying not to think of Nora in an intimate tangle with the man.

"Wrong. Best friend. Name's Sammy Halvorsen. And I know you're the fancy lawyer who's here to offload his family's house for a quick buck. Nora has a soft heart for all her bluster. Take a word of advice and leave as soon as you can. We don't need people like you in Emmett's Mill and neither does Nora."

"Nora's an adult, she can make up her own mind," he answered calmly, though a slow, angry burn was searing his chest. "I'd thank you for the advice if it were needed, but it's not, so in the interest of preserving our working relationship, I'll just ask you to mind your own business and leave it at that. What happens between Nora and me is private and will remain private. Do we understand each other?"

Sammy's sardonic chuckle made Ben want to jab him in the gut with his crutch. "You've got a lot to learn about small towns," he said. "Nothing's private. If you're planning to stay you'd better get used to it."

He scoffed. "What makes you think I'm staying?"

"Because you seem to have a thing for Nora and nothing short of dynamite is going to blast her out of this town. She has something you'll never understand— pride in her roots. That's why you're going to leave and she's going to let you."

Ben swallowed at the man's uncanny insight, but refused to give him the satisfaction of knowing he'd hit a nerve. "Well then, I won't keep you from your work," he said coldly, allowing the door to slam behind him.

He didn't want to stay; she didn't want to go. He

didn't want the white picket fence and she didn't want a relationship that didn't hold the promise of marriage. She was smart to cut things off; a part of him appreciated her fortitude for ending something that held no future, but every time he considered walking away from her—as he should—he found himself fighting for air. He was scaring himself.

Heading to the office that was beginning to feel more comfortable than his corner office at the firm, he grabbed the phone and prepared to haggle with his client, knowing the battle was a suicide mission; Ed Wallace wasn't only a dumb son of a bitch, he was greedy, too.

He thought of Buster and how the man had integrity in spades yet little cash and wondered how his perception of people may have been altered if, instead of being kept from knowing his grandparents, he had been allowed to see them every summer. Would his view have differed? For the first time in his life, he allowed his mind to briefly consider what it would be like to have a wife. Nora starred front and center in his fantasy and he had to admit it didn't instill the knee-jerk reaction of distaste that usually followed, but he couldn't bear the thought of watching the love shining in her eyes slowly wither and disappear until they were sitting opposite one another in a courtroom, haggling over who got the furniture.

And kids? He closed his eyes against the vision that popped into his head of a towheaded little girl with Nora's spirit and inquisitive nature and a boy with his smile.

What was wrong with him? He jumped out of the chair as quickly as his injury would allow and limped out of the room as if that action alone would erase the image stuck in his head. Nothing short of a lobotomy was going to get rid of that tempting vision. And even then…who knows?

CHAPTER SIXTEEN

THE NEXT DAY, Nora dragged herself out of bed and prepared to go to work, and although she knew she had to face Ben sooner or later, she'd been hoping for later so that when she did see him she didn't do something rash.

And when it came to her mercurial moods, the definition of *something rash* had a wide range of possibilities.

It was time to take Ben to Doc Hessle's for a checkup and since she was Ben's number-one taxi service, it was up to her to get him there.

Of all the stupid scrapes she'd put herself into, this one certainly took the cake. For the first time ever, she was tempted to walk away from the job and refund Ben his money, but her pride prevented her from doing it, so as she climbed into Bettina, she tried not to notice that she'd put a little extra effort in her appearance today, arguing she wanted to look nice for Doc Hessle.

Yeah. That's why she'd dragged out her antique curling iron and tried coaxing her wild hair into some kind of style. Yep. For the doc.

Fine. She did it but for Ben, but only so that he knew right away what he was missing.

Slightly mollified by her logic, she backed out of her driveway and then pulled onto the highway.

As she pulled into Ben's driveway, she saw the work Sammy had finished yesterday and an ill-contained sound of joy escaped her mouth, as the rest of the old shrubbery had been cleared away, and the earth was clean and bare, ready for the plants she had waiting to go into the ground.

Corrinda and B.J. would've been thrilled. A small tear fell from the corner of her eye at the memory of the old coots and it took her a moment to get under control. She didn't want Ben to see her blubbering. The selfish prick would probably think she was crying over him.

And she so wasn't.

Bettina screeched in protest as Nora opened the driver's-side door and popped out of the truck. After promising the old girl a squirt of WD-40 when they got to town, she strode to the front door. She walked inside and hollered.

"Taxi's here, city boy. Get your butt in gear, this ride's taking off in two minutes."

Ben appeared, looking adorably rumpled and disheveled, and she wondered for a split second whether he'd slept in his clothes. But even as she thought it, she stomped the concern down with the vicious intent of a child stepping on a colony of ants collecting food for the winter. He wasn't worthy of her anxiety.

"I overslept," he said, his voice as bleary as his eyes. "I need to shower."

Nora looked at her watch. "Five minutes, no more."

He eyed his cast and shook his head. "I need more

time than that to shower with this thing on my foot. It'll take at least five minutes to wrap it up. Unless—" his expression turned suggestive as he added "—you want to help."

She hit him with a scathing look and sniffed. "Take as long as you need. You're the one who has to deal with the doc, not me."

"Forget it. I'll just wash my face real quick."

"And hopefully brush your teeth," she said under her breath, but Ben's look told her he heard her comment just fine. She suppressed a smile and turned her attention to the window facing the side yard, sighing with annoyance at the delay.

"Make yourself at home," Ben said caustically as he slowly disappeared to change.

Resisting the urge to respond by sticking out her tongue, she turned on her heel abruptly and headed for the kitchen to check his food stores. Peeking her head into the fridge, she noted with satisfaction that he was getting low on milk and butter—though not eggs, thanks to Buster's faithful deliveries—and wondered when she'd become so mean. The man had to eat and he was stranded, for crying out loud. If her mom were alive Nora would probably go deaf from the lectures she'd give on being a good Christian.

Well, she'd never been particularly pious, and her mom knew that, but she had to give the woman kudos for never giving up.

A surprise smile lifted her mouth as she closed the fridge. Her mom would've loved Ben. She'd always held out hope her youngest daughter would meet and settle down with a nice boy. Ben gave off that impression—too bad it wasn't real.

Ben reappeared through the breezeway and she sucked in a hungry gasp at his appearance. On second thought, she mused, deliberately averting her gaze, she preferred the rumpled look over the quickly cleaned one. He smelled like soap and his black hair was shiny from the hasty dousing, which only made him look all the more like some Calvin Klein model. As if he needed help in that department.

The man should seriously rethink his decision to procreate. His babies would be lovely.

"Let's go," she demanded, stalking from the room, determined to get this day over with. "Some of us don't have all day."

"I'm right behind you," he murmured and his tone made her distinctly aware of his hot gaze on her backside.

She whirled and hissed, "And don't stare at my ass!"

He chuckled and smiled, knowing he'd been caught, and the temptation to push him down another hill was only tempered by the secretly giddy pleasure that she affected him the same way he affected her.

At least that part of their relationship wasn't one-sided.

The ride was silent, though Nora was nurturing a wildly destructive hope that Ben might try to strike up a conversation just so she could shut him down. By the time they arrived at Doc Hessle's office, she was sullen and disappointed.

"I'll stay out here," she said in the waiting room,

flopping into the nearest chair and refusing to look at Ben as he hobbled to the front desk to talk with the receptionist.

Mabel, the doc's wife, chatted with Ben as if she wasn't aware that he'd completely cut his grandparents out of his life, when Nora happened to know Mabel and Corrinda had been bingo buddies.

Ben disappeared with a nurse and Nora grabbed an outdated *National Geographic* and tried burying her nose in it, but Mabel had spied her and appeared to be in the mood to chat.

Not that the older woman was ever not in a mood to chew the fat—Mabel was the resident gossip—but she seemed overly pleased to see Nora had brought Ben.

"He's a looker, isn't he?" Mabel gushed, prompting Nora to lift the magazine higher to dissuade any further conversation. "Nora Marie, I know you see me. Come over here and chat a minute," she instructed sternly, and Nora grudgingly put the magazine down.

"Isn't there some rule about chatting while working?" Nora asked.

"Not that I'm aware, at least not in this office," she answered with a cheeky grin.

"Maybe there should be," Nora grumbled. "How are you, Mabel? Win anything good lately?"

"Actually, funny that you should ask…I won a really wonderful toaster oven but I already have one I like so I gave it to Sunny Watkins. Since her husband died last year, she said she can hardly bring herself to cook, so I told her a toaster oven was perfect for fixing meals for one."

"That was nice of you," she said.

"We haven't seen you around the senior center much lately. What's got you so busy that you can't play a round of bingo now and then?"

She must've let her gaze stray to where Ben had disappeared, for Mabel immediately got a knowing look. "Oh honey, I don't blame you—he's cuter than a frog's ear. I think he looks a little like B.J., don't you think?"

"Uh, maybe a little?" Nora wondered if Mabel had been a little sweet on old B.J. Harmless flirtation was Mabel's middle name no matter her quarry's age. "Although he doesn't have his integrity," she said under her breath.

Mabel didn't seem to catch Nora's comment and continued to prattle. "I don't know about you, but if I were your age—and single, of course—I'd hook that boy faster than you could blink. He's a major prize. Good-looking, smart and with a fine job, you could do a lot worse." Mabel's voice dropped an octave in the interest of privacy. "And he's single. Not like that last man you set your sights on."

Nora colored and wanted to drop through the floor. No such thing as a secret in a small town. "Yes, well, he has the manners of a dog that hasn't been housebroken. I pity the woman who does try to catch him. She's in for a world of heartbreak."

Mabel looked taken aback. "That's a shame. He's so cute."

"Yeah, so are puppies until they pee on the rug."

Mabel tittered and Nora resisted the urge to roll her eyes. There was more to life than a guy who wasn't hard on the eyes. As Mabel so eloquently pointed out, Nora should know.

Ben walked out with Doc Hessle, and Nora did her best to appear disinterested, bored even, by his return. She checked her watch. "Done? You're still on crutches?" she noted in disappointment.

"Doc says I'm not quite ready for a walking cast yet, but my ribs are healing up nicely."

"Ankles are tricky buggers. Are you staying off it like I told you?"

"More or less," Ben answered, and Nora wanted to snort but didn't because if she did, she'd have to admit she was to blame for some of that activity.

"Well, keep doing what you're doing," Doc advised, and Nora almost choked on her own spit when Ben cast an eager look her way.

"I'm doing my best," Ben answered solemnly like a good boy, and Nora glared.

Oh, puhleeze. If only Doc Hessle had an inkling as to what Ben hoped to continue doing—mainly her!— he'd probably snap Ben in the ear for getting fresh.

"I suspect another two weeks and you'll be ready for a walking cast. You have great healing capacity," Doc Hessle said, clapping Ben on the back and causing him to hold his smile with difficulty. "Some people take forever to heal from the smallest of wounds, but others mend quickly—that's a sign of a healthy body and good genes."

"Is that your scientific or medical opinion, Doc?" Nora asked wryly.

"Both, smart aleck," the doc retorted, eliciting a

wider grin from Ben. He turned to Nora, serious. "You're doing a good thing helping this man out. Think you can hang in there for a little while longer?"

No. "As long as he continues to pay me," she answered sweetly.

The doc laughed. "In that case, keep your checkbook handy, Ben. This girl is all business."

Ben arched his brow so that only Nora would catch the subtle meaning, and if it weren't for the doctor standing there, she might've broken his other ankle.

"So are we done here?" she asked, eager to leave. Doc Hessle nodded and she smiled. "Great. Let's get moving. I have work to do."

"You and me both," Ben declared, earning a black look from Nora.

From behind the counter, Mabel made a clucking noise and they turned to find the older woman giving her husband a conspiratorial look. Nora's stomach was uneasy. Those two were up to something. "Mabel, Doc, whatever you two are thinking, you can just forget it because I'm not interested."

"Aw now, Nora, don't be like that," Mabel said. "I just had a fabulous idea and it wouldn't hurt to hear me out. Jim and I have been looking for a replacement couple for the bingo tournament because we can't make it tonight on account of unexpected plans to have dinner with the Johnsons, but if we give up our spot, we'll be out of the tournament."

"Mabel," Nora said plaintively, shuddering at the thought of spending an entire night at the senior center playing bingo with Ben. "That's kind of last minute. I'm sure Ben already has plans…"

Ben made a fair show of checking his memory and if she hadn't been royally annoyed with him she would've appreciated his playing along but then he ruined any good feelings she had by grinning widely and proclaiming he was free for the night.

"Excellent," Mabel exclaimed, turning to her husband. "We're still in!" She looked at Nora and gave her a bright, thankful smile and that, at least, was genuine. "We really appreciate this. We're in the top tier. I have my sights set on that plasma television. Tonight could be the big night."

Ben arched a brow. "A plasma television at bingo?"

Mabel nodded her head vigorously. "Oh yes, it was donated, of course, but it's a top-of-the-line model that we'd never feel right spending the money on for ourselves but would love to win. Jim likes to watch his *CSI* on a nice screen," she added with a wink. "I'll call Mary Alice—she's the bingo coordinator this round—and let her know that you'll take our place."

Nora's mouth worked but no words actually came out. The woman was a master. Somehow Nora had been roped into playing bingo and she wasn't even sure how it had happened. Doc caught her dumbfounded expression and rubbed her shoulder in understanding.

"You didn't stand a chance, sweetheart. She's been looking for our replacements for weeks. You were in the right place at the right time."

"That's debatable," she grumbled, shooting Ben a

look that promised retribution for not helping her out. She sighed. "What time are we supposed to be there?"

Mabel grinned. "Seven sharp, dear. And remember to dress lightly, the air conditioner is having fits again and can't seem to handle all the excitement of bingo night."

Ben's amused smile made her want to plant her foot in his behind. He thought he'd won that round. Well, he'd discover soon enough it was a dubious win, for she doubted a night with the elderly of Emmett's Mill was high excitement for the silver-spooned city boy. By the end of the evening, she'd be the one laughing.

IT TOOK SOME EFFORT but Ben convinced Nora to meet him at the house so they could drive together. Even though he couldn't get himself there it felt good to climb into his car and look across the way and see Nora sitting beside him.

He wasn't sure if it was a deliberate attempt at making him drool or if she dressed like this every time she went to play bingo, but he could barely keep his eyes where they belonged.

She wore a light, gauzy top that exposed the tanned, sultry skin of her neck that he vividly remembered kissing and nipping. Her delighted moans echoed in his memory and his jeans tightened as his groin remembered as well. He shifted discreetly, glad her attention was focused on driving the high-performance sports car and not on the suspicious bulge in his trousers. Light khaki capris and flirty sandals finished the look that was relaxed yet feminine, and her hair was loose and framed her face in beautiful waves. She wasn't wearing earrings but there was a light gloss slicking her lips that made him want to sample that delectable honey one more time. Who was he kidding? One more time? Try a thousand and even then he wasn't sure that would be enough to sate the hunger raging inside him.

They entered the senior center recreation hall and Ben was amazed at how bustling the room was, given the average age of the people inside. There was a blue-haired woman operating a smoothies bar and another couple selling kettle corn, the warm, sweet smell wafting through the air and giving the place a festive feel.

"Lively group, aren't they?" he observed, watching in amusement as a couple two-stepped past them to the music playing in the background. "And nimble," he added as the elderly man dipped his partner as if they were Fred Astaire and Ginger Rogers.

Nora allowed a small smile, but it was clear by the warm reception she wasn't a stranger to this group. "I like bingo," she admitted, moving away quickly before he could comment. He watched as she maneuvered her way to the lead announcer—who must've been Mary Alice—and after a short conversation and a lot of head bobbing, Nora returned with a set of playing boards. She handed him his and gestured to a free spot. "We'd better get a seat. This place fills up fast."

"Who knew bingo was such a draw?" he joked, pausing to pull out her seat before sitting in his own. She hesitated at his gesture but took her seat and scooted closer to the table. "So how do you play?"

"You don't know how to play bingo?" she asked incredulously, but he tried not to take offense. He was fairly certain there were things he could do that she could not.

"Do you know how to play water polo?" he retorted.

"Why would I know how to play water polo?"

"I could ask the same about bingo."

She snorted. "Apples and oranges." Then for reasons he wasn't sure, she switched gears. "All right, let's get down to basics. Mary Alice will select the numbers from the tumbler and read them out loud. You check your playing board for the number and if you've got it, place your chip on the number. Bigger places use a special marker on the playing board but we're not that sophisticated. The middle spot is your free square and then it's up to you to pay attention. When you get five in a row, yell *bingo*."

"Sounds fun," he said with a grin. "Any other special bingo lingo I should know?"

She cracked a smile and shook her head. "Just pay attention. And if you yell bingo, don't knock your chips off the board, because someone will come and check to make sure you're right."

He leaned over to whisper, "I'll bet that's a common problem with this bunch."

She giggled but immediately sobered as if realizing she was having fun and said, "There are people in this room who run 10ks and bike cross-country. Don't let their age fool you. These people don't let a number drag them down."

"Point taken."

"Good. I should also point out that Hugh—" she pointed discreetly to a spry-looking gentleman with waves of white crowning his head "—is a master at jujitsu."

He eyed the man. "Also good to know. Thanks."

Suddenly excitement flared in Nora's eyes and she gestured toward Mary Alice as she took the small stage where the tumbler was sitting on a table. "Get ready to experience senior center bingo, Emmett's Mill style," she added with a superior smile. "I guarantee you've never seen anything like this."

He was ready—or so he thought.

Hours later, he was wiping away the sweat beading on his brow and chanced a glance at Nora who was eyeing her board, memorizing her open spots so that, if by chance her number was called and she got bingo, she could scream it out faster than anyone else in the room. Judging by the past rounds, that was quite a feat. He was sitting in a good spot—he could get a bingo with two different numbers, but so was Nora. Her tongue snaked along her bottom lip and her fingers clenched the tiny chip in her hand and every muscle looked tensed and ready to go at the slightest provocation. If she won, he worried she might shoot out of her chair like a rocket.

It was the final round and the television was on display. Ben wanted to win so he could give it to the doc and his wife, but the competition was fierce.

"Here's the next number," Mary Alice said, pulling a ball from the tumbler. "Everyone ready? Lucky number B-thirteen!"

A bingo sounded from Ben's left amid the loud

groans of disappointment and Nora was craning her neck to see who had won. Mary Alice hurried over to double-check the numbers and announced, "No win! Sorry, Stan. You must've thought I'd said B-seven when I actually called *B-eleven*."

Stan lifted his hands in chagrin, but otherwise seemed to take his mistake well.

"There's still a shot," Nora said, concentrating so hard Ben actually wondered if she was trying to telepathically communicate the numbers she needed to the caller.

"Using the Force?" he asked playfully and he gestured toward her intense expression and clenched fists.

Nora loosened up—a little—and returned to her board. "C'mon D-fourteen or F-twenty. Mama needs a new plasma television."

Ben laughed but Nora's ardent plea to the bingo gods sent a dark thrill twisting through his insides. Mama…she'd make a fun mom. Possibly not the type to be the PTA president, but definitely one all the kids loved because she went out of her way to ensure everyone was having a good time. He pictured her laughing, cuddled with a blond-haired boy and a little girl dancing with a puppy—a snapshot of familial bliss.

Nora gripped his arm and he realized she was pointing wildly at his card. Breaking from his disturbing thoughts, he glanced at his card and realized Nora was saying he'd won.

Holy crap… "Bingo!"

Mary Alice hurried over and after a quick check, declared him the winner of the plasma television.

"I can't believe you won," Nora said, bordering on a dark glower that was completely adorable. He loved her competitive nature—even at a bingo game. "You must have the luck of the Irish," she pouted. "Well, let's go see how to collect your prize."

Ben and Nora went to Mary Alice, and after signing a release stating it was now his property and not subject to return because it was a donated item, Ben asked if he could leave the television overnight because his car wasn't large enough to transport it.

Mary Alice grinned knowingly. "You must be the one with the fancy sports car. I figured as much," she said. "No problem. Here's my number, just let me know when you want to pick it up."

He smiled his thanks and steered Nora to the smoothies bar. "Thirsty?"

"Parched."

"Strawberry banana or strawberry banana?" He read the choices and she laughed. He nodded, saying to the lady behind the counter, "Two strawberry bananas, please."

"Coming right up, handsome."

He caught Nora tossing her hair and fought the urge to plant a kiss straight on her mouth. "C'mon, admit it, you had fun," he teased.

She sent him a cool look. "Of course I had fun. I'm a regular here."

"I gathered from all the warm hellos. Now don't get me wrong because this was an unexpected treat, but you're about three decades too young for this crowd. Why don't you hang out with people your own age?"

He wouldn't have been surprised if she told him to mind his own business but she didn't. She accepted her smoothie and after a sip, answered blithely, "Because unlike people my own age, what you see here is what you get. These folks have lived full lives and no longer see the value of lying. I trust them."

As they walked to the car, he realized her honesty covered a bigger truth—a wound she was protecting. He waited until they were on the highway to return carefully to their previous discussion. "That guy you were seeing—the married one, he hurt you pretty bad, didn't he?" Her guarded expression was all the reply he needed. "What did you like about him? What was so special about him that you let your guard down?"

She sighed and shook her head with a self-deprecating smile. "I don't know. Bad timing. He was funny and confident and sexy. We got along so well, and he never showed any outward signs that he was married. He didn't wear a ring and he never had any pictures in his apartment that I could see that would make me suspicious. And I never asked."

"He had his own apartment?" he asked.

She nodded. "Cute little place in Elk Grove. Later, I learned he kept his own place but he kept the house with his wife in Woodland Hills. Never figured our paths would ever cross."

Ben shook his head at the embarrassment he heard in Nora's voice, hating the guy for hurting her. "You know all guys aren't like him," he reminded her gently, though to what purpose he wasn't sure. She'd already stated her adamant desire to stay away from him.

She forced a chuckle. "A lawyer *and* a shrink? Your clients are so lucky. Listen, Ben, I know all guys aren't like Griffin, but I haven't found another I'm interested in taking a chance on." She chose not to look at him when she said that, and Ben sensed she was lying. She'd been willing to take a chance on him but he'd dropped her as badly as Griffin, with one exception, he defended himself—he'd never promised her a future. Still, he had let her down.

She pulled his car into the driveway of his place, and he invited Nora in for a nightcap. To his surprise, she accepted, though he wasn't about to question her motives. Frankly he didn't care.

Nora wandered into the darkened sitting room and, after lighting a single lamp, relaxed into an overstuffed lounge chair with a sigh. She didn't look like a guest but rather the woman of the household. Ben backed out of the room to clear his head and returned with two glasses of red wine.

She accepted the glass and smiled shyly. "Thanks for going to bingo with me. Mabel and Jim are going to be over the moon that you won that television."

He grinned and savored a swallow of wine. "I'm actually excited about seeing their expressions when I tell them tomorrow. You should come with me."

"Maybe. I have a lot of work to do."

She dipped her head and inhaled the woodsy scent of the wine, enjoying the way the smooth alcohol soothed her tensed muscles and eased her concerns that coming inside was a bad idea. She finished her glass and watched as Ben made his way toward her, unbuttoning the first two buttons of his shirt to expose a glimpse of his smooth chest.

"How's your foot?" she asked, but her gaze was nowhere near his ankle. She knew what lay beneath that shirt and the knowledge teased her senses and messed with her ability to think clearly.

He eased into a wing chair. "Not bad. It feels weak and there's a twinge now and then, but other than that, I guess it's doing better."

She smiled but her mind was far from the doc. She bit her bottom lip. "Glad to hear it." As if suddenly seeing herself and her actions if she stayed, she mustered the strength to end the evening and slowly stood. "I should go," she announced almost painfully.

He nodded as if it was a good idea, but then must've changed his mind, for as she walked past him, he gently grasped her hand and pulled her to him until she was in his lap. It felt entirely too good to be cradled in his arms.

"Ben…"

"Shhh…" he murmured, stealing her breath with the soft press of his lips against hers. "I've been wanting to do this all night," he admitted. "You're so amazing. So unlike any woman I've ever known…" He deepened the kiss with almost savage intensity. She responded greedily, a part of her brain wailing at the lack of control she was exerting, and a second later she turned and straddled his hips, placing her knees on either side of his thighs. He looked into her eyes and she nearly melted at the wonder she saw there. "Woman…" he said, cradling her with both hands. "You're under my skin and I don't know what to do about it."

"That makes two of us," she admitted, sliding her hands up his chest and fighting the purr she felt rumbling in her throat. Too many clothes between them, a voice whispered, and she was inclined to agree. Sliding carefully off his lap, he watched warily as if he was afraid she was going to leave. She smiled and held out her hand. "Let's go complicate things."

He didn't hesitate and accepted her hand. She pulled him out of the chair and smack into her mouth. *A perfect place to be,* she thought fuzzily as desire blotted out anything that didn't involve their bodies rubbing against each other.

They managed an odd kiss-and-stumble to his bedroom before they fell onto the four-poster bed and the gauzy netting draped the bed, but Nora only felt Ben's fingers divesting her of her clothes until she was bare to his hungry gaze, loving the way he seemed to drink her appearance like a starving man. Never had she felt so desired, so wanton yet so safe. With only a few choice curse words as his cast hindered progress, Ben had shucked his own clothing and carefully climbed the length of her body until he was above her, staring down at her as if she were a prize he'd won in battle and meant to treasure. She realized hazily, she could happily drown in a look like that.

"You're so beautiful," he murmured, sealing her mouth with another searing kiss before gently capturing both of her hands and pulling them over her head so that she was helpless to escape even if she'd had the wherewithal to try. The simple action sent a dark thrill spiraling down to her toes and her breath hitched in her throat.

With one hand free, he gently massaged her breast until her nipples puckered painfully, aching for the hot slickness of his mouth. She didn't have to wait long. Seconds later, he descended on her breast, laving it with his tongue until she writhed against the hold he had on her, and her hips bucked against the erection she felt against her thigh. She bit her lip against the urge to beg.

He released her arms and she wound them around his neck so they could roll together until she was on top.

She grinned devilishly, knowing exactly how to move to put him over the edge, but he surprised her by flipping them again. "Not so fast," he said, exciting her with his control. "You're not getting there yet."

He slid down her body, stopping at the juncture of her thighs, and hooking his arms around her legs, he lifted her until her most private part was exposed and ready for his mouth.

Nora groaned and sank into the pillows as his tongue touched her with alternating strokes that within moments had her panting and gripping the bedcovers against the building crescendo waiting to explode within her body.

She tensed and her heart seemed to stop as stars burst behind her eyes with the force of her climax. She shuddered and came back to earth slowly, opening her eyes sluggishly in time to see Ben poised above her. She grinned and accepted him as he slid into her body in one slow push that seemed to fill her completely. She reveled in the way his eyelids fluttered shut with a groan that she felt rock her soul. This was what it felt like to make love, she thought in a heated fog, the realization intensifying the physical sensations rioting through her body.

"Nora," he gasped her name, burying his face against the crook of her neck as he slid in and out with strong, powerful strokes. "Oh…"

He tensed and shuddered before collapsing against her, their hearts perfectly aligned and beating wildly together, raining soft kisses along her collarbone before uttering a single word, "Amazing…"

He didn't know the half of it.

CHAPTER SEVENTEEN

NORA WAS NEVER a cuddler, but as soon as Ben pulled her to him she curled against his body as if it was the most natural thing in the world, and simply enjoyed the feel of his skin against hers.

He kissed the back of her neck and she heard him inhale softly. "You have the most intoxicating smell," he murmured against the shell of her ear, causing her to shiver. "I can't quite describe it. It's just you and I can't seem to get enough of it."

She smiled. "Maybe I should bottle it and try to market it somehow."

He growled. "I don't like to share."

A tingle warmed her belly at his statement and she settled into her pillow, her eyes drifting shut. "Neither do I," she countered softly.

She was nearly asleep when his voice brought her back to consciousness. "What did you say?" she asked with a small yawn.

"Nothing. Go back to sleep."

There was something troubling about the timbre of

his voice but she was too tired to rouse herself to find out. Whatever it was, it could wait until morning.

And then she dropped off into the most restful sleep she'd ever had.

EARLY THE NEXT MORNING Ben rose and made Nora breakfast while she slept. He didn't sleep very well and he wished he could blame his restless night on Nora's snoring but he couldn't. He loved the way her body curled into his in a completely trustful manner and he was racking his brains to find a way to extend their relationship into more than his short stay in Emmett's Mill would allow. Ben wasn't accustomed to wooing a woman and he didn't know where to start. But he'd find out, because he wasn't ready to let her go.

He hobbled to the bedroom with a laden tray just as she woke, stretching and making little noises like a sated cat after a bowl of cream, and he nearly dropped their breakfast on the floor.

"Good morning, sexy," he said, coming to set the tray before her. Her eyes widened and her gaze flew to his as he grinned. "Denver omelet, the sequel. This one you'll be able to eat."

"God, that smells good," she said, taking the fork and, without a hint of bashfulness, sectioned off a piece. She groaned when she popped the food into her mouth and speared another piece. "Perfect," she said with her cheeks full. "But you shouldn't be moving around so much. If Doc Hessle knew how much you were doing, he'd give you an earful," she admonished as Ben grabbed his own fork and followed suit. "But you are a fabulous cook. Of course, you probably know this, but I don't mind saying it again—you can cook for me anytime."

His gaze narrowed at the innocent comment and she stopped. "Did I say something wrong?" she asked.

"No. I'd make anything your heart desires," he answered honestly. "All you have to do is say yes."

"Say yes?" She swallowed with difficulty, her eyes widening. "What do you mean?"

"Nora, will you be my girlfriend?"

The light dimmed in her gaze and he realized his question hadn't been the one she'd been hoping for. She speared another bite and chewed slowly, careful to avoid his eyes. "Ben, we've already covered this topic."

"I didn't like the outcome," he said, watching her closely, noting her demeanor had changed and she'd returned to her naturally guarded state. The change disappointed him but he didn't give up. "Why not, Nora?" he pressed.

He read the hurt in her expression. "Because I refuse to start a relationship that has no hope of going further. It's pointless."

"Why?" he asked, frustration at her argument coloring his voice. "Who starts a relationship with the expectation that a walk down the aisle is inevitable? Wait, don't answer. Apparently too many, which explains the rampant divorce rate in California. That's the moment they come to their senses and realize they never should've tied the knot in the first place."

He got up from the bed and she pushed the tray away. Anger crept into her cheeks, dusting her face with hot spots of color. "And who starts a relationship with the knowledge that it's destined to go *nowhere?*"

"I can't believe a woman as highly educated as yourself is refusing to go into a relationship with a man whom you're clearly attracted to just because he doesn't want to get married!"

She swung her legs over the side of the bed and jerked the bedsheets around her naked body. He only had a moment of regret in losing sight of her luscious figure before she was stomping past him with the ire of a woman scorned.

"Screw you, Hollister," she snapped, and he couldn't help the snarl that followed.

"If I remember correctly, that's exactly what you did last night and I didn't hear any complaints!"

She skewered him with a glare before slamming the bedroom door. He quickly followed.

"Where are you going? You're naked!"

Nora glanced down at her body and her lips tightened as she realized she'd left her clothes behind. She would have to push past him to return to the bedroom, but he knew she'd rather walk on hot coals than go anywhere near him and for once he was glad. She wouldn't dare leave wearing only a bedsheet and he wasn't finished with the conversation.

He took a deep breath to cool his temper and tried again. "Nora, we're good together. We share a connection that makes the sex between us out of this world. We both enjoy each other's company. We're intellectually compatible and certainly compatible in bed—why won't you just give it a chance?"

Her eyes brightened suspiciously and he realized Nora was on the verge of tears. The urge to cradle her in his arms was strong, but not stronger than his need to hear her agree to give his way a shot. "Honey, I'm not like that other guy. I'll never lie to you and pretend to offer something I have no intention of sharing. Does that mean nothing? Why won't you give me a chance?"

Nora stiffened and glared. "Because you're worse."

"Worse? Worse than the guy who used you?" He took offense. "How? I've been nothing but honest with you from the very beginning. I desire you unlike any woman I've ever met and I know you feel the same about me. Why are you fighting it when it's so good?"

Her jaw hardened. "It's good for *you*, Ben. I've already told you it's not good for me. That's your problem. You're so accustomed to looking out for yourself you don't take the time to consider how someone else might feel." She tugged the sheet closer around her body. "And I'm not interested in your offer. Contrary to what you think, you're no different than Griffin. You just have a different way of asking for the same thing. You want me on your terms, no matter the cost to anyone else. I'll tell you what I told him. Whatever we had is over. Goodbye."

And then she did exactly what he didn't think she would and marched out the door.

NORA REFUSED to cry—at least that's what she told herself fiercely as tears stung the back of her eyes. She had a knack for picking the biggest jerks on the planet.

If there were a market for such a talent, she'd be a millionaire. But no one wanted her gift—least of all her.

Her heart wailed as she drove, and she used the edge of the sheet still wrapped around her body to wipe at her nose. She should've stuck to her original plan and ignored him, but damn if he didn't worm his way back into her good graces. Manipulative lawyer scum, she wanted to scream, but her throat closed as another wave of sadness threatened to drown her. What was wrong with the men she was attracted to?

Bettina rumbled into Nora's driveway and kicked up a cloud of dust as she pulled in. Nearly tripping in her haste to get into the house, she yanked at the caught bedsheet and ran in, hating Ben, hating men, hating her inability to spot a decent man amongst the snakes curling around her.

BEN STARED IN SHOCK as Nora jumped into her battered truck and sped down the driveway. Spurred into action a second too late, he managed to get outside in time to eat a cloud of dust.

Stumbling into the house, he winced as his ankle protested the action. Once in the study he riffled through papers on his desk, looking for Nora's business card. Finding it, he grabbed the phone and dialed her cell phone. As he expected, it rang four times and then went to voice mail, which meant she'd just screened his call. He tried again. This time there was no ring, only voice mail, telling him she'd shut off her phone. Reaching for the business card, he read the address printed on it.

Grabbing whatever clothes were within reaching distance, he threw them onto his body and scrambled to his car. This was not over—not by a long shot!

He stared down at his foot and weighed his options. He could kill himself trying to drive with this stupid cast. The manual transmission didn't lend itself to accommodating a crippled foot. Dammit! A crazy thought came to him and as he practically dragged himself back into the house to the office, he knew this idea was a long shot.

Pulling Nora's estimate from his desk, he flipped through to the page listing her subcontractors and found the contact number for Sammy Halvorsen. The guy didn't like him very much, but maybe luck was on his side. Ben could only hope.

"You want me to what?" Sammy asked incredulously once Ben got him on the line and explained the circumstances. "You're nuts."

"I can't drive and I have to talk to her." He tried a little harder to appeal to some sort of guy loyalty. "Have you ever met a woman that gets under your skin so bad that it goes beyond any pleasure or pain you've ever felt?"

There was a long pause on the other end, and Ben had the sinking feeling he'd banked on the wrong emotion until Sammy sighed and a forced chuckle followed.

"Man, do I ever. All right, here's the deal. I'll help you out, but you better not hurt her or you'll be dealing with me, got it?"

"Deal. Now hurry up and get over here. She's already got a ten minute head start on us."

AFTER A NAUSEATING half hour of navigating twisting country roads, Sammy pulled into Nora's driveway and said he'd wait outside. "Good luck, city boy."

Ben accepted the dubious offer of luck and wondered if he'd ever earn a different nickname around this town. He made his way to the front door, giving it a sharp rap before entering the house.

"Nora?" he called out, going from room to room until he heard the faint sound of sniffling. An abrupt detour later, he found Nora in the bedroom, curled on her side and crying into her pillow. The sight tore at his heart. He swallowed the lump in his throat and said, "Please come talk to me. I don't want to end this on such a bad note."

She lifted her head, shocked to see him standing there. "What are you doing here? How did you—"

"I talked Sammy into bringing me," he answered.

She narrowed her gaze and snorted. "Some best friend he is," she added with a watery sniff. "If you've come to retrieve your bedsheet, I threw it in the trash."

Startled, he said, "You threw it in the trash?"

"I was all out of lighter fluid," she retorted.

Right. Focus. "Okay, you're mad. I get that."

She popped up, indignation flashing in her eyes. "Mad? I'm more than mad, you idiot. I'm hurt."

Chagrined, he tried again. "I'm sorry. I didn't mean to hurt you. I was trying *not* to hurt you."

She made a face. "Well you're terrible at it."

"I know. I have a talent for honing in on someone's vulnerable spots and poking at them. I've been trying to change…that's why I wanted to open my own firm. I'm tired of being the ruthless bastard I'm known as."

She wiped at her tears, still listening. That gave him courage to continue. "Nora…when my last girlfriend broke up with me, I swore I wouldn't get into another relationship unless she knew from the start that I wasn't the kind of man who wanted marriage and kids. I didn't tell my last girlfriend and we ended a relationship that I thought was pretty good, until I realized after a year she was waiting for me to pop the question. I didn't want to hurt you like that."

She swallowed and her expression looked wounded, not for herself this time but for him. "My parents were married for forty-seven years before my mom died of pancreatic cancer. I thought my dad was going to climb into the grave with her he loved her so much. My sister Tasha and her husband, Josh, were high-school sweethearts who never stopped loving each other and ended up married almost twenty years later, still so in love it hurts to look at them. My other sister, Natalie, is married to a man who thinks the sun rises and sets in her smile and doesn't mind that she's a worrier and wound too tight. Love is real, Ben. It's out there. Has it ever occurred to you that what you see is only a skewed version?"

Ben's lips clenched together and his heart thumped painfully against his chest. She didn't see the ugliness he saw every day. "What if you're wrong, Nora? What if what *I* see is the norm and not the exception? It's a scientific fact that love is a chemical reaction in the brain that can be simulated in a lab. How romantic is that? Love can be induced in lab monkeys, but that's not something we want to put on a greeting card, now is it?"

She drew back in shock and he cursed under his breath, hating that she'd hit a nerve. "Nora, once my parents were happy. I have good memories of going to the park for picnics, boating on a Sunday afternoon, and my mother teaching me how to ride my horse. But they're overshadowed by the bad memories of a marriage disintegrating before my eyes as two people who were supposed to love each other 'till death do us part' started their own War of the Roses. I refuse to go through that myself. It's better to stop while you're ahead."

"Life without love isn't worth living," she said sadly.

"That's your opinion," he retorted coldly. "And a naive one at that. Contrary to what you may believe, love doesn't make the world go round—money does. And we all know there's nothing warm and fuzzy about the pursuit thereof."

She looked at him reproachfully, but he refused to give in to the pull of regret. Perhaps she was right. They had no future. He was stupid to have come hoping otherwise. He should let her go, both professionally and personally.

But she beat him to it and he didn't like the sound— or feel of it.

"Ben, I quit. You're going to need to find someone else to finish the job. I'm sorry. I've never quit a job before, but I can't work with you there. It's too hard."

He swallowed at the quiet anguish in her voice, knowing how difficult it would have been for Nora to admit such vulnerability and his opinion of himself took a nosedive.

"Please don't quit," he said, despite her protests. "It's not necessary. I'll leave in the morning. You can finish the landscaping without me around. I'll leave a check on the hallway table."

"Ben, you don't have to leave. It would be easier to replace me. Besides, you can't leave yet. You can't even drive. Who will take care of you?"

Ben chuckled blackly. "Nora, don't be ridiculous. Your work is almost finished. It would be twice as expensive to hire someone new, and if I can pay you to take care of me, I can find someone else to do it for a short while."

He didn't mean to make it sound as if she was easily replaced, but the pain in his chest made it hard to temper his words.

"Sounds like you have everything figured out," she said icily. "Your ride is waiting."

In other words: get the hell out.

He stiffened and with as much dignity as a man on crutches could maintain, he walked out.

What he didn't say but certainly believed was that Nora would be impossible to replace in his life. He wouldn't even try.

He climbed into the truck and Sammy regarded him curiously. "Didn't go well?" he surmised.

"You could say that," Ben answered.

Sammy put the truck in Reverse and chuckled lightly. Ben gave him a sharp look. "What's so funny?"

"Life. You never know when it's going to throw a curveball."

Ben snorted. "This is no curveball—it's a goddamn train wreck."

CHAPTER EIGHTEEN

THE NEXT DAY Nora went to Ben's and found his car
gone and a fat check on the hallway table just as he'd
promised. Her immediate thought was how he'd
managed to drive the car, but figured he'd paid someone
to take him back to the city. As he said, he could
probably find anyone for the right price. Forgoing the
check, she wiped at her eyes and wandered the house,
feeling her heart break for his absence. Hopefully his
new driver cost him more than an arm and a leg—a
kidney, perhaps.

It was several minutes before she could focus on the
day ahead. Ben was right about the job—it was nearly
finished and it was silly to hire someone else. Plus, for
selfish reasons, she hated the idea of someone else
coming in and putting their mark on her work, so she
put her heart on hold and her head on track. This was
something into which she could pour her energy.

Nora lost herself in planting rows of cheery yellow
spring primrose and orange marigolds along the side of
the house, when the sound of a car caught her attention.
Pausing long enough to see if it was Ben, she returned
to her planting when she saw it was not.

"I've been calling your cell and it's just going straight

to voice mail," Sammy complained as he strode to her. "What gives?"

She shrugged. "Didn't feel like talking. Especially to you," she added pointedly.

"All right. I'll take that hit because I drove him to you, but he sounded so pitiful he tugged at my heartstrings."

"I didn't know you had heartstrings to pull," she said, still angry and feeling betrayed. "What do you want? Like I said, I don't really feel like talking."

He did a double take. "Since when? I believe Nora Simmons not feeling like talking is the fifth sign of the apocalypse."

Nora didn't have the will to chuckle at Sammy's joke. "What did you need, Sammy?"

He came to squat beside her, squinting against the sun. "I haven't talked to you in a while and needed a girl's perspective, but it doesn't look like you're up to dispensing advice. Listen, I'm sorry that city boy broke your heart. I thought, maybe, I don't know, there might be something between you guys. I thought you might be in love with him and were just too stubborn to admit it."

"So you sold me out on the premise of love?" she asked but she'd lost some of her fire. "Whatever. It doesn't matter. He's gone."

"So…good riddance, right?"

She looked at Sammy sharply and he lifted his hands in defense. "Don't bite my head off, just following your lead. What happened?"

She sighed and wiped her brow with her wrist before sitting back on her haunches. "You were right. I fell in love with him. Stupid me, huh?"

Sammy sobered and gestured toward the house. "He got beer in his fridge?" She nodded and he helped her up. "Then let's go snag a few. You and I've got a lot of catching up to do."

Nora smiled, grateful for a friend as solid as Sammy and followed him into the house.

Cracking open two dark import beers, Sammy and Nora found themselves back outside on the porch, commandeering chairs they found in a shed.

Sammy dusted hers off, saying, "A little dirt never hurt anyone. C'mon, let's talk."

"There's nothing to talk about, Sammy. He practically warned me at every turn not to fall in love with him because he didn't believe in love or marriage, and I did it anyway. What can I say? I'm an idiot."

"No, you're not. You're a closet romantic," Sammy countered. "Always have been. It's just that most people don't dig hard enough to reach that soft underbelly of yours. Unfortunately, the two that have, happened to poke at you with a sharp stick."

She exhaled. "All right, wise one…enough."

"Well, all I'm trying to say is there's nothing wrong with you. If this man of yours is too dumb to see what's right in front of him, that's his problem. And that other guy, what was his name? Grissom? Grendel? Gristle—"

"Griffin."

"Whatever. He was just a jackass and you're better off without him."

"I know. But I thought Ben was different. I really did." She refrained from describing the connection she'd shared with Ben, it only made her feel worse. "It's going to be hard letting him go."

And this house, she realized. It had long ago started to feel like her home and the thought of someone else walking the halls and enjoying her koi pond made her want to weep.

Stupidly she'd started to picture the halls filled with family—her sisters and their children—maybe her own. She tipped the beer back and closed her eyes against the tears threatening to fall.

Sammy wisely remained silent and she struggled to get a grip, refocusing on what was important. She cleared her throat, but a catch remained in her voice as she said, "Ben paid me. I'll cut you a check tomorrow for the backhoe work."

He waved her away. "I know you're good for it. Whenever."

She smiled her gratitude. He instinctively knew she was putting off cashing that check. It was illogical, but somehow she thought if she didn't cash the check, Ben's leaving wasn't real. That he'd have to return at some point. But the very fact that she was clinging to such a ridiculous hope made her angry at herself.

Finishing the rest of her beer, she handed Sammy the empty bottle and stood. "Break's over. I have new sod coming tomorrow. If you're available, I could use an extra back."

"You got it, friend. Need anything else? Like someone to pummel that ex-boyfriend of yours?"

Her smile was brief. "He wasn't my boyfriend."

He wasn't anything.

BY THE TIME Sammy showed up the next morning, Nora had been at the job for two hours. She hadn't been able to sleep and didn't see the point of lying in bed staring at the ceiling when there was work to be done. Her cell phone remained off and she was afraid of turning it back on. What if he called? Worse, what if he didn't? Either way it was safer to keep it off.

Sweat poured down her back and soaked the waistband of her jeans but she didn't stop. Laying sod was backbreaking work but she welcomed the physical exhaustion. Her muscles screamed as she pulled another layer of sod from the pile and laid it into place, covering the freshly installed sprinkler system in neat rectangles.

Sammy sensed she was in a rhythm and didn't start the morning with chatter. They worked side by side like robots until noon and the entire lawn was done. It looked glorious, but Nora wasn't sitting back to admire her work. The gazebo was also arriving today and she needed to clear the area so they could carry it in. She also had to fill the koi pond and drop in the fish—they were waiting in a special container, but couldn't stay there long.

Nora and Sammy were hefting the gazebo into place when a Honda Accord drove into the driveway. Nora glanced up and looked to Sammy. He broke into a nervous grin and gestured for the driver to come over.

"Who's that?" she asked, though she had a fair idea and she wasn't in the mood to entertain guests.

"Take a break," he suggested, but Nora waved him away. "C'mon, I want you to meet someone."

"We've already met, remember?" Nora said sourly,

not caring that she sounded like a shrew. It was fitting. She felt like one. "Go ahead, I can finish."

"Nora, it's important to me," he said, his suddenly earnest tone catching her ear. "I need you guys to get off on the right foot." He gestured to the woman getting out of the car. "Dana, come on over. Watch the grass, though, it's new."

Dana, the bossy paramedic, made her way over to them and for a second the two women simply regarded each other warily, as if waiting to see if defensive maneuvers were warranted. Finally, Dana extended her hand to Nora. "We haven't been formally introduced, but I've heard a lot about you."

Nora shook her hand. "Don't believe everything you hear," she said, shrugging. "Then again, maybe you should. Half of it's right, the other half's wrong but you never know which is which."

"Samuel speaks very highly of you," she said, smiling at Sammy.

Nora angled a look at Sammy. *Samuel?* He grinned sheepishly. *So that's how it is.* "Nice to meet you. Sorry about my behavior earlier. I was under a lot of stress that day with my client falling down a hill and nearly killing himself. He wore the wrong shoes," she said as if that explained it all.

"Nora, we wanted to tell you something in person because the news we have just doesn't seem right to say over the phone but the last few days you've been hard to track down," Sammy said, and Nora blushed, knowing exactly what she'd been doing. Dana slipped her hand into Sammy's and Nora got a queasy feeling.

Not now, she wanted to groan, but Sammy was beaming like a blooming idiot. "We're getting married."

"You and her?" she asked, cringing seconds later when she realized how rude that sounded, but she was tired and cranky and even on the best of days hardly tactful.

Dana stiffened but Sammy rushed to smooth things over. "Try to contain your joy. It's damn near contagious. C'mon, usually congratulations are in order."

Inexplicably Nora's eyes watered and she nodded, ashamed of herself for feeling so bitter inside when her best friend was sharing the happiest moment of his life with her. "Congratulations, Sammy, Dana. I hope you're very happy together and it's not just a chemical reaction in the brain!"

Spinning on her heel she ran into the safety of the house and buried her face in Ben's pillow, inhaling his lingering scent and hating that she missed him and was tempted to agree to any term he liked as long as he came back to her. Pathetic, but true. God help her, how pathetic.

BEN CLOSED his briefcase and prepared to leave the courtroom but his client, Ed Wallace, was spitting mad.

"You rotten bastard, she took half my estate!" he said, spittle flying from his mouth to land on his expensive tie. Wallace glanced around and readjusted his suit before continuing in a malevolent hiss. "I'll see you out of a job by the end of the day for your incompetence. By the time I'm through, you won't be able to give legal advice at a free clinic. Mark my words, Hollister. You're career is *over*."

Ben ignored the malice in Ed's voice. "I told you to settle. I'm not a miracle worker. You should've heeded my advice before she wised up. Better luck next time."

"If you think it's a coincidence that she found out about my account in the Cayman Islands, you're royally screwed in the head. I'll have you disbarred for sharing confidential information with the enemy," Ed vowed, nearly vibrating with anger, but Ben could care less. He felt oddly liberated despite the fact that Ed Wallace would most assuredly end his legal career in the Bay Area. He'd think about that later.

He moved past Ed and walked over to opposing counsel, surprising both the former Mrs. Wallace and her attorney. He shook her attorney's hand and offered a smile that was more relieved than professional though he hoped they saw only the latter. "Don't waste a moment worrying about Ed. Men like him always land on their feet. Good luck."

Mrs. Wallace met his gaze and smiled tremulously, communicating she was grateful but if she knew the identity of the man who'd provided her the confidential information she needed to win, she'd never tell.

He inclined his head and left.

Ben was halfway to his office when he spotted the lithe figure of Elise Birkeland standing beside one of the senior partners. He offered a wave and cloistered himself inside.

Isaac Franklin, senior partner of the firm, walked in unannounced, but Ben wasn't surprised. "Isaac, what can I do for you?" he asked congenially, steepling his fingers as he waited. *This is the part where I'm fired,* he thought to himself.

"Ed Wallace is ranting and raving about how you sabotaged his case. Is this true?" Isaac asked point-blank.

Ben considered his answer and opted for a variation of the truth. "I told him to settle. He refused. The man's a greedy bastard and he got what he deserved."

"It's not our job to determine morality. It's our job to win," Isaac reminded him, his gaze shrewd. "And you didn't answer my question. Is there any validity to Ed's claim?"

He looked Isaac straight in the eye and imagined saying yes, that he'd deliberately offered information that would sink his client, but he wasn't stupid. "No." He leaned back in his chair. "You and I both know Ed Wallace is stupid and prone to bragging. He could've blabbed about his offshore account to the tart he's seeing or any other person who might've been impressed by that sort of thing." He shrugged. "I did the best I could with what I had to work with."

Isaac grunted an acknowledgment. "You've a point. We'll get the bill out quickly before he starts moving money around. Good job, Benjamin. It was a tough case but in light of the circumstances, I don't think anyone else could've done better."

Ben let the praise bounce off him, knowing it meant nothing. Next week, he'd get another case just like this one and he'd be expected to win, no matter the cost.

Closing his eyes, he tried to savor the look on Mrs.

Wallace's face when the judge ruled in her favor, but Elise's entrance interrupted him.

Her svelte beauty did nothing to arouse him, which he noted was probably a travesty in some neck of the world, but it was true. The only woman that turned his head was miles away and out of reach.

"You were missed, darling," Elise said, coming to sit on the corner of his desk, her expensive couture suit smelling of money and power. Her ice-blue eyes were watching him closely. "Are you healed from your injury?"

"Just a twinge now and then."

"So glad to hear of it. It must've been dreadful tucked away in that mountain town with your country girl," she mused. "So nice to be back in civilization, yes?"

Yeah. What's not to miss about bumper-to-bumper traffic, graffiti and crazy people talking to themselves? "There were some things I enjoyed about the mountains," he admitted. Like Nora. Waking up with her in his arms, listening to her snore, even arguing.

She waved away his answer. "Pooh on that. Clean air, quaint lifestyles, too *Green Acres* for the likes of us. We thrive on what the city can provide. Come to the theater with me tonight. I have box seats and Isaac has made other plans."

"So you're seeing Isaac now?" he asked and she lifted one shoulder in a delicate shrug.

"He amuses me. For the time being. You know how it goes. He's here today, perhaps not tomorrow. I don't waste time chasing one man when there are so many more out there to choose from." She tapped his desk, demanding his attention. "Come with me, yes?"

"Another time," he suggested, though they both knew he wouldn't.

She sighed and rose from his desk. "Go back to your country girl," she directed with an air of bored indifference. "She has sucked all the fun out of you."

He chuckled at Elise's pique. She would forget about him within seconds; her interest in anything was fleeting. But she'd managed to zero in on one essential truth—Nora had done something to him. He was different. And the change might just be the best thing that had ever happened to him.

CHAPTER NINETEEN

"NORA," GUSHED HER SISTERS as they surveyed the finished grounds. "God, it's gorgeous!"

Nora smiled with pleasure at her sisters' praise and agreed silently. The finished yard was a dream. The koi were swimming in their new habitat, their flashes of brilliant color peeking out from beneath giant floating lily pads, and the fountain gurgled as if chortling with delight over its new polished and buffed exterior.

The lawn extended around the house with an arbor leading to Nora's herb garden, and the air was sweet and fragrant with the varied flowers and foliage. They were right; it was gorgeous.

Yet her heart felt like lead in her chest. Ben was not here to enjoy it with her. She'd given up hope that he'd at least call, and she expected the last she'd hear from him would be when he received her final invoice and cut the check for the expenses. Leaving her sisters to explore the grounds, she wound her way down the newly constructed pathway to the creek and found a place to sit beside the water.

The blackberry bushes were beginning to bloom, and come summer they'd be bursting with fresh berries, though it was likely only the wildlife would enjoy them.

The creek ran swiftly, still swollen from the winter runoff coming off the mountain but Nora was safe in her spot. It wasn't far from here where she first met Ben. Drawing her knees against her chest, she sank into her sorrow and wondered if she'd ever be able to look at this creek again without wanting to burst into a horrible display of girlie tears.

"I rather like the stairs after all," a voice said behind her. She whirled and saw Ben, of all people, standing on the last step, smiling, cast free. "It seems you were right after all."

She wiped at her eyes and stood stiffly. "What are you talking about?" she asked, trying not to notice how her heart had tripled its beat. "What are you doing here? I would've mailed the key back to you if that's what you're worried about."

"Now, where would the sense in that be?" he chided her, further confusing her and setting her nerves on edge.

"Have you lost your mind or started doing hallucino-genic drugs? You're not making any sense. Of course you need your spare key." Unless the house had already sold. She faltered, her dreams crashed and burned. She blinked back tears. "What's going on?"

He stepped forward and came within touching distance. She couldn't retreat without landing in the water. She glared at him for invading her space. "It seems you were right and I was wrong about a number of things," he began. "Starting with the stairway, herb garden and koi pond. The house looks fabulous."

She relaxed only a little. "Anything else?" Damn, was that her voice that sounded so hopeful?

"Just this…" His voice softened and her heart did a strange little skip as he pulled her to him, his gaze caressing her face. "Love *is* more than a chemical reaction. It's real and it's been with me ever since I left this place."

"Ben, if this is some kind of joke, I'm not laughing."

"I hope to God you don't think this is a joke because I'm about to ask you to spend the rest of your life with me. I've quit my job at Franklin, Mills & Donovan, and I'm going to open up shop here, in Emmett's Mill. I figure this town could use someone to fill my grandfather's shoes and I know I'm the only man for the job. I even parked the Beemer and bought my own car. An SUV with monster tires in case it snows around here."

She gasped. "Are you serious?"

He gave her a look that melted her heart. "I've never been more serious in my life. Will you make an honest man out of me and promise to tell me when I'm being a jackass until the day I die?"

Nora beamed, unable to believe what was happening. She wrapped her arms around his neck as pure joy cascaded through her body. "Only if you promise to love me every single day of those years together."

"Is that a yes?" he asked a bit anxiously, and she answered him with a kiss.

"Yes, Benjamin Scott Hollister III," she said against his mouth. "Yes, yes and God, yes!"

EPILOGUE

"A WEDDING IN September?" Natalie groaned. "It'll be so hot. Why not next April? What's the rush?"

Nora sent a secret smile to Ben and his gaze settled on her stomach. No one knew yet, but she was three months pregnant and if they didn't tie the knot soon, her father would be ordering a shotgun wedding.

Tasha smiled and reached over to pick up Justin Cole from his swing. "I think he's teething, Nat. He's drooled all over his front," she observed, accepting a clean onesie from Natalie so his auntie could change him.

Gerald was bending Ben's ear about something that had him riled and was no doubt pestering him for legal advice and Josh and Evan, her brothers-in-law were exclaiming over Nora's herb garden and asking if she could help them plant their own.

"Smell this oregano," Evan said, pushing the herb right under Natalie's nose until she sneezed. "Can you imagine a spaghetti sauce with some of this in it?"

She waved it away from her nose. "Sounds great." When Evan wandered off to finish his exploration, Natalie leaned over to Nora and whispered, "No oregano. I'm allergic."

Nora smiled, her heart full to bursting. She'd never

seen herself as the type to cherish home and hearth like some people, but until she had something worth cherishing herself, she'd never known what she'd been missing.

She had the house she'd always wanted, but better than that, she was living the dream she never truly knew she wanted until it had almost been taken from her.

She let her hand slide surreptitiously to her still-flat stomach and her gaze returned to her soon-to-be husband. Now she knew.

And life was great.

* * * * *

Valentine's Fortune
by
Allison Leigh

"Miss?" The deep voice seemed to come at Bethany from a long, hollow distance. "I'm with the Red Rock Fire Department. You're safe now. Just open your eyes."

Her throat hurt. Breathing in made her nose burn. She wanted to sleep. How long had it been since she'd had a decent night's sleep? Since before…before what?

Her brain searched, but all it found was fog. Thick, choking fog.

"Come on now, darlin'. Open your eyes for me."

She was floating in the fog. Was she flying? Someone had told her if she flew in her dreams that meant something good.

A dream. That was it. She was dreaming.

"Dammit, make a hole," the deep voice barked. "She needs air."

She winced. She wanted to shrink away from the harsh command in his voice. Didn't he know she was sleeping?

"Breathe through my mask." The voice was low again. Intimate. "It'll help."

Something covered her face. She pushed at it. Tried to protest. Sucked in oddly sweet air. She turned her head away. "No." The word scraped her raw throat.

"That's it, Miss. Come on back to us. You're doing fine now."

She could follow that voice anywhere. Even up and out of her dreaming fog.

"You're safe now," he coaxed softly. A lover's whisper.

No. That wasn't right. Her lover was…where?

She frowned at the pain inside her head. "No."

"Yes, you are safe. I promise. Just open your eyes. You'll see. Can you tell me your name?"

Bethany. The name sighed through her. *My name is Bethany.*

She jerked, her eyes flying open to stare into the face of the man speaking to her.

Voices. Shouting. Sirens. Smoke. Flashing lights.

It all accosted her in that instant and fear shot through her, making her stiffen. She tried to work her hand to her abdomen, but couldn't seem to manage it. "What?"

"Can you tell me your name?"

Relief was swift, but fleeting. She hadn't said her name. Or if she had, he hadn't heard it. Not over the incredible clamoring confusion surrounding them.

She started to clear her throat. Coughed. What was the name she was using? "Barbara," she finally supplied. Her voice wasn't much more than a croak. Her brain just didn't feel like cooperating. "Burr—" *Not Burdett. Not Burdett.* "Burton." That was her borrowed name. "What happened?"

"Don't worry about a thing now, Barbara. You're safe," was all he said. "I've got you now."

He was carrying her, she realized, and just as quickly she

felt consumed with dizziness. She closed her eyes, but that didn't help. "I feel sick."

The floating, rocking motion ceased. "I'll bet. I'm going to put you on the stretcher now. Just relax."

She opened her eyes again as he settled her on a firm, blessedly steady surface. "What happened?" she asked again. He had streaks on his face. Like war paint. And shoulders wider than a linebacker. He looked armed for battle.

She realized vaguely that a large white van was next to them.

"I almost didn't find you when we were clearing the restaurant." He'd leaned down closer to her and his voice was softer. Impossibly gentle.

Comforting.

She blinked. Rubbed her eyes. Realized that they were watering.

"The smoke was thick in there. You were unconscious," he said. "They're going to take you to the hospital. Just as a precaution. Make sure you're all right."

She didn't want to go to the hospital. She wanted, she wanted…she didn't know what she wanted. "A fire," she said, stupidly. Thickly. Even now, she could see the lick of hungry red lighting the sky beyond the van—an ambulance. And beyond that, a rise of thick, cloying smoke.

Oh, God.

She slid her hand over her abdomen. Please, *please* be all right. "I came for an enchilada."

His teeth flashed. "Afraid you'll have to wait a while for that. Inhaling smoke the way you did can make you pretty woozy," he said.

It wasn't war paint on his face. It was soot. And the armor he wore was a fireman's uniform.

"*You* rescued me?"

"Yes, ma'am." She realized his grin was slightly crooked. "And you're gonna be just fine, Barbara. D'ya have someone you want us to call? Husband? Boyfriend? Who were you with at Red?"

Red. The restaurant. She'd been treating herself to the first meal out she'd had since she'd landed in Red Rock. A woman only turned twenty-five once in her life, right?

"Barbara?"

Her mind was wandering. She knew it. She just couldn't seem to make herself stop. "I'm not married." It seemed to be the only clear thought in her head. "There's no one to call."

"We've got her now, Darr." A woman and another man appeared beside the stretcher and before Bethany could marshal another coherent sentence, they pushed the stretcher and she felt herself slide smoothly into the rear of the white ambulance. The woman followed her.

But Bethany wasn't looking at her.

She was watching the fireman, still standing there.

And then the ambulance doors closed and she wanted to protest, but it was already too late, because she could feel the vehicle begin to move.

The ambulance attendant closed her cool fingers around Bethany's wrist. "What's your name, ma'am?"

Bethany closed her eyes again. In her mind, though, was the firefighter's crooked grin. His deep, gentle voice.

"Barbara." Again, the lie scraped along her raw throat. "Barbara Burton."

2 FREE BOOKS
AND A SURPRISE GIFT

We would like to take this opportunity to thank you for reading this Mills & Boon® book by offering you the chance to take TWO more specially selected books from the Special Moments™ series absolutely FREE! We're also making this offer to introduce you to the benefits of the Mills & Boon® Book Club™—

- **FREE home delivery**
- **FREE gifts and competitions**
- **FREE monthly Newsletter**
- **Exclusive Mills & Boon Book Club offers**
- **Books available before they're in the shops**

Accepting these FREE books and gift places you under no obligation to buy, you may cancel at any time, even after receiving your free books. Simply complete your details below and return the entire page to the address below. You don't even need a stamp!

YES Please send me 2 free Special Moments books and a surprise gift. I understand that unless you hear from me, I will receive 5 superb new stories every month, including a 2-in-1 book priced at £4.99 and three single books priced at £3.19 each, postage and packing free. I am under no obligation to purchase any books and may cancel my subscription at any time. The free books and gift will be mine to keep in any case.

Ms/Mrs/Miss/Mr _____ Initials _____

Surname _____

Address _____

_____

_____ Postcode _____

Send this whole page to: Mills & Boon Book Club, Free Book Offer, FREEPOST NAT 10298, Richmond, TW9 1BR